**Three vulnerable, lovely and spirited women
are looking for a few good men with
marriage in mind....**

Groom #1: Cattle-station owner. Untamed, fierce,
smoldering, dangerous. A man to be
reckoned with—and needing a wife for
his child....

Groom #2: Diamond mine owner. Tough,
successful, powerfully sensual,
attractive, determined. Gets what he
wants—and who he wants!

Groom #3: Vineyard owner. Aristocratic,
handsome, elegant, commanding,
arrogant. Was he already married...
to *her?*

ANN MAJOR

lives in Texas with her husband of many years, and her three college-age children. She has written more than thirty-four novels. A premier Silhouette Desire author, her larger-than-life characters, compelling plotlines and sensual prose have touched the hearts and emotions of millions of readers all over the world. Whether she writes a simple love story or a more intricately plotted tale of romantic suspense, she always delivers unforgettable stories. Her books have repeatedly placed at the top of national and international bestseller lists.

EMMA DARCY

nearly became an actress, until her fiancé declared he preferred to attend the theater *with* her. She became a wife and mother. Later she took up oil painting—unsuccessfully, she remarks. Then she tried architecture, designing the family home in New South Wales, Australia. Next came romance writing—"the hardest and most challenging of all the activities," she confesses. With over fifty novels and over five million copies of her books in print, fans of this bestselling author are delighted she persevered!

ANNETTE BROADRICK

has shared her view of life and love with readers all over the world since 1984 when her first book was published. In addition to being nominated by *Romantic Times Magazine* as one of the Best New Authors of that year, she has won the *Romantic Times Magazine*'s Reviewers' Choice Award for Best in its Series, the *Romantic Times Magazine*'s WISH Award and the *Romantic Times Magazine*'s Lifetime Achievement Awards for Series Romance and Series Romantic Fantasy.

ANN MAJOR
EMMA DARCY
ANNETTE BROADRICK

THE MAN SHE
MARRIED

Published by Silhouette Books

America's Publisher of Contemporary Romance

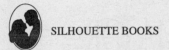 SILHOUETTE BOOKS

ISBN 0-373-20161-3

by Request

THE MAN SHE MARRIED

Copyright © 1999 by Harlequin Books S.A.

The publisher acknowledges the copyright holders of the individual works as follows:

WILDERNESS CHILD
Copyright © 1989 by Ann Major

THE WEDDING
Copyright © 1992 by Emma Darcy

MYSTERY WIFE
Copyright © 1994 by Annette Broadrick

Look us up on-line at: http://www.romance.net

Printed in U.S.A.

CONTENTS

Dear Reader,

Wedding bells sing the song of love. I enjoy weddings because by celebrating the bride, they celebrate all women and the transformational power of love. When a woman falls in love with a man, this exhilarating experience is, at first, magic and personal. When she marries him, families come together; families expand.

There are so many sorrows we can do nothing about, so it is truly wonderful to be able to share the happy events in peoples' lives. I try to attend every wedding I can.

Tad and Jessica are a special pair of lovers. Long ago, Tad loved her, but she set him up by allowing her identical twin to change places with her on their wedding day. On his honeymoon he discovered he'd married the wrong sister.

Now that's a lot to forgive. But weddings say that true love is about forgiveness, compromise, renewal, endurance and hope. It's easy to fall in love; it's harder to stay that way. Weddings symbolize that we believe love can last.

Sincerely,

Ann Major

WILDERNESS CHILD

Ann Major

To Ted…

Prologue

The sun dipped below the broken battlements of the mountains. Half an hour later, the west wind, hot and fiery from its passage over a thousand miles of Australia's Never Never, died.

The pilot's glazed eyes were red-rimmed. His body movements were slow and deliberate because he had fought the heat and the head wind for hours.

The red sky was edged in opalescent colors. The mountains and gorges changed from scarlet to mauve to purple, and the wild night creatures that had been sheltering in caverns began to stir. No native creature ever traveled in the heat of the day.

Only the white man.

The plane was flying low, too low, following a north, northwesterly course home. The airborne Geiger counter went wild as the plane crossed the remote northern tip of Jackson Downs, forbidden territory. The pilot's pulse began to pound in his temples as he observed the high reading. He raised his hand and gnawed at his torn nails. Then he circled, flying even lower over the vast Jackson cattle station. Twice more he circled. Each time, the Geiger counter's readings soared. His hands were shaking. There had to be an immense deposit of uranium down there. There had to be.

The pilot looked down. Beneath the twin-engine plane stretched a million acres of baking-hot, blood-red desolation darkening in the twilight. And beyond those acres of eerie, undulating rock formations, were a million more. And beneath them—a fortune in uranium.

He could not wait to get back to the station and tell Noelle. At last she would see him as a man and not a boy.

Even though his brother had stupidly sold this hellish land and it no longer belonged to them, he could not contain his excitement.

For it would.

Again.

No matter what he had to do.

Just for a moment the pilot considered Tad Jackson, the owner. There was no man tougher, no man anywhere around this desolate emptiness who was more respected. Jackson, his wife, his kid, all of them would have to be crushed.

The pilot had started his climb when before him, out of nowhere, loomed a mountain, its violet razor edges higher than the rest. In his excitement, he'd failed to keep a sharp eye on his altimeter.

He pulled the yoke back to make a steep, climbing turn, but nothing happened.

Uranium!

He wasn't going to crash into a damned mountain. Not tonight.

The razor-red edges of the mountain rushed toward him. Life had never been sweeter. Nor crueler.

The plane was like a dead weight hurtling through the sky.

In those last seconds, he wondered as he'd done so many times before—why was it always like this for him? Just when everything was beginning to go right for him, everything went wrong!

Noelle! Oh, God! Noelle!

The plane exploded against the wall of rock.

The man-boy inside was devoured in a billowing blossom of flame.

A flock of galahs rose screeching with doleful, disturbed cries from their nesting places in the cliffs. They soared and flapped wildly about like crazed bats above the petals of fire.

Then the flames died away, and the birds settled upon their gnarled perches in the casuarinas and stringy barks.

Flying foxes and euros, the small, gray mountain kangaroos, came out to forage and drink from a dark pool where cloyingly sweet applethorn was in flower.

There was a great quietness, and all became darkness except for the hard glister of a narrow moon that rose and swam through a sky that was as black as jet.

One

"Why isn't that the Yank that killed..."

"It's hard to tell with his beard."

"I think you're right. That's him. That's the one! Jackson—bloody murderer."

The women's voices were high-pitched, curious, not in the least embarrassed, and they cut Tad Jackson to the quick. The hurt was immediately followed by fierce, murderous anger.

All eyes fastened upon the lean, golden-haired giant in the denim trousers and khaki shirt, that ubiquitous uniform of the Australian bushman. His skin had been burned and his hair bleached by too many hot, southern suns. Leather hat in his clenched hand, he was slouching negligently in the shadows while he waited for an elevator.

They had noticed him, of course. Right away. The moment he'd come into the building. Women always noticed him. Even now, despite his beard.

A look of quick, smoldering anger hardened his carved features, and his silvery blue eyes narrowed. His sensual mouth thinned. He moved his head slightly and a silken lock of gold swept across his forehead. There was a recklessness in his dark face, something intangible that was wild and dangerous, something hostile that exuded virile masculinity, and that special, barely tamed something had always been irresistible to women.

Once he'd considered all that an advantage, but for the past year it had been a curse. Why couldn't they leave him alone? Why did every man, woman and child in Australia want to nail him to a cross?

Wasn't it enough that he and his family and men had been terrorized for two years? Enough that his fences were routinely cut, his livestock shot, his stockmen ambushed, and the road trains carrying his cattle to market attacked? A year ago his wife had become so terrified she had taken their daughter Lizzie and run away. She'd come back, stolen money from him, and then run away again. He had loved his daughter, but not his wife. Then the rumors had begun to fly about that he'd killed them. But he hadn't. He wanted desperately to know where they were.

The women were staring at him in fascination and horror.

Heat stained his cheeks. Tad let his hot, blue gaze slide over them. Then his mouth curled as he strode past the pocket of women waiting for the elevator.

Maybe some day one of them would take a wrong step and learn what it was to be persecuted for a crime she hadn't committed.

As he pushed open the door to the stairwell, he stopped and turned. Forcing a bitter smile, he touched a tanned finger to his brow and muttered a savage, "G'day, ladies."

His greeting was Australian; the slurred drawl, Texan.

But it was the white grin in the bitter, male face that brought startled little gasps of fear.

"He heard us!" There were more frightened titters.

He forced himself to keep smiling even though he felt as if the walls of the stairwell were closing in on him. God, was this nightmare never going to end? He had come to Australia because he'd wanted to be his own man, to stand alone. Because he'd never fit in with his own family back in Texas—at least, not with his older brother Jeb running things. Tad had brought Deirdre here, ruined her life. For what? He was ready to sell out, to pack up, to leave this country and go back to Texas. Even if it meant taking orders from Jeb again.

He could feel the women's eyes drilling into his back like the sharpest bits.

"The Yank killed his wife, they say. And probably his nipper, too. On one of them fancy resort islands off the Great Barrier Reef. There was something about it in *The Australian* again only last week."

"How horrible."

"He wasn't even charged. They never found her body."

"Poor little sheila. And they won't find her, either. Not with the sharks where she disappeared. And their child. The little lass disappeared without a trace. Good-looking devil, though, isn't he?"

Tad let the door bang behind him, and he raced up the stairs, his long legs taking them two at a time. He ran up eight flights. He ran till his heart felt like it was bursting in his chest. Then he stopped and leaned against the wall to run a shaking hand through his hair. He reached in his pocket for a cigarette, lit one, took a single drag and then, when his throat burned, he remembered his cold and that he wasn't supposed to smoke. The cigarette made the pain in his chest worse. He tossed the cigarette to the concrete and squashed it out with the heel of his boot.

He'd always been a loner. He'd thought he didn't give a damn what people thought of him, and he hadn't until now.

Ian better have a good reason for demanding that he leave the station and fly into Brisbane. Every time Tad came to town, it got worse. People stared at him, talked about him, actually accused him of killing his wife and his daughter. They were driving him from the country where he'd made his home for the past eight years. As if he could ever hurt a woman, or a child. His Lizzie…

Most of his friends had deserted him. Even Ian, his own lawyer, half believed he'd killed Deirdre. It was Ian who'd talked him into selling out and quitting Australia.

Tad walked up the last flight and barged into Ian's outer office and past Ian's receptionist who was carefully styling her billowing tufts of cotton-candy white hair. Her overblown, Kewpie-doll brand of beauty would have stopped most men dead in their tracks.

As Tad rushed past her, she dropped her brush. Her mouth formed a wide baffled O that would have made a perfect target for a blowie had she been in the bush. Then she jumped up, all flutters and big-eyed alarm. Just as his hand touched Ian's door, Tad heard the pit-a-pat of her heels behind him.

"Wait! Mr. Jackson, you can't go in there!"

He whirled, and she almost ran into him. Her neon-bright fingertips flailed wildly to avoid him. His narrowed gaze met the frightened baby-like brown dazzle of hers. As she shrank from him, he grinned bitterly. "You going to stop me, sweetheart?"

If he'd been a mulga snake towering twenty feet high and about to strike, the poor girl couldn't have looked more terrified. Tad's expression softened. "Why don't you go back to your desk, honey, and tackle something you can handle?" He shoved open Ian's door.

The office was opulent and felt as safe and silent and as insulated from the real world as a bank vault. It was January, and the sun outside would bake a man alive. Inside this cell of urban splendor, blasts of icy air cooled the plush carpeting, rich, lustrous mahogany walls and floor-to-ceiling sheets of glass.

Ian was one of the richest men in Queensland. Unlike Tad, Ian had started with nothing. Nothing but greed and ambition, Tad thought bitterly, two of the most powerful forces in the world. Ian had grown up in Queensland on a cattle station, the son of a horse-breaker and a shepherd girl. At the age of six Ian could track a lizard across rock better than most Abos. At the age of ten the station had been sold to American investors and Ian's family had ended up destitute on the streets of Brisbane. Ian wasn't forty, but he'd done well.

On one wall were maps of Queensland and the Northern Territory where Ian had colored in the properties he owned. He owned stations that totaled in the millions of acres. He was into ore, salt, gypsum, cattle and wool. "You name it and I'll own it" was his motto. He was the best lawyer in Queensland, but despite his upper-class pretensions, he was a street fighter at heart. He'd been one of the first friends Tad had made upon coming to Australia to take over the management of his family's holdings.

Tad studied the maps rather than the magnificent views of Brisbane's sprawl, the famed Story Bridge over the wide, curving river, the moored yachts, the snarl of river traffic. Tad saw that Ian was expanding his operations, and the fact was like salt in the wound of his own failures.

One of Ian's cigars was smoking in an ashtray. Ian was

on the phone, barking orders. He was short
and he exuded the raw, animal power of a
His eyes were as bright as twin dark coals a
with fierce intelligence. He had a hard, bluntly ꞏꞏꞏved face,
bushy black brows and a thick frizz of prematurely gray
curls. He took one look into the wild blue eyes of his client,
growled an abrupt goodbye and slammed the phone down.

"This had better be good, Ian."

Ian was as cool and serene as his client was irrational.
The lawyer picked up his cigar and puffed great clouds into
the air before replacing it in the ashtray. "Oh, it's better
than good," he said slowly. "Sit down, and I'll tell you."
Ian paused. "Coffee?"

"Coffee!" The single word was an explosion. "Hell,
no." Tad sprawled violently into the leather chair across
from Ian's desk. "Well?"

Ian grinned. He was never intimidated by Tad's outbursts. Tad thought he took a perverse delight in drawing
out this moment of suspense.

"Jackson, can't you ever relax?"

Never, when he was closed in by walls, by people, by
the city. Never, when his lawyer demanded he fly into
town.

"I thought you'd feel better," Ian persisted, "once you
decided to sell."

"Who decided? I was driven to sell. I don't like quitting,
but I'm not running a station out there anymore. I'm fighting a war. My men are armed to the teeth. None of us dares
leave the homestead alone. I just wish I knew who I was
fighting. They come out of nowhere. It's always a strike in
the dark when you least expect it. One week they cut
fences; the next they blow up a bore. The other property
owners have had their troubles, too. There's the drought.
My cattle are dying, but every time I try to ship them the

ad trains get attacked. It hasn't rained a drop on Jackson Downs in months. I've been heavily in the red for the past three years. I just flew across a thousand miles of spinifex, scorched bush and dying cattle, and you say relax!''

"Things haven't eased up, then?"

"Eased up? Hell. Ever since Holt Martin's plane was sabotaged a couple of years back…''

Ian ran a hand through the gray frizz. "So you think it was sabotage?"

Tad's face darkened. "Who knows? The bush coppers, acting officious as hell, poked around the wreckage for a while, came by the station in their new Jeeps and wrote up a report. Then we never heard from them again. I didn't think it was sabotage then, but all I know now is that that was the beginning of it all. Holt was a harmless sort, poor bloke. A geologist. Always out poking around where he didn't belong, exploring for minerals. Never found much. I guess he never knew what hit him.''

"You don't have any ideas who's behind this mess?"

"I have a few, but I can't prove anything. I don't trust any of the Martins. Not even their American cousin, Noelle.''

"You've been down on women ever since I've known you.''

"Ever since I stuck my head in the noose and married one of them. But I can't forget that we didn't have any trouble till Noelle turned up. Now it's brother against brother, property owner against property owner. We used to trust each other out there. With every property under attack, nobody trusts anybody anymore. Hell! Who knows? Anyway, I didn't come here to rehash my problems!''

"Well, I called you because I've got good news." Ian's grin broadened. "One of my men found Deirdre.''

Tad sprang out of his seat and leaned across the desk.

Forgotten were the killers that stalked him night and day. Forgotten were the Martins and the drought.

His fear was an icy, suffocating mist that seemed to mingle with the noxious curl of acrid cigar smoke, gagging him.

"What?" he rasped. "You mean her body? Where? It must have been badly decomposed. Lizzie..." He hardly dared breathe his daughter's name.

Ian leaned forward, too, his grin intact. His dark face was placid. Only his sharp black eyes belied his outward calm. "Not her body, you bloody bastard. Her." He seized Tad by the forearm and held it in a death grip. "She's alive. So's your kid."

"Alive..."

Ten thousand pins seemed to pierce him just beneath the surface of his skin. He couldn't believe it. Tad didn't want Deirdre dead, but he didn't want her back in his life, either. He just wanted Lizzie.

Deirdre had to be dead, or she would never have left Australia without the money. And he had found the money in the cottage.

Images of that nightmarish time nearly a year ago came back to him. The bush coppers had seized him and flown him to the island, to her cottage. He could still remember the way her suitcase had lain half open on the rumpled bed with her lacy garments dripping out of it. The rest of her things had been scattered untidily about on the rose-patterned carpet and couches. Meticulous about her person, Deirdre had always been messy when she traveled. They had told him she'd probably drowned.

He could almost hear the rush of the sea sounding through the windows, almost smell the salty dampness of it seeping inside. He had picked up her lavender silk blouse, which had fallen carelessly beneath the white wooden rocker. He had caught the faint, lingering fragrance of her scent. She had been wearing that blouse the last time he'd seen her alive, the afternoon three days before when she'd come back to the station on the pretext of discussing their problems and telling him where Lizzie was. Only what Deirdre had really been after was the operating cash he kept in his safe. She'd stolen the money—all $75,000 of it, and his plane—and run out on him again. She'd emptied their joint checking account in Brisbane. He hadn't had the vaguest idea where she'd gone until the coppers had come for him.

He remembered standing in that cottage. He had felt her presence everywhere. It was as if she had only gone out for a minute and would be back in a little while. Only there was an eeriness about her absence that had told him she would never come back. And she hadn't. Nor had his child been found.

He had told the police to look in the lining of Deirdre's suitcase because he'd known her to hide things there before. When they found the money, they'd considered that incriminating evidence against him.

Apparently she had gone diving alone, the police had said. Or someone had made it look like she had. Did he know why she'd come to the island, alone, with the money? Where had he been at the time of her disappearance? What was his alibi? They had found bits of what might have been her diving gear washed up on the beach. A battered yellow tank. A piece of black hose. They weren't sure. Like Lizzie, she had disappeared without a trace.

Then they had begun to torture him with questions about Lizzie. Where was she? All he could tell them was that he didn't know. Deirdre had taken her.

"It is no secret you and your wife didn't get along, Mr. Jackson. No secret that you hated her."

Hate. The single word was inadequate to describe the complex snarl of emotions he had felt toward his wife.

"You say she took your child. She took your money. Did you follow her here? Did you kill her?"

They'd crucified him on that last question.

Tad had hired professionals to look for Lizzie. When they'd failed to find her, he'd retreated to his homestead, into his own pain and silence for nearly a year. There'd been times he'd been grateful for attacks against his station because at least they'd distracted him from wondering about Lizzie.

"There's no way Deirdre's alive," Tad whispered to Ian.

No way he was taking her back if she was. He was through. Through with all women, for that matter.

Ian's expression was intense, odd. "So you don't think she could come back?"

"No. It's a trick of some sort. A lie."

"It's no lie. You're lucky as hell she turned up, mate. You can quit hiding out on your property, and you can shave off that damn beard." Ian thrust a series of photographs in front of Tad. "My man took these yesterday."

Tad stared wordlessly at the pictures. A beautiful woman—if it wasn't Deirdre, it was an exact duplicate of her—was standing on a beach in front of a towering rain forest. Except for her dark eyes, she was tall and golden like a Valkyrie; sleek, slim and yet amply endowed where a man most wanted a woman to be. Her long, blond hair was glued to her shapely neck and head. Sparkling rivulets of water slid down the curves of satin-gold legs. She was wearing a one-piece black bathing suit that fit her body like a second skin. She was comforting a wet and frightened Lizzie in her arms.

Usually Deirdre had found other things in life infinitely more diverting than her child.

"Oh, Lizzie…" Tad breathed. His hand began to tremble. For the first time he allowed himself to believe she was
really alive.

"Lizzie." He ached to hold his daughter as the woman
was holding her. To touch her soft red curls. To hear her
quick, lilting bursts of laughter. To watch her dart about in
her dinosaur suits. He would relish even the sound of her
tears, even the hot outbursts of her temper so like his own.

In the picture Lizzie's hair was the same brilliant copper
red, but she was older, six now. Her hair was longer, tied
back with purple ribbons. Of course, purple, only purple.
She'd always had a fixation about anything purple. And
dinosaurs. He realized with a pang how long a year was to
a little girl. Would she even remember him?

He devoured the pictures of her. In one she was holding
a starfish and studying it. In another the woman was bending over her and lovingly examining a hurt baby toe. The
look of trust and devotion between the woman and his child
touched something deep and longed for in his own soul.

Jess…

The forbidden name sprang from some place deep within
him.

Jess, Deirdre's identical twin.

Dear God. Quickly he closed the door on the treacherous
emotion Jess alone could arouse in him.

The woman, whichever she was, had his child. She had
deliberately kept his child from him for nearly a year.

The last shot was of Lizzie alone.

Tad stared at it until the familiar upturned nose and red
curls blurred. The excitement, the relief of knowing she was
alive was unbearable. He felt a vague reeling sensation. He
tried to focus, but the image of his daughter swam before
his eyes. He could no longer ignore the woman who held

his child in her arms. Lizzie looked happier than she'd ever looked with Deirdre. He forced himself to concentrate.

He picked up the picture of the woman and stared at it hard. With avid dislike, his eyes ran down the slim yet deliciously curved body. *Jess...* He knew it was her.

Just as he knew how the long, blond hair would blow in the wind, just how silky it would feel if he were to run his fingers through it. Just how hot her skin would be to his touch, or how cool. Just how warmly those dark, gold-flecked eyes could sparkle when she laughed. Just how treacherously she could use such beauty to twist and manipulate a man. Once he'd been bewitched by this woman. Her touch alone had enflamed him.

His heart filled with a savage, dark anger. Never again.

He studied the beautiful face, the magnificent bust, the cinched-in waist, and his mouth twisted with pain as he remembered.

Deirdre's face.

The face that had launched his life on a collision course with disaster.

Only it wasn't Deirdre.

It was her twin. His sister-in-law. Dr. Jessica Bancroft Kent.

A muscle in his stomach pulled.

Even more than Deirdre, he detested her.

Because it was she whom he had loved.

Years ago when he'd been hardly more than a kid himself—when he'd been in school at the university back in Austin, Texas and before he'd married Deirdre, he'd been thoroughly tricked by Jessica Bancroft. Though Bancroft had posed as a do-gooding intellectual bent on becoming a doctor and saving the world, he'd discovered that she was every bit as much a liar as her sister.

For it was Bancroft who'd played the starring role in the

trick that had induced him to make the worst mistake of his life. Her excuse had been that she had been helping her sister. The knowledge of her betrayal lay as heavy as stone in his stomach.

Help... That was the catchword that gave people like Jess the excuse they needed to meddle in others' lives. Tad had always believed that if people would just mind their own business, the world would run a lot more smoothly.

Although Jess and Deirdre had kept up through the years, Tad had avoided Jess. He had never given a damn how Bancroft might feel about him. All he knew was that she had helped Deirdre trap him into his hellish marriage. Then Jess had gotten married herself. Not that she'd ever acted like a wife should. She'd run all over the world doctoring the poor, leaving her husband and son to fend for themselves.

Three years ago Jess's husband and their only son had been killed in a car accident in Austin. Deirdre had gone and stayed with Jess, but it hadn't bothered Jess enough to keep her from taking off almost immediately on another of those ill-advised, medical-missionary sprees of hers. She wasn't a woman, with a real woman's heart.

Sure, Bancroft had a meddlesome, do-good facade. The truth was she was bossy as hell. She was just conceited. She liked inserting herself in poverty-ridden villages where no one knew nearly as much as she. There she could strut about, filled with self-importance, as she taught those wretched creatures to boil water and wash their hands, as she delivered their babies, as she bullied them to her heart's content until they recovered from cholera or whatever blight had made it necessary for them to endure Jess's ministrating presence in the first place.

Deirdre had come home after the funerals, and after that two-month absence the sense of isolation she'd always felt about living in Australia on a remote cattle station with him had worsened.

Tad hadn't minded Deirdre being away. As always when he had had the station and Lizzie to himself he'd felt relief. That absence had been a turning point, and after it their marriage had gone steadily downhill. It was as if they had both known it was over and they had given up.

Holt Martin had crashed into Mount Woolibarra. Deirdre had flown to Brisbane and begged Ian to convince Tad to leave Australia or consider a divorce. Then the war against himself and his property had begun, and the tensions in his marriage had increased.

Tad stared at the picture in his hand. If Deirdre was dead, this could only be Jess. After a long time, he set the picture down beside the others.

A chill ran down his spine. It was as if the ghost of something he wanted dead had fluttered willfully back into his life. He tried to tell himself that it didn't matter. All that mattered was that she had his daughter, that his Lizzie was still alive.

"It's amazing," Tad whispered. "Truly amazing... Lizzie... Deirdre..."

"So you think it's Deirdre?"

Tad didn't look up. "Who else could it be?"

There must have been something odd in his face because Ian was watching him, examining every nuance of his expression.

"It was so strange. I got this call. A woman talked to my secretary and told her that a client of ours, Tad Jackson, would be very interested in what she had to say. The woman was an American; the take-charge sort. Bossy as hell. You know the type—the kind who makes her presence felt wherever she is. She wouldn't hang up till she got me."

So it *was* Bancroft. Cut loose from her do-gooding mission and thereby free to meddle in his life.

Dear Lord! Oh, yes. He knew the type.

His jaw clenched. Just the memory of her still cut him to the quick.

But she had Lizzie! And it was obvious from the pictures they were getting along famously. Something in him that was fatherly and possessive glared at the redheaded six-year-old in the purple swimsuit as if she were a traitor.

Then his gaze returned to the blond who was to blame, and that was a mistake, because he couldn't stop himself from staring at the snug swimsuit where it clung to the soft swell of her breasts.

Those breasts! Damn her! They were magnificent! He had a weakness for the exquisite proportions of well-endowed women. He told himself it was a general thing. Still, a hot tingle of something he didn't want to feel tightened every muscle in his body as he remembered a night he'd vowed to forget.

A magical night when orange blossoms had bloomed on a verdant lawn that swept down to Town Lake in Austin. A night when moonlight was blue dazzle on rippling waters. An unforgettable night of unusual and tantalizing pleasure.

Jess Bancroft had been too damned good to forget.

Who would have thought a Puritanical do-gooder like Jess would be a wanton in the sack? He had been stunned by her primitive, abandoned passion.

She had made him think it was Deirdre he was making love to. For that, he could never forgive her.

Tad frowned uneasily.

Ian said, "She said I ought to come to a certain place. That I'd find something of interest. I thought it was some sort of hoax, but I sent a man down there just in case. And he took those snapshots.''

Tad sank slowly back into his chair. He was numb with shock. His face was white, sick-looking. He could feel the violent thudding of his heart, the perspiration beading on his forehead. Was it his cold that was suddenly making him feel so ill or the murderous all-consuming fury anything that reminded him of his wife or her twin could arouse?

''Where were these pictures taken?''

''I really don't think you should see her,'' Ian replied coolly. ''At least, not for a while. Not...not till you calm down. Your face is purple.''

''Achoo!'' A raspy curse vibrated behind Tad's sneeze.

''She's my...er...wife, damn it. She's put me through hell, and you really don't think I should see her! I'll strangle her with my bare hands, that's what I'll do.'' Tad was getting carried away, but he couldn't stop himself. ''I'll strangle you, if you don't tell me.''

''As your lawyer, I didn't hear that, and I advise you not to go around saying things like that to other people.''

''Okay. Okay. But you're my lawyer, not my keeper. No one runs my life but me.''

''You've sure done one hell of a job.''

''Where is she?''

Ian hesitated. ''Maybe she doesn't want to see you.''

Fat chance. Jess Bancroft hadn't come to Australia to count legs on starfish or coo over Lizzie's injured baby toes. ''She called you!''

Ian was regarding him coolly. ''That's the odd thing I can't figure. Why did she call me...and not you?''

''Ian, for God's sake! She's got Lizzie! Have you never felt a single overpowering emotion in your well-ordered life?'' Tad's hard gaze was riveted to the map with the colored pins on the wall. ''Besides greed?''

Ian smiled grimly, "Not since I was young. Not since my home was sold out from under me to some Yanks, and my parents and I were out on the streets starving. Not since my sister died on those streets. I learned to channel my emotions, not to act on them. I married a woman who likes to stay home. A woman who understands that this is a man's world. She knows her place—and mine. While you... You married the most beautiful creature on earth. A goddess meant to dazzle and be admired. Then you buried her alive on Jackson Downs with nothing but cows and termite mounds and goanna lizards scuttling about for company. And then people started shooting at her. So she got a bit jumpy."

"If I had it to do over, I would run like hell from anyone who even remotely reminded me of Deirdre."

For a moment two pairs of male eyes were drawn to the voluptuous image of golden female beauty in the photograph. Then both men looked away—too quickly.

"I wonder..." Ian folded his hands beneath his blunt chin in that curious attitude of prayer that meant he was thinking.

"You've got to tell me where they are, Ian. What if she takes Lizzie away again?"

The world was full of wretched niches where a doctor of Bancroft's curious bent could hide indefinitely.

"They're on the island," Ian said.

"What?"

"They're staying at the cottage—alone."

"She's crazy to go there."

"It's almost like she's tempting fate, isn't it?" Ian mused.

Tempting fate was exactly the sort of sport Jess Bancroft liked best. Aloud, Tad said, "It's the last place I would have thought to look."

"You're as crazy as she is if you go there. What's going to happen to Jackson Downs with you gone?"

"My brother-in-law, Kirk Mackay, is there, and there's no man alive I'd trust more to see after things."

"You should meet her on neutral territory. This could be a setup of some sort."

Tad's icy blue stare went over the slim, golden woman in the top photograph one last time. He remembered the way her body had fitted his. Rage flamed in his heart, but he could not stop the memories of her. He could almost feel her rosebud nipples pressed into his chest. Despite those immense breasts, she had been slender, lovely, instilling in him a hot, pulsating urgency and then fulfilling him beyond all his wildest expectations. She had been so good, so sweet—that once. Taking her had been so easy. Forgetting her so impossible.

Because he had loved her.

He'd been looking for her that night. She had said she was looking for him. Only when she found him she deliberately pretended to be her twin, Deirdre.

Her twin, Deirdre, whom he'd married because of that one night of ecstasy.

His wife, Deirdre, who had been frigid, at least in his bed, for ten years.

His spoiled, selfish wife, who had married him only for his money, who had taken his child and run out on him at the first sign of trouble. He flinched as though his chest had been stabbed by a knife of ice.

Ten years ago his relationship with Deirdre had been over until Jess had deliberately seduced him, pretending she was Deirdre, and then Jess passed him back to her sister as though he had meant nothing.

Tad smiled grimly as he pocketed the pictures.

Oh, it was a setup all right.

Only this time…

Two

The scent of mimosas and oleander and hibiscus mingled with the perfume of the sea.

Everyone else on the island was relaxing.

Everyone except Dr. Jessica Bancroft Kent.

Everyone except the aboriginal child with the matted gold hair who was watching her from the rain forest canopy of giant bloodwoods and ironbarks.

The hordes of tourists from the resort hotel at the other end of the rocky island were either swimming, snorkeling, windsurfing or viewing the wonders of the Great Barrier Reef from glass-bottom boats. But Jess had not come to this thickly wooded paradise of dappled sunlight, with its flitting blue butterflies and magnificent beaches, as a tourist. She was a woman with a mission.

And the word relax was not in her vocabulary.

She almost wished it was. Her heart was pounding violently from her exertions, and she was so hot she felt she might explode.

Then the child peeped out of the jungle. Their eyes met—the woman's and the boy's. Jess smiled, and as always whenever Jess made any attempt to communicate he became frightened and ran away. Sturdy brown legs flew past her down the trail of white coral.

Alone once more, Jess felt like she was in a steam bath. It had just rained. The fierce summer sun beat down on the tropical island with deadly intensity. Even in the dense shade of the rain forest—the Australians called it scrub— that skirted the rocky road where she stood huffing and puffing as she leaned against the mower she'd been pushing uphill, the heat was stifling. The narrow path was made narrower because some untidy individual, no doubt male, had parked a bulldozer square in the middle of it.

Jess's hair had come loose from its pins, and great globs of it were glued to her neck and forehead. Her khaki shorts and blouse were as wet as if she'd showered in them, and the blouse clung disgustingly across her too-ample bosom.

Even now, all these many years since school, her play-mate-of-the-month figure remained a secret embarrassment. It was something to be hidden beneath high-necked blouses or baggy clothes. It galled her that her breasts were the first thing men noticed about her, her brains the last.

"I've got brains of my own, honey," had been one boy-friend's crude gem.

She tugged at the clinging, sticky-wet fabric and then gave up the attempt to loosen it from her skin and fanned herself with her fingers. She had lost all enthusiasm for the prospect of mowing the overgrown lawn surrounding Deirdre's cottage. Jess could have gladly turned around and pushed the mower back down the hill except she was too stubborn to face Wally's boyish smirk of male triumph.

He had warned her, hadn't he? And like all men, even a green chauvinistic pup like himself, he would take great delight in being right.

She cringed as she remembered their conversation once she had lured him away from the contractors involved in the hotel's expansion.

"The motor mower's too heavy for a woman to push over that hill."

"For a woman..." How she detested superior, limiting, masculine phrases of that variety.

His eyes had fallen from her stern face to those two protruding, softer parts of her anatomy that always drew male eyes the way magnets attract iron filings.

"If you'll just wait till Hasiri comes back—" he said.

"Nonsense," she had replied crisply. "If I wasted my time waiting for all the Hasiris of the world to come back, I would have gotten very little done."

The handlebars of the mower had slid so easily from Wally's grasp into hers. He had managed to bring his gaze back to her face and keep it there.

Wally was a gentle soul. She almost wished now that he'd fought her a little harder. Not that it would have done either of them a particle of good. It was never difficult for a woman with even a bit of backbone to best the Wallys of this world, and Jessica had much more than a bit.

Not that she was a man-hater, despite the innuendos of more than one member of that sex over the years. She had found, however, starting with her handsome and dynamic father, that few persons of the male sex were to be trusted. Later experiences had merely confirmed her opinion.

She smeared the back of her arm across her damp brow. The rain forest was abuzz with insects—some of them huge, voracious, exotic-looking creatures that made her think she should carry a rolled newspaper at all times, especially when lifting toilet lids. Something horrendous flew past the tip of her nose, and she swatted at it. Suddenly she longed for a cool drink and a shower; she longed to be back at the cottage with Meeta and Lizzie.

Nearby in the dense tangle of bloodwoods and gum trees, a twig snapped. Every muscle in her body went rigid. For the first time it occurred to her how remote her end of the island was, how lonely this particular part of the trail was, how dark the shadows of the jungle had become.

She'd come to this island and asked a lot of questions, perhaps too many, about her sister who'd died violently.

Jess's stomach felt hollowed out, that overpowering indication of fear, of the hunted realizing she was hunted. She instinctively knew it wasn't the child. The boy crept stealthily through the jungle without making a sound. This was something bigger, something clumsier.

Jess swallowed. Normally she wasn't the shrinking, terrified sort of female her father had taught her to despise. Hadn't she fearlessly braved the slums of Calcutta for the past two years? But those garbage-strewn alleyways had been familiar territory. And those teeming slums, for all their filth, weren't nearly as dangerous as most downtown American streets after dark.

A brooding atmosphere hovered in the dark rain forest. The green-breasted parrots had stopped their raucous squawking. She was a stranger to this country, to this island, to jungles and their dangers. Obviously, she was not nearly so talented at playing detective as she'd naturally assumed she'd be. She peered warily into the darkness and listened to the eerie quiet.

An explosion of white burst from the jungle.

Jess screamed, jumping back as feathers brushed her cheek.

"Silly goose!" She chided herself shakily as she

watched a cockatoo, its crest sulfur yellow, flutter grace-fully down from the branches of a firewheel. "It was just a bird."

She had let go of the mower, and it began to roll back-ward toward the edge of a six-foot cliff.

"Be careful with it, love," Wally had said. "Believe it or not, this is the only working motor mower on the is-land."

"I always take excellent care of every item I borrow," she had promised faithfully.

She lunged after the borrowed item that she was taking such excellent care of, catching it just as it tilted precari-ously over the edge. Once her pulse had calmed, she began to tug on the mower with all her strength, but its wheel was jammed in the crevice between two rocks.

It was then that the unmistakable sound of a human sneeze issued forcefully from the jungle.

"Achoo!"

She nearly jumped out of her skin, and the mower lurched even more dangerously.

"Achoo!"

This second sneeze was followed by a man's quick, low, snarled curse. "Damn."

A ripple of fear raced up her spine.

There *was* someone! Someone who was deliberately hid-ing in the trees.

Paralyzed, she clung to the mower. "Who's—"

A dark cloud came out of nowhere and obliterated the sun.

She yanked at the mower but it wouldn't budge.

If she let go, it would fall. If she didn't...

More than once in the span of her twenty-nine years, her audacity had carried the day. "Come out of there, whoever you are," she called softly in what she had intended to be her I'm-not-afraid-of-anything tone, "and help me with this mower."

No answer. Not even a sneeze. There was only the thudding of her heart. Only the silence—thick and cloying like the heat, like her terror. Only the one motor mower on the island, heavy as lead, its wheel sliding out of the crevice and rolling downward over a large, slippery rock, pulling her with it toward that shadowy ravine.

She screamed as she felt a wheel go over the edge.

Something heavy jumped out of the rain forest behind her. Before she could turn around, an arm went around her waist like a steel band, pinning her arms to her side. She felt his fingers settle beneath her breasts.

That was the one place she didn't like men touching.

She let go of the mower with a yelp and watched in a horrified daze as it hurtled slow-motion past a strong brown hand over the edge of the cliff and smashed itself on the rocks below. Before she could scream, that same calloused hand clamped firmly over her mouth.

Her body was arched against a solid wall of muscle and bone. Hard male fingers burned into her breasts.

"Stop fighting me, you silly fool. I'm not going to hurt you," a deep, vaguely familiar masculine tone growled.

She forced her panic to subside, and when it did she stopped struggling so frantically.

Her attacker gallantly relaxed his grip, and that was his mistake. Jessica was a student of the martial arts. From then on it was pure, delicious instinct.

Teeth into brown fingers. A deft twist. A knee in his groin. A sharp blow with her heel in his solar plexus.

He doubled over in a spasm of agony. She kicked at his shin. He lost his footing, and the great, bearded giant was tumbling over the rocky edge after the mower.

He bellowed like an injured bull all the way down.

Till he hit bottom with a sickening thump.

Though she hadn't heard Tad Jackson's voice in over four years—she'd thrown him out of her house on that last memorable occasion for a barrage of chauvinistic insults about busybody females galloping about the world like a herd of misguided mares, pretending to help others when all they were really doing was running away from their own personal problems—no other human alive could make that particular howl of frustration and fury except him.

There was an awful silence.

Then a parrot squawked. In the distance a lone windsurfer streaked past on the glittering ocean.

She was shaking, but the pure horror of what had happened did not strike her until she stepped out onto the ledge and peered down at him.

In spite of his beard, she recognized him instantly.

Jackson!

Dear God!

His great, muscled body lay sprawled as still as death across the bleached coral beside the mower. A faint breeze blew the bright mass of gold back from his tanned brow, and she saw the blood.

Terror gripped her.

What had he growled into her ear? "Stop fighting me, you silly fool. I'm not going to hurt you." And she knew that despite all her brother-in-law's character defects—and they were too numerous to catalogue, not that she hadn't made the attempt on more than one occasion—he would never have physically hurt any woman. Not even her.

For four days she'd waited for him. He needed her help—desperately—but he was so stubborn it was the last thing he would ever willingly seek. For that matter, it was the last thing she would ever have willingly given him. For four days she'd expected him to barge into the cottage like a great giant roaring to the rooftops in one of his high rages, demanding his daughter and demanding Jess's own departure from his life.

Instead, like most men, he had taken the most unexpected, the most foolhardy and the most calamitous course of action. He had snuck up on her in an idiotic macho attempt to bully her. And she had bested him in physical combat.

If he lived he would add this to his lengthy list of unforgivable things she had done to him.

If he lived...

She scrambled down the cliff after him.

Three

Tad lay on the rocks in a blur of agony. Vaguely he was aware of his surroundings. The resort was expanding. Bulldozers had gouged great chunks out of the jungle, but they'd left the cliff with its famous Aboriginal rock art intact. Crudely painted crocodiles and kangaroos and other unknown animals that recalled the Aboriginal creation myth of the Dreamtime loomed above him. But he was not admiring this splendid example of rock art; he was concentrating on her.

Pain splintered through his battered body. He had hit his head when he fell, and it was a struggle to focus his eyes on the she-devil. He watched, though, as she climbed as nimbly as a goat down the rocks—no doubt, to finish him off.

He'd been following her all day, trying to figure out her game plan, trying to figure out when and where to confront her, how best to seize the advantage. Then he'd gotten soaked in that shower which hadn't helped his cold, and he'd sneezed and given himself away.

He'd only jumped her because she was so stubbornly determined to save that rattletrap mower—he'd been afraid she was going to let it drag her over the cliff. Instead, she'd shoved him off it.

Jess-of-the-jungle grabbed a spidery vine and with an agile jump made her final descent. She landed light as a feather. Was there nothing that woman couldn't do?

Through half shuttered eyes, he watched her sink to her knees beside him. Her immense breasts heaved beneath her damp shirt. He could make out the outline of taut nipples thrusting against wet cotton. He knew better than to watch those, so he gritted his teeth, fighting to concentrate on the danger of her proximity, fighting to ignore the fiery, pulsating pain in his leg and lower hip.

It would be so easy to grab her by the throat, to pull her down, to scare her witless and thereby make her pay for what she had done. He almost succumbed to this nearly irresistible temptation, but some part of him was curious as to what she planned to do next. Besides, to lie still was the easiest and least painful thing to do.

To his surprise, instead of picking up a rock or a stick to pound him with she gently lifted his hand, her practiced finger searching his wrist for a pulse. She mashed her magnificent breasts against his chest.

Her own hand felt as cool as springwater against his blazing skin. How could anything alive feel so cool and nice in this heat? Her cotton blouse was as wet as his own soaked shirt, her breasts soft and deliciously warm.

How could Jess…feel so nice?

Jess, whom he hated even more than he'd hated Deirdre.

Jess, who had betrayed him, who had tricked him into marrying Deirdre.

Jess, whom he had loved as he'd never loved Deirdre.

Jess, who had just pushed him over this damn cliff.

What the hell was Jess doing here anyway—besides trying to kill him?

The she-devil lowered her head to his chest and listened for his heart, and he was forced to endure the lustrous tangle of her soft, blond curls tickling his chin and nose.

When he thought he couldn't hold back the sneeze that threatened a second longer, she lifted her head and brought her face closer to his. He was aware of her lips hovering, lushly half opened, tantalizing, a scant inch above his. He could smell her, and her nearness stirred old, long-forgotten memories. No…

Not forgotten. Never forgotten; just repressed because they had hurt too much to remember. He could almost taste her.… He wanted to, and he loathed himself for that weakness.

She licked her lips, and he watched the curl of her pink darting tongue follow the lush curves of her perfectly shaped mouth. A fingertip dubiously touched his beard and then withdrew.

He caught the scent of something sweet, like orange blossoms. Her scent, enveloping him.

"Jackson," she whispered. The sound was ragged with fear. Through the dampness of their clothes, the points of her breasts shuddered delicately against his hard chest muscle. Her warm breath caressed his throat.

The jungle was a beastly sauna.

He could hear her labored breathing. Or was it his?

"Jackson, can you hear me?"

No use to answer. They'd quarrel, and he felt weak, too exhausted for one of their battles.

When he clung stubbornly to his silence, he heard her muted cry of remorse. "Dear God!" Her fingertips stroked his cheek. ''You big, impossible lug, I never meant to hurt you.''

She—who'd been the cause of all his hurt—had never meant to hurt him.

He studied her through the thick veil of his almost closed lashes, and he felt twisted with conflicting emotions. The sunlight was in her hair. Her wet blouse outlined her lush female shape. Even in a state of dishevelment, she was golden, lovely.

He didn't want his thoughts journeying down that fatal path, but a man's thoughts are not so easily whipped onto the path of his choice when the woman he doesn't want to think about is right there pressing her breasts into him, distracting him. So he kept looking at her, thinking about her.

Hell. Jess certainly wasn't her usual prim and proper Puritanical self. She was badly shaken, soft and vulnerable. Indeed, she looked exactly like she'd stepped out of the centerfold of a men's magazine and come to life.

She sat up, this tabloid fantasy that he knew from past experience was no tabloid fantasy, and he closed his eyes with a faint groan, but not before he'd gotten a good look at her beautiful, anguished, tear-streaked face.

He wanted to hate her. He was determined to.

But it was hard to hate a woman, no matter what she'd done, when she was crying over you.

Instead of hatred he felt the dangerous pull of that old indefinable power that had crawled inside him and eaten him alive—body and soul—until there had been nothing left. For years he had told himself he was glad she was out of his life, glad that whatever had been between them was finally over.

But memories of her had haunted him. Sometimes he'd dreamed of that night ten years ago, the one night he'd had

her, the night that had made him want her forever—he'd
dreamed hot, lascivious dreams in which Jess crawled all
over him in wanton abandon.

He had married the wrong sister. Damnation! Was that
why he hated Bancroft even more than Deirdre?

The jungle was hotter and more oppressive than ever.
There was a smell in the heated air that was very Australian, a thin, subtle odor of the scrub, an unmistakable pun-
gency of aromatic oils stealing out from the trees. Tad began to perspire, and the faint breeze trickling through the
trees from the ocean made his skin feel like ice.

Her fingers sifted through his golden hair and probed the
burgeoning lump and the hot stickiness surrounding it. He
groaned aloud, and she drew her hand away as if burned.

"Don't be such a sissy," she whispered. "I don't want
to hurt you. I have to do this."

Sissy! It was all he could do not to grab her and make
her pay for that one.

The hand came back, gently probing his eyelid open so
she could check the dilation of his pupil. She opened the
other eye. Then she ran her hands over every part of his
body, examining every bruise, every scratch. It was hard
for him to remember she was a doctor and that it was the
doctor touching him, not the woman. When she finished,
she observed his still face thoughtfully.

"Jackson..."

Her low, melodious voice wasn't nearly so bossy as
usual. Yes, she had clearly been shaken off her know-it-all
pedestal.

He felt her fingers touch his cheek. "Jackson, if you can
hear me, would you please..."

She took his hand and gripped it again. He felt her other
hand push his hair from his brow and remain there. Her
cool touch was gentle, infinitely sweet, comforting.

"Jackson, your pulse is strong. I don't think you're hurt too badly. You're going to be okay, but I'm going to have to leave you here for a little while. I'm going to the cottage to get someone to help me carry you."

Her voice went on, but the sound seemed to drift in and out. He could only hear snatches of it. He tried to open his eyes, but when he did, he couldn't see her anymore.

Suddenly he wished he hadn't been so obstinate. He wished he'd spoken to her when he'd been able to. He was afraid that he was bleeding internally and that he might never get the chance again.

He wanted more than this abrupt finality with her, more than one of those endings without a goodbye. Without even an I'm sorry. Suddenly he knew that he wanted much, much more than a goodbye with her.

But there was only a whirling blackness sucking him under. Only a numbing pain that seemed to engulf his whole being. Only her hand clutching his as she tried to pull him back.

"Jackson, you stubborn fool, why didn't you speak to me?" she screamed.

He could barely hear her, but he tried to make his lips form the words. "Because…because…"

Because he had wanted to so much.

When he came to again, he felt faint with agony. And yet relief.

He was still alive. He was in the cottage. Safe after an eternity of danger.

Here there were no guns. No one was stalking him. Only this woman.

It was night. The heat of the day had lessened. Moonlight slanted through the shutters. The air was dense and humid and smelled sweetly of rain and pungent, wet gum leaves.

The jungle was alive with a riot of bird sounds. Above the bed, the blades of a ceiling fan stirred lazily and cast flickering shadows against the ceiling. Even in the darkness he could see that the room was neat, tidier than it had ever been when he'd stayed in it with Deirdre. Jess was a fanatic when it came to neatness.

From downstairs came the scent of something cooking, something that reminded him of sweet long-ago things when his life had been simpler—Texas, his mother, home. Of being a little boy. Of happiness. Of that pleasant time before his parents had separated, before all the loneliness, before Jeb had taken over and made him feel like an outcast among his own family.

Chicken soup.

Jess always knew how to get next to him. Deirdre had never cooked chicken soup. But Jess, for all her faults, had a couple of saving graces. Those breasts... He pushed that thought aside and concentrated on the delicate aroma of chicken soup. She could cook better than any woman he'd ever known. And he had a weakness for good cooking.

He watched the blades of the fan; he watched their shadows on the ceiling. He wished he didn't have a weakness for big breasts and good cooking. He tried to concentrate on the faint throb of music drifting from the hotel's bar at the far side of the island. Then he heard Lizzie's laughter downstairs mingling with Jess's stern voice.

Lizzie... He struggled to sit up, but he was too weak to manage it. Slowly he became aware of his circumstances. He was lying upstairs in the master bedroom, and he was naked between crisp white sheets.

Naked!

The she-devil had stripped him and robbed him of his clothes! At the thought of her hands going over him he went hot all over.

She had no right to touch him! But the memory alone made him rock hard.

Vague memories, like those from some barely remembered dream haunted him. Long, slim fingers, cool fingers, had slid over the hot skin of his body, touching him everywhere. He remembered scissors snipping away at his trousers. Cold points, needle sharp, had teased his burning skin. He remembered icy cloths being pressed against his forehead, against his neck and shoulders. He remembered a gentle Indian girl in a scarlet-and-gold sari. Most of all he remembered Jess's voice. She had talked to him in the darkness, talked to him until the gentle sound had lost its soothing quality and had become raspy with weariness.

Jess had managed to get him to the house, to carry him up the stairs, to undress him, to put him to bed. As always—when she put that very determined mind of hers to it—she was a whirlwind of efficient, competent energy.

That same whirlwind of energy had kicked him and sent him whirling over that cliff.

God, he needed a cigarette! But where were they? She had taken everything.

How long had he been here? Hours? Days?

He heard her footsteps on the stair, and a child's lighter, faster steps dashing in front of her.

The door burst open.

The doorknob banged against the wall.

He closed his eyes.

Jess's urgent whisper across the darkness. "Lizzie! Careful!"

Then a breathless silence.

A knot of suspense formed in his gut. He didn't know what to say to either of them.

He was a man used to the vast expanses of the outback, a man who could go for days sometimes without talking as he traveled from cow camp to cow camp, a man who did not mind such long silences.

Everyone in the room waited. There was only the whir of the ceiling fan rotating lazily.

Then a tiny, impatient hand with cold, sticky fingers curled tentatively, gently around his little finger.

The nightmare of the past year was over.

He opened his eyes, hardly daring to believe the angelic vision of bright red curls tied back in a lopsided purple bow. Big, dark eyes glowing with joy and yet mirroring his own uncertainty.

"Daddy!" The uncertainty was in her voice, as well.

This bright-eyed waif was wearing a crinkly green-and-yellow dinosaur raincoat and holding a half-eaten grape Popsicle that was melting all over her hand. She brought this dribbling delicacy to her lips and licked greedily.

His child.

He was not a sentimental man. His grip tightened on hers.

"He's awake," Lizzie squealed, jumping up and down.

"It's about time," Jess murmured drily. She, too, looked excited, pleased, proud that he was better, though she was attempting to appear stern.

"Aunt Jess!" Lizzie whirled, then turned back to her father. "Aunt Jess, he's crying." Lizzie's eyes were wide; her low tone awestruck.

"Nonsense, darling," came Jess's crisp, firm tone, removing the Popsicle and giving her charge a much needed tissue.

"Lizzie…" His voice was so deep and hoarse with emotion he hardly recognized it. His hand closed over the smaller one, careful not to crush it.

Very gently Jess lifted the child up so that she could put

her arms around him and press her face against his grizzled cheek.

"Daddy, I missed you something awful." Green-and-yellow plastic crinkled as she squirmed closer. Jess stepped back.

His fingers tangled in her curls. "I missed you, too..."

Did those words convey the emptiness of the past year? The helplessness? The sick, gnawing fear? On top of it all, everything he'd loved had been under attack. "You look wonderful," was all he said.

Jess seemed to be staring out the window as if she, too, were deeply moved. He remembered she'd always tried to hide her sentimental nature.

"Daddy, I know why Mommy never came back. But why did she take me away? I wasn't scared of the bad men."

Jess's head pivoted sharply. "Not now, Lizzie darling," came Jess's voice, still raspy with exhaustion. "Remember what I told you about not upsetting him."

Lizzie lapsed into silence. As though bored, the child brushed a finger through his beard and pulled it back. "Sticky. I don't like it. You didn't have it before."

"Then I'll shave it," he muttered, unhappy that anything about him should displease his Lizzie.

Lizzie touched the bandages on his head. "How'd you get hurt, Daddy? Aunt Jess said..."

His eyes rose to Jess, who had become rigid behind Lizzie. Jess was prim and proper now, dressed in a white poplin blouse with a high collar. The blouse buttoned practically all the way to her nose. She wore navy slacks, and her hair was neatly bound at the nape of her neck. The hairstyle couldn't have been sleeker if every hair had been glued in place.

The schoolteacher look! He didn't like it. He'd liked her

better in the clinging, wet blouse with her hair streaming down her neck. With her body hot and breathless against his. With tears of passionate concern for him streaming down her cheeks.

At Lizzie's question the look of excitement and shining pleasure in her aunt's eyes died. A guilty flush came into her face.

"What did your Aunt Jess tell you?" He kept staring at Jess until the color in Jess's cheeks deepened.

The line of Jess's mouth tightened. "Tell her whatever you want."

"Oh, I will." His voice was husky. "I will." His velvet tone went softer. "All in good time. But first, I'd like to hear your Aunt Jess's version."

Lizzie got down off the bed and eyed her aunt dubiously. Jess's cheeks remained as bright as a pair of beets.

"She said you fell off that cliff with the big pictures where she keeps telling me to be careful."

Tad's eyes slanted toward Jess, who seemed to be holding her breath as she looked past him out the window. A sliver of moonlight molded the lovely curve of her neck. He smiled crookedly.

"I fell, did I? What an interesting…er…interpretation of events."

More blood seemed to gush into Jess's face. She started to back away from the bed, but he lunged forward and seized her wrist.

They screamed together—she in surprise, he in agony. One glance at his white face, and she stopped fighting him.

Pain shot from his hips and thigh, but even as he sank back into the bed, he clung stubbornly to that tiny bit of female flesh and bone, pulling her closer.

The scent of orange blossoms and soap enveloped him. Her scent, treacherously pleasant. He fought to ignore it.

What he couldn't ignore were those two temptingly soft parts of her anatomy that spilled over his chest.

"Send Lizzie away," he croaked hoarsely into Jess's ear.

A golden tendril came loose from her stern hairdo and blew softly against her cheek.

"You need to lie still, Jackson," Jess murmured, not in the least intimidated by him. "You're too hurt and weak for this idiotic macho behavior—as if it hasn't already gotten you in enough trouble."

This reminder of how easily she'd bested him only served to make him madder.

"Get Lizzie out of here. I have to talk to you alone."

His eyes burned into Jess's for what seemed an eternity.

At last Jess averted her gaze and whispered softly, "Lizzie, darling, would you be a little angel and run down to the kitchen and tell Meeta to heat the soup I made for your Daddy? I'll come down for it in a minute. I need to check him first."

That sweet, hypocritical, ladylike voice that made him want to snap her head off! But it fooled Lizzie, who dashed out of the room.

When they were alone, his grip relaxed ever so slightly upon Jess's wrist, but he kept on holding her. "Bancroft, just what do you think you're doing?"

"For the last twenty-four hours—nursing you. Believe me, that was hardly a prize assignment. Like most men, you were no use in an emergency. You've been very difficult. First you refused to walk. We had to carry you. Uphill. You're heavy as lead."

"Good!" His blue eyes glinted with savage pleasure at having put her to trouble. "You probably broke both my damn legs when you pushed me."

"You're exaggerating—as always."

"All I know is that I was in perfect health until I met up with you."

She snorted. "Perfect health! Ha! Jackson, you had a case of walking pneumonia. A fly could have pushed you over that hill."

That stung. "I had a cold!"

"Pneumonia. You probably kept working and smoking—"

"Naturally I kept working and smoking."

"More of that idiotic machismo you take such absurd pride in! Even a fool such as yourself should have had better sense. Well, you won't smoke now. It was clear someone had to take charge of you. It was equally clear there was no one but me to do so. I tore up both of the packs of cigarettes you had in your pocket."

She was just like his older brother, Jeb, who was always telling him what to do.

He felt apoplectic. "You what?"

"They're the last thing you need in your weakened condition. You were on the verge of collapse."

Her smug superiority was more than he could endure. What did she know of his hardships? "No, *you're* the last thing I need." He yanked her closer so that her soft body fitted intimately to his. She felt cool to the touch—ah, too pleasantly cool; his body was racing with heat. "You tried to kill me, you witch!"

"A fate you brought on yourself when you attacked me!"

"I didn't attack you. I was trying to prevent you from going over the cliff with the mower."

"Well, it doesn't matter now," she said softly.

"Doesn't matter?" he exploded.

"For once, you might surprise me and try thinking rationally," she continued in that cool know-it-all tone of hers that would have been a needle in any man's ego. "We can't alter what happened, can we? Besides, you're not hurt all that badly, despite the way you're carrying on about it. Like most men, you're a big baby when it comes to illness."

"A big baby!" He'd been fighting a guerrilla war all by himself for nearly two years. If he was sick, it was because he'd driven himself so hard.

"A few bruises, a slight bump on the head, and you carry on like it's the end of the world."

"A slight bump! I'm seeing two of you. Believe me, that's more than any man could stand!"

She went on. "A slight bump, a very mild concussion, a pulled muscle in the groin—that's all that's wrong with you."

"My groin!" This time it was he who was blushing. "For God's sake, I hope you didn't examine me there."

"Naturally I examined…"

The thought of her fingers probing around there made him go hot beneath his beard.

"Jackson, the reason you feel so rotten is because of the pneumonia, and you brought that on yourself. You've been burning up with fever. I had to pump drugs into you to get it down. I bathed you with cold cloths all afternoon and last night. Then this morning, your fever went back up and we had to do it all over again."

For the first time he saw the dark shadows beneath her eyes, the lines of weariness etched into her face. Somehow, this evidence of her dedication toward him made him want to attack her with an even greater ferocity.

"Don't expect gratitude or an apology from me," he jeered.

She pursed her lips.

So… She had felt at least a glimmer of doctorly compassion toward him because she'd nursed him through a crisis. He watched that sentiment die completely.

Her eyes were cinders. "Common courtesy, dear brother-in-law, is the last thing I'd ever expect from you," she replied coolly, in a miffed, hurt tone. "Not that you should feel you owe me anything. I would have done the same thing for a sick dog."

His fingers tightened around the slim wrist. "I want Lizzie, you man-hating witch. I want you out of my life. I have enemies enough without taking you on."

"I know." She lifted her chin and stared at him down the length of her nose. "For once we are in agreement," she answered, this time in that infuriatingly placid tone a schoolteacher might use with an upstart youngster.

As he watched her flatten one of the tucks in her blouse with her free hand, he felt a wild jubilation. Nothing had ever been this easy with her. Then he grew aware that something in her smug expression didn't fit with her words. He realized she had caught him off guard.

"What do you mean?"

She smiled sweetly. It was the smile he most distrusted.

"Only that this once we both want the same thing, Jackson." She pressed her fingertips beneath her chin in that cool, determined manner of hers.

She was finished with the tuck. But not with him.

"You see, Jackson, I want Lizzie, too. I'm here to help you."

Four

Tad's hand was a claw gripping Jess's wrist. He felt the warmth of her breasts spilling voluptuously against his chest. Her body was soft and inviting. Too bad her head and heart were as hard as flint.

"You see, Jackson, I want Lizzie, too."

Jess's velvet voice seemed like a living thing, a hateful sound lingering in the darkness.

Her mouth was set, and she was looking down the length of her shapely, upturned nose at him again. Dear God! Of all the ills in the world, surely there was none worse than an interfering female who's made up her mind to bully you.

The ceiling fan droned. The moonlight was a halo of silver in her hair.

Tad could not get her statement out of his mind.

Her face was pale, her eyes darkly glimmering pools. The wisp of her hair that had blown loose wrapped around her neck.

In the smoldering silence that fell between them, they studied one another warily. It was as though so much was at stake, neither dared say more. It was as if a bomb was about to go off, and they were both in such a state of shock all they could do was listen to the ticking.

"What do you mean, you want Lizzie?"

"The same thing you do, Jackson."

"Lizzie is my child."

"Your child. Not your possession," came that precise schoolteacher tone he so despised.

Despite her air of moral superiority, she was the one who had stolen his child! He wanted to scream, "Mine! Mine, you fool!" and be done with it. But that would never work with Jess. He had to progress logically. Logically—whatever that meant to her.

He began in what he hoped sounded like a calm tone. "Surely you don't think a person should just take a man's child and keep her for a year without even telling her father where she is."

Darkly defiant gold-flecked eyes met his. "For pity's sake, Jackson, that's deplorable—even from you. I didn't take Lizzie. Deirdre entrusted her to me because your station was a war zone and you weren't doing anything about it."

"Not doing anything! I was fighting back with all I had. Then my sweet wife just took Lizzie and vanished."

"I don't blame her. Like all men, you see only your side. Deirdre was scared witless, and you couldn't protect her. You were always an impossible husband—even in the best of times. Of course she ran."

He controlled his rage and continued, his voice bitter. "When she ran short of money, Deirdre came back to the station and stole my operating cash and one of my planes."

"She needed money to live on."

"She left me nothing. She emptied out our joint checking account, too. After that she came here and never returned."

"Because she was killed!"

"My child was gone, and the only person who knew where she was was dead. My station was a battlefield. Everyone thought I killed them both. My own child! There was no way I could defend myself. The only thing that stood between me and prison was Ian McBain, my lawyer. Believe me, his legal fees, on top of all my other expenses, have dealt the station a death blow."

Jess's expression was odd. "Deirdre mentioned Ian."

Tad's mouth thinned. "Do you know what it's like to be hated and despised for something you didn't do? What it's like to live with the terror that your child is somewhere hurt or dead and there's nothing you can do? To go to bed every night looking at her picture, wondering if you'll ever see her again? That ate at me more than living with the constant violence."

He felt Jess flinch. The moonlight seemed to bleach all color from her face.

Her voice was smooth and unemotional. "I'm sorry."

"You'll have to do better than that," he murmured tightly. "I'm sorry's have never cut any ice with me."

"I-I didn't know what to do," Jess said at last. "When Deirdre didn't come back for Lizzie I did make inquiries, and I found out you were in terrible trouble."

"Trouble?" He sneered. "I was in hell. You knew! And still you didn't bring Lizzie."

"You have never exactly been my favorite person."

"You didn't even write! Not a line to tell me she was alive."

"But then you would have known where we were."

"So you admit it—you deliberately kept her—knowing what I was going through?"

"What else could I do?"

"You could have brought her home!"

"How? I was working in Calcutta at a clinic. I couldn't just leave. I came as quickly as I could find a replacement."

"No, you were too busy saving the world to give a damn about the one man whose life you've been set on destroying ever since you first laid eyes on him."

"That's not true."

"It damn sure is."

"How could I bring Lizzie to you? Not after what Deirdre said about you. Not when she made me promise—"

"And I'll just bet she said plenty! My sweet wife had the habit of blackening my name to anyone who would sit still, and I'm sure you enjoyed listening when she aired all the dirty laundry of our marriage."

Jess's eyes grew huge, intent on his face. "Would you believe me if I said you're wrong about that?"

"Deirdre doesn't matter anymore. Whatever she told you doesn't matter."

"It does to me. A year ago, to help her when she came to me and said you both were in trouble, I accepted responsibility for her child. Lizzie's been through a rough year."

"Tell me about it," he said caustically.

"It wasn't easy for me, either. I was in India working fourteen hours a day in a clinic. I-I was trying to forget about…the accident. Deirdre left a five-year-old child and never came back. And Lizzie, who just happens to take her willful disposition after you, is hardly the most easily managed child. My life was turned upside down, and I had to make changes. Lizzie was separated from her home, from everyone she loved, everything familiar. I understood her loss. For several months I thought Deirdre was coming back. Then I found out that Deirdre was dead, that there were rumors about you having had a part in her death.''

Jess stopped, and the tortured look on her face that he read as disgust and fear made him writhe inside.

"So you, too, think I killed her?''

When Jess didn't answer, he yanked her closer to the bed, so close he could feel the heat of her body, the intoxicating scent of her perfume. Her haunted eyes were filled with some emotion he did not understand.

"Answer me,'' he demanded.

"No, I don't.'' She lowered her lashes.

He could not stand her cool remoteness. "You do!''

She forced herself to look at him again. "I never lie,'' she whispered.

"That's not true.''

Her face went blank. Her eyes glittered darkly in the queer light of the moon.

"You did. That once,'' he said, "ten years ago.''

She shook her head in denial, but he kept glaring at her until she flushed guiltily.

"All right. Yes. Back then maybe, but not now. I don't know what happened to Deirdre. Except I know...I know you didn't kill her.''

"Then why are you looking at me like that?''

"B-because I know what it's like to take the blame for something terrible like that. You see when Jonathan and little Benjamin were killed...I was driving.''

His grip tightened. "It wasn't your fault.''

"I wish I could be so sure. All I know is that if I could undo what happened that night I would. But we make mistakes, and sometimes there are no second chances.''

He felt a strange pull from her, a crazy desire to drag her into his arms, to touch her, to caress her, to comfort

her. Unknowingly she caught her lower lip with her teeth
and a sudden tremor shook him.

He stared at her. She believed him! When everyone else
doubted him. She had known what it was to suffer, to be
blamed for something she hadn't done.

A wild elation filled him that someone understood, even
if it was only Bancroft, who was his enemy. It pleased him
that she didn't think he'd killed Deirdre. For the first time
in a year, some of his loneliness left him.

He wanted to seize Jess and kiss her. Immediately he
realized how absurd such an impulse was. This gorgeous
blonde whose voluptuous curves fitted him so enticingly
was none other than his conniving, bullying sister-in-law.

He wanted to throw her out of the room and never lay
eyes on her again. The last thing he wanted from her was
kindness. And yet there was an ache in his gut that told
him it *was* the one thing he wanted.

He remembered how she hated sentimental fools. He
hated them himself.

"So you see, I know you'd never hurt anyone...not like
that anyway. Still, I can't just turn Lizzie over to someone
who..." Her voice caught. "I can't send her to Jackson
Downs with all the violence, back to you, when I know
you won't see after her properly."

"I'm her father," he said roughly. "I'll be there, damn
it. She's my responsibility, not yours."

He could feel Jess's hand trembling in his. She was as
deeply upset as he.

"Then we're at odds," she said firmly. "As usual. Because I consider her my responsibility, too."

"And you take all your responsibilities seriously."

"You know I do." She hesitated. "Especially this one.
Jackson, I don't want to fight you."

He studied Jess's still, white face, and he knew that his

sister-in-law was just as determined as he. And just as stubborn.

"I don't want you in my life," he said. But he gripped her hand like it was a lifeline.

"I didn't ask Deirdre to make Lizzie part of my life, but Deirdre did it anyway. I-I never wanted to love another child again. Not after..." Her voice broke. "And especially your child. B-but I do. I won't let you take her and ruin her the way my father..."

A cloud passed in front of the moon, and Jess's face was lost in darkness for a few seconds. Then the moonlight shone through the shutters once more, brighter than before, and he saw the terrible vulnerability in her eyes again.

He was not the only one who had lived in hell.

With his free hand he reached up and traced a finger against her jaw, along the sensitive skin beneath her chin and neck. He felt her pulse leap in response. He saw her lower lip quiver. Then she fought to control it.

His own pulse started to throb, and he tore his finger away from the tantalizing softness of her throat.

She took a breath and then lost it. He felt her stiffen. The wrist he held had stopped trembling and was again cold and rigid with tension. He struggled to control his own emotions.

There was going to be a battle. The fiercest he'd ever fought.

"You kept my child," he said, "for a year, without ever letting me know where she was."

"Someone had to look after her. It was obvious that her parents were too wrapped up in their own problems to do so."

He'd been ambushed more times than he could count. "You dare imply that I was not a good father?"

"Let me go, Jackson," she whispered. "We'll talk about this tomorrow."

"I want to finish it now."

"You're as weak as a cat." She twisted her wrist and broke free of his grip. "See!"

It was humiliating how easily she had freed herself.

"Tomorrow," she insisted, backing into the shadows. "You must go to sleep now."

Then she was gone.

All through the night Jess's words thrummed like staccato heartbeats in Tad's fevered brain.

I want Lizzie, too. I want Lizzie, too. The words mingled with the raucous thunder of parrot sounds outside and drummed even louder.

Another, more dangerous sensation thrummed in his blood like the rain that pattered for a time against the roof and thick clusters of broad banana leaves.

She had commanded him to sleep. Even if he'd been the kind of man to let a she-devil boss him, how could he sleep with her words whirling in his head? How could he sleep when the scent of orange blossoms lingered in his bed, when she'd left behind her an aura of sensuality that stirred forbidden memories? But it wasn't only her beauty that haunted him, it was the sadness he'd seen in her eyes, the terrible longing in her soft voice, the way her skin had been like hot silk beneath his fingertips.

All he wanted to feel for her was a cold, hard anger, and an even colder satisfaction that her life had gone as badly wrong as his. But something stronger than hate was in his heart, something that filled him with fear.

He told himself that it was the stifling heat that made the bedroom so unbearable, and not this new unwanted emotion. It was the moonlight, slanting across the bed, right in his eyes that made it impossible to sleep.

Restlessly, he threw off his sheet and lay sweltering on top of the narrow bed, fighting not to think of her.

He could think of nothing else. He hadn't had a woman in over a year. Maybe that's why he kept remembering how beautiful Jess was, with her pale hair shining in the darkness, with those flyaway wisps blowing against her face. He couldn't get her out of his mind. He remembered the way the poplin material had stretched across her breasts and pulled at the row of buttons, and a fever throbbed in his blood. He clenched his fists and willed himself to forget. He hated her. He hated that stubborn, willful streak in her that refused to bend. At the same time he ached to take her in his arms and hold her all through the night. He wanted to comfort her. He wanted to make her forget Jonathan and Benjamin. Never again did he want to see that terrible look of anguish on her face. He knew too well the pain she must have suffered.

The fan blew across his skin, and he started to feel cold. So he pulled the covers over him again. No sooner than he got warm, he was too warm.

Some time in the night he got up, bundling the sheet around his waist. He tore open the shutters and opened the doors that led out onto the veranda. There was no breeze. Only the thick, wet heat seeping out of the jungle. He felt faint, sick, drugged. The black trees seemed to whirl like towering giants.

It was Bancroft's fault! She had plunged him into this hell. She'd taken his child. She'd pushed him over that cliff. She'd given him all that medicine.

He almost fell down. He lunged wildly to save himself, and crashed into the shutters instead.

Wood splintered. One of the shutters drooped crazily.

He knew he should go back to bed.

He stumbled outside anyway.

Five

It was after midnight. Jess lay awake, absently twirling a strand of her hair as she glared at a ribbon of moonlight on the wall. She'd been awake for hours, her mind stewing endlessly about Jackson. From where she lay, she could see the dark rain forest clearly.

She had known when she came to Australia that Jackson would behave in his inimitable deplorable fashion. She had never expected him to willingly cooperate with her.

Blast him! Why did he have to be so impossibly macho and stuffed to the core with his own pride? Despite all his ferocious strutting and chest-thumping, he was only a man. But what a man. She smiled weakly, and not the usual sweet, superior smile that Jackson hated. Her lips felt hot and fluttery as she thought of his long, dark fingers, holding her prisoner, of his immense bronzed body coiled into hers, of how deliciously small she'd felt as she'd lain on top of him. Her stomach felt hollow and clammy.

Dear God, what was happening to her? How could this perverse man still affect her in the same way he had when she was a girl? For all her blustering determination when she'd been with him, the truth was she was actually afraid to go to Jackson Downs with him.

Why did he have to be so excessively masculine? So disturbingly male that even a woman with a character as strong as her own still found him exciting? She lay in her empty, cold bed and wadded her top sheet restlessly as she thought of him alone in his. Her heart throbbed dully as she remembered his tight fingers gripping her wrist, his hard body beneath hers.

Why him? Why did he alone have this power over her? He was a hunk of muscle and conceit—strong-willed, grouchy, selfish, stubborn, spoiled. The list was endless. He didn't care a whit for the world or its problems. Only his own. She'd grown up abroad, seen the world and its problems; she'd wanted to make a difference.

But she had to help him—because of Lizzie. It wasn't going to be easy. Like all men, of all colors and all nations, he was unable to accept the unpalatable possibility that an intelligent woman might be able to put his affairs in order more capably than he.

For all his strutting and chest-thumping, he had certainly made a mess of things. His station was under siege. He was suspected of murdering his own wife. He'd had a year to clear his name, a year to resolve the conflict at Jackson Downs, and what had he accomplished? The violence was accelerating. He was living under this terrible shadow and he expected Lizzie to live under it, as well. Did he intend to hide out on his station forever in the hope that the sordid rumors would die down? She'd heard he might sell out if things didn't improve. That was no way for a child to grow up. At least not for her own, darling Lizzie.

Jess traced the heavy thread of stitching along the sheet's edge. Her Lizzie. His Lizzie. Whether he liked it or not, they were all in this together.

There was, no doubt, a simple solution to this whole affair. Someone had to ask questions, investigate, think. Men always used force when sometimes a fresh insight, a different tack, would make all the difference. More guns! was their cry when usually what they needed was more brains. There wasn't a man alive who could do much without a woman behind him. Nor a country that could be a great nation without allowing women to realize their full potential. Through the centuries men had warred and strutted, while women had quietly done the really important work—taming and civilizing and promoting culture. Not that men or the history books written by men had ever given them due credit.

Something small and dark moved beneath the spreading branches of the flame tree. The child was at his post again, like a silent sentinel, watching her. Moonlight shone upon the bright thatch of matted curls.

Jess had talked to Wally and to everyone else on the island and learned nothing. This child had followed her everywhere. Why? Did he know something? Why was he so afraid of her?

Jess determined to take him something, a present of some sort, in an attempt to win his trust.

She went out onto the landing. On the stairs lay several of Lizzie's toys. Lizzie had so many.

Jess picked up a small, stuffed pink brontosaurus with a purple ribbon around its neck and carried it down to the flame tree. As always the boy disappeared at her approach, but Jess was sure he couldn't have gone far. She laid the dinosaur down in a nest of tall, damp grasses and then ran back inside the house and up to her room.

No sooner was she inside than there was a crashing sound against her bedroom door. She flew to the window, thinking it was the child. At first she saw nothing but night and stars. Nothing but the Southern Cross blazing overhead like a great brooch on a black velvet canopy.

She opened the door out onto the veranda. The floor planking creaked, and suddenly a huge, ghostly apparition loomed out of nowhere, filling the darkness. She heard the dry rustle of the creature's white gown as it was dragged behind him. She almost screamed before she realized it was Jackson sleepwalking on the veranda. Because of the white sheet wrapped at his waist like a flowing skirt, he towered darker, bigger. Jess's first impression was of a primitive male, powerful and dangerous, sinewy muscles rippling in the moonlight. Then he wobbled against the railing and she was terrified he was going to fall.

The child was forgotten.

"Jackson."

It was a cry, and yet it was softer than velvet in the darkness. She did not recognize it as her own.

His unseeing gaze swept the shadows, fixed upon her, and drank in the sight of the shapely perfection of her female form clearly revealed by her transparent nightgown. The blatant sensuality of the look unnerved Jess.

Her heart froze and then began to pound more violently.

"Jess…" He tumbled toward her.

Her outstretched arms went around his muscled waist. The shock of unexpected contact with his virile body made her gasp. A tremor went through her and through him, as well. The sheet fell away, and cool fingers touched hot, naked male skin. Yet even though her pulse was racing, she did not shrink from touching him. He was burning up.

She was afraid as she'd never been afraid before.

"I thought I heard something," she said, alarmed. "You should be in bed."

"I'm not going to give Lizzie to you!" he roared.

"Dear God," she moaned, "you're delirious again."

He staggered, and they both nearly fell.

"I've got to get you to bed," she said.

His room was too far. She led him to her own and helped him into her bed. To get him onto it, she collapsed on top of him. When he kept holding her, she could not get up.

In the struggle her corn-silk hair came loose and fell in a mass against his throat, where it was glued against his hot brown skin. She wore only a thin nightgown, and the filmy thing rode up to her thighs. Her legs were spread open across his, and she was straddling him provocatively.

The coarse hair of his muscular legs scratched the satin smoothness of her thighs. Her senses catapulted in alarm as she felt the force of his earthy, pagan attraction. She remembered another night when she'd lain on top of him writhing with ecstasy. That terrible night when she'd betrayed her sister and in doing so had destroyed them all.

He was sick, she fought to remind herself, attempting to break the spell. She struggled, but he merely tightened his grip and aligned her body more closely to his.

Arousal sizzled through her like an electric current, but fortunately his mind seemed on something else.

"Lizzie... Don't take her away from me again," he pleaded desperately.

He was so helpless, so sick. Deirdre had obviously put him through hell. The past year, when he'd been accused of her murder, had not been easy.

Despite her stubborn will to resist his appeal, a great tenderness welled in Jess. Gently she brushed his cheek, his lips. "I'm not going to take Lizzie away from you."

"No?"

"No," she whispered.

He breathed more easily.

Again she tried to rise, but he drew her inside the steel circle of his hands, flattening her once more against his chest. "Don't go," he said. She felt his warm breath waft against her throat. "I need you—now. I've been alone so long."

She knew all about being alone. For years, even when she'd been married, she'd felt alone. Jackson seemed so lost, so vulnerable. So hot and ill.

Another involuntary impulse of exquisite tenderness toward him seized her. She wanted to help him, more than she'd ever wanted to help anyone. He was much more charming and trustful delirious than he ever was when he was feeling well. She bent closer to him, meaning only to trace her fingertip across his brow. Instead she found she could not resist kissing his dark lashes. Then her mouth grazed his bearded cheek and last of all his lips, lingering for a timeless moment on their hot sensual fullness.

He opened his mouth, inviting her to deepen her kiss.

Violent tremors of fresh desire warmed Jess's melting flesh as her mouth lingered on his. She felt his fingers stroke her hips. Her heart fluttered with a strange, thrilled wildness. She caught herself sharply, stunned by the intensity of her emotion. The way she lay against him, it was easy to pretend he didn't really hate her. It was difficult to remember how impossible he would be when he was himself again. He was so sweet, like a sick child.

She felt the hard, muscled contours of his shape burning against her body.

He was no child; he was all man. It was the curse of her life that she had always wanted him.

His fingers wound in her hair. "Don't go," he whispered raggedly again.

Nothing seemed to matter at the moment. The only reality was his touch, his caress, his burning mouth beneath hers tasting faintly of the sugared medicines she'd forced down him.

"Don't leave me."

"You needn't worry about that," she murmured, loosening his hand, making her voice light even though she was more shaken than she would have ever admitted. "Tonight I'm going to take care of you, and when you're better I'm going with you to your property and help you make Jackson Downs safe for Lizzie." She stroked his forehead.

"Dangerous," he muttered thickly. "It's too dangerous."

"Nonsense! Why should you men have all the fun?"

"You're the most meddlesome…" His voice died away.

Jess knew he was too delirious to remember anything, but she kept talking to him because she always talked to patients in his state as if they were perfectly rational. "She needs both of us right now. I know you dislike me."

"I don't dislike you," he muttered passionately.

If only he didn't. If only she didn't long to feverishly draw him closer. If only she didn't enjoy quite so much the press of her warm, soft flesh against his.

"Well, even if you do, your property is so enormous—nearly a million acres? When we aren't actually battling, we shouldn't have to be with one another too often. You see, Jackson, I'm writing a book, from the journals I kept in India. And I've got a recertification exam to study for. So during the lulls, I'll have plenty to do. As you know, I don't believe in wasting anything so precious as time."

"Then why did you let us waste the past ten years?"

You were the one who married first, she wanted to say. The one who always belonged to someone else. Instead, she whispered, "We'll take care of Lizzie together."

"Together," he groaned.

Whether this was a groan of affirmation or misery Jess couldn't quite tell, but she thought he'd agreed. His single word was deep and long and husky before it died away.

His body went limp.

He lay so still that for a moment horror gripped her. She took his pulse. It was rapid but steady. Then she loosened her body from his and stumbled downstairs to get his medicine, water and some towels.

She chopped his pills, put them into a spoon filled with sugar and water just as she would have done for Lizzie and forced his mouth open. He knocked Jess's hand aside and sent the spoon and medicine clattering to the floor.

Jess thought of how docilely the hyperactive Lizzie took her pills. Like all men when ill, Jackson was more difficult to manage than the most obstreperous child. As always, such resistance increased her determination. She commanded Meeta to come up, sit on one of his arms and squeeze his nose tightly shut. Jess tied his other hand to the bed, pried the spoon between his clamped teeth and made him swallow the second dose. Although he twisted his head and coughed and sputtered and growled like an angry bear, she succeeded in getting it down him.

"Madame doctor," Meeta whispered in her perfect English as Jess was untying him, "he seems very sick again."

"He made himself sicker by trying to bully me. There's no real danger. He's as strong as an ox. Besides, though I deplore a certain tendency I have to brag, I'm on the job."

The worry went out of Meeta's dark, pretty face, and the flash of her sudden white smile was luminous as she looked up at Jess in that awestruck manner that Jess found so engaging. "You do not brag. I have seen you save so many who were not so strong. My brother..."

Images of frail brown bodies, young and old, lying outside on the pavement of her clinic flashed in Jess's mind's eye before she suppressed the pain of those memories.

"Hush," Jess whispered. Effusive sentimentality always embarrassed her.

All through the night the two women sponged the man with the hard, beautiful body that seemed to have been cast from bronze. Jess tried to ignore how muscular he was, how shapely. But as always when she touched him, even now when he was so sick, something outside herself took hold. She was aware of a ripple of excitement in the center of her being, of a treacherous softening toward him. Even when he was in the middle of one of his childish tantrums, she sometimes experienced this same keen excitement. Indeed, never except when in his presence did she ever feel so vitally alive.

She had spent her life chasing restlessly about the globe searching for something that was always just out of reach. Only when she was with him did she feel some sense of being where she really belonged. Now he was in trouble, and she was determined to help him.

It was almost morning when his fever broke. Jess sent Meeta downstairs, and because Jackson was holding onto her hand she allowed herself to collapse beside him.

He flung his arms across her waist and drew her close. She was supremely conscious of the feel of his large body all around her as he held her enfolded against him.

"No-no," she protested wearily.

But he was a man, used to getting his way. A man who had never learned to take no for an answer.

And he was stronger than she.

Deep within her was the desire to lie beside him and never leave the contentment she would know there with him in that soft, warm bed.

His arms locked around her silken body and she could

feel the moist heat of his bare chest burning through her gown to the skin of her breasts.

She couldn't move even if she'd wanted to.

She struggled no more.

The cotton sheets were cool against her body as Jess dreamed of Jackson. She was back in her college days at the University of Texas when she'd been young and naive, sure that all the world needed was Jessica Bancroft to solve its problems.

It was a bustling Saturday morning in October. There was the hint of fall in the air, and the tennis courts were crowded with students who had no Saturday classes and were killing time until the football game and fraternity dances that night. The U T tower chimed the quarter hour.

Jess was sagging against the net while she waited for her twin to return. Deirdre had said she wanted a Coke. In reality she'd stomped off the court, mad about a line call.

The clay court burned through the rubber soles of Jess's tennis shoes to her toes. Impatiently she glanced at her watch. Her own temper was rapidly becoming as fiery as her feet. Then Jess heard someone on the court behind her. Thinking that it was Deirdre, Jess had squared her shoulders and prepared herself for battle.

Without warning a golden giant of a man in faded jeans and scarred boots loped across the court and swatted her affectionately on her behind. Furious, she whirled. He took one look at her scowl, laughed, threw his cowboy hat to the ground and pulled her into his arms, crushing her against the granite wall of his chest.

Never in all her life had Jess felt anyone who was so lean and rangy, whose skin was so hot, whose body was so brick hard. He was not the usual UT sort, but a kicker, a man used to the open ranch lands of Texas. His hands were callused but his touch was gentle.

"This court's taken," she hissed.

"I don't want the court. I want the woman," he drawled cowboy-style, smiling down at her.

His smile lit up a pair of beautiful blue male eyes. She couldn't think for the bewildering waves of warmth that heated her trembling body.

His features—the wide forehead, the carved cheek and jaw, the strong chin and straight nose—seemed chiseled from dark stone. He was blond, and he kept smiling. Cowboy or no, he was gorgeous, too gorgeous to smile in such a crooked, sexy way.

He wore a washed-out blue cotton shirt that stretched tautly across powerfully muscled shoulders. She felt mesmerized, frightened. She wanted to look away. To catch her breath. But when he didn't release her from his level gaze, she found herself gaping at him instead.

"Darling," the charismatic stranger drawled. "Don't get so riled."

Her face flamed. "Darling?"

She echoed his endearment in a dumbstruck tone, but apparently he thought she was using it in the same seductive manner he had.

"God, you're beautiful," he murmured in that deep voice that made shivers crawl up and down her spine. "What do you say we kiss and make up?"

"Y-you're crazy."

A lazy look of wickedness and delight stole over his face. "Only about you."

She shoved at him, but it was like trying to move a mountain of rock.

"One kiss," he whispered, grinning down at her in a manner she found absurdly engaging.

His long fingers wound into her thick hair, gently pulling her head back so that the curve of her slender neck all the way down to the provocative swell of her breasts was exposed. He lowered his mouth to hers.

She caught the heady scent of his after-shave, and it worked on her shattered senses like an aphrodisiac.

She swayed closer. Why wasn't she doing anything to stop him? Why was she just standing there with her lips pursed in readiness?

Like one hypnotized, Jess watched the tantalizing descent of his beautifully sculptured lips. At the last second, in a frenzy she tried to twist away but that had only made him more determined. His lips ruthlessly zeroed in on hers.

She opened her mouth to scream, but his tongue merely slid inside it. He tasted faintly of cigarettes. She could smell his hot, masculine scent, and the odor was warmly erotic. She felt the heated dampness of his skin under her fingertips. His wide brown hands shaped her against him, and every bone in her skeleton turned to wax.

She felt a quickening deep inside her, a longing so intense that she felt faint. He was breathing unevenly himself.

One kiss with this brash, blond, suntanned cowboy, and she was dissolving into him. One kiss was merely the appetizer that whetted her appetite for the whole meal.

Alarm bells were ringing in her ears. But she ignored them. Her arms circled his neck with a moan.

She felt him shudder and her heart leaped as she realized he felt it, too.

Suddenly he released her.

He had that lopsided grin plastered on his gorgeous cocky face again. His golden hair fell in sexy tangles across his brow.

"God, you're hot," he whispered, his low tone huskily

pitched. "We shouldn't waste this on tennis. Your place or mine?"

His insolence snapped her out of her hypnotized state. She had no idea who this impertinent sex maniac was and why he might be kissing her, nor why she was so crazed by his kiss that her mind refused to work logically.

The most appalling thing of all was that she was actually tempted!

His place? Dear God!

Utterly shaken, her reaction was pure instinct. Her hand slammed into his brown cheek with all the force she was capable of. "Just who do you think you are, you lunatic?"

That got his attention.

His sheepish, charming look died instantly. He stared at her for a long moment as he rubbed the red mark on his face, his blue eyes smoldering with a rage equal to hers. "What the hell's the matter with you?"

"What the hell's the matter with you?" she snapped back.

"Darlings!" Deirdre popped out of the cabana with two iced colas. "Hey, great! Tad! I see you've decided to forgive me."

Jess and Tad glowered at one another, stunned, as the truth dawned on them both.

Whoever he was, he'd mistaken her for Deirdre.

And that kiss, that incredible, melting explosion of body and soul had been Deirdre's kiss! Not hers! For some idiotic reason, Jess felt like weeping.

Deirdre looked trim and cool in her white tennis shorts. She had brushed her hair, and it shone like puffs of gold. She handed Jess a Coke, sharing her own with Mr. Beautiful. "You two getting acquainted?"

"You could call it that," Jess replied coolly.

"Tad, meet my twin, Jessica Bancroft. Jess, my new

boyfriend, Tad Jackson. He's on loan from A & M University for a semester.''

The man and woman who'd just tasted each other's mouths inside and out stood as still as statues, glaring at one another under that hot October sun.

''An Aggie,'' Jess wailed with fresh despair.

There was an ancient pseudo-friendly rivalry between UT and A&M.

''And proud of it,'' Tad murmured drily. To Deirdre he said, ''We already introduced ourselves.''

''Is that what you call it?'' Jess grumbled.

''Great!'' said Deirdre.

''Why the hell didn't you tell me you had a twin?''

''Why didn't you tell me you had another boyfriend?''

These two questions were blurted by both injured parties at once.

''Because Jess always hates my boyfriends,'' Deirdre explained.

Jess felt the man's blue eyes assess her from that hard, sun-dark face with a sweeping, superior coolness.

''This once I wanted the man in my life to make a good impression on Jess,'' Deirdre explained.

''Well, you damn sure made one,'' Jess said slowly and distinctly.

''Did I?'' He met Jess's boldly inspecting stare and returned it with a mirthless quirk to his mouth.

''Don't mind Jess. All she does is study. She thinks she hates men. Especially Aggies.''

Tad's hand went back to his cheek. ''I can tell,'' he murmured. ''Still, the women who protest the most are usually the most susceptible to us.''

''Men take up too much time,'' Jess said stiffly. ''I'm going to be a doctor.''

"All I want is to get married, but our Jess is going to save the world," Deirdre said laughingly, sipping her Coke.

Tad set his hot, insolent gaze upon Jess until she blushed. "Well, the world certainly needs someone to save it. But my personal motto is every man for himself."

His gorgeous voice was low and disturbing, and the vaguely possessive note in it sent quivers down Jess's spine, especially since he kept looking at her.

Jess's face felt warm, too warm, and not entirely from the sun. "I could tell that the first minute I met you," she said, feeling as if she were on treacherous footing as she baited him. "But it's not a very original motto, Mr. Jackson. It happens to be what nearly every human who has ever lived has thought also. Which is exactly why the world is in such a deplorable state."

Jess would never have insulted him had she known that there was no surer way to inflame his interest.

Tad forgot Deirdre and loomed nearer Jess, his mouth tight. "So you're blaming me for the mess we're in?"

"In a way."

His dark brows shot up. "And you're going to change it all?"

"Is it so wrong to want to make a difference?"

"No. But maybe it's just a little hypocritical of you. What can one person do? One…woman?"

She shook with temper and reaction. "How dare—"

He moved nearer. "You see, I could tell—the first minute I met you—that you were a woman with selfish impulses of your own. It's just that you're not as honest about them as I am." Again he let his hot, liquid blue eyes wander boldly over her body. "I know what I want." His gaze lingered on her breasts. "You don't."

"Not so honest," she'd sputtered, furious. She whirled

on her twin. "Deirdre, th-this conceited…individual is the worst boyfriend you've ever had."

His smile broadened. "I take that as a compliment," the conceited individual whispered so close to Jess's ear that his warm breath tingled on her neck. "There's nothing I like better than standing apart from the crowd."

His gaze slid to her lips, and Jess had to fight the impulse to moisten them. She remembered his kiss, and the memory caused a curling sensation in the pit of her stomach.

She was hungry. But not for food. For him.

He was watching her. There was a musing curiosity about the look he gave her, oddly warm and gentle.

Deirdre put her arms possessively around him. "Please, Jess, please quit picking on him!"

Picking on him!

He laughed and lowered his golden head toward Deirdre's so that she could pet him more easily. But his blue, amused gaze was on Jess.

He was horrid! But as she watched the manicured fingers stroking his brown neck, caressing the strong jawline, Jess wanted nothing more than to have the right to touch the smirking devil like that herself.

The sunlight made his hair gleam silvery gold. His dazzling eyes blazed at her, mocking her. His white smile was equally dazzling and equally mocking. Aggie or no, she caught her breath at the masculine beauty of him.

Never in all her life had Jess felt more rawly vulnerable.

She spun on her heel and stomped toward the chain-link gate.

But their voices followed her.

"Oh, dear! I so wanted you two to get off to a great start," Deirdre moaned.

"Well, at least it was memorable," he replied huskily, unperturbed.

"But I don't think she even likes you."

"I think she does," came that silken, know-it-all tone.

Anger boiled up so violently it practically choked Jess. She wished the earth would open up and swallow her because the galling reality was that he was right. On that hot, miserable morning Jess had met and fallen irrevocably in love with the exact sort of scoundrel she'd always told herself she despised. And if that wasn't bad enough, he was an Aggie who belonged to her twin.

Forbidden fruit. Was that why his kiss had been sweeter than candy? And hotter than fire?

Was that why even as Jess quickened her steps across those white-lined, baking green rectangles of clay, deep in her bones, she already craved the sweet hot taste of him again?

Lying in one corner of the court was a brown, crisply creased Stetson with two jaunty turkey feathers sewn into the headband.

His hat!

Suddenly all Jess's frustrations were focused on that wide-brimmed hat with its saucy feathers. She took a sharp detour and made a flying leap right in the center of it and jumped up and down on the crown until it was as flat as a pancake and the quills of the feathers lay limp and broken.

"Jess!" Deirdre yelled.

Jess just dashed toward the gate like a naughty child.

"I can't believe she mashed your hat," Deirdre cooed. "And look what she did to your feathers!"

His laughter was a deep, reverberating bass. "What's one ornery tea-sipping girl to a hat that survived a stampede of ornery bulls?" He shoved a fist into the crown to straighten it. "But I will have to pick up a couple of feathers somewhere. Deirdre, darling," Jess heard him say. "How many boyfriends have there been—I mean—before me?"

So that dart had found its mark, Jess thought with grim satisfaction.

"None that counted, darling," Deirdre purred. "She just said that to stir you up and make you mad."

He placed his crumpled hat with the broken turkey feathers on his head at a jaunty angle. "Well, I don't know about mad, but she damn sure stirred me up."

Jess slammed her car door.

All the way home Jess told herself that she hated him.

But why, oh why, did she keep picturing him in her mind's eye? Why did she keep remembering the piercing quality of his shattering blue eyes? Why did she keep remembering the way his hair had slid like silk through her fingers? Why did she keep shivering every time she remembered his lips on hers, his hands roaming her body?

She clutched the steering wheel and groaned. "Why him? Dear God! Why him?"

Tad Jackson did not even remotely resemble the kind of person she had intended to choose for the role of her leading man. Hadn't she always dreamed of someone tall and dark, a paragon of easygoing affability and charm? Someone who cared about the poor? Someone sensitive and kind who would court her gently? Someone who shared her views, or at least someone who could be persuaded to share them? Someone, although she did not admit this to herself, with a tractable disposition whom she could easily bend to her will? Only recently she had begun to date such a man— Jonathan Kent.

Tad Jackson was the epitome of everything she hated.

But he was tall, whispered a treacherous little voice in the back of her mind. And quite handsome.

But he was blond, and Jess had never had any luck with blonds.

He has the most devastating smile, said the voice. And he knew how to kiss.

But he was a smart aleck. He was also irascible, arrogant and selfish—the conceited sort of male chauvinist who was used to bending women to his will. An Aggie with tunnel vision.

But Tad Jackson had stormed onto that tennis court and taught her that most unforgivable lesson of all.

The truth.

With one kiss that had burned all the way through her to her soul.

With one kiss that had taught her that she did not know herself at all.

With one kiss that had made her betray her only sister.

After that day, Jess had pretended she hated him, but every insult she'd hurled at him had been a lie. Jess had wanted him, and because she had she had ruined all their lives. For that, she had never forgiven herself.

And neither had he.

Six

Tad thought he was dreaming when he awoke in a shimmer of moonlight and felt his hard body nestled into the softness of a woman's. Long strands of glimmering golden hair lay across his arm. In the darkness his fingers had tangled in the gleaming lengths of silk.

Jess. The one woman he hated. Her arms were around him. He lay beside her on a narrow bed. Hers, he realized. In her sleep she had cuddled trustingly against him.

What were they doing here together? Vaguely he remembered her nursing him long into the night. She must be exhausted.

He hardly dared breathe for fear of awakening her. Carefully he slipped his arm beneath her head to hold her to him and then he lay there, savoring the warmth of her nearness, thinking he was crazy to do so.

The sheet was drawn back, and the strap of her gown had fallen down her arm. He could see the movement of her breasts through her thin nightgown; he could see the darker circle of her nipples, their beaded tips pressing against the gauzy fabric every time she breathed.

He inhaled the dizzying sweetness of orange blossoms. And even though he knew the scent and her beauty were a fatal trap, his arm slid beneath her neck and drew her closer.

She moaned softly, and her mouth brushed his temple in an attempt to fight him. "Jackson..."

He liked hearing his name, even his last name, from her lips. Dear God! What was happening to him? That he could feel such tenderness toward this woman who had betrayed him into a marriage that had nearly destroyed him. A phony do-gooder. A woman who'd deliberately kept his child from him for a year.

He hated her. But that didn't stop him from wanting her warmth and nearness now.

Jess opened her eyes and stared at him in sleepy bewilderment. Her muscles tightened and she began to withdraw from the encircling fold of his arms and body. She started to say something. If he gave her half a chance there would be a lecture. He could feel her beginning to struggle. He grabbed her wrists and held her fast.

The velvet moonlit darkness cast a magic spell. The soft night breezes blew through the window and caressed their bodies. Tonight, this moment, there was no hate between them. He did not mind so much that she was meddlesome and determined. Still, if she talked, they would quarrel.

He felt a quickening emotion. Something deep inside him, something he did not understand at all wanted her with him as she had been in her sleep, silent and trusting. She was the wrong woman. He knew this in his bones. But he needed her, as he hadn't ever needed anyone else.

Like an animal following some primitive instinct, he

brought a callused fingertip to her mouth, gently shushing her before she spoiled the mood with some tart comment. He no longer held her by force but by the terrible strength of his will. He kissed her brow tenderly. Then her eyelids. His hand lightly caressed her cheek.

She tried to pull away, but he dragged her back. For a long moment they stared into one another's eyes. With a drowsy sigh of defeat, she closed hers.

They slept again.

When Jess awoke, she could not imagine where she was. She was tangled in Tad's brown arms and legs, her head resting on his shoulder. His beard was tickling her cheek. One of her arms was thrown across his waist; his legs were sprawled on top of hers.

Dear Lord! He looked so dark and virile against the white sheets. Against her paler body. She flushed as she became shudderingly aware of his nakedness and maleness.

He was sound asleep, his skin cool, his breathing even.

Thank God for that. But she couldn't let him find her like this. He was so abominably conceited, he would brag most obnoxiously about how she'd nestled up so close to him. He would never believe that he'd been such an impossible patient, she'd been exhausted from nursing him and had simply collapsed beside him.

Funny, how warm and safe she felt in his arms. It would never do to dwell on that! Cautiously she slid her legs from under his. Once safely out of the bed, she couldn't resist hovering above him for a moment.

How tired he looked, even in sleep. He didn't seem quite so arrogant. The agony of the past year was etched into his lean, dark face. There were new lines beneath his eyes; his tanned skin was stretched across his cheek bones. His hands were callused from hard labor, his skin peeling in places on his palms. She fought against some idiotic instinct to brush the golden hair away from his forehead, to smooth the lines with her fingertips. He drove himself—and everyone else—too hard.

Only minutes before she had felt so safe and contented in his arms. Now she wanted to protect him from the world, from the lies, the betrayal, from everything that had destroyed his life.

"You sentimental fool!" an inward voice scolded. "He hates you."

He must never never know how profoundly he stirred her.

She bolted from the room and from the house as soon as it was daylight, determined to face Wally about the mower.

In the gloom of the gum-scented rain forest, she stared at the shattered mower. It was ten o'clock in the morning and although she'd only gotten a few hours' sleep, Jess felt unusually vital and alive. Behind her, watching her from the cliff was the silent child, with the stuffed brontosaurus clutched in his hand.

The bulldozer had excavated more deeply since she'd been here last. Her gaze ran up the height of the jagged coral cliff where sunlight flickered across the path of torn vines and rock art. Jackson was luckier than he deserved. Any other man of a less stubborn will and constitution would have died from such a fall.

Unfortunately, the mower had not fared nearly so well. The housing was cracked; the blade and the crankshaft were bent. She picked up a wheel and tossed it back down beside the broken aluminum carburetor.

There was nothing for it but to confess to Wally and pay for the mower. Nothing for it but to scramble back up the cliff and head to the hotel. She grabbed hold of a thick vine to pull herself up.

Without warning the sky darkened, and the birds stilled. A sudden eerie silence charged the atmosphere. Normally Jess was not superstitious, yet she sensed something.

A warning.

It was ridiculous. Unscientific. Illogical. The type of superstition or paganism that might lie dormant in the palpitating breasts of other ninnies but never in hers!

A sudden gust of wind stirred the hot, humid air.

The child vanished into the scrub.

Jess felt Deirdre's presence—warning her. Her twin had been here. Something terrible had happened to her here.

Jess's heart beat faster. Her trembling fingers tightened with determination on the vine.

Ninnyville! Poppycock!

For an instant the powerful tug of some dark force battled with her equally powerful will. With a cry Jess flung the vine and its snarl of emerald leaves aside and clambered ungracefully up the cliff. Branches tore at her clothes and skin. The roughened edge of a tree limb nicked her cheek, bloodying it, but she struggled upward.

Above her, Jess heard a footfall. It stopped cautiously. A tiny rock tumbled downward through the vines. There was only silence.

"Hello there," she called out. Then she parted the vines and pulled herself the rest of the way to the top.

There was no one there.

And yet she knew there had been someone. Someone who had not wanted to be caught watching her.

Tad sat at a wicker table in a high-backed wicker chair. Where was Jess, damn it?

The tropical sunlight streaming across the veranda was

bold and hot, and yet without Jess to battle, the morning lacked sparkle.

Her presence was everywhere. The gray painted floor had been mopped with something that made it gleam. No cobweb dangled from the eaves or from the shaded corners. Tad noted these details with amused respect. Jess, and her Dutch-housewife mania for housekeeping. In the past he had loathed this nit-picking trait of hers. A bit of dirt never hurt anything. For an instant he reflected on Mrs. B., his housekeeper, who preferred complaining about all the housework she had to do instead of doing it. What would Jess make of the shambles he'd allowed his homestead to fall into in the past year? Not that he'd ever allow her to set foot on his place, of course.

Jess. Where was she? He had felt out of sorts ever since he'd awakened and found her gone.

Tad sprawled in the wicker chair and rubbed his clean-shaven chin. Lizzie had watched him shave—fascinated. The skin was paler there than the rest of his face, but it felt good to be almost himself again.

Around him a profusion of begonias, spider lilies, cunjevoi and orchids bloomed beneath ten-foot-tall tree ferns. The flower beds near the house had been recently turned, and not a single weed grew among the blooms. Jess had doubtless been busy there, too, after she'd finished with the porch. A high weed-infested, emerald green lawn stretched to the dense scrub where the parrots were conducting a symphony—the lawn that she had meant to mow.

Tad's fever was gone. He was miraculously better. Naturally, he took full credit. His well-being owed nothing to Jess's nursing. He refused to dwell on the memories of how she had hovered at his bedside.

He told himself that he had the constitution of a horse. It took more than pneumonia (he still didn't believe that diagnosis from Dr. Know-it-all) and a kick off a cliff from a she-devil to get him down. Except for being a little sore, he felt invigorated from a night of rest, from a hearty breakfast of eggs, toast, butter, jam and purple passion fruit.

He sipped his coffee and felt bursting with energy.

He was a new man—ready for a cigarette. He fumbled defiantly in his pocket and then remembered that there were none.

A new man, more defiant than before, after that empty pocket, ready for battle with the she-devil.

If only there had been a she-devil to battle. He was almost in the mood for one of her lectures.

Grumpily he eyed the vacant wicker chair across the table. Where was she, damn it? Messing around in someone else's business, no doubt. With her gone, there was no one to fight. And that bothered him even more than the nagging urge he felt for a cigarette.

What did Jess have? The minute he was around her she crawled inside him and took him over until his every thought, his every emotion, centered upon her.

He hadn't seen her since that last hour before dawn when he'd awakened in the moonlight and discovered her nestled in his arms. Vaguely he'd been aware of her getting up some time later, after the sun had risen above the trees. She had crept stealthily out of the room as though she were ashamed of having slept beside him. She had cooked his breakfast, but Meeta and Lizzie had served it.

"Madame doctor went to the hotel to tell about mower you broke," Meeta had explained in her curiously precise English, when Tad had demanded to know where Jess was.

So, now it was the lawn mower *he* broke! Well, when was she coming back? How long did it take to walk two miles to the hotel, fabricate this half-truth, pay for the blasted thing and return? Usually she was efficient as hell.

Though he felt bored and irritable, he decided to waste no more time while she was away. If he was going to wrest control of his daughter from Jess, he needed their passports. That way Jess couldn't disappear with Lizzie the minute she decided to.

He hobbled to Jess's room and began going through her suitcases and briefcases. While he searched, he discovered several journals in which she'd made notes about her experiences in India. Vaguely he remembered her saying she was writing a book.

He found letters from the Indian government warning Jess that she had been admitted as a tourist to India and not as a missionary, that she had no right to operate her clinic even though the neighborhood wanted her to. As if legalities would stop Bancroft!

At last he located Lizzie and Jess's passports in the side compartment of one of her briefcases. Just as he pocketed them he heard a sound outside.

Lizzie bounded into the room, then came to an abrupt standstill when she caught him rummaging through Jess's papers. Two untied purple ribbons dangled from her hair.

"What are you doing in Aunt Jess's room, Daddy? She told me never to…"

He started guiltily, but he couldn't help feeling more secure since it was he who now possessed Lizzie's passport.

"Aunt Jess came to Australia to help us."

"That's what I'm afraid of," he muttered.

"She better not catch you! Come on, Daddy, I don't want you to get into trouble."

"I'm not afraid of her," he roared. Nevertheless, when Lizzie took his hand and pulled him firmly away, he let her lead him downstairs to his wicker chair.

He lifted her onto his lap. "All I want to do is take you home, Lizzie. Is that so wrong?"

"I heard you fighting with Aunt Jess last night. Daddy, you were so mean to her!"

"I wasn't mean. It was your Aunt Jess! She kicked—"

"You were too mean!" Lizzie gave him a long, searching look. Then she jumped off his lap and went to watch a weird bug inch its way across a fern. "Why don't you want Aunt Jess to come? She can take care of me. She can write her book."

The last thing he needed was Dr. Know-it-all setting up a command post at his station.

"I'm going to take care of you," he stated emphatically.

"I want her, too! I'll be scared when you're gone. I need her."

There was no way around the fact that Jess had been the only mother Lizzie had known for the past year. Tad remembered Deirdre's neglect. The only mother ever! No wonder Jess held his daughter's heart in a stranglehold.

Lizzie's childish mouth trembled. "Will you go away and leave me alone all the time, the way you used to? What if the bad men come while you're gone?"

He knew too well from his own childhood what abandonment felt like. He thought of how lonely he'd been the year Lizzie had been away. A vertical crease of worry formed between his brows. He'd been thinking of sending Lizzie to school until the station was safer.

"Aunt Jess pays attention...just to me. You never did that."

"Jess has her clinic in India," he said lamely. "What would all those sick people do without her?"

"She got another doctor to come for a while and take her place. Daddy, you don't know her like I do! She'll be sad and cry if I go away and leave her."

"Somehow I can't imagine your Aunt Jess crying."

"But she does. When it's dark and she can't fall asleep,

when she thinks nobody knows. I saw her one night when I sneaked up to tell her I wanted a glass of water and I couldn't find my purple cup. She was in her bed looking real sad and holding Benjamin's picture. She showed it to me and let me climb in bed with her. Then she told me about him. He was her little boy, but he was killed. She'll never see him again. That's why we can't go away without her. She'll be all alone.''

At the thought of Jess crying over Ben's picture, a strange feeling gripped Tad. He'd known long, sleepless nights the year Lizzie had been gone. He remembered the shimmer of desperate loneliness he'd seen in Jess's eyes.

There were quick, brisk footsteps on the stairs. The light patter of sound grew louder.

Bancroft.

He had learned the sound of her years ago and he felt cheered, much more than he wanted to. She was back. Safe. For the first time he realized how worried he'd been.

Behind him the footsteps stopped. She had seen him.

He inhaled the scent of orange blossoms. Jess's presence hovered in the air, electrifying him. He had difficulty trying to breathe and there was an odd tightening in the pit of his stomach.

''Bancroft?''

''You're better, I see,'' came her crispest, no-nonsense voice.

He turned and saw her. The expression in his eyes grew momentarily soft.

She was standing in a shower of sunlight. Her hair in its prim knot was as bright as gold. Her cheeks were radiantly flushed. As always she wore a white poplin blouse buttoned all the way to her throat. Only this one had a torn sleeve. He saw a tiny scratch across her cheek.

"Did you hurt yourself?" he began, his voice filled with concern.

"I—I tripped," she said. "I—I'm okay."

In his mind's eye he saw the broken bits of rubber hose, Deirdre's diving gear scattered upon the sand. "Where were you?" he demanded.

"Paying for the mower that you—"

"That *you* broke," he finished. "It damn sure took you long enough."

"Wally got to talking about the hotel expansion."

"And no doubt you insisted on seeing the plans and sharing a few of your own ideas."

"As a matter of fact I do know a thing or two about building. I couldn't resist helping the poor, befuddled—"

"I knew it!" This was a roar. "You are the bossiest! The most impossible—! Poor Wally!"

Jess's face darkened.

"Aunt Jess, please don't mind if Daddy gets grumpy and picks quarrels with you. He's been sick, and he always gets like this when he sits around by himself and starts feeling lonesome."

"Grumpy?" Tad almost snarled the word. "Lonesome? I was as happy as a lark while she was gone!"

Lizzie bounded into her aunt's arms to protect her.

"You're right, darling," Jess agreed in her sweetest, most galling tone, petting her niece and retying the purple ribbons as she ignored Tad. "He's impossible now." Jess hesitated. "The pity of it is that he's even worse when he's well."

"Worse!"

Lizzie snuggled even more tightly into her aunt's arms, and Tad reined in his fierce desire to rant endlessly as he observed the easy affection and trust between the two of them. With a pang of something that felt almost like—like jealousy—he watched Jess stroke the bright red curls tenderly, her face softening.

"Look, Aunt Jess! He shaved it off!"

"So I see."

Jess's expression was an attempt at sternness, as she studied him. Suddenly she smiled, that charming smile that lit up her eyes. His own anger and jealousy vanished. He stared at her, dazzled.

"I'm glad to see that you haven't acquired a double chin since I saw you last, Jackson," she murmured drily, coming nearer, inspecting the hard line of his clean-shaven jaw with disturbing intensity. "Or a scar."

"What?"

"In fact, I'm surprised." She squinted, studying every detail of the hard jawline, the stubborn, clenched male mouth. "I was afraid you must be hiding some new defect. Why else would a man as vain and cocky about being handsome as you are cover your face with those beastly whiskers?"

He dismissed vain and cocky and beastly.

Handsome. He felt inordinately pleased by her backhanded compliment. In spite of himself, he grinned at her. "I'm glad that you…approve of my face."

There was a brief silence. Lizzie, who had tired of being hugged, bounded exuberantly outside to chase blue butterflies across the lawn. For a moment Jess's gaze followed the child. Then she turned back to the man.

"I'm sure most women who do not know you as well as I do approve of your face, Jackson."

"Ah, but you who do know me, and quite well…" He let his eyes flash with delicious, joyous insolence. "You approve, too."

"That would not be my choice of term. I heartily disapprove of your conceit, of your arrogance… In short, of the multiple defects in your character. And character is what really matters in a man.''

"Well, at least there's something about me you like.'' He grinned at her. "That's a start.''

"A start?''

The most horrendous, the most outrageous idea had popped into his head. He was remembering the way Jess's eyes shone every time they touched Lizzie. He was thinking of his own excitement every time he found himself in this impossible woman's presence. He was remembering how the station had been this past year. He was bored with the dreary sameness of his lonely existence. And sometimes when he was bored he did crazy, crazy things.

"A start in the right direction,'' he replied casually. Tad's heavy-lidded eyes swiftly appraised the slim, full-breasted woman standing before him. She was wearing her khaki shorts again, and a great deal of honey-toned leg was exposed. But he wasn't looking at her shapely legs. He was studying the stretch of starched white poplin across her breasts.

He remembered those breasts, those ripe, lush breasts with their enchanting strawberry tips, rising and falling against the hot skin of his chest last night. He thought of her narrow waist, her curving hips, the long, luscious legs and he became uncomfortably warm as he remembered how marvelous she was in bed. Despite all the reasons he had for hating her, despite her contrary disposition, she excited him as no other woman ever had.

He had always wanted her.

He had just been tricked into taking the sister instead.

Jess's lashes fell before his bold, deliberate scrutiny, and she held her breath in an agony of embarrassment and irritation. He lowered his gaze—not a second before she would have blasted him with a barrage of temper.

He was insane—to even think of it. But at the mere thought of it, his blood tingled through his veins, setting every nerve alert.

His eyes rose to her breasts again.

He thought of the danger.

But there would also be the opportunity for revenge. She had betrayed him. She had made love to him, made him love her, and then... He remembered the years of bitter, soul-destroying pain with Deirdre.

Quickly he looked away, but he had made up his mind in that instant.

He was going to take Bancroft to the station with him. What were bullets and bandits to someone like Jess? It was time he took the upper hand with her and used her for his pleasure in the same way she had used him.

He wasn't going to fight her about it, after all. He was going to placidly agree to her plan. Of course, they wouldn't get along. He would have to endure her busybody presence. She'd insist on running things. So would he. They would fight like tigers.

But that's what tigers were meant to do.

He smiled back at her. He was drowning in the inky, gold-flecked darkness of her sparkling eyes. Long ago she'd looked at him in that same way when he'd made love to her, the night she had betrayed him.

"I see my medicines and my nursing have done the trick," she said, congratulating herself immodestly in that manner of hers that usually annoyed him.

Naturally, like any man with a dash of conceit in his nature, he felt it his duty to eradicate such an abominable trait when he found it in a woman.

"I wasn't very sick," he said huskily, deliberately goading her. "I'm healthy by nature."

She frowned slightly. "Oh, really?"

"Really. I didn't even need a doctor."

Her eyebrows arched. She pursed her lips at his conceit and ingratitude. "Yesterday you thought you did."

"You may be interested to know that I've decided to let you come with me to Jackson Downs," he said magnanimously.

"You already agreed to that last night."

"What?"

"When you were delirious. You practically begged me."

"When we were in bed," he amended. "At such times, a man will say anything."

Her narrowed eyes went from deepest black to fiery gold—her haughty-empress look. And yet beneath the look, he sensed a profound pain.

She moved jerkily, turning her back to him and crossing the veranda to the side door.

"I'm sorry if I embarrassed you," he pursued softly. He said that only to prevent her leaving.

She stopped.

"No you're not, Jackson. You're used to treating every woman as if it's your intention to seduce her."

"Not every woman," he said thickly. "I already succeeded with you—once before."

She sucked in a quick breath. Her fingers trembled as she struggled to open the door.

He jumped out of his chair and sprang toward her. She backed against the wall.

"Y-you're just saying this so I won't come," she said.

"Am I?" He towered over her, laughing, conscious of a hot male excitement. Once she had made him want her, and she had used his desire for her to destroy him. "Maybe I'm saying it so you will."

Scant inches separated them. She was so beautiful, like a goddess, with the sunlight turning her hair to glowing gold, with the color high in her cheeks. He longed to trace a fingertip gently across the jagged cut on her cheek. She turned from him and struggled with the door.

Dimly Tad heard the doorknob rattling furiously, but he was overwhelmed by an urge to touch her. Instead of doing so, his brown fingers clasped the brass doorknob, and twisted it. "Here, let me help you."

She yanked her fingers away, but not before his had touched them. Her face was as vividly red as a bush fire. He was afraid she might pop a blood vessel if he delayed her exit a second longer. Still, under the circumstances, a parting shot was irresistible.

"You know what they say?" he whispered silkily.

"No. And I don't want to know, either!"

He studied the curve of her full, lush lips. He longed to kiss her. It would be so easy to pull her into his arms. So easy to see if he could turn her blazing anger into blazing passion.

"I'm going to tell you anyway," he said. "They say the second seduction is usually easier—the philosophy being that a fallen temple is more easily plundered. Anyway…I'm looking forward to your stay at Jackson Downs. You said you were writing a book. When you're not doing that and I'm not fighting thieves and murderers, I'll have more than enough time…" The passion in his dark, hot look mesmerized her, and she swayed toward him. His voice was low and charged with emotion as he finished his taunt. "More than enough time to take a tour of the temple…and explore all its charms before conquering it completely and making it mine."

Her face went as white as the painted boards behind her. Her mouth was trembling with rage.

He was filled with an overpowering urge to seize her, to

taste her. Would she melt in his arms? Or would she fight? Either activity would have been most enjoyable.

"You look faint," he murmured solicitously, staring sympathetically at her.

"I've never fainted in my life!"

"Still, you'd better get out of the heat." He opened the door.

She stormed inside.

He heard her brisk footsteps leaping up the stairs, taking them two at a time, and he obligingly slammed the door after her.

Then he sank down in his wicker chair and chuckled softly.

She would be his.

Correction. She already was.

She was just too stubborn to admit it.

And when he was through with her, he would force himself to turn his back on her, as once she had rejected him. He imagined himself in that pleasant moment—satisfied, proud, thoroughly finished with her. In control.

Then a cool wind whispered across the veranda, and the shadows from the rain forest crept across the lawn.

Now that she had gone inside he felt alone, and the same dismal darkness that had filled his heart for the past ten years filled it now—jealousy, rage, love and betrayal. Most of all there was an all-engulfing sensation of hopelessness.

He told himself it was time she paid for what she had done.

Seven

Damn her. It was time he seized control.

For two days Jess had sulked. For two days Tad had endured nothing except stony silence from her, nothing except dark, closed looks of deep animosity every time he attempted to break through the barrier of her tenacious will and tease her. When he addressed her, Jess would answer him only if Meeta was nearby. Then Jess would point her pretty chin high in the air and say in her sternest, bossiest tone to Meeta, "Tell Mr. Jackson thus-and-so." Before he could reply, Jess would turn on her heel and huffily march away to some safer quarter.

For two days Jess had clung stubbornly to her anger.

Despite his frustration, Tad had never admired her more.

He was also pleased by her reaction. For he was sure that no woman could stay mad so long over so little if she were not deeply involved with the man she was mad at.

Every time he was with her he had felt a new and furious tension in her.

The trouble with her was that she was mortally afraid of having her temple sacked. Or maybe she wanted it sacked and hated herself for wanting it. This second analysis was just the sort of conceited idea that appealed to him most, and he chuckled at the delicious thought.

But enough was enough. He was tired of her sulking and her pointed chin. Tired of getting nowhere when he baited her. On that third morning he stomped through the house looking for Jess.

Instead he found Meeta in an emerald-and-gold sari feeding a mulish Lizzie in the kitchen. Lizzie always bounded out of bed before dawn, only to pout and be difficult. "Purple!" Lizzie screamed. Only when Meeta smeared grape jelly on her eggs would Lizzie touch them.

Sugar and eggs. It was disgusting.

"Where is Bancroft?" he thundered, his deep voice unusually resonant in the quiet house.

Lizzie dropped her spoon, and grape-spattered egg hit the floor. At this sudden eruption of sound in her peaceful kitchen, Meeta's liquid dark eyes rose swiftly to his. "Madame Doctor has gone swimming," Meeta replied in her gentle, soothing tone. She looked slightly frightened.

It was impossible to shout at such a woman. He softened his voice. "Swimming? You let her go alone?"

Meeta nodded meekly. "I can't stop Madame Doctor."

Like most bullies, Jess always surrounded herself with human doormats who were too afraid of her to oppose whatever outrageous behavior she might dream up.

"Daddy, don't you be mean to Aunt Jess!"

"Mean?" He was all innocence. "Me? I'm never mean."

"You are to her!"

Bancroft had turned his own daughter against him!

"You eat your eggs, young lady!" He grabbed the jelly jar. "Without this!"

Lizzie was screaming the frantic word "purple" as Tad stormed out of the house and ran down to the beach. An endless expanse of glimmering turquoise stretched toward the horizon where a red sun hung low.

Jess was nowhere to be seen. The sun was turning the water a vivid red. A tremor of anxiety traced through him. He was remembering another time, another woman who had gone swimming alone, a woman who had never returned. If he had to stalk the whole island looking for Bancroft, he would. And when he found her...

He began to stomp through the thick sand, mindless of it until the coarse stuff practically filled his boat shoes and ground painfully against his bare toes. Half an hour later he was drenched with perspiration.

He was about to give up when he found her, dripping wet, kneeling in a spot of dappled sunlight where thick jungle and a jewel-red hibiscus grew to the beach.

He frowned fiercely, feeling so annoyed he fairly radiated grumpiness. She had already been swimming! He felt a sick sensation in the pit of his stomach.

Bancroft's thick, lustrous gold hair was wet and lay glued against her neck. Water glistened on her golden arms. She wore a plain black suit. This scrap of thin, wet stretch fabric was plastered to her well-endowed curves so snugly almost nothing was left to his imagination.

He was struck anew by how lovely she was despite her bossy, hell-on-wheels feminism. She looked deliciously damp and flushed from her swim. She couldn't have been sexier if she were nude. He didn't know what he really wanted to do most—to throttle her or to enfold her in his arms and kiss her good morning.

Her fingers were sifting the sand that wasn't sand at all, but tiny pieces of coral. She held her hand to the sun and looked at all the strange patterns and shapes of the tiny broken pieces. Her snorkel and fins lay half buried beside her.

He moved toward her until his shadow fell across her, and she looked up to see him looming tensely over her, his mouth tight, his face dark.

The sand trickled through her fingers, some of the grains sticking to her wet skin.

His gaze flickered briefly across her lips, which were as full and luscious as a fresh rose. God, she was a beauty. Some day, when he was in the mood for that particular battle, he would tell her that it had always been his opinion that she'd make a perfect centerfold.

Her eyes were wide and dark and frankly curious.

"Hello, Jackson," she said. Those were the first words she had deliberately addressed to him in three days.

He felt a fresh surge of anger that she had been swimming alone. "What the hell do you think you're doing?"

She glanced at him without even a trace of her sulky attitude. "Swimming."

"Do you think I'm blind?"

"You asked."

"Don't you know anything, Bancroft? You shouldn't swim alone. Especially since you're a woman."

Usually she would have bristled at such a tyrannical tone. Usually she would have jumped at the chance to defend an attack against her sex, but she seemed in an odd mood.

"I wouldn't think you'd care, Jackson."

He shouldn't, and the realization that he did terrified him.

She seemed worried about something. "You know I—I usually don't have a superstitious bone in my body."

"I know."

"So this is going to sound ridiculous—coming from me."

"Well?"

"Something drew me to this place."

"Something drew you..." He started to shake like an engine about to explode. "You little fool, this is where—" He stopped himself. Behind her he saw a small black face in the rain forest. Then the child darted away.

"I didn't go far," Jess said. "I stayed in shallow water. Just a few feet away in that clear water there are the most wonderful fish. They are beautiful colors and they all play around like friends."

"Friends?" He snarled the word. He remembered that other morning when he'd come to this same beach and the coppers had shown him the bits of rubber diving hose, all that had been left of his wife.

A shadow must have crossed his face because Jess got up slowly and came to him. "Where did Deirdre die?"

For a long moment he stared at the sand, at the way bits of it were stuck to Jess's slim wet ankles, at the way her thighs glistened.

"Here?" she whispered.

He looked up at her, into her solemn, dark eyes. "Yes."

She came to him and touched him gently on his arm, and he shuddered at even this light brush of her fingers. He sprang back from her.

He wanted revenge, power over her. Not the opposite.

"I sensed something," she said softly. "I don't know how, but I did."

"She was scuba diving not far from here," he muttered.

"Alone?"

He nodded. "She did it often."

"You're sure? Did she have...a friend...on the island? Anyone she might have gone with?"

"Not that I know of."

She was regarding him thoughtfully. He didn't think she quite accepted his answer. "It's a dangerous sport even when you go with someone else. Why would she come here? Why would she risk—"

"Didn't you know your twin, at all, Bancroft? She always did what she wanted, without regard for the consequences." He stopped himself and wearily raked his hand through his hair. "Hell. What am I saying? I never understood her. I only married her."

"Maybe you should have tried harder."

His mouth thinned. He turned away abruptly, not liking the sharp note of accusation in Jess's voice. He was uncomfortable talking about his marriage with anyone, especially Jess, the one woman who'd deliberately set his life on the wrong course. But Deirdre had talked too much, and to Jess. For the first time in a year he felt the need to say something in his own defense. So instead of walking away and repressing his feelings as he usually did, he squared his shoulders and turned back to her.

"Look, I'm not in the habit of talking about my marriage. Not to anyone."

"I know that," she whispered.

"So I don't know why I'm talking to you—of all people!" He stopped and clenched his jaw so tightly he could feel the muscles of his cheek jumping. "Whether you believe me or not, I swear I wanted to make her happy. I tried as hard as I knew how. Nothing worked. We both tried, but we never really touched each other as people. Not even in the beginning...before all the trouble."

"And I always thought you two were so happy back then."

"Happy?" Low, harsh laughter came from his throat. "We were in hell."

"But Deirdre told me—"

"Damn it! Forget what she said! She only wanted everyone to think we were happy. Especially you. Because of..."

Because of that night, he'd almost said, remembering the night when he'd made love to Jess.

He struggled to go on. "I wanted people to think we were happy, too. We had everything money could buy—rich friends, parties. At first Deirdre was insatiable for all the things she'd grown up without. But eventually she wanted more than just the trappings of a successful marriage, and I couldn't give her that. There was an emptiness between us, a coldness."

His gaze was tortured. He stared past Jess as if he were looking back into the misery of that time. "She had other men. She kept a place in Brisbane. Despite its vast size, Australia is a small country in a sense. Rumors got back to me. Sometimes she would stay away for weeks. Then she would come back and things would be better for a while. But the inevitable dissatisfactions always returned. I was the wrong man. Our life was the wrong life. I got so I wanted to bury myself in my work and never leave the station. Lizzie was caught in the middle. Then when the trouble started—" He stopped himself. "If you want to know the truth, the amazing thing about our marriage was that we stayed together ten years."

His mouth was compressed grimly with the memory of that time.

Jess took hold of his wrist and laid her other hand palm-to-palm over his large brown hand. He felt her gentle warmth seeping into his skin.

"I—I'm sorry," she said. "I always thought..."

"Jess—" he began, his head moving to the side in a hopeless gesture. "I know there's no way you could possibly understand."

"But I do."

He saw her loneliness. He sensed that she had known deep unhappiness in her own marriage, as well.

He felt the pull of that special something between them. He wanted to take her in his arms. He wanted to bury his lips against her throat where her pulse throbbed unevenly.

She held her breath. So did he. They both felt themselves inexorably drawn against their wills. Silence crashed around them, and for one long, self-conscious minute they both stared longingly at one another.

Abruptly she pushed him away, her fear of sharing any intimacy with him as great as his. Her brows knitted. Firmly she clasped her hands together and tamped down her feelings. In her most matter-of-fact voice she said, "Jackson, you two stayed together because you were both too cussed and stubborn to quit. There's not anything amazing about it. Not when you consider that you're about the most ornery, the most mule-headed person I've ever known."

His eyes flashed. "Oh, really?"

A gust of wind blew across the beach, and she shivered. He leaned down and picked up her towel, unfolded it and drew it gently around her shoulders. Her skin was icy cool beneath his hot fingertips.

He felt a rush of excitement. He wanted to draw her into his arms and warm her with his body heat.

"I hope you don't mind if I return the compliment and say that you are the most ornery and the most mule-headed person I've ever known," he said lazily, gently.

She smiled at him. "I know all about trying to make my life and myself into something they can never be."

"Truce?" he whispered.

There was a momentary silence as his eyes ran over her from the top of her golden head, down the thick, concealing drape of towel to her shapely calves and ankles. She had long slim feet. Elegant feet. He watched one of her bare toes curl and uncurl in the sand. Even her toes seemed sexy to him.

"Truce." She nodded in agreement. "For now. Until you misbehave again."

He watched the sexy toe bury and unbury itself in the soft, warm sand. It was a good thing she couldn't read his mind. A good thing the thick cotton towel he'd covered her with hid those parts of her anatomy that so tempted him and so embarrassed her.

"Knowing me that won't be long," he said. "Only this time, you're going to misbehave, too."

"Not me. I always behave myself."

She shifted from one foot to the other, and the towel dropped a couple of crucial inches. He saw the erect button tips of her nipples straining against her thin black suit.

With shaking fingertips he jerked the towel upward so that she was completely covered once more. Again his hands brushed her body. Again he felt her cool skin, hotter now, beneath his unsteady touch.

It was getting harder and harder to remember how she had wronged him. Abruptly he drew his hand away. She was watching his clumsy movements warily.

She repeated, and more emphatically. "Jackson, I'm determined to behave myself."

His gaze traveled over the soft roundness of a breast. "That's something I'm about to change," he muttered hoarsely.

Her eyes shot sparks. Then she picked up a great lump of sand and threw it at him. That sent him half skipping, half hobbling out of her range toward the cottage.

"Don't run," she shouted after him bossily. "You'll just get sick again. The last thing I want is to have you lying in your bed again and me doing your bidding."

That stopped him. He turned back with a smile. His look was long and hard, but there was laughter in his voice.

"Honey, you should never have put an idea like that in my head—me in bed, you doing what I say for once."

She was scowling. "And don't call me honey! You know I hate it."

"That's only because you haven't heard it often enough."

"I have no intention—"

"Honey," he drawled huskily, "you're going to do a lot that you have no intention of doing. And soon, my love. Soon..."

Later, as Tad was servicing his Cessna, he was coldly furious with himself. Every second he spent with Bancroft increased the level of intimacy between them.

Dammit to hell, anyway! It wasn't as if he didn't know how treacherous she was. Why couldn't he leave her alone? Why couldn't he just pack his bags and take Lizzie and return to Jackson Downs?

He knew too well all the complications a woman of Bancroft's infuriating inclinations could cause in his life if he let her. But even as he told himself this, he remembered the feel of that soft, silky body clinging to his when she'd slept with him in her bed. He remembered how she'd nursed him so carefully.

And more than anything he wanted to banish that glazed look of haunted sadness he saw so often in her eyes.

Eight

"**O**uch!" Tad shouted, strangling. "Take it easy! I'm a convalescent, you know."

Jess jammed the cold metal spoon into his mouth, and a bitter glob of medicine burned all the way down his throat.

"Really?"

Tad was sprawled across the bed, on top of a pile of plumped pillows. He swallowed the last bit of medicine and wrinkled his nose. This nasty grimace was so overdone that even she laughed, flushing prettily.

Her face lost all its primness, and when she started to move away he grabbed her hand. "I know something you could do, if you really want to make me feel better," he whispered.

The pulse in her wrist quickened beneath his thumb. Then she stiffened and tried to pull away. He just held on, grinning.

When she saw that there was no way to escape until he let her go, she sank down on the edge of the bed.

"All right," she said. "Since you're set on being stubborn I guess this is as good a time as any to talk about Deirdre."

"Again?" he thundered, letting her go. "Hell! More than anything, I want to forget her! Bancroft, why are you so obsessed with her and the way she died?"

"I'm going to swim there again," Jess confided. "Only this time I want to go all the way to the reef."

"What? There are great whites out there."

"There's something about that place that bothers me."

"Something bothers me, too! Deirdre died out there," he growled.

"I'm not so sure about that. Besides, just because you're a man, you have no right to boss me."

He gritted his teeth and sat up amidst the tangle of pillows on the bed. "Does everything always come down to that—man against woman—who's bossing who?"

"With a male chauvinist such as yourself—yes."

He struggled for control.

"Like most men, you think you know more. Just as you think you should be obeyed."

Beneath the sheets he clenched his hands into fists. His mouth twisted into an unpleasant scowl. Dear God, she was impossible! How had he ever imagined for a minute he could keep her safe on Jackson Downs if trouble started?

She leaned over him to straighten a pillow.

"I learned long ago that I was perfectly capable of running my own affairs," continued Dr. Impossible.

She bent lower, and her breasts accidentally grazed his bare arm as she put her hand to his forehead. His skin flamed to her touch.

And he was supposed to be conquering her.

With the dizzying smell of her so close, it was difficult for him to concentrate on her inane arguments, but he managed. "As well as running the affairs of everyone else you happen to encounter."

She drew her hand back from the pillow. "The world could do with a smart woman to run it. You men have had your chance. That's why it's in such a deplorable state! I'll bet it won't take me a week to set things straight at Jackson Downs."

His dark face turned a bright tomato-red. Just as he was about to shout his rebuttal, she returned to their original topic—her swimming.

"It'll be all right, Jackson, if I swim there again."

"I said no!"

"I've got to find out what really happened to her."

His hand closed roughly over her arm. "And I don't want what happened to her to happen to you!"

"It won't."

"If this is a battle to see which one of us is the more thick-headed, it's me!" he yelled.

"I never doubted it for a moment."

He ignored that. "I'm going, too." He shoved sheets and medicines aside and leapt from his bed.

He never wore much to bed, and he was suddenly conscious of her gaze raking his broad shoulders, of her gaze running lower, following the ripple of muscle-ridged abdomen even lower to the white elastic band of his jockey shorts. He felt hot blood crawl up his neck to his cheeks. Damn, he was blushing! Like a high-school kid. He grabbed the sheet and covered himself.

She watched this evidence of modesty on his part with suppressed amusement.

Damn her for being a doctor.

She said only, "This is just the sort of macho nonsense

I'd expect from you, Jackson. If you go swimming, you'll have a real relapse in an hour."

He was hopping around in the sheet, still blushing like a boy, looking for his clothes—which she had hidden. "What do you mean—real?"

"You know what I mean, you big malingerer."

He smiled sheepishly. Then his gaze darkened as he took in the sensual beauty of her. Her golden hair fell about her shoulders in silky disarray. He decided it was time to show her who the boss was. "Can I help it if—for some quirky reason—I don't want you gobbled alive by sharks? If I want you near me?" he whispered huskily. He let his sheet drop a little.

Jess's eyes fell from his face to his brown chest again. She caught her breath. "I know too well what you want. You told me, remember? I'm a temple and you're the barbarian who wants to sack me."

"And you sulked over that for two days." The soft sound of his laughter taunted her.

He came closer. His sheet fell lower. He was as hot as fire. As hard as stone.

She backed away. He had her on the run. Now it was she who was blushing.

God, she was beautiful. So beautiful, he was almost tempted to drop his sheet and let her see how much she aroused him.

"If I was sulking," she said in a prim but slightly breathy tone, "it was because you were so obstinate there was no other way to communicate with you."

"Never mind!" he rasped. "All that matters is what I want now."

Involuntarily her hands came to rest on her hips. Her gaze drifted sensuously up and down his seminude body. "What do you want...now?" she whispered.

The air between them was charged.

"The same thing you do, honey."

Like one spellbound, she came a step closer.

Her mouth was a lush, pearl-flushed pink. Her silver-gold hair fell wildly about her neck.

What he wanted, what he ached for, was to kiss her. To feel her lips quiver beneath his, her arms tighten around him, to feel the press of her soft breasts against his solid chest. He almost groaned aloud, so acute was his torment.

She expelled a sharp breath. "What I want is to go swimming. By myself!"

He had followed her into a dark corner. Her eyes widened as he placed one hand on the wall behind her with studied casualness and leaned forward so that his great body towered over hers. Less than an inch separated them. They were so close he could feel her body heat. So close the scent of orange blossoms invaded every cell in his system. So close the dark intensity of her gaze mesmerized him.

He lifted aside the molten gold of her hair, pushing it away from her neck. "Jess..." He said her name in a gentle tone, reaching for her, lowering his lips.

She swallowed and stood very still. Gently he tilted her chin back. His unerring mouth found the sensitive place at the base of her throat, and he kissed the fiercely quivering pulsebeat there.

She gasped as she felt his wildness. Heat spiraled crazily inside him. Then she drew away.

Desire for her was melting his bones. With a low groan he let her escape.

"I'm going to swim alone, Jackson."

His features hardened. He shrugged. "Okay! Heaven help the sharks!"

Nevertheless, he wasn't nearly so indifferent as he pretended. With sulky misgiving he followed her about the house. He stomped, slammed doors, and made every remark he could think of to goad her as she got ready.

She ignored him. All too soon she was in her sexy, glove-tight black suit and marching officiously out the door carrying her snorkeling gear. Quickly he went to his bedroom, gathered his own gear, put on his suit and raced after her.

When he got to the beach she was already walking knee-deep into the waves. Her smile triumphant, she waved to him as he hopped about on the hot sand. He was furious as he struggled into his own flippers. He watched her disappear beneath the smooth, placid surface.

Then he waded into the shallow water. She swam farther and farther away, with him snorkeling behind her at a grudging distance. It took them a quarter of an hour to reach the reef. They swam amongst a school of fish that cavorted so enthusiastically they roughened the surface of the ocean.

A nagging worry plagued him—hordes of small fish brought bigger fish.

It was difficult to keep his eye on her in the rough water. He watched the school of fish stir the water. She kept swimming onward.

Just as they reached the reef, he saw the elongated dark body of something huge roll beneath them in the water. Another immense sea creature slid by him. A shark! Doubtless, there were more he couldn't see.

A pair of dolphins cavorted in the distance. Dolphins or no, he didn't like swimming with big things.

At just that moment Bancroft dove. Her black fins flipped water and then disappeared beneath the turquoise waves. Something immense brushed his leg. What was it? Where was Jess?

Hell!

What kind of wimp was he to let her run things? Rage strangled all his other emotions. He quickened his speed to catch her, using long, hard strokes to cut the water.

He waited for her to surface. Then he grabbed her by the hair.

She thrashed wildly in his arms.

He let her go. He ripped his mask off his face. "Swim back to shore," he yelled.

She pulled her snorkel out of her mouth and lifted her mask. "What?"

"Sharks!"

"I'm not afraid…"

"Swim back or I'll drag you back. If we splash a lot that attracts them."

"I know that! What do you think I am—some idiot?"

"Honey, you just read my mind."

If they'd been on shore, she might have slapped him. Instead all she could do to show her anger was to narrow her eyes and tread water mulishly.

"Swim or I drag you. It's your choice," he growled.

"Some choice." But something in his fiercely determined expression startled her into obedience. She swam toward shore. He followed her, keeping a wary eye on those large, dark shapes darting about making a meal of the teaming fish.

When they reached shallow water and Jess was trying to race ahead of him, Tad caught her and yanked her into his arms. The heat of his body burned into hers.

"You could have gotten us both killed!" he bellowed. "Those sharks—"

"Shark," she hissed nastily. "I just saw one, and he was only a baby. The rest were dolphins. If you're so scared why didn't you just stay on the beach?"

His blue eyes flamed as they swept over her flawless womanly form. He wanted to hate her, but his hatred had blurred and changed into a new, more powerful emotion that he could not recognize. All he knew was that she was Jess. His Jess. Infuriating, stubborn, impossible…and yet his stomach felt hollowed out at the thought of something happening to her.

His grip was making reddish marks on her arms. "I came after you because I didn't want you to die…the way Deirdre died," he muttered roughly.

His words fell away, fading into the silence of the glimmering afternoon, and yet the low, throbbing emotion that had governed them remained.

Her face was soft, sad, hauntingly lovely.

The familiar gnawing ache her nearness always aroused was back in his gut, only stronger than ever before. There was a wildness in him.

An answering wildness was shining in her eyes.

He jerked her closer, his large hands spanning her waist, their imprint burning through the wetness of her suit. For once, she did not resist him. His skin was mahogany dark against her paler body; his muscles sinewy and dangerous, her curves soft and feminine, molding him.

The sensation of her body pressed into his inflamed him. The creamy mounds of her full breasts pushed against the hard wall of his chest. Every muscle in his body tightened, and slowly his gaze lifted to her face. She began to tremble as the full force of his passion jolted through her.

Her dark, glowing eyes met his, and he felt her soul reaching out to him even as she fought an inward battle against the arousal of her senses. The wildness was drumming in his own pulse.

He knotted his fingers into the tangled masses of her hair.

He pulled her closer until he felt the taut, quivering warmth of her body responding to his.

It was as if every moment of his life had been leading to this moment. Waves crashed against white coral. It was all he could do not to resist pulling her down in those warm, roiling waters and taking her. But anyone could see them. He had to take her somewhere where they could be alone.

Her fingertips came up tentatively and brushed the wiry vee of wet curls that grew on his chest, and she pushed at him to disengage the arms that locked her body to his.

Her touch set him on fire. He tightened his grip and drew her even closer.

Her eyes widened as she felt beneath her fingertips the flexing of his muscles, smooth as hammered steel, latent in their sexuality.

He could feel her heart racing; her breath quickening. Her fierce excitement mingled with his own.

Their eyes met and held. He felt the power of her stubborn will battling against her desire.

Her body stiffened.

"Don't," she whispered. "You don't really want me! You never did. You were hers! Always hers! Never mine! You blamed me for ruining your life! Well, what do you think you did to mine? You used me! I never loved Jonathan. And I ruined his life because I couldn't."

His hands bit into the soft flesh of her upper arms as she tried to pull away. "No."

"I—I want to talk about Deirdre right now. Not us. Or at least I want to think about her."

"Deirdre!" Damnation! "Now?"

Jess's big, grave eyes implored him. "Now."

Every male nerve in his body was aroused. He felt enflamed, enraged. He was so frustrated he wanted to smash something to bits if he couldn't have her. Instead he watched the surf breaking on the reef.

Reluctantly, gently, he let her go.

For a long moment she looked at him. Then she walked slowly toward the beach.

He felt like a bottled-up volcano.

He bit his lip until he tasted blood. Until pain brought back his self-control. Then he went after her, throwing his snorkeling gear in the sand beside hers.

Their eyes met again, and they both felt the new awkwardness between them.

"It's gorgeous down there, but eerie," she said in a strange, unsteady tone.

"Hell."

"I could almost hear things breathing, sucking in and out like a respirator. I mean everything under there is eating everything else, and when you watch it for a while, the beauty turns into ugliness. It's sinister. Something beautiful will lure something equally beautiful to its death."

"It's the cycle of life and death," he said. "Deirdre loved it here. She loved the reef."

Jess's mood was pensive. "Why did she take the money and then come here? Why? I have so many unanswered questions. I don't think she died in the water. I wish now that I'd known her better. But I never really could because except for a few summers and college we grew up apart. She and Mother always had so little money that they had to live with my uncle in New Orleans. I stayed with my father and grew up in oil camps and lived all over the world."

Damn. Tad didn't want to talk about this. Aloud he said, "I know. She envied you and what she imagined as your exciting life."

"Exciting! Ha!"

As always Jess's haunted, lonely eyes touched some deep chord within him. He knew too well what it was to feel starved for affection.

"You survived," he said.

"Yes, but I dreamed of being part of a real family."

"I was part of a real family. It only makes it worse when your own marriage fails."

"Maybe. All I know is I always wanted to feel close to Deirdre. But I just couldn't somehow. Maybe it was a mistake the way our parents split everything, even their daughters, equally when they divorced. Dad believed in clean breaks. Anyway, my only chance to get close to her was when we were in college, but she always resented the fact that Dad and I had so much more money than she and Mother. She knew nothing about the loneliness of my childhood, of the sadness and guilt I felt about the poverty I saw in all those countries where we lived. Deirdre thought I had everything. But she was wrong. And now she's gone. So utterly gone."

A single tear trickled down Jess's cheek and she tried stubbornly to brush it away with the back of her hand before Tad could see.

But he saw. "Hey, it's okay to cry," he murmured.

"I—I don't know why I'm acting like a sentimental fool when I didn't shed a tear when I found out she was dead." Jess was weeping in earnest now. An incoherent torrent of words mingled with her sobs.

His fingers curled and entwined with hers. "We both lost her long before she died," he said gently.

"I think that's what hurts the most."

"It always hurts when you can't love a person you want to love," he said huskily, taking her in his arms. He smoothed her damp hair out of her eyes.

"But you, of all people! To think that you should see

me like this, that I should actually seek comfort from you,'' she wailed piteously, unable to stop the tears.

"Really, Bancroft, your manners are every bit as atrocious as mine," he admonished gently. "And as for gratitude that I'm here to wipe away your tears—"

"Oh, do shut up." She tilted her head back, but her attempt at a watery scowl disintegrated into fresh sobs.

Again she made no objection to being folded more closely in his arms. Indeed she clung to him, and he could not ignore how delicious and hot her body felt pressed into his.

The light was fading. The jungle was deep and dark. The child had not returned. The hushed, silent atmosphere was charged with emotion. Tad knew Jess was vulnerable. Just as he knew that he was probably taking advantage of that vulnerability.

But such a moment might not come again.

Jess—soft and gentle seeking his comfort. He might wait for years for another such moment.

He wanted her. He had wanted her for years, and because he had, his marriage had been a double torment. He had been forced to endure the presence of a woman who resembled Jess so exactly, he had never been able to forget her.

Jess's sobs were subsiding. In another moment she would regain her composure and her independence and push him away.

He locked his arms more tightly about her. He felt the lush, overflowing fullness of her magnificent breasts against his chest.

He was a healthy, red-blooded male.

He had never been a man to waste his opportunities.

It was time he taught her she was his.

Without a word, he lowered his hard mouth to hers and kissed her. She fought him, but he kissed her until she began to tremble again. He kissed her until she was breathless, until she was limp and dizzy and clinging to him. Until her fingers were curling weakly against his neck and into the thick wetness of the golden curls at the nape of his neck.

Then he lifted her in his arms and carried what was surely the most stubborn bundle of femininity in all the world into the jungle.

It was the golden hour of his revenge.

No hour had ever seemed sweeter.

Nine

The sun sank like a ball of flame behind the coral hills, and the moon came up to fill the velvet darkness with silver-spangled fire.

The jungle was hot and silent. Tad was burning with a strange heat that centered in his loins.

His blue eyes fixed Jess like piercing shards of glass. Her own dark gaze widened uncertainly. Without a word, he carried her deeper and deeper into the thick, blackening shadows.

He knew his life was plunging down a fatal course. This woman was all wrong for him. But all he saw was her brilliant eyes, her mouth, soft and inviting. He slid his hands along the velvet heat of her body. A soft sigh escaped her moist half-opened lips. He trembled from the intense shock of his ravening need.

"We shouldn't," Jess protested as he lowered her to the towel that he'd thrown down to cover the soft sand.

She was so right.

"Don't you ever give up, Bancroft?" he whispered, nuzzling her throat hungrily, his mouth hot against her skin while his hands cupped her breasts.

"Give up? Never!"

But he felt her convulsive movement, when the palms of his hands grazed her nipples.

"So you intend to defend the temple to the last?"

"Yes, indeed." But her arms wrapped around his neck as if she would never let him go.

"The hell you say," he whispered, crushing her to him.

"The hell I say," she murmured with a languid sigh of defeat.

He kissed her throat more fervently.

"After this, I'll be the boss," he murmured.

"That's what you think." She flung her words at him hotly. "Jackson, tomorrow you'll pay—"

His long, strong fingers with their faintly callused tips ran possessively over the crests of her breasts in the wet bathing suit. He felt her quiver.

"I'm willing to face the consequences, honey."

His mouth hovered above hers. The fight was gone from her. And from him. For the moment.

She opened her mouth to him endlessly and let his tongue slide inside. She was hot and honey-sweet. He felt the savage building fire of her response.

"I've wanted you," he whispered, "for years. No one but you. Although Deirdre looked exactly like you, she could never take your place. Not in my bed. Never in my heart." What traitor made him say such things? He didn't know. He didn't care.

His fingers closed over the black spaghetti straps of Jess's bathing suit. Her breath caught when his knuckles brushed the smoothness of her shoulders as he lowered the straps. She grabbed his hand, stopping him when the top half of her breasts were revealed. Her breathing was coming in tiny gasps and her pulse was racing out of control.

"No," she whispered bossily.

"Your body's nothing to be ashamed of, Bancroft," he murmured. "You're lovely. Lovely. Your breasts..."

"They're too big. Vulgar."

"Sexy," he argued. He pulled the bathing suit lower.

"They make me feel...dirty, somehow. Men always..."

"They're beautiful. Magnificent. You're beautiful. I want to love them. I want to love you. All of you."

"If I could have had a say in the creation of my shape, I would have asked to be made as flat as two pancakes."

"Thank goodness, then, that for once you weren't around to give your bossy opinion."

She had many faults, but her breasts were all his torrid adolescent fantasies come true. Somehow he controlled his pulsing male instinct to hurry. He touched her, his hands trembling.

Easy. He had to go easy.

And his tender caresses, his hands, his lingering kisses, his sweet murmured endearments—all served their purpose. He took a nipple in his mouth and she gasped. At her response, fire shot from his belly to his thigh. He buried his lips against her tender, voluptuous flesh and suckled her like a babe until she gave out whimpering sounds of ecstasy.

Tad felt so full with male need he strained against his swimming trunks. Still, his shaking hands were gentle as he lowered the straps and removed the clinging wet black cloth. Shifting, he yanked his suit off while she lay back, watching him with deep, dark, languorous eyes as he undressed. Moaning, she pulled him back until he felt himself hard and hot and naked, pulsing against her thigh.

At last she sighed again, softly in surrender.

And so began a long hour of bittersweet delirium for
them both. In no time their stubborn wills were swept aside
before the power of an inexplicable bond. All their differences became nothing. She was sweet; he was tender. For
a timeless, unforgettable moment they were one.

He made love to her in a fever. They came together, flesh
to flesh, gasping, sighing, clinging to each other as if to life
itself, making each other whole, her response as searingly
white-hot as his.

Their hellish private lonelinesses fell away. Never before
had either of them felt anything remotely like it. It was as
if some vital part of them had been dead and was now
brought to life. That other time, ten years ago, had been a
dream to them both, something they hadn't let themselves
believe in.

With bruising kisses, he tasted the salt tang of her skin.
Gently he kissed her slender throat, her trembling breasts.
His tongue dipped deeply into her navel. She opened her
legs, and his lips moved lower to devour that sacred dewy,
musky essence that was hers alone. She was a fire in his
blood, a steaming, pulsating part of him, completely his.

Then she kissed him back, tentatively at first, on his lips,
then everywhere just as he had kissed her. She trailed light
kisses down his belly. There was no part of him which that
succulent, feminine mouth did not lick and nuzzle. Soft
lips, the tongue darting out, traced the back of his earlobe,
curved into the hollow of his throat, traced a tingling path
down his chest to his stomach and lower. Soft lips, hotter
than fire, tickled him until he was wild for her.

Suddenly he could contain himself no longer. He rolled
over, pulled her snugly under him and thrust deeply.

That first moment, inside her, was ecstasy. She was tight

and small. Woman. His woman. Velvet warmth and soul-destroying sweetness.

His salvation.

His damnation.

God, she felt good—tight and all-enveloping, her nipples pressing into his chest, her satin skin, smooth beneath his fingertips.

Then he began to move, too fast.

She cried out. He forced himself to stop and be more gentle even though every nerve in his body throbbed with urgency. Their hearts beat as one. Her hands stroked the damp curls that fell over his forehead. He opened his eyes and lost himself in the blazing darkness of hers.

"Bancroft..." he whispered in a voice so tender he did not recognize it as his own.

All of her primness and bossiness were gone. She was blushing and shy and yet a wanton.

His wanton.

"Jess..." she corrected. A fingertip toyed with his hair. "You are mine.... Darling Jess."

"Mine," she said with those glowing, earnest eyes.

Whether this was in agreement or a possessive statement of her own, he did not know. Or think to care.

He began to move slowly again inside her sensuous warmth. He was careful, matching his rhythm to hers, until passionate waves swept away all restraint and his control broke. Then they were two beings, caught in a cataclysmic swirl of flame and darkness and unwanted passion that carried them out of themselves to a place of exploding ecstasy.

When it was over, they were left shaken and clinging. Vaguely he grew aware of her whimpering softly beneath him, of her body shuddering delicately, of her nail tips pressing lightly into his back. His body felt unbearably heavy and wet with sweat. She lay in his arms, her eyes closed as if she were in a torpid state of insensibility.

There was no strength in any of his muscles. He felt drained, content, unable to move, wishing never to let her go, never to leave this moonlit bower.

And in that moment he knew he was doomed. Dimly it occurred to him that he who had thought to possess was himself utterly possessed.

He shrugged his misgivings aside, and stretched his lean, muscled frame out next to hers. Gradually his body cooled and he drifted to sleep, holding her warm body.

He awoke to a lovely dew-moistened morning. The leaves and branches of the ironbark were black filigree against the red dawn of a brightening sky. He felt balmy, at peace, more self-confident, happier than he had in years.

That was before he reached for her and found that she was gone.

She had done it again!

He jumped up, an angered, naked, abandoned giant. He was alone in the long shadows of the thickly wooded rain forest. She had left him. Without a word. Just like she had before. Why? Damn it!

He had been a fool to have had anything to do with her. He saw his involvement with Jess Bancroft like catching some dreaded disease; once you got it, it never went away. It just kept getting worse.

Where the hell was she?

He grabbed his bathing suit. It was gritty and cold, but no colder than the fury filling his heart as he slapped the suit hard against a gum tree so that zillions of particles of silvery sand rained down onto the beach towel. Then he yanked it on.

He felt the same total despair and rage she'd plunged him into ten years ago when she'd made love to him and then run off and served him up on a silver platter to her sister.

It didn't matter that Jess had given herself to him. All that mattered was that she'd left him. Again.

He should have taken Lizzie and thrown Jess out the first chance he'd gotten. That's what he would do now, as soon as he found her.

Quickly he raced up the trail that skirted the cliff. Halfway to the cottage, he came to the place where she'd shoved him off the cliff. The bulldozer hovered precariously beside the cliff's edge. He was about to hurry onward when he was startled by two things. First he saw a man stealthily climb out of the bulldozer and sneak down the shadowy trail.

Tad was about to yell at him, when he heard the secretive sound of Jess's voice coming from below.

Tad peered through the vines but could see nothing. Then he pulled himself into the bulldozer which commanded a better view. He could see Jess bending over a child. Had the man in the bulldozer been watching Jess, listening to her? With what intention?

A key dangled from the ignition.

The bulldozer was parked on the very edge of the cliff.

The bloody bastard!

An ice-like throbbing started in Tad's stomach. He sucked in a hard breath. All it would take was a flick of the wrist, and the thing could be started, put in gear, and it would have driven itself over the cliff and smashed whomever was down there. In his mind's eye, Tad saw Jess, still and white, crushed beneath the bulldozer.

He thought of his road train, which had been blown up on Jackson Downs. The cattle had all died. The driver had been severely injured.

In an instant Tad's fury toward Jess died, and he knew

that he wanted to protect her at all costs. Even at the risk of his own life.

The bastards! Had they followed him here? Were they after her, too?

Tad wished he'd chased the man and beaten him until he found out who he was and what he wanted—who had sent him here. And why.

With a shaking hand he parted the thick green vines. Jess was kneeling beside the wall of rock art, looking as prim as always in her baggy shorts and white poplin blouse. Her face was serenely unaware of the slightest danger. For all her courage and stubborn will, she was a fragile woman. He was determined to protect her.

With one hand she picked up a thick bouquet of wild flowers. In the other she was fingering a tiny, shiny object that gleamed in her open palm. A child with matted yellow hair hovered at the edge of the trees. He was clutching a stuffed toy with a tattered purple ribbon against his bony chest as if it were very dear to him.

"So you thought I was a ghost?" Jess asked gently.

The child nodded. "I'm glad you're not her. I didn't like her. You gave me..." The dark hand tightened on the animal pressed close to his heart.

"And you gave me this." Jess took one last look at the bright object she was holding and then carefully pocketed it. "Thank you. She was my sister. Do you know what happened to her?"

The big liquid-black eyes rolled in terror.

"Tell me," Jess pleaded. "Don't be afraid."

"He come back, too," the boy whispered.

"There are no such things as ghosts." The boy merely listened. "She didn't go swimming, did she? Not that last day. She came here to meet a man. A man who..."

"He come back, too."

"What happened to her?" Jess pleaded. "Please tell me."

"She fell down. He hit her with rock."

"Where?"

The boy caught sight of Tad through the vines and pointed at him, screaming incoherently.

Jess turned. Tad sucked in a deep breath. Damn! Was that brat trying to frame him for Deirdre's murder? Was Jess encouraging him?

Tad grabbed the vine and crashed down beside them. The child took one look at the flying male figure. The whites of the boy's eyes rolled. Then his high-pitched wails began again. "He come back, too! He come back, too!"

Tad lunged for the child, but the boy made an agile side-step and ran. Tad raced after him through the rain forest, crashing against trees, stumbling over roots, but the boy was faster and nimbler. He slipped between a crack in the forest wall and disappeared soundlessly into the gloom. In his panic he had dropped his stuffed dinosaur.

Panting and breathless, Tad leaned down and picked up the dinosaur. "The little lying thief! This is Lizzie's."

Jess was right behind him, panting and breathless, too. "I gave it to him, you big idiot!" Jess snatched the animal from him. "What do you think you're doing?" She placed it back on the ground so the child would find it when he returned.

Tad was equally enraged. He yanked her into his arms. "What's going on here? 'He come back!' What's that supposed to mean—that I killed her?"

Jess caught the wrenching agony in his low tone.

"No, you dope. The kid was so scared, there's no telling who he thought you were! But I might know if you'd kept quiet and let me play detective a bit longer. As it is... Oh, Jackson, why must you always be so difficult?"

"Me?" His tone was offended. She was the one who'd abandoned him! If he hadn't come along, she and the boy might have been crushed under that bulldozer. His hand dug bruisingly into her arms.

"These things take subtlety, not Tarzan machismo coupled with one of your childish temper tantrums," she hissed. "I was trying to help you."

Her dainty chin was thrust out. Her offer to help was the most provocative remark she could have made.

"Damn your help! I don't want it! I'm not some poor, starving, diseased native. What on earth makes you so conceited that you think you can manage my affairs better than I can? You who know nothing of Australia?"

"I have lived all over the world. People are the same everywhere."

"These people are dangerous."

"I've dealt with dangerous people before."

"Damn! Why did you run away without telling me?" All this was a muted roar. He did not tell her of the man who'd been watching her.

She smiled sweetly, having regained control of her temper. "I couldn't sleep, and you looked so tired I didn't want to disturb you."

He didn't believe her. Not for a moment. But he let her go on.

"So I got up. When I got to the cottage, the boy was there. I dressed and followed him here because I think he knows what happened to Deirdre. I was on the verge of something important, if only you hadn't decided to be Rambo."

"Deirdre." Tad ground out the name. "It's always Deirdre. She's dead. Why can't we just forget her?"

He held Jess close. He should have cast her aside and walked away. If he were smart he would never see her again. But his eyes were drawn like magnets to the luminous pain he saw in her dark gaze.

He buried his face against her throat with the profound despair of one totally lost. "Dear God, I want to forget her." Dear God, no matter what Jess had done, no matter what she would do to him in the future, he didn't want to lose her, too.

"I can't, till I know what happened to her."

"It's too dangerous, you fool." His mouth came down on Jess's, kissing her fiercely.

Her hand caressed the sandpaper roughness of his cheek.

"Damnation!" he growled. "You're the sexiest, stubbornest... You're driving me crazy. I can't live with you. I can't live without you."

"We can't shut out the world and pretend it doesn't exist, Jackson."

"Damn it, I don't care how she died anymore. I don't care if my station goes up in flames."

"I care."

"Damn. Why can't you understand it's too dangerous for you to get involved?"

Ten

"**D**on't give me another one of your bossy lectures!" Tad yelled.

For once she obeyed him and stopped talking. Jess stood on the other side of the white-sheeted bed and smiled at him.

She was so damn beautiful it hurt.

The thought of anything happening to her...

Tad's fear was a knife severing every vital organ in his gut. Why was she always so set against what he was for?

The rosy morning sunlight was like flame in her tousled hair. A pink stream of light sifted through the bedroom shutters behind her, revealing the outlines of her body.

Tad clenched his fists to keep from grabbing her and pulling her toward the bed. He could still taste her deep inside his mouth. The scent of her still lingered on his skin.

Why her, dear God? He hadn't wanted any woman in his life. Ever again. Why her?

He opened his eyes once more and began to perspire as he studied her. The glimmering backlight gave her the appearance of a voluptuous angel.

He was still furious, but more than that he was scared. In the jungle he had begun to realize he was beginning to care for her more deeply than he had ever intended.

Hell.

He was scared of caring, scared she would do to him what she had done before. Scared that she would stay with him only for a little while, just long enough to ensnarl every emotion in his heart. Then she would flit off and leave him to try to put together the shattered pieces of his life again.

What a fool he was. He'd thought he could have sex with her and be done with it. Never with any other woman had sex come with such an emotional price tag.

One taste of her, and he wanted her completely—not only for her body but for her stubborn mind and soul.

And she knew it.

He kept staring at her. Inside the bedroom it was as silent as a tomb. The only sound came from the breeze outside rustling in the rain forest.

Then Jess spoke. "You are the most stubborn man on earth. Why can't you understand that I came to Australia for the sole purpose of helping you and Lizzie? That's not such an awful thing."

The muscles in his throat tightened. At last he rasped, "I don't want your help!"

"I don't care. I'm here to stay."

"Deirdre was my wife. What happened to her is my problem."

"She was my sister, and she came to me for help. She told me something—"

"I won't have you interfering."

"You can't stop me," she whispered.

"I'm trying to protect you, you little fool."

"I've managed very nicely all these years without you around to protect me."

"Forget Deirdre."

"Okay. For now." Jess kicked her damp leather sandals off, arched her feet and wiggled her toes against the bare wood floor. "You want me around more than you'll admit."

"What?"

Her luscious mouth quirked in a seductive smile. "You do. I can tell."

"The hell I do!"

She just stared at him and wiggled her naked feet. Then she lifted her fingers to her hair and shook it so that it fell in a heavy, silken mass over her shoulders. Slowly, sensuously she combed her fingers through it. It was gold and silver, alive, on fire.

His heart began to pound, and he could think of nothing but his desire to shove his hands into her hair. He stood stock-still, looking at her.

Her eyes were half closed, her skin flushed a glowing rose. She pulled her hand from her hair and let it trail down her bare throat to the shadowy place between her breasts. She unbuttoned the first button of her blouse.

He wanted to rip the rest of the buttons apart. To shred her blouse. To clasp her to him. To feel her naked body beneath his again.

"What are you doing?" His voice was harsh. "Damn you! Do you really think you can get around me with sex?"

That quirky smile again. "Probably."

He was intoxicated by the sight of her, even though he could feel the danger, close, too close, swirling around them like a treacherous mist. Somehow the bastards had figured out that she mattered to him, and they would use her—to get to him.

He was on the verge of yelling, of smashing something, of doing anything to distract himself from the hot, sensual tension between them, but the narrow bed at the center of the room made him remember the night they'd slept together there, her body pressing into the heat of his.

He knew why she had brought him here. She knew his weaknesses.

"Quiet," she whispered, touching a vertical fingertip to her lips and then blowing him a wanton kiss. "No more of your pompous shouting. You'll wake Lizzie."

Pompous! His eyes traveled up the curved length of naked, honey-toned legs to the cuffs of her baggy shorts, and he forgot the insult.

He should never have followed her to her bedroom.

It was too late now.

She softly crept toward the bed and leaned back against a bedpost, watching him with her dark eyes as she began to unbutton the rest of the buttons of her blouse.

She arched her spine, stretched. Her breasts jutted towards him. White cotton peeled away to reveal the lush honey-gold fruit of her silken body.

Inch by inch, the poplin shirt was coming off. He watched cool ivory cloth slide slowly against fiery hot, womanly skin as she pushed the fabric down her shoulder. Carelessly she tossed it away into a pool of darkness. Her breasts were covered by wisps of beige silk and lace. He could see the outline of her nipples, delicate and dusky pink pushing against the silk cups.

An unwanted thrill coursed through him. He muttered a low, strangled curse.

"And you don't want to wake Lizzie, do you?" Jess

murmured. "Not till we…" The sensual promise of her unfinished sentence hung in the hushed room.

He made no further sound. Their eyes met. Hers were blazing, and they lit a fire in him. If she was trying to break him, she was succeeding.

With a lingering fingertip she slowly traced the swollen roundness of a breast. The movement was intended to arouse, to primitively provoke his male mating instinct.

And it did.

Normally she was so shy about her breasts. This about-face held the tantalizing allure of the forbidden.

"Touch me," she pleaded.

He wanted to so badly he hurt. His senses reeled with his longing. A muscle ticked savagely along his jawline as he struggled to withstand her. He balled his fingers into fists until he felt hard bone bite through flesh to bruise bone. His chest swelled with a deep, hard breath. He let it out with a groan. His mouth felt as dry as dust. It was no use.

Her striptease had him mesmerized. His eyes were riveted on her long, graceful fingers unhooking the dainty catch of her bra between her breasts.

She stepped forward, her movements slow and seductive, just enough to make her breasts bounce lightly. She came out of the darkness, into a shower of rose light that touched her hair, splashed down the length of her golden arm, spilled over the voluptuous softness of her breasts.

Everything in the room blurred and dulled and darkened except her. She was at the center of a brilliant fire, and the heat of her was filling him, too.

He was full and hot, ready.

His gaze was drawn to her breasts, to her narrow waist, to the curve of hip and thigh. She was radiant, lovely, and his body was racked with pain from his desire.

She had him right where she wanted him.

Her fingers on the tiny clasp moved; her breasts jutted free of restraining lace. Slowly, tantalizingly she removed her bra all the way, letting the filmy object dangle from her hand for a long second before she tossed it aside.

She wore only her baggy shorts. It was the sexiest outfit he'd ever seen on any female.

He was caught in her spell; furious, yet totally aroused.

It wasn't supposed to be this way. She wasn't playing by his rules. She was playing by her own, using the splendid beauty of her body to captivate him. He felt his will, his intractable, stubborn will, dissolving in the heated mist of his desire. It galled him that she could so easily provoke in him white-hot adolescent emotions and use them to control him.

She laughed softly, touching his chest with hot, featherlight fingertips that traced a ridge of muscle until she made him groan.

"You've got a lot to learn about women," she whispered. "It's time for you to abandon all your outdated notions." Her hand explored the athletic hardness of his muscled shoulder. Her gentle voice went on. "Love is more than sex, more than words."

"Who said anything about love?"

"Me. It's two people sharing, trusting, working together to accomplish common goals. It's commitment."

So expert were those hot feminine fingertips, he could hardly think, much less talk.

"Damn. Why are you so determined to complicate everything? I don't believe in love. All I want to do is protect you."

"Right." Jess lifted her long-lashed eyes mockingly to his. Her fingernails lightly raked the length of his spine. The hunger that filled him was a fierce stirring in his vitals.

Her creamy skin glowed rose from his look.

She was so beautiful, he hurt all over.

Tad closed his eyes to shut out the hot, dazzling vision of her.

But that was his mistake.

He smelled the beguiling sweetness of orange blossoms. He felt her fingernails dig into him lightly with that faint promise of passion to come. Then she kissed him. He felt her tongue move across his chest; her mouth sucked his nipple. A bolt of electric excitement coursed through every nerve ending.

He felt her fingertips again, gliding over his taut stomach and narrow hips. Then she pressed herself into him. She was molten satin against him. There was no escape.

He lowered his lips to hers. His tongue plunged into her mouth, tasted her, and she began to tremble.

His hands were in her hair, combing through the silken tresses. Loose pins rained onto the floor and waves of sweet-smelling gold flowed through his fingers.

He kissed her mouth, ate it with his lips and tongue; kissed her face, her ears, her throat. He bent low and softly kissed one shell-pink nipple. He picked her up and carried her to the bed. Then he pushed her down on cool cotton sheets and covered her body with his.

Her cheeks were rose-colored like the dawn. Tousled gold curls lay in a riot of glimmering waves on the pillow. Her gaze was deep, dark, intense.

A vast silence seemed to envelop them.

Possessively she circled him with her hand and guided him toward her.

Then it began—the throbbing urgency that blocked rational thought. The hot, insistent craving that possessed every nerve in his body.

There was only woman. Only this woman. Only his

fierce, raging need. It no longer mattered that she refused to behave the way he thought she should. He wanted her exactly as she was.

His hands were eager, trembling. He kissed her, roughly, softly, with a keen, seeking urgency, fusing their two naked bodies together.

He moved over her.

Her hands came together in an urgent knot at the base of his spine. She opened her body endlessly to his.

And he felt the world slip away.

She touched him everywhere.

The room whitened and exploded in a sudden and all-consuming, soul-filling lava fire.

And two wary, stubborn spirits were molded into one—for that brief instant.

A damp sheen of perspiration covered them both.

Tad wanted to own her, but he knew he never could.

He clasped her tightly, burying his face in her hair, inhaling the smell of her, the scent and feel of clean, silken hair and sweet, voluptuous woman flesh, the exquisite sensation of her sated body against his.

She began to laugh softly, a bit too conceitedly he thought. "That was really something," she purred. "I..."

"Yes. You're quite something. I know you just did that to throw me off balance."

"You were screaming and ranting the whole way back from the jungle. You refused to listen to my very logical lecture. I had to get your attention."

"You damn sure got it."

"You wouldn't listen to reason."

"Neither would you," he whispered against her ear.

"I wanted to show you that we are partners. We belong together."

"I always knew that."

"But I mean together—in everything. Not just in bed. We will be equals."

"A woman can never be equal to a man."

"Nor a man to a woman—literally, but I want to help you raise Lizzie. I will always have my career, my work outside our relationship that is as important to me as yours is to you. But first, I want to help you find out what's going on at the station, what happened to Deirdre..."

He had bedded Jess twice. So she thought she had him.

He sat bolt upright, his body tense. "Why can't you understand that this is my battle? This is Australia."

"The male chauvinist's last domain," she murmured with gentle sarcasm. "But don't you see, Australia's no different than any other place. It's you and I who matter. If we love each other, your battle is my battle. And vice versa. I love you, and that means there is nothing, nothing I wouldn't do for you."

She said this sweetly with her warm eyes caressing him. But he knew that honeyed tone and that velvet gaze were like the sugar she used to coat her bitter medicines. Beneath the feminine wiles she meant business.

Our battle. Hell! She was so strong, so certain. But she knew nothing of what she was getting herself into.

He felt strange, unsure, not himself at all. He was possessive, jealous, protective, sick at the thought of something happening to her. He hadn't wanted another woman in his life, ever again. Especially not one like her. He was fiercely independent. He didn't want her meddling in his life, but he didn't want her out of it, either.

They were at an impasse. Each eyed the other warily, and while they did they lapsed into an uneasy silence.

A long time later she said, "I know it's probably hard for you to trust...a woman...after your marriage to Deirdre.

Especially to trust me. But don't you see, trusting you is not so easy for me, either. You ruined my life, too. Only I'm not the sort to cling to a grudge the way you do.''

As always it galled him the way she saw herself in a superior light to him. "I ruined your life?" His eyes darkened to midnight blue. "That's a joke."

"When we were all in college, you used me to get Deirdre."

"What?"

"You wanted to make her jealous so she'd marry you."

He laughed harshly in disbelief. Gently, roughly, he gathered Jess into his arms. "I never used you. And I never lied. It was the other way around."

"No!"

"Then explain why you went to bed with me, pretending you were Deirdre."

"Jackson, you knew who I was all the time."

"No I didn't. Not until after I married Deirdre."

"She told me you did…after…"

"I don't give a damn what she told you!" He was silent, his face dark and tensed.

Jess wrenched herself free and escaped to the farthest edge of the bed. "I remember that night like it was yesterday. I loved you. I thought you loved her."

"That sounds about normal for our relationship."

"Don't be sarcastic, Jackson."

He nodded grimly for her to go on.

"Well, that night I was in my lab studying. Deirdre stormed in, sobbing out some nonsense about you having broken up with her because you loved me. I was stunned. You and I always quarreled. You had never even hinted you loved me in any way. I decided it was just some trick of yours to make Deirdre jealous. I swore it wasn't true. Then I went looking for you to have it out with you for using me in one of your lovers' quarrels. I didn't realize until later that I had accidentally picked up her sweater instead of mine.''

''It was dark,'' he muttered. ''So when I ran into you outside your dorm in her sweater, I assumed you were her. The way I did that first day on the tennis court. Why the hell didn't you tell me who you were?''

''I don't know. I always acted crazy when I got around you. Maybe because I thought I could get to the bottom of what was wrong between Deirdre and you better if you thought I was her. Maybe because I was mad. I just asked you if you really meant it when you said you were in love with Jess.''

''And I said I did.''

''That made me even madder. I thought you were trying to make her jealous. I started to cry and begged you to stop tormenting me. You took me in your arms. You thought you were comforting Deirdre. Things got pretty hot between us very quickly.''

''They always do. I don't know why that didn't tip me off.''

''We made love,'' she whispered.

''And all the time I could hardly believe it was the same Deirdre I'd jilted. Always before she'd turned to ice when I touched her. The Jackson money was the only thing about me that ever turned her on,'' he said bitterly.

''Yes, but you see, I didn't know that then. Just as I was about to tell you who I was, you stopped me, and said, 'Marry me, Deirdre. I only said those things about Jess to make you jealous.' Jackson, in that instant my heart froze. It was like death.''

''All I knew was I had to have the woman who set me on fire. I really did think you were Deirdre.''

''Don't lie to me!'' Jess cried.

"I'm not." His hand clamped savagely around her wrist. "I didn't know till the honeymoon that I'd married the wrong twin. And then I hated you because I thought you'd slept with me to trick me into marrying her."

"Dear God. Oh, Jackson. I loved you so much. After you asked me to marry you, thinking I was Deirdre, I was so hurt. You loved her, wanted to marry her, but I'd slept with you. That's why I ran away.

"All I could think of was Deirdre. How was I going to face her with what I'd done? I couldn't at first, so I just sat in a café drinking one coffee after another. Finally I realized there was nothing I could say. I just had to face her. But when I got back to our room, Deirdre was gone."

Jess's voice became desolate. "She'd left me a note thanking me for fixing everything. The note said that you'd just said you loved me to make her jealous. That I'd seduced you, and you'd known all along who I was."

"Damn her." He slammed his fist against a bedpost.

"I felt so cheap, so used. She told me she and you had run away to get married. She and you...together... I—I didn't know what to do. For days I was filled with the most bitter despair. After that, nothing mattered any more. I tried to tell myself that you were the wrong kind of man for me, that we were both better off. Eventually I married Jonathan. But, it's never any good—fooling yourself. My marriage didn't work out. I began my career, had a child. You know the rest. Deirdre finally told me most of the truth last year in Calcutta."

"Deirdre..." Tad's features twisted with bitterness. The memory of her filled him with black emotion. "All the time I blamed you for ruining my life, when it was her. I should have known."

"The past is behind us," Jess whispered, but her voice was haunted. "You really loved me?"

Her pale, distraught face touched Tad, and the layer of icy distrust in his heart began to melt.

"Yes, I loved you. Only you," he whispered. "Always. Only you. Even when I was married to her. Even when I hated you."

Her face remained bloodless.

He took her cold hand in his. "We were both such fools. But it's over," he said gently. He brought her fingers to his warm lips. "All that matters now is our future."

"Yes," she said, "our future."

"You will leave Australia, take Lizzie, and I will follow after I've taken care of things here."

Her hand tensed, and although it was small and delicate in his larger one he felt her strength. Her warm, resolute gaze moved over him lovingly.

"You still don't get it, do you? I mean how it's going to be with us?" she asked quietly. "I stay. Beside you. Always. I could never feel safe anywhere if I were afraid for you."

He felt vaguely alarmed. "You talk like a man," he muttered uneasily.

"No, you're just a male chauvinist clinging to the dark ages." She lifted her arms high above her head and stretched languorously. "You're a man, but that doesn't make you my superior or my boss. And thinking that you aren't doesn't make me any less of a woman." The brilliant morning rays shining through the shutters bathed her body in a soft, golden, iridescent glow. "Or haven't you noticed?"

His eyes ran boldly over her. He kept watching her. She moved, smiling knowingly up at him, and the morning sun gilded her soft, lush curves, warmed creamy, pale flesh.

"I love you," she said, "and that makes us one."

Did it? Could he accept her on her terms? Had they in

reality always been his terms, too? Did she know him better than he knew himself? All his life he'd been alone. Until now. With her.

But could he risk her safety?

He could feel the danger, all-enveloping, a menacing presence in the bedroom. She might think she was tough, but the bastards would kill her in a second, if he gave them the chance.

He was about to argue, but she melted against him, nestling her body between his thighs. As always she was a perfect fit.

She caressed his powerful, muscular chest with light fingertips.

He couldn't think.

"We are one," she said. "Partners."

"But…"

She began to stroke him. His body turned to flame.

"Partners for life," she said. "In everything."

She lowered her hand and touched that one part of him that electrified every cell in his body.

"It won't work," he growled weakly.

She bent her face to his cheek. "Wanta make a bet?"

He felt that moist, feminine tongue, seeking and searching near the sensitive spot beneath his earlobe, turning his blood to rivers of fire.

Even as he was protesting, he rolled her beneath him.

Sun-darkened skin covered her paler, silkier flesh.

"No." He whispered. "No."

But his body said yes.

Eleven

A mist rose from the damp earth of the rain forest, and under the flame of a new sun the trees wore a mantle of glowing wet.

Tad sprinted soundlessly down the narrow trail. It was still and hot. Muggy. His cotton shirt was glued to his body from his long run. But he didn't care. The weather forecast was perfect for flying.

He was leaving Jess! There would be hell to pay!

Tad remembered all her fierce arguments about her determination to help him fight his battles. He felt like a heel, running away from her, pretending he was going fishing with Wally when in reality he was flying back to Jackson Downs. But late yesterday afternoon, he'd gotten a message through Wally from Kirk that things were heating up on Jackson Downs. The Martin homestead had been attacked, and Noelle and Granger were on guard against the threat of another. Tad had called Ian McBain, and Ian was flying to Jackson Downs to assist in the signing of all the legal documents in regard to the sale of the station.

Tad was determined to keep Jess from meddling in his dangerous affairs. It was time she learned she could only push him so far.

Tad didn't trust the Martins, even though they were the prospective buyers for Jackson Downs. It was odd that Granger was buying him out. Granger had always had a weak stomach for violence. Odd how his determination had never wavered despite all the trouble. Odder still, when not so long ago it had been Granger selling out to him. And yet, if Granger were behind it all, why would he attack his own homestead?

Tad heard his Cessna even before he saw it. That was the first inkling that something was wrong.

His heart raced with panic as he slung his duffel bag over his shoulder and began to run even faster down the narrow path through the rain forest. He broke through the trees and saw his white, orange-trimmed plane.

The propeller was a big fan. The blades blurred, turning, thinner and faster as the engine sound grew stronger and deeper.

Who the hell had dared...

Tad remembered the man in the bulldozer. Was he back, sabotaging the Cessna?

Then Tad saw her.

He should have known.

Jess waved jauntily to him from the cockpit. A pale-faced Meeta and an excited Lizzie were bundled into the seats behind her.

Rage filled him. He should have realized getting away from her had been too easy.

How sleepily she'd lain against the pillow this morning. The smell of orange blossoms had been dulled by the warm, male scent of him still clinging to her skin. How docilely she had allowed him to kiss her goodbye before he'd left, jogging the long way to the resort as a safety precaution, and thereby giving her enough time to dress and beat him to the plane. He had planned to leave her on the island in Wally's care because Wally had assured him there wouldn't be a boat or plane to or from the island for three days. Somehow she'd gotten around Wally.

Jess opened the cockpit door and smiled down at him brightly. And her smile made him volcanic.

Bancroft was in his plane, disobeying him, having done God alone knew what to a delicate piece of machinery he'd babied for years. She stuck a denim-clad leg out of the door and he grabbed her by the thigh and pulled her, kicking all the way down, to the ground.

She threw him off balance, toppling him and sending him sprawling so that he lay flat on his back beside the chock. She fell on top of him, straddling him. He had a fleeting sensation of her softness fitting his tight, straining male muscles. He seized her wrists and held them fast so that she couldn't escape.

"What do you think you're doing?" he yelled over the roar of the engine.

"Going with you, you low-down sneak," she yelled back.

"I told you yesterday, you were to take Lizzie to Calcutta while I went back to the station."

His jeans were skintight. He could feel the warmth of her seeping inside him.

"But I never agreed," she began.

"That's why I was leaving without—"

"I'm not letting you sell out. What will that settle?"

"Everything! I've been losing money for three years. People are getting killed."

"No."

"What do you mean *no*? We're talking about my property!"

"I mean we're not leaving till we know what's going on!"

"I'm tired of fighting everybody in this country all alone." A muscle ticked in his hard jawline.

Her expression softened. "You're not alone—not anymore."

His eyes moved slowly over her with insulting deliberation. His hard mouth thinned as he regarded her usually sleek hair tumbling about her shoulders. His gaze fell to her heaving breasts beneath her tight cotton shirt. He thought of the dirty bastards getting to her in some way, touching her, hurting her. Damnation! For all her courage and heart, she was only a woman.

"And that terrifies me more than anything," he said, not ungently. "Don't you see, I can't stand it if they use you. If you and Lizzie are there, I won't be able to think."

"We're in this together."

"No."

"Deirdre was my sister. She was probably killed because of what was going on at Jackson Downs."

"And I don't want you to die the way she did."

"If you think I'm the kind of woman you can safely jettison like an unwanted bundle of cargo behind the lines of battle, you're crazy."

"If you give a damn about me or Lizzie, for once you'll do what you're told."

"I'm not a coward—even if you are."

"What?"

"Who's the brave boy that's selling everything he and his family owns and clearing out?"

"It isn't like that."

"Oh, it isn't? Then tell me how it is."

"It's none of your damned business."

"You can't shut me out, the way you always shut Deirdre out. I'm making it my business. I love Lizzie like she was my own."

"Sweet Jesus. I won't have you meddling in my life."

"You and Lizzie are my life, so it's my life, too."

"If we're ever to have a future together..."

"Don't threaten me with that, you low-down bully."

He continued. "You're not coming to Jackson Downs, and that's final. I won't have a woman running my show. What I'm saying is that if you do, we're finished. Do you understand me? Finished!"

A string of violently muttered curses burst forth from the pilot. This fresh outburst made Jess's heart grip with pain. She tilted her head just a little and caught a sideways glance of the irascible Jackson, who sat stiffly beside her at the controls wearing a look of sour gloom. He was doing everything he could to inflict his dark mood on her and make the journey as abominable as possible.

He really did look like he hated her. She turned away before he could see how nervous her forced smile really was.

The four of them were in the plane high over the flat red parched endlessness of Queensland's center, having left the dazzling aqua waters and all greenery behind hours ago.

In the back Lizzie and Meeta were as quiet as mice. Poor Meeta was probably terrified. She was too kind and too obedient. Inconvenient character traits when it came to dealing with a man of Jackson's stubborn temperament.

There were times when a woman had to assert herself. Jess had done the only sensible thing. There was a crisis at the station. Jackson had been too caught up in his chauvinistic views of gallantry to be reasonable. Clearly someone needed to take charge; clearly she was the one to do it.

He would have to forgive her eventually. But every time she looked at him and saw his black expression of fury, she paled as she considered the faint possibility that he would not.

Jess had to fight to maintain a triumphant attitude, a pretended eagerness for every detail of the monotonous scenery. She and Jackson had flown in tense silence most of the way. Like all men, Jackson was able to sulk ferociously when he didn't get his way. Well, that was just fine—even if his sulking was a constant oppressive force. Even if his doing so was ruining what might have been her first exhilarating view of Australia. Even if it took all of her considerable willpower to act like she was happy despite him.

His black mood and her determined cheerfulness were each weapons in a fierce battle between two stubborn wills.

They were flying over sparsely covered ridges of stringybark tress.

"Down there!" Tad pointed grimly, breaking the silence. "That's where Martin Reach ends and Jackson Downs begins."

She nodded, glad that he'd decided to speak to her at last.

"At the turn of the century that used to be lush home paddock," he said. "Now it's desert. The sheet erosion has stripped the topsoil from the underlying clay and degraded the rich pastures of Mitchell and Kangaroo grass."

The landscape beneath them was indeed forlorn: five-thousand acres of bare pans dusted with salt and ringed by yellow samphire. The illusion of limitless space in the small, manmade desert was at once fascinating and daunting.

His voice was cold. Her own heart fluttered painfully. But she kept her chin as high and proudly defiant as his.

Everywhere there was the sad evidence of the drought. The sky was a pitiless copper-blue, and the few clouds seemed to scoff at the dry, cracked earth with their dry, cotton puffiness. Tad flew low over his dams, which only had a little water in the center of them. The creek was a string of muddy water holes.

Again his frosty, toneless voice broke the silence.

"We have twenty bores, pumps, windmills, but when it gets like this, water alone will not sustain cattle because they can't find forage. We've got to provide feed, but when it doesn't rain, feed's too high to buy. The cattle die. Out here the distances to market are enormous. This is a heartbreaking business in a heartbreaking country. A few years ago a lot of Aussies began selling out to Americans. Now the Americans are selling. Six years ago I was buying land from the Martins. Now they're buying mine."

"Surely there must be something else you could do."

Tad just looked at her, his expression so dark and hard and cynical that she glanced out the window, chagrined.

The land did seem big. Ruthlessly big. Bigger than any one man. Bigger than any group of men. The kind of land that had broken the backs and the hearts of the grittiest of adventurers. There was a reason why most Australians chose to cling to the green fringes of their continent rather than venture into the interior.

"In America, our desert, our West has always inspired us with a sense of freedom," he said. "Maybe because it was the path to California and a new life. But the Aussies have never seen their outback in that same light. This was a convict nation, and the Never Never was like the bars of a prison. They've always been scared of it."

Beneath them the forbidding landscape became wrinkled by deep-scored gorges, cliffs, ravines and mountains.

"I wouldn't want to crash here," she said.

"As a matter of fact this is where my neighbor Holt Martin's plane went down a few years back. He died instantly, and that was probably a lucky thing. The wreckage of his plane was in a ravine and couldn't be seen from the air. He would have needed to climb out of the ravine to signal, and it's almost always suicide for a man to abandon his plane or vehicle in the bush. We're a hundred miles from the nearest cow camp or homestead. Noelle didn't find him for nearly a month."

"Noelle?"

Tad's face darkened. "His American cousin. She's probably behind everything that's been happening."

"You would blame a woman!"

He muttered a low, mercifully inaudible curse. "You would turn this into another one of your sexist battles."

"Why are you so sure it's her?"

"Well, she's a newcomer."

"Circumstantial."

"Do you always make up your mind in an instant?"

"When the facts are as nonexistent as these, yes."

He made a sound like he was grinding his teeth. "All I know is we didn't have any trouble till she got here. Her family threw her out of Louisiana, and it wasn't because she was behaving herself. She's the type who causes problems wherever she goes. Ever since Holt died, she's been poking her nose around where it doesn't belong."

"She sounds like me."

He made a grimace. "That's hardly a recommendation. Before Holt died, she even stirred him up against his brother, Granger. And Granger against me."

"I thought he was buying your land."

"He is."

"Why couldn't it be him?"

"His property's been hit nearly as badly as mine."

"I thought you said he was sick of Australia. Why would he be buying more land?"

"Damn it, if I knew the answers, I wouldn't have a problem."

Turbulence shook the plane, and Tad lapsed into his stubborn silence once more. Hours passed, and he didn't speak again. Not until the sun was so low and so bright he could no longer shield his eyes from it. And then he wasn't addressing her.

"Damn!" he muttered as he squinted into the sun.

At first she thought he meant the sun as he leaned forward. Then she saw a thin, black coil of ominous smoke against the fiery sky.

"What's that?" she whispered.

His mouth thinned, but he said nothing.

Beneath them was an immense two-story house and its outbuildings—the store, office, quarters for the staff men, laundries. They seemed to cower under an eerie, deepening twilight. Beyond she saw the stables and stockyards.

One of the buildings was burning. Men were running about wildly.

"It's the homestead. Jackson Downs is on fire," he said grimly.

Then he set up their approach.

The Cessna bumped its way to an abrupt stop on the dirt runway. Tad threw open the door, jumped down into the whorls of choking dust. Then he turned to help Jess and the others down.

The landscape was bleak, desolate and vast—cut off from civilization by hundreds of miles of dry, baking land.

The air was oven hot. The red dust seemed to have settled on everything—the buildings, the scraggly trees, her clothes. Two Land Rovers and a forlorn Jeep looked like they had just come out of a red brick kiln.

The gritty hand Tad gave Jess jerked her roughly to the ground. For an instant her weight dangled against him in an undignified manner.

For a fleeting moment she was aware of how beautiful the house was, even covered as it was with its mantle of dust. It was an oasis in the middle of a desert. The two-story house had adobe walls two feet thick with wide, shaded verandas along every side. The house was set high on a rise of red earth and nestled amidst the shade of tamarind trees. Despite the steaming heat and her own wretched exhaustion, Jess felt drawn to it because it was Tad's home. She was determined to make it hers, as well.

She caught the faint scent of spinifex resin, the stronger smells of smoke and fire. The desert was like an inferno suffocating her, making her tongue go dry and tacky in her mouth.

Nearby horses screamed in terror.

"The stables!" Tad yelled before he cast her aside and broke into a run.

Jess chased after him.

A huge wooden building with a rusted corrugated-iron roof was the source of a fountain of orange flame and black smoke spurting fifty feet into the air and billowing higher. As they reached the building, Tad shouted at a bulky man who was fumbling with the locked doors of the stable.

"What the hell do you think you're doing, McBain?"

Ian whirled, his hard face panicked. Tad reached him, and the two of them managed to shove the doors aside.

A dozen horses stampeded out the open doors. Tad grabbed Jess and shielded her with his own body. Chasing after this terror-crazed herd was a tall, dark man whose shirt was ablaze. He cracked a whip in the air.

As soon as the man got outside, he crumpled to the ground in agony and used the last reserves of his strength to roll himself in the dirt.

Tad and Jess reached him at once. His ruined shirt hung in ribbons upon his broad, muscled back. His handsome face was contorted with pain and exhaustion and covered with black grit and red dirt. Rivulets of sweat had etched crazy grooves into this fierce mask of accumulated grime. There was the scent of singed cloth and flesh.

Other men came running up, jackaroos, the native children who'd been silently watching the fire. Jess was scarcely aware of them as she knelt with Tad beside the injured man.

"Kirk! You fool!" Tad began to swear softly to himself as he and Ian helped his brother-in-law stagger to his feet. "The bloody bastards!"

"I told you things were heating up," Kirk said, sagging against him. "You damn sure took your time getting back here. What kept you?"

Then Kirk cast his beautiful black-lashed, green eyes upon Jess. "Deirdre... You found her..."

"No."

"You crazy bastard," Kirk said to Tad.

Black lashes sealed over the dazzling green. Kirk's voice became a whisper as he fainted.

Jess leaned closer and caught the faint name that was the last sound from his lips.

"Julia..."

Jess stared questioningly at Tad.

"She's my little sister. His wife. And she's back in Texas, pregnant. If anything happens to him..."

"But I thought she died when she was a child."

"That's what we all thought, but she survived the kidnapping. Kirk went through hell to get her back for us. It's a long story." Tad winced as he inspected his brother-in-law's wounds. Then Tad's hand closed over Jess's. His gaze was intense, pain-filled.

"Please," Tad begged, "don't let him die."

Twelve

There is nothing like a medical emergency to give a doctor total power. With horror Tad saw that despite everyone else's terror, including his own, the opportunity to boss him and his employees had put Bancroft in an excellent humor. Her smug little smiles told him that she was enjoying herself hugely, while she mined this rich vein of drama for all it was worth. He could do nothing but grit his teeth and pray she was as good as she conceitedly thought she was.

Tad's scowl was bitter as he watched Jess bark orders and two of his jackaroos scurry away from the sickroom at a dead run across vast expanses of cool, terra-cotta-tiled halls. His two toughest, hardest jackaroos, men who never let a woman boss them, scampered like children every time Jess's voice rose above a whisper.

In less than an hour, Bancroft had taken over his house, his station, his men. What made him maddest was that he was used to being the one in command. She made him feel useless and…yes, jealous. Oh, sure he'd begged her to save Kirk. Sure, he'd done what he could himself. He'd sent his stockmen after the runaway horses and had guards posted at every outbuilding as insurance against another attack. But in everyone's eyes, it was Bancroft who was the heroine of the hour.

While Tad had been occupied outside with his stockmen, Jess had entrenched herself firmly inside his homestead. Every one of his thirty employees, including the lazy, fat Mrs. B., was in complete awe of her. Jess had won the older woman over with a single sympathetic remark about her plight as the victim of oppressive male tyranny. Mr. B. was as gentle as a lamb! Mrs. B. was the wolf!

"More cold towels, please," Jess ordered crisply.

Mrs. B. didn't even frown as she usually did when commanded to do something. Indeed, she nearly knocked Tad down as she rushed past him to obey this order. Hell, never once had she jumped like that to obey one of his orders.

Ian, too, was impressed as he watched Jess gently work over Kirk who lay sprawled on his stomach across Tad's bed. When McBain's hard gaze shifted to Tad's glum face, the lawyer all but laughed out loud at him. No doubt McBain thought this woman was probably running him, too.

Well, wasn't she? But what could he do? As long as Kirk was down, Tad's hands were tied.

Kirk's gray face was beaded with perspiration. Tad had promised Julia that he would get Kirk back to Texas safe and sound before their baby's birth.

"How is he?" Tad muttered ungraciously, conscious of an acute annoyance toward Bancroft because she had proved herself so thoroughly indispensable so quickly.

"He's going to be okay. He's in pain, but his burns are pretty superficial. What he needs now is rest."

Tad cleared his throat, started to say something, thought better of it and slouched deeper into his chair by the bed.

"We need to leave him alone, now," she commanded softly, ushering everyone into the hall. "You, too, Jackson."

"All right. Damn it." He got up quickly. "It's not as if I don't have a million things to do—things that are more important than supervising you." He slapped his thighs and a cloud of red dust issued forth from his jeans.

She watched the dust settle on the furniture, the floor.

"So do I," she murmured with that irritating tone of self-importance. Then she smiled quirkily, cockily, making him even more furious.

Did all doctors think they hung the moon the way she did? Such conceit was insufferable.

"Leave Jackson Downs to me," he growled. "I won't have you taking over."

"I'm here to help you," she whispered defiantly.

Tad was aware of Ian watching them from across the hall.

"Just remember one thing," Tad said. "I didn't invite you here. As soon as this is over, I want you gone." Her face went very white. "I was through with you when you got on that plane. You proved then that this thing between us won't ever work. I don't give a damn how good you are in bed or what you do here to help me."

Her eyes flared brightly with hurt, and although that silent look of pain got to him, he forced himself to go on. "Nothing you do is going to make a bit of difference. You're just too damned bossy—I mean, for a man like me."

"Admit it, Jackson," she said softly. "What makes you maddest is that you know you need me. You know you want me, and not just in bed. Do you really want a woman who'll let you bully her? You walked all over Deirdre, and you weren't happy with her.''

"That wasn't the reason!"

"This is a big place. Do you really want to run it all by yourself? Kirk—"

"To hell with Kirk. You're just using him to get power over me."

"Jackson, that's unfair—even from you."

He knew she was right, but he was tired of her always being right, of her always being wiser. Tad stormed out of the room, determined to get as far from her as he could.

But he was aware of her, of her brilliant, pain-glazed eyes, of her competent efficiency, of everything she'd said and done the minute he'd turned his back on her.

Ian stopped him on his way out of the house. "Hey, Jackson, what about the papers?"

Tad was tempted to agree to everything just to be stubborn and show her, but he turned back and saw Jess in the shadows at the far end of the hall. "I'll sign them tomorrow," he muttered roughly.

Jess's low gasp knifed through Tad.

"What?" Ian was about to go on. Then his thoughtful gaze shifted uneasily to Jess and then back to Tad.

"I need a night to sleep on it," Tad insisted.

"But you already agreed."

All Tad could see were Jess's haunted eyes.

"Damn it, Ian. I said I need a night."

Tad slept in the bunkhouse that night, if one could call twisting and turning on that wretchedly narrow, rock-hard bunk sleeping, and it wasn't selling Jackson Downs that was worrying him. The air conditioner that was fueled by his own natural gas wells was broken, and the holes in the screens let in some persistent blowies. They kept up a per-

petual buzzing at his mouth and eyes, and he kept up a
nearly constant swatting at them. If it hadn't been for the
bottle of whiskey he kept taking frequent swigs of, he'd
never have made it through the long, dark misery of those
hours.

The yellow porch light was on. Every time he opened
his eyes, his gaze fell on a poster-sized picture of a sexy
nude blonde opposite his bed. The lady was a bit of provocative decoration that the jackaroos had nailed to the
wall. The trouble was that this particular big-breasted starlet
bore a too-striking resemblance to Jess, and it was torture
to look at her and to remember Jess asleep in a soft, clean
bed somewhere in his cool house. Only last night he had
had her—again and again. She'd been a wanton, wild for
him. Sexually they were a perfect match.

Just the memory of her and his throat felt hot and dry,
his body tense and aching. He loathed himself for the power
she had over him. He liked good, hot sex; it was something
he'd done without too long.

It was infuriating that just a female image on a scrap of
paper, just an image that only faintly resembled the warm,
luscious woman asleep in his house could arouse him so
that every time he looked at it his insides quivered hotly.

Damn her. There would be no peace in his life until she
was gone.

He kept opening his eyes, staring at the feminine image
on the wall that so taunted him, saluting it with his bottle.
It was hell remembering, hell fantasizing, hell doing without the one thing he really wanted.

In the end he resorted to drink to dull his senses, but the
drunker he got, the hotter he became every time he looked
at the picture, until every muscle was so tense he felt like
he was going to explode. It was almost dawn when he

finally fell fitfully asleep, but in his dreams he couldn't fight her off.

Jess came to him, and her eyes were as darkly passion-filled as his own. When she began to strip, he welcomed her into the narrow bunk. She crawled on top of him and drove him wild, so wild that he awoke thrashing. Ned, who was in the bunk under him, had slugged him in the arm to make him stop kicking their bunk.

"Some dream," Ned joked, his dark, chubby face too close.

"Shut the hell up."

The next day there was no new violence on Jackson Downs or Martin Reach, and yet the unspoken threat of it hung menacingly in the air.

Maybe that was what set everybody on edge. The jackaroos seemed to find special delight in tormenting Tad by speaking with amazement of Jess's accomplishments. Their praise made Tad want to howl with rage over Jess's clever treachery. She was killing him, killing them all with her kindness, with her usefulness.

"MacKay's doing real good today. He was on the radio talking to his wife in Texas for an hour, though. And the doctor's on a rampage, cleaning your house," Ned told him that morning while he was still in the bunkhouse nursing his hangover.

"I liked it the way it was," Tad muttered in a low voice. He plunged his painfully throbbing head into a lavatory and ran tepid water through his hair.

"She's even set Mrs. B. to work."

Tad jerked his head out of the water and banged it into the faucet—hard. "Ouch! Damn it! What?"

Mrs. B., Felicity Binkum, by name, Tad's housekeeper, was well over sixty and had gray hair that looked like she

trimmed it with tin snips. Mrs. B. had a forceful, dominat-
ing, poor-me personality and was always at outs with her
long-suffering husband, Mr. B., the best damned foreman
Tad had ever had.

Mr. B. was the only reason everyone on the station was
forced to endure the lazy, whiny domination of the inces-
santly complaining Mrs. B. He was the only reason Tad
had endured the sloppy condition of his house for years, as
well as the thinly veiled insults Mrs. B. assaulted everyone
with—including him.

Every time any new violence occurred she always eyed
Tad and muttered to herself just loud enough so he'd be
sure to hear, "Some men would do something."

"Boss, you wouldn't know Mrs. B.," Ned taunted.
"She's as sweet as sugar. None of her two-edged barbs
today."

"I don't believe it." Tad was gingerly rubbing the lump
on his wet head.

"Believe it, mate. Doctor knows how to handle her."

Damn right, Bancroft could handle her. They were two
of a kind—both man-haters from way back.

Tad snorted belligerently, but Ned wasn't one for taking
hints. "Mrs. B.'s mopped every floor. Stripped and waxed
them. Scrubbed the walls. Washed everything in the
house—sheets, drapes, rugs. Got the jackaroos helping her.
You wouldn't know the place. She's cooking up some meat
pies. Best-smelling pies! Doctor's a damned good vet,
too."

"You haven't turned her loose on the livestock?" This
was a yell. He tossed his towel on his bed and yanked on
his shirt.

"No, but she sure cured Dane's dog. Wheeler fell into
the cattle dip and got himself snakebit last week, and if she

hadn't treated him, he would have died for sure. The boys and Lizzie sure would've been brokenhearted.''

Wheeler, a Queensland Heeler, was a great favorite on the station.

"You ought to see how she is with Lizzie."

"Damn. I don't want to see it."

"Doctor's the busiest sheila I ever saw."

She damn sure was.

"Hey..." Ned's speculative gaze swept from his boss to the girlie picture of the half-naked blonde that had taunted Tad all night. "That looks likes her, don't it, boss?" Ned's white grin became a leer in his plump, dark face.

Jealous rage washed through Tad as his own gaze followed Ned's. How dare Ned think dirty of Jess. It was all Tad could do to keep from going after Ned's thick, sunburned throat with his bare hands. Instead, Jackson's violence found another outlet.

"Damn it," his deep voice boomed. "What the hell do you blokes hang filthy trash like that on the wall for?" With a single, fluid leap of fury, Tad lunged across the narrow room, ripped the paper from the wall, tore it to bits and threw it into the garbage can. He grew aware of his men's lean, dark faces—hard, set, yet intently curious as they watched him, read him—before they averted their gazes to the rude plank flooring.

Afraid of what he might do or say next, he flung the screen door open and strode outside into the thick dust, flies and suffocating heat.

The door banged; he heard their snickers behind him.

"Now what the hell got into him?"

"It don't take no genius to figure that one out, Ned."

There were guffaws and laughter.

"She's one hell of a woman. Nothing like the other one.''

''The boss has met his match for once, and it don't seem as if he likes it none too much.''

The boss damn sure didn't. Beneath the darkness of his tan, Tad whitened. The smell of livestock was suddenly overpowering. The liquor churned in his belly like acid. The wooden planks of the unswept porch flooring seemed to swim. He felt a hot, nauseous sensation crawl up his esophagus and he had to grab the railing for support.

''Damn them. Damn them all.''

Slowly his weakness ebbed, and after it had, Tad felt like going back inside and using his fists to teach them all a thing or to about what he didn't like too much.

Instead he slammed down the wooden stairs and stepped onto the rocky earth. Brawling with his own men was not the thing to do. Especially since the only crime they'd committed was speaking the truth.

At the bottom of the stairs Tad reached in his pocket and brought out a cigarette. Very slowly he lit it and inhaled deeply. The cigarette made him sick all over again, and he threw it to the ground and squashed it violently with his boot heel.

He had known it would be a mistake to bring Jess here. He just hadn't known how quickly she would take over, how quickly she would challenge his dominion over his own world. Over his own men. Worst of all—his dominion over himself.

She got to him worse out here.

Maybe it was because everyone but him seemed to think she belonged.

Tad refused to let himself be driven out of his house forever. So that night he came in for supper. His intention was to get down to business with Ian, sell the place and ignore her.

But her presence was everywhere.

He was a stranger in his own home.

The house was sparkling. So was Mrs. B. The tin-snip hairdo was wavy and almost becoming. For the first time in years she seemed almost happy with Mr. B. Tad found the contented older couple in one of the screened courtyard gardens, sitting beneath the tamarind trees drinking grog together. He left them before they saw him and went in search of Ian.

Jess was in the kitchen.

Tad meant to stride past the open door and avoid her, but the aroma of roast beef, Yorkshire pudding and lemon meringue pie was too much for him. Damn her. Why was she so good at everything that mattered to him?

His boots made hollow sounds on the cool terra-cotta tiles as he stepped inside and then leaned back against the doorjamb. He was hot and dirty, a grim, angry male presence in the neat domesticity of her kitchen. He knew he smelled of dust and the animals he'd been vaccinating. He could still taste the whiskey on his breath from last night.

She looked up from her cookbook, smiled quirkily at him, and said, "Hi, there."

Just "Hi, there," bold as brass, after what she'd put him through. But his heart filled with a wild, thrilling joy.

"Where's Lizzie?" Tad demanded gruffly.

"In her room reading. I got down a book about dinosaurs."

"Oh."

His intense blue gaze couldn't get enough of Jess. She looked fresh and quite glamorous in Deirdre's riding clothes. She'd probably slept like a baby last night—without him. Beneath a lacy white apron, she was dressed in exquisitely cut cream-cord jodhpurs, elastic-sided riding boots and a clingy, red silk shirt.

A searing pleasure coursed through him.

"I missed you," she said as she put down her spatula, undid her apron and came across the kitchen into his arms.

He felt her trembling, and he was tongue-tied at the beauty of her.

For years he had lived in this house, but never until this moment had it felt like home.

He buried his face against the sweet-smelling satin of her throat. His arms closed around her. "Oh, dear God," he said hungrily, defeatedly. "I'm lost. Truly lost."

For years he had blamed Jess for all that had gone wrong between them. But the blame was as much his as hers—for not seeing the truth, for not wanting to see.

"That's exactly the way I felt—all night," she whispered.

"I missed you."

"I missed you, too. Why didn't you come to me?"

"Because..." His large brown hands ruffled her hair. "Because I was too cussed stubborn."

He knew he would never rule her, just as he knew he could never stop trying. They would always have their battles. But in that moment he didn't care. She was precious to him. He had to have her at his side. He wanted to please her—in everything.

"Hell. I shouldn't be touching you. Not till I've taken a shower. I'm the only dirty thing in this whole blasted house."

He started to pull away, but she wouldn't let him.

"Just hold me," she begged softly.

His finger traced the sensitive skin from her jaw to her chin and then back, a caress that tantalized them both. He could feel her pulse throbbing.

She licked her lips.

And then he kissed her.

In that moment he knew that as long as she was with him, he could never sell Jackson Downs. It was no longer a million acres of drought-stricken desert plagued by perpetual violence. It was his home. Hers, too. And he was going to do what she wanted. He would fight for it because she wanted him to.

Even if it cost him everything.

But he was going to fight for it his way.

Not hers.

Thirteen

The three of them were alone in Jackson's tiny office. A thick, noxious spiral of smoke rose from Ian's cigar that he had set down in the ashtray.

''What do you mean—you're not going to sell?'' Ian's voice was as violent as a rapier slicing through the hostile silence.

Jess coughed lightly and fanned the smoke away.

The best supper Tad had eaten in years was over and Mrs. B. could be heard in the distant kitchen doing the dishes, for once without complaining.

Ian, Tad and Jess were glaring at one another across Tad's desk, which was stacked high with legal documents.

Tad leaned slowly back in his cracked leather chair. ''Hey, hey. Easy, Ian.'' Tad took a long sip on his beer. ''You're just my lawyer, remember? I make the decisions governing Jackson Downs.''

Ian shot a telling glance toward Jess. His low voice got nasty. "Not all—apparently."

The jeering masculine insult went through Tad's vitals like a bullet. Ian had known it would.

Bull's-eye, you bastard. There had always been some barely understood, male rivalry lurking just beneath the surface in his relationship with Ian.

Not by the flicker of an eyelash did Tad let the gray-haired man know his slight had hit the mark. Slowly Tad tipped his chair forward and set his beer bottle square in the center of the most important document so that it ringed it. He said only, but with more stubborn determination than before, "I never wanted to sell. That was your idea."

"Nothing's changed since you decided."

Tad reached across the desk, lifted a legal paper, looked at it, considered the months of tedious negotiation that had gone into drafting all the documents, and then flipped it airily toward the wastebasket. He picked up Ian's cigar and stubbed it out in the ashtray.

Ian lifted his bushy black brows.

"Nasty habit—smoking," Tad murmured.

Ian laughed. "You smoke."

"I've quit." He hadn't made up his mind on that issue until that instant.

"That your idea or...your doctor's?"

"What does it matter, as long as it's a good one!"

Tad took Jess's hand in his and turned it over and thoughtfully studied the smooth, pale, delicate fingers intertwined with his larger, darker, callused ones.

His icy blue gaze met Ian's. "You're wrong, McBain, about nothing having changed. Everything's changed. I'm not fighting this thing alone any more."

Jess's fingers wound more tightly into his.

Ian sprang to his feet. "I wasted a trip. It'll cost you."

"It always does."

"I only hope you won't be sorry."

Tad attempted a thin smile. "Thanks for the concern."

Tad pulled the half-empty pack of cigarettes out of his pocket, looked at it and then wrinkled cellophane, paper, and tobacco into a ball and pitched it toward the wastebasket. A moment later he brought Jess's hand slowly to his lips and kissed it.

It was nearly four in the morning when Noelle's panicked call came over the radio.

Jackson woke up slowly, not aware at first that it was the radio that had broken through the layers of his unconsciousness. Jess lay beside him. He caught the faint scent of her skin—that lingering fragrance of orange blossoms. He felt her breasts pressed into his side.

They had made love for hours and fallen asleep together in a blissful stupor of exhaustion—a dangerous thing to do under the circumstances. He felt drugged. He wanted to stay beside her forever.

And yet he felt the danger. Nearer than ever before.

He got out of bed, careful not to disturb her, and went to the radio.

Noelle's voice was so soft, and the transmission so filled with static, that he could barely make her out.

"Granger's gone crazy. Jackson Downs, do you read me?"

She sounded terrified. Either Noelle was the best damned actress he'd ever heard, or someone was really after her.

Tad flipped the switch and mumbled something to reassure her.

"Granger's got a gun. Please…"

The sound of a beautiful woman crying out in the night for his help was impossible to ignore.

But it was a trap! Jackson felt it in his gut. Before he could think through what he wanted to do, he heard Jess behind him, flipping the switch again, speaking into the mike.

"Jackson Downs to Martin Reach. Stay calm. We're coming to save you. Over."

Tad whirled, his anger instant and fierce. As always, Jess was taking over. This was no medical emergency. This was his kind of emergency.

Through the red mist of his rage he could barely see Jess's pale face, stricken with fear and alarm. "Why did you tell her that?"

"You can't just leave her out there all alone!"

"What if she's lying?"

Jess flinched. "What if she isn't?"

His vision cleared and although Jess's beautiful face was half in shadow, he saw her for what she was, a frightened woman, pleading for him to help another. And yet he saw her courage, too.

His expression softened. He reached for her and pulled her closer. Mere inches separated their bodies. She wore only that diaphanous, floating nightgown. Her extravagant, voluptuous breasts were clearly revealed. He could feel the heat emanating from her skin. He remembered the way she made his body pulse with passion. She wanted him to help Noelle—Noelle, whom he'd never trusted.

A heavy sigh broke from him, and he paused before answering. "I'm going, then," he said grudgingly. "If that's what you want."

Dark, gold-flecked eyes were shining now as they met his. "Thank you."

"But you're staying."

Her fingers tightened reflexively on his arm. "Jackson…please… I want to help you."

"We're doing this my way—for once." He stared at her long and hard. "This could be dangerous. Very dangerous."

"Okay."

Nothing was ever that simple with her. "Do you really mean that?"

Her eyes shone trustingly, obediently. She nodded.

He was filled with immense male satisfaction. This was the way he wanted her, docile, sweetly doing things his way. "I love you," he said gently. "You're much too precious for me to risk."

"I love you, too." Tenderly she touched his unshaven cheek. "Even now when you're impossibly macho."

He touched her lightly, lifted her chin. Then he kissed her until they both began to tremble. "Oh, Jess..." He murmured her name with a sigh of regret. He didn't want to leave her, but he unwrapped his arms from her warm, lush body and set her away from him. "You're going to stay here and keep Lizzie safe for me. And that's an order."

"Aye. Aye." She gave him a mock salute.

"We're doing this my way."

A funny kind of smile came over her face. Tad was so staggered that for once she'd agreed to obey him that he didn't think to distrust it....

Not till hours after he and his men and his two planes were already at Martin Reach did he distrust it. Not till he'd been shot at. Not till he'd freed a terrorized Noelle from the attic where she'd been handcuffed to a pipe and a time bomb. Not till he'd defused the bomb and was chasing Granger down with one of Granger's own Jeeps did Tad remember Jess's funny, crooked smile. Only then did he know to distrust it.

And then it was too late.

After setting Noelle free and leaving her at Martin

Reach, Tad and his men and their Abo trackers chased Granger, their Jeeps making sweeping, zigzag patterns across an endless bleak landscape of night desert. The moon was a sliver, but the Southern Cross was blazing. The two wildly jouncing vehicles raced bumper-to-bumper. Twice Granger had tried to trick Tad into running over the side of a cliff. Panicking, Granger tried to blast Tad's tire with his gun. Tad rammed him in the rear. Granger's Jeep swerved too sharply, and his tires went over an embankment. The vehicle flipped end-over-end, and Granger wound up pinned beneath the roo bar.

The acrid scent of burning upholstery and oil filled Tad's nostrils as he got out of his own Jeep and strode warily, shotgun in hand, toward the upside-down Jeep.

"Pull me out," Granger screamed hoarsely from beneath the torn canvas tatters of the roof.

Tad was breathing hard from the chase. His shirt was wet with sweat; his face black with grime. He wiped his sleeve across his brow. The first shell of lethal buckshot made a hollow sound as he racked it into the chamber. "I'll show you the same mercy you would have shown Noelle if we hadn't gotten here in time. The same mercy you showed when you set my stables on fire and damn near killed MacKay."

"For God's sake, mate," Granger yelled, "it wasn't me. I didn't want any part of that. I never wanted to hurt Noelle. But she kept snooping around."

Tad kicked a rock with the toe of his boot and sent it skittering past Granger's face. "Then who?"

"Help me, please."

"Tell me, and I'll tell Ned and the boys to pull you free."

Granger was a weakling—city-bred. He had always been a coward. His face contorted in fear.

"Tell me or you'll fry to death the way Holt did. Did you kill him, too?"

"My own brother, dear God!" Bitter, hopeless tears were in his choked voice.

Tad swaggered up to the Jeep, leaned down and grabbed Granger by the throat and squeezed his larynx hard until Granger began to choke. "No use blubbering like a baby. Talk if you're going to. The fire's almost to the fuel tank. I'm not sticking around to get myself blown apart."

Tad let go of him so abruptly that Granger's face fell into the dirt. Granger whimpered with pain. Tad turned on his heel in disgust and strode away until the darkness swallowed him. "Come on boys."

Granger's gaze went to the thread of blue-and-gold flame creeping ever closer. Then he became crazy with terror all over again. "Okay," he blurted. "You win. Jackson... Jackson! Don't leave me."

There was an eerie silence. Twin threads of flame licked the black night.

"Jackson!"

Out of the darkness came two words. "Tell me."

And Granger whispered a single name.

And to Tad that name was a knife blade of betrayal. Because it belonged to the one man in Australia Tad had trusted. Maybe he hadn't always liked that man, but he had trusted him. Jackson's pulse throbbed unevenly, sickeningly. He stood frozen in the darkness.

"For God's sake, get me loose!"

"Let him go, Ned!" Tad hissed. "Quickly!"

Ian McBain. Friend. Confidant. Fighter for justice.

Ian McBain. Murderer. Betrayer. Ambusher. Vandal. Deirdre's lover.

The damned bastard had been bolting MacKay inside the stables, not letting him out of it!

It didn't fit.

And yet it did.

Ian!

Why?

The Jeep exploded, and while he watched it burn, Tad staggered backward. He was remembering Jess's funny, sweet smile.

She had known all along.

She was back at Jackson Downs—with him.

Rage filled Tad, but it was instantly obliterated by a far more powerful emotion that held his heart in a tight-fisted grip—terror.

Ian McBain.

Tad felt like he'd just been punched hard in the gut.

Deirdre must have told Jess something in India.

Something that had made her go to that island.

Something that had made her call Ian in the first place—instead of him—when she'd first come to Australia.

Tad stared a moment longer at the burning Jeep. Why hadn't he seen it?

Tonight Jess had deliberately put herself in danger. She'd put his child in danger, as well as everyone else he'd left behind at Jackson Downs. For that Tad would never forgive her.

She'd done this to him for the last time! She had proved that she could never be trusted. If he got her out of this alive, he was through with her forever.

Jess had betrayed him, betrayed his trust, betrayed him in the single way that could most hurt him. And yet all that he could feel was the same nauseating fear Granger had known as he lay pinned beneath that burning Jeep.

Ian had Jess. Tad remembered what he'd done to Deirdre. Deirdre must have loved McBain. She'd gone to the island, trusting him, and he'd murdered her. What would he do to a woman as mule-headed and feisty as Jess?

Fear was bile boiling in Tad's stomach.

Jackson doubled over, sick with fear, and threw up on that dry, barren ground. Then he started running.

Jess was quite calm as she stole silently through the house with Lizzie sleeping in her arms. Meeta raced behind them, carrying blankets. The feeling of calmness had crept over Jess gradually as she'd listened to the vanishing drone of Jackson's planes when he'd flown away.

She had deliberately let herself be trapped at Jackson Downs with a man who might be a murderer, with the man who might have cold-bloodedly taken Deirdre's life. It wasn't something Jess had deliberately planned, although Tad would undoubtedly believe she had. That cry for help from Noelle had been real. Jess had had to send Tad to help her.

But now there was no one to save this sleeping child in the trailing purple nightgown, no one to save the others. No one except herself.

She had five minutes. Max. Before Ian made his move. If it was Ian.

Her day of housecleaning had not been in vain. She had discovered beneath the oldest part of the house a cool cavernous basement that was naturally ventilated. With its great doors locked from the inside, it was a natural fortress. In it she had stored food and water, guns and ammunition for just such an emergency.

After she'd placed Lizzie with Meeta on a pallet, Jess went and brought Mr. and Mrs. B. downstairs to guard them.

"You must do as I say," Jess ordered crisply.

The two days Jess had spent bossing everybody about

until they were thoroughly under her control had not been wasted. The B.'s would not have argued with her if she had told them to burn the house to the ground and bury themselves alive beneath it.

"Do not open these doors unless you hear three gunshots followed by a fourth. If someone forces this door, shoot to kill."

Mrs. B. picked up the gun and stared at Jess with wonder and admiration. "You would think the men would do something," she muttered.

"It's up to us—to the women," Jess said in a conspiratorial tone that won Mrs. B. completely.

Jess closed the door, and she heard Mrs. B. order Mr. B. to bolt the doors from the inside.

Jess had given Kirk a powerful narcotic. Her belief had been that if he posed no threat to the murderer, he would be in no danger, either.

Jess went back to Jackson's bedroom and locked the door. She pulled on a black shirt and a pair of black jeans. She got the loaded .38 that she had hidden out of the drawer, tucked it inside the waistband of her jeans, and softly raised the window. If she could just get to the desert, maybe she could hide until daylight. Until Jackson got back from Martin Reach.

Outside the sky was as black as old, congealed blood, and a sliver of moon hung in that menacing curtain of death like a wicked dagger's blade.

She threw a leg over the windowsill.

She was halfway out of the window when he seized her.

Ian grabbed her gun and shoved Jess mercilessly forward toward one of the great outbuildings.

He was hunched forward as he walked, his lips drawn back over his teeth in a savagely crazy grin. "You're too smart for your own good. You were on to me from the first.''

''Not from the first. Not till now. But I was almost sure, when you were bolting Kirk inside the stables. You killed my sister.''

''You won't get a confession out of me.''

''I won't need one. Wally's going to find her body with his bulldozers before too long. The black boy saw you kill her, didn't he? You've been back to the island, and he saw you then. I don't imagine it will be too hard to get him to talk. He gave me her wedding ring. You were her lover. Why did you kill her?''

''Everybody was her lover.''

''But it was you she went to meet on the island.''

''Maybe.''

''She came to you in the first place because she was afraid of the violence on the station. You seduced her.''

''Don't kid yourself there. She was willing.''

''Then she came back to Australia because she loved you, and you had promised to follow her if she left Australia. You sent her to Jackson Downs to steal Jackson's operating cash—to cripple him.''

''Deirdre couldn't have told you that,'' Ian said with a smile.

''She told me enough so that I could figure out the rest for myself.''

''You should have stayed in India where you belonged.''

''I belong here.''

He grabbed her arm and held it bruisingly. ''No, I belong here. This land was my family's long before the Jacksons.''

''It's over, Ian. Too many people are involved now. Maybe this started out as simple greed or revenge. Maybe you just wanted the land the Jacksons took from your family, but you went too far.''

He flung open the door to the outbuilding. It smelled of hay and heat and animals.

"A little gasoline and this place will go up like a torch, the same way the horse stables did."

"Why, Ian?" Her voice was pitched higher than she intended. It sounded shrill and hysterical. "You don't strike me as a sentimental man. I can't really believe you want this place because you lived here once. Why did this land suddenly become so valuable to you after Holt Granger died on that mountain? He was a geologist, wasn't he?"

Ian smiled pleasantly and kept pushing her. "You figure it out, Miss Know-it-all." He shoved her inside. "Now it's your turn to answer my questions. I want the kid and the old couple. Where are they?"

She cringed away from him, but he shoved the muzzle of his gun into her belly.

"I can't have any witnesses." His trigger finger jumped, and the gun made a menacing click. "Tell me, damn it."

He grabbed her blouse to pull her closer, and the flimsy material tore. She shuddered from his closeness, from his hot, vile touch, but he yanked her toward him. The back of his hand gripped the creamy top of her lacy brassiere. She stiffened with alarm when she felt his hand, hard as a hot steel claw, there.

"You're a damned beautiful woman," he muttered, drawing her even nearer to his own bulky, powerful body. She shuddered again. "Damn beautiful."

She felt his fingers tighten on her blouse. "Tell me where his kid is. You can die quickly, or you can die so slowly you'll pray for death to come."

She paused and took her time considering both charming possibilities.

Then in answer she leaned forward and sunk her teeth into his fleshy wrist so hard that he flung her back against the wall. A burning pain shot through her head when it bounced off wood. She could feel a hot stickiness trickling through her hair. Everything started to swirl and darken.

"So you want it slow," he murmured viciously.

She had to stay awake. She had to keep him distracted from Lizzie. Until Jackson could get back from Martin Reach.

That could be hours. Hours… It was hopeless. She would be dead by then. More than anything, before she died, she wanted Jackson to hold her. Just one more time.

Her thoughts began to fade.

Dimly she was aware of Ian looming over her, his hands fumbling at his belt buckle.

What was he doing? Something too horrible to contemplate.

She lay in the hay, helpless, broken. No… If he touched her, she would kill him.

Then she heard a sound at the door. Ian must have sensed it, heard the rush of hot wind or seen a blur of ghostly movement behind him, because he turned.

Buckshot was racked into a shotgun chamber. There was an explosion like an incendiary bomb. Then a shotgun blasted wildly a second time into the ceiling.

The silence afterward was numbing, deafening.

A pile of hay began to burn. The flames cast eerie shadows. In the leaping light Jess could make out Jackson's tall, broad-shouldered form just inside the doors. One of his sleeves was torn halfway off his bronzed arm. His handsome features were wild with hate.

"Let her go, McBain." Jackson's hard voice vibrated like angry thunder in the empty building.

Flames raced up the wall behind Jess.

Ian leaned down and jerked her savagely to her feet. She could hear him laughing softly, nastily against her ear.

"I said let her go!" Jackson raged, aiming his shotgun at them. "My men are outside."

"I've got a gun to her head! I don't have to take your orders, you bastard!" Ian shrilled.

"Let her go or I'll kill you, McBain!"

The heat was like a furnace, and Jess began to cough from the billowing black smoke.

"It's the other way around! Throw your gun down! Or I'll kill her!"

The two men were staring at each other across the darkness, the smoke, the flying sparks and the flames, each man screaming crazily.

The atmosphere was insane, highly charged, electric.

Something had to happen, and soon, or they would all die.

But the tense, silent moment dragged itself out in slow-motion while the flames flew higher.

Then a stray spark landed on Jess's blouse and she jumped. Ian ground his blunt nails into Jess's neck and she screamed in terror.

With a cry Jackson threw his shotgun to the ground.

"No," Jess moaned in defeat as she watched Jackson's gun fall. They were lost. Dear God! They were lost.

Ian yanked her closer to his own body in savage triumph.

"You said you'd let her go, McBain."

"I lied." Ian held Jess so tightly she screamed again. Then he pointed his gun at Tad.

"Why, Ian?" Jackson demanded.

They were surrounded by racing, shimmering walls of fire. Sweat ran down Jackson's handsome face in glimmering rivulets.

"I grew up on this land. You Yanks took it. I always wanted it back. That's why I was so anxious to make your acquaintance when you came over here to run things. Holt

Granger worked for me. So did Martin. Holt was looking for uranium before he died. After his plane went down, I sent another geologist into Woolibarra with a Geiger counter. There's uranium down there, all right. Mine. I tried everything I could think of to keep you distracted so you couldn't discover it for yourself. I got Martin to make you the offer to buy you out. I already owned his land, you see. He was just a front for me. Martin set up the attacks. But you kept fighting. Noelle kept snooping around, pestering Granger. She got on to him there at the last, and I ordered him to take care of her. Deirdre came to Brisbane seeking my help. She played right into my plans. Not that she knew what I was really up to. I had to kill her when she finally figured everything out. She was more loyal to you than either of us ever realized.''

Ian was backing out of the burning building with Jess. Leaving Jackson to die.

"Well, this is goodbye, Jackson. You're too damned stubborn for your own good. You should have cooperated a long time ago. Get over in that corner."

Tad backed slowly into the corner. "Just let her go."

Ian gripped Jess's arm. "No way. I need her to get out of here. Then I'll have to kill everybody."

"You're crazy."

"Don't say that!" Ian smiled. "I need her to get your little girl. If I can break you, I can break the old couple guarding her."

Something inside Jess snapped. She had been listening to everything he'd been saying limply, lifelessly, enduring the unendurable heat. But his last, gloating threat brought the will to fight charging back to life inside her.

Ian was going to kill them all! If she didn't do something, he was going to kill Lizzie!

Long ago, when Jess had been living in Indonesia, her

father had taught her how to fight. What had she been waiting for?

For the right moment. For the exact second when the murderer was so sure of his success that he relaxed his grip on her just a fraction.

She screamed, a high-pitched Oriental yell that was louder even than the roaring fire. Then she kicked Ian hard in the groin. She whirled like a dervish, jumped and jabbed her heel into his throat. He dropped his gun. She grabbed it.

Jackson lunged at Ian and sent him toppling. The two men rolled over and over, fighting, grunting, grappling.

Above them the roof was on fire.

Jackson was younger, stronger, and he wasn't writhing in pain from Jess's blows. Jackson straddled Ian and began pounding him with his fists. Then Jackson's fingers circled Ian's thick throat and squeezed until Ian's face turned purple. Jackson's expression was hard and savage with fury.

Jess rushed to them and tried to pull them apart. "No! Jackson! You're killing him!"

Outside the night filled with bobbing flashlights. Jackson's men came running into the barn.

Jess turned to them pleadingly. "Stop him! Please!" Ned lifted her into his dark arms, held her close against his clumsy body, then carried her outside. The other men grabbed Jackson and Ian, pulled them apart and hauled them bodily outside.

They had hardly stumbled to safety when behind them there was a terrible, rending sound, a rupture that sounded like the end of the world. Flames shot even higher into the black ebony of that long night.

Then the roof caved in. The ground shook with an awful thud as the building collapsed.

Jess scarcely felt it or saw it. She had eyes only for Jackson. Jackson would not even look at her.

"Jackson."

His grimly handsome face was streaked with grime. He gave her a long, hard stare.

Then she remembered that she had defied him.

He was done with her. She could see it in his eyes, and his harshness was killing her. He had come back to save her, risked his life to do so. He would have gladly died for her in that burning barn. All that she saw. But he didn't want her any more because she hadn't told him of her suspicions about Ian.

Jackson was too proud, too stupidly masculine.

He turned and began to walk slowly toward the house.

She had never been more aware of how heart-stoppingly virile he was until that moment when he was leaving her. Through the mist of her tears and pain she devoured that male swagger in those skintight jeans.

Damn him. A sob caught in her throat. She wasn't going to let him just walk out on her. This wasn't just his show. He still hadn't learned, had he? He wasn't the only one who was going to make the decisions in their lives.

She raced across the hard-packed dirt and flung herself into his arms.

For a moment he was stiff, unrelenting.

"I love you," she cried, touching him pleadingly. She felt him flinch when her fingers grazed his shoulder where the shotgun had kicked him. "Whatever I did, I did to save you. I love you. Doesn't that mean anything?"

For a long moment he studied her tear-streaked face. She could feel her hair, soft and streaming in the warm breeze. She was aware of his height, of the way he towered over her, making her feel smaller than usual. She was aware of the tension in him. It seemed that his emotions were strung as tightly as wire.

"I love you," she said. "I would do anything...anything for you. Why won't you see I'm the right woman for you? The only woman..."

The silence between them stretched until it was almost unbearable. After that agonizing length of time, she finally felt the terrible tension drain from him. A gentle, almost loving look came into his eyes.

"Dear God," he muttered.

Her heart skipped a beat.

"Dear God..." His eyes and face took on an expression that made her feel very odd, as though she'd never be able to take another breath. Slowly, carefully he folded her into his arms.

She laid her head against his chest. He held her close, so tightly she could feel the hard rhythm of his heart pounding fiercely in unison with her own. She felt his hands move gently beneath her hair.

"Oh, Jackson," she wept into his chest. "Don't leave me."

"As if I could." There was a new, softer tone to his voice that Jess had never heard there before. He was surrendering to a force that was stronger than he. "I love you, too," he said simply. "You may as well hear the truth although I know it will make you even more unbearably conceited than you already are—and conceit is an abominable trait in a woman. I can't fight this...this... damn...whatever it is...any longer—although I tried mightily. It's in me, through and through, this love thing. I can't fight you. I can't fight myself. I have to have you—even if you are stubborn and impossible and bossy."

She was weeping, just like any ordinary, sentimental

woman, and it was almost pleasant because he was cradling her in his arms so gently, so protectively.

"When Ian had that gun on you, I knew if he killed you I'd die, too," he whispered. "You're a part of me."

"I felt the same way," she said.

"My sweet, impossible, meddlesome darling," he murmured, and no love words had ever sounded dearer. His mouth covered hers. He kissed her, holding her tightly.

At last he released her. There was an interval of tender, joyous silence.

Someday he would tell her that it was not her fault that loving came so hard to him. Not her fault that as a boy he'd idolized his own father till his father had walked out on his mother for another woman. He'd felt that his father had abandoned him, as well. Even after his father had come back, the hurt had stayed there, buried. Subconsciously he'd probably felt safer believing the worst of Jess, blaming her. Safer marrying Deirdre, a woman he couldn't love.

"Lizzie?" Tad whispered.

"She and the B.'s and Meeta are locked safely inside the basement. I gave Kirk morphine so he wouldn't get into any trouble."

"If only there was a pill we could give you." But Jackson was grinning down at her lovingly.

"Are you mad because I let you go even though I suspected Ian?"

"At first I was. But I'm still too damned scared to be mad. That was a hellishly stupid thing to do. Maybe later when I calm down, I'll get mad. Then there'll be hell to pay."

"I promise, from now on, I'll do exactly as you say."

"I don't believe you, Bancroft."

She clung to him tightly.

"But you know something?" He tilted her chin back.

"What?"

He was staring deeply into her eyes. "I don't care any more. What really matters is what you did a while ago. No woman's ever stood up for me the way you did. You said you'd fix things in a week, and you damn sure did. I guess I never knew till now the kind of woman a man needs out here. I love you. I want to marry you."

Her heart gave a leap of joy. "Do you really mean it?"

"Honey, I feel sorry for you." His voice was warm, husky, tenderly amused. "Who'll marry you if I don't? Who else in all the world is cussed enough, and stubborn enough, and ornery enough to put up with a woman as impossible as you?"

A tremulous smile curved her lips, a wild song of joy singing through her veins. "There isn't anybody who can hold a candle to you in that contest."

He smiled sexily, charmingly. His hand reached out to tentatively smooth back the tangles of gold at her temple. Her dark eyes glowed in response to the caress.

In the next instant his arms were tightly around her, and his mouth came down hungrily on her lips.

A long time later she said, "Let's go tell Lizzie."

"And after that..." he said, his voice thickening.

"Yes, after that...we have till dawn."

Her eyes warmed. Her quick smile held the most tantalizing promise.

Epilogue

It was the first of June, and it was Tad and Jess's wedding day, as well. They were in Texas at the Big House on Jackson Ranch, having been married in the family chapel.

The house, the glittering chandelier, the wedding party—everyone and everything was decorated lavishly in purple satin. The groom's cummerbund and bow tie were of that color. Even the bride's gown was the palest shade of lavender. The bouquet was of white flowers and purple ribbons.

Tad had grumbled at first when Jess had begged him to give in to Lizzie's outlandish wish for the color scheme.

"It's my wedding," he'd howled, "you spoiled imp."

"Our wedding," Lizzie had asserted just as firmly. "You didn't even want her to come to Jackson Downs."

"Because I was afraid you two females would put a ring in my nose and I'd find myself led around by you both for the rest of my life."

Jess and Lizzie had merely glanced knowingly at one another and smiled.

Jess was having the most abominable effect on his child. Every day she got bossier and more muleheaded.

The wedding was purple, a child's fantasy of delight, and Tad was no longer against it. The great mansion was filled with an almost childish, fantastic happiness. And filled with familial love, as well.

For the first time in years Tad felt at home. Almost satisfied to be in Texas. It seemed a long time ago that he'd grown up here, a lonely child, a younger brother, who'd idolized his father and felt abandoned when his parents had separated. With his father's absence, Jeb, his masterful older brother, had begun to dominate everything until Tad had felt he no longer belonged. Later Deirdre hadn't fit in, either.

But now with Jess everything seemed different. He was at peace with himself and with his family, as well. His parents were happier than ever before, and marriage to Megan MacKay had mellowed Jeb.

Upstairs the nursery was filled with babies. Mercedes had shown off her brood of grandchildren to all the guests. Amy and Nick's tiny daughter, Merry, lay napping in a crib beside Jeb's feisty son, Jarred. Kirk was upstairs with Julia, guarding their own newborn son, Jack. Tad swore that it wouldn't be long before he had a son of his own.

Tad asked Jess to dance and soon they were dancing down the length of the ballroom toward the solarium. He could smell her bouquet of orange blossoms. Purple streamers fluttered against his neck and shoulders as Jess waltzed. Suddenly, he was aware of Noelle Martin's shining, dark gaze. She was watching them intently, sadly, from where she stood arm-in-arm with her famous father who had long been a senator from Louisiana. Her still-beautiful mother was sipping champagne as she chatted with Mercedes and Wayne Jackson.

Noelle had been Jess's maid of honor. It was just like Jess to have defied him and befriended the wild, titian-haired Noelle in Australia.

"Noelle is not what you think," Jess had said enigmatically, "not what you think, at all."

Tad clutched Jess closer and forgot Noelle. For a bossy woman, Jess followed his lead divinely. "I hope Lizzie outgrows this purple thing before she's old enough to get married herself," he whispered into Jess's ear.

"I'll save my dress just in case."

"Jeb won't let up teasing me about you. He says you made us more money in the month you were at Jackson Downs than in the entire eight years I was there running things without you. He said you're a wonderful addition to the family."

"Discovering a uranium mine did help. Still, I'm glad he approves."

"He just approves of you to goad me."

"I'm sure you're wrong."

"I've known him longer than you."

For a long time they danced, until Jeb himself strode across the ballroom and cut in. Tad asked Jeb's wife, Megan, to dance, and he saw his brother Nick dancing with the beautiful Noelle.

All too soon the reception was ending, although not soon enough for the impatient bridegroom.

Tad lounged negligently on the balcony and sipped champagne as he watched Jess teasingly assemble the unmarried girls below in the foyer. Gaily she held her bouquet to her lips and kissed it. Then she turned her back on the cluster of girls and flung the white blossoms and purple satin ribbons high into the air.

Every girl ran and jumped toward the flowers.

Every girl but one.

Noelle stood apart, looking grave and lovely in her purple gown. Tad had seen that expression on her face before, many times. Any time a jackaroo had flirted with her. Any time her thoughts had turned to the past.

Not for the first time his curiosity was aroused. As well as an unwanted pang of sympathy.

The flowers flew through the air, glanced off Noelle's listless hands and fell to the floor at her feet.

Lizzie rushed toward the bouquet. "It's yours, Noelle!"

Noelle shrank from the flowers. "No... Give it to someone else."

Jess was there in an instant, seizing command—as always—but more gently this time, though. She quieted the disappointed flock of girls and placed the bouquet in Noelle's hands. Jess's words floated up the staircase. "Seek your destiny." Then she kissed Noelle's cheek.

Jess was rushing up the stairs to Tad.

"You threw those flowers to Noelle on purpose. Why? To defy me?"

"You have a complex about female defiance, my love."

"If I do, you are the female who has given it to me."

She kissed him.

"Why Noelle? Why were you determined to throw the bouquet to her? 'Seek your destiny!' What did that bit of theatrics mean? Tell me, Jess."

"It's a long story. A love story. Very romantic. Very tragic," Jess said mysteriously. "Someday I'll tell it to you. But now..."

Her fingers grazing against his tensed in the way he'd come to think of as her nighttime touch.

"Yes, now..."

''Have you forgotten that tonight is our wedding night?''
Her voice was soft, husky.

His arms went around her, and he lifted her easily and
began to carry her up, up those endless darkened stairs to
the upper story and the bedroom they would share until
they left for their honeymoon the next day.

When he reached the door, he kicked it open. Once inside he swiftly locked it behind them before he set her
down.

After weeks of wedding madness—relatives, children,
Lizzie—they were alone.

Her dazzling golden hair fell in tumbled disarray upon
lavender lace.

She was his wife. Really his. Forever.

At last.

Suddenly he felt a wild thrill such as he had never
known—joy, excitement, fear—a powerful happiness surging through him.

He was shaking so badly he couldn't move.

Gently she put her arms around his neck. Her mouth was
reaching up to meet his. He felt her lips trembling hotly
beneath his. Her fingertips caressed his jaw.

He clung to her. To life. To love.

She was everything.

He knew that as long as he had her, he would never be
afraid of love again.

*   *   *   *   *

Dear Reader,

There is an immense pressure to go through with a wedding once all the arrangements are in place, time is running short and one feels as though expectations have to be fulfilled.

I well remember lunching with my husband-to-be the day before our wedding, having a dreadful argument and suffering the awful stomach-churning thought of telling my parents everything had to be canceled. Happily we did resolve the problem and our wedding day will always be a joy to remember.

But what if there had been good reason not to get married?

In *The Wedding,* Tessa finds her fiancé in bed with another woman. It's impossible to go ahead...until her employer, Blaize Callagan, steps into the breach and offers himself as her bridegroom. A man Tessa has always thought of as every woman's fantasy.

A wedding can take on a powerful life of its own—as it does in this story. But is it a fantasy fulfilled or the deep and meaningful commitment it should be...has to be...for ever-after happiness?

Emma Darcy

THE WEDDING

Emma Darcy

CHAPTER ONE

HOW COULD HE?
How could he!

The refrain had pounded through Tessa's head all night. It had punctuated the rattle of the train trip to North Sydney from her sister's home in Chatswood. It was still throbbing through her mind as she entered the huge CMA building that housed the headquarters of Callagan, Morris and Allen, the engineering and architectural company that claimed her services as a secretary.

That any man—but most particularly a man who said he loved her—could do such a thing! It was beyond Tessa's comprehension.

Tears pricked her eyes again. She determinedly blinked them back as she strode across the foyer. No more tears for Grant Durham. He didn't deserve them. He didn't deserve anything from her, ever again!

She entered an empty lift and jabbed the button for her floor. As the doors closed she vehemently vowed she would close the door on Grant Durham and never let him back into her life. Never!

She had issued the ultimatum last night. Out! And if Grant was not out of her apartment by the time she got back after work today, she would—she would... Well, she didn't know what she would do, except the scene that would follow would be dreadful.

Her stomach twisted. Her heart ached. Her mind reeled

weakly for a moment, then clutched at an even fiercer self-determination.

The lift reached her floor and Tessa stomped down the wide corridor to Jerry Fraine's executive suite of offices, stoking resolution with righteous and furious indignation as she reviewed the degrading humiliation of the previous evening. No more pain, she told herself. No more anguish over him. Grant Durham was finished. FINISHED! In her mind's eye the word looked better in capital letters. No forgiveness. Not for any reason. Never. Four years of her life she had wasted on him, on and off, but this was THE END! Not another day more!

She threw open the door to her own little office and hurled it shut behind her. That made her feel better. She needed to give some vent to the churning emotions she had been trying to contain. Converting pain into anger was very good therapy. Tessa tried a bit more of it.

She threw her weekend bag into the corner beside the filing cabinet. She opened the large bottom drawer of her desk, dropped her handbag in, kicked the drawer shut. She opened the top drawer, snatched up the keys to the filing cabinet and banged that drawer shut as well. She unlocked the top file drawer, withdrew the folder of reports to be processed and slammed the drawer in. The loud metallic crash was very satisfying.

"Not happy this morning?"

The mild inquiry came from the doorway to the executive office. It startled Tessa for a moment. She hadn't expected her boss to be in. The Japanese conference started today, and normally the executives of the company would be meeting in the boardroom before flying off in the company helicopters. She pasted an extra-bright smile on her face and swung to greet him.

Jerry Fraine was a big man with the kind of looks that

suggested a cuddly, comfortable bear. He had frizzy grey-brown hair that stood out like a halo and a plump genial face that invited friendly confidences. He also had a razor-sharp mind, which could negotiate around the trickiest deals and land them. This made him the envy of the other ambitious executives of Callagan, Morris and Allen. All of whom had one ultimate ambition: to impress the managing director, Mr. Blaize Callagan.

Tessa liked being Jerry Fraine's secretary. He was appreciative of her skills, he was kind and considerate, and he had a dry sense of humour that made working with him a pleasure. He didn't try to lord it over her, and, most importantly, he was happily married and not the least bit addicted to any playful slap-and-tickle around the office, thank heaven! It made for an easy relaxed atmosphere between them.

Tessa took a deep breath. "Never been happier," she tripped out airily. "Overflowing with buoyant spirits. God's in His heaven and all's right with the world." But if there was any justice, a bolt of lightning should hit Grant Durham right where it would hurt most!

Jerry grinned at the flaring glitter in her tawny gold eyes. The tigress in her was certainly running rampant today. Good, he thought. That should liven up proceedings. Perhaps it might even draw a little blood from Mr. Blaize Almighty Callagan. Although Jerry was careful not to let that thought show.

Tessa Stockton might be pocket-sized, but she was feisty, high-spirited and, in Jerry's mind, utterly delightful. A lovely woman. A real thoroughbred. Whose sharp wit was an amusing bonus to her sharp efficiency.

He observed, in secret amusement, that she was in a force-ten hurricane over something. Her long glossy brown hair was pulled tightly into a ponytail, a sure sign of furious impatience. Her tip-tilted nose was scenting battle. Her very sweetly curved mouth was stretched thin over a row of small white teeth that looked ready to bite. The delicate pointedness of her chin was decidedly thrust forward in a most aggressive manner this morning. Her long neck was stretched taut. Her exquisitely feminine body was quivering with tension.

"A slight twang of pre-wedding nerves?" he teased.

"The wedding," Tessa said through her teeth, "is off. O-F-F off!"

Jerry's eyebrows rose above his gold-rimmed spectacles. His mouth pursed. "It's quite normal, you know. Little tiffs do happen in the final rundown to the marriage ceremony."

Tessa's heart cramped. Infidelity was not a little tiff! It was on the tip of her tongue to say exactly that but she bit the words back at the last moment and clamped her mouth shut.

No need to say anything. No need to go public yet. No need to castigate Grant Durham for what he had done. Although he certainly deserved every bit of castigation he could get. To Tessa's mind, castration was probably better than castigation!

The humiliation searing her soul was too painful to discuss with anyone. She hadn't even told her sister when she had taken refuge there last night.

"Perhaps a little separation will help cool things down," Jerry went on smoothly.

Tessa gave him a blast with her eyes. The thick dark fringe of her eyelashes did nothing to fan the heat of molten gold.

Contrary to his own expectations, Jerry Fraine was not fried on the spot. He did a hasty reappraisal. He didn't relate to anger, and he liked to run a smooth ship. What employees did away from work was none of his business, and right now he had a problem. Which had to be addressed without further delay.

He relaxed, projected geniality, a soothing composure. "We have an emergency situation, Tessa."

She paused in mid-step between the filing cabinet and her desk. She looked at him, really looked at him for the first time this morning. When Jerry Fraine put on that bland face and used that quiet voice, Tessa knew it was serious business. Her mind instantly changed gears; anger pushed out, concentration forced in.

Knowing that he now had her full attention, Jerry went on. "You're needed for the Japanese conference. Today. Right now, in fact."

Tessa was dumbstruck. "Why?" she croaked, unable to comprehend what was happening.

"Rosemary Davies was involved in a car accident on her way in this morning. She's in hospital. Nothing too serious but…"

Rosemary Davies, the ultra-cool, immaculately groomed, beautiful blonde, who was personal secretary to Blaize Callagan!

"I've chosen you to replace her."

Tessa's jaw dropped open. In her world, this was like trying to fly, then suddenly soaring to the sun. Jerry Fraine was an important man. Tessa thought she had reached her career heights when she was seconded to him. But Blaize Callagan—he was the absolute top! Only rarely did she see him, tall, powerful, riveting, a man who stood out amongst other men.

"You're free to be away for the three days of the conference, aren't you?"

Tessa unlocked her jaw. "Yes. Yes, I'm free." Very definitely free, her mind added savagely. Her ex-fiancé had no further say in her life.

"Take a taxi home," Jerry instructed. "Pack fast and be back here in Blaize Callagan's office at ten-thirty. Not a second later."

Tessa jerked into action, wheeling around to shove the folder of reports into the filing cabinet and lock the drawer. Her mind was in a fever. She was going to fill in for Blaize Callagan's secretary. She would be in close contact with *him* for three whole days. Lord above! Her knees went weak even thinking about it. It would be a miracle if she didn't melt into a heap at his feet. If ever there was a man made for female fantasies, Blaize Callagan was *it!*

"And, Tessa…"

"Yes?" She tore the key out of the drawer and swung around, still dazed by the prospect ahead of her. "Yes, Jerry?"

"Please don't stuff up." He lifted his hands in imploring appeal. "I *am* a married man. I *do* have children to support."

"Well?" said Tessa, trying to get the point.

"I don't want Blaize Callagan to think I can't choose an efficient secretary."

Tessa pulled herself together. Forget the fantasies. This was business. Big Business, with capital *B*s. Blaize Callagan might be lethally attractive, but he was way out of her league, and all he wanted from her was her secretarial skills. If she acted like a star-struck idiot and messed up, it would reflect badly on Jerry Fraine. Not to mention the fact that it wouldn't do her own career any good, either. Since marriage was no longer on her immediate horizon, her career was all the more important to her, and she had better concentrate pretty fiercely on it.

"I'll do my best," she promised grimly.

"Better get moving, then," Jerry advised.

Tessa snatched her handbag from the bottom drawer of

her desk and raced for the door. It was only when she was in the corridor she realised that she couldn't possibly go home to her apartment to pack the clothes she would need. If Grant was still there… If that big-boobed floozy was still there…

Revulsion cramped Tessa's stomach as rage billowed through her mind once more. How could he do it? With that overblown creature in *her* bed! Between *her* sheets! It was the absolute pits of crass insensitivity! Which just went to show what a low-down rotten louse he was underneath all his surface charm!

It made Tessa positively ill to think that if she hadn't come back from her parents' place a day early, she wouldn't have found out what she had almost married. All these years thinking he was the only man she wanted, and she had been over the moon with happiness when he had finally proposed marriage to her. Yet here it was, only seven weeks to the wedding, and he could do that! He might even be creep enough to think he had free slather in her apartment today, since her ultimatum had given him until this evening to be out.

In retrospect, that had been wrong. What she should have done, of course, was hurl him and his floozy out there and then! Stark naked into the street! Except Grant was stronger than she was. And she had been so shocked, so outraged, so upset, that she hadn't been able to think straight. She had hurled a barrage of missiles at them, then stormed out of the apartment, feeling it was too contaminated to stay there.

She couldn't face that again.

She just couldn't!

There was nothing for it but to buy some clothes. That boutique up the end of the road, Executive Class—she would go there. It would probably cost her the earth, but so what? She no longer had to pay for a wedding dress.

Tessa worked it all out as she rode the lift to the ground floor. She had all her toilet things and make-up in her weekend bag. Enough underclothes for three days. She needed three outfits that would go with her black high heels and handbag. Certainly the skirt and top she was wearing at the moment did not rate as suitable wear for Blaize Callagan's secretary.

Her heart fluttered in nervous anticipation. Blaize Callagan! Good Lord! How was she going to live up to *his* expectations? Well, she just had to keep her head and give it the best try she could, she told herself sternly. Jerry was counting on a good performance from her. For her own self-respect she had to perform well. She needed to feel good about something!

Forty minutes later, Tessa walked into the CMA building, wearing a black linen suit that hugged her figure in streamlined class. It was teamed with a pin-tucked, high-collared blouse in fine white lawn. The outfit had cost her four hundred dollars but it made Tessa feel like a million dollars, so to her mind it was worth every cent. As were the two three-hundred-dollar outfits in the shopping bag she carried.

There was something very uplifting about being sinfully extravagant. Freedom, she told herself. All the scrimping and saving she had done for a future with Grant Durham was a thing of the past. It was her money now, to do with as she liked. She was no longer accountable to anyone but herself! Perhaps she would blow the rest of her bank account on a trip somewhere.

Meanwhile, this conference trip was a real godsend. It got her out of the city, away from any contact with Grant, and no doubt Blaize Callagan would keep her so busy she wouldn't have much time to think depressing thoughts. She hoped Grant would do one decent thing and get out of her apartment before she got back. Her continued absence for three days ought to hammer that message home to him.

Tessa arrived in her office with twenty minutes still up her sleeve. She quickly repacked her weekend bag, putting the things she wouldn't need into the plastic shopping bag. She was cramming that into the bottom drawer of her desk when she noticed the vinyl pouch that contained her "professional" glasses.

There was nothing wrong with Tessa's eyes, but the glasses were sometimes useful in projecting an image. She had first bought them when she came to Callagan, Morris and Allen so that she could keep other men from bothering her while she concentrated on Grant Durham. What a mistake that had been! But the glasses did give her an aura of serious reserve, helped along by the thick tortoiseshell rims. She suddenly thought it might be a very good idea to wear them as Blaize Callagan's secretary.

Her hair needed attention, too. Tessa wound her ponytail into a neat topknot, which she fastened with hairpins from her toilet bag. Then she tried on the glasses and examined the effect in her little hand mirror. They certainly helped to make her look a bit older than her twenty-four years. Gave her a more serious, earnest look, particularly with her hair up instead of falling loose. No one looking at her now could possibly think she was anything but a career professional.

She checked her watch. Five minutes to go. She zipped up her bag and set off for the lifts again, satisfied that she looked every bit as elegantly professional as Rosemary Davies, even though she was considerably shorter and nowhere near as upper class. However, there was nothing she could do about that.

Tessa worked on her composure as she rode up to the twentieth floor where Blaize Callagan reigned in the managing director's suite. Cool, calm and collected, she recited, like a mantra that would soothe all manner of palpitations.

Unfortunately, it didn't really work. Not once she was ushered into Blaize Callagan's office and she came face to face with him. It ran through Tessa's mind that there wouldn't be a woman in the whole world that could stand in front of Blaize Callagan and not suffer at least some palpitations.

He rose from his desk as she entered, six feet of masculine virility that had lost nothing in thirty-six years of high-powered living. His physique alone had strong sex appeal, lean enough to lend him a lithe elegance in the superbly tailored suits he wore—charcoal-grey today—yet with that hint of danger in the hard muscularity, which proclaimed him superbly fit and ready for any type of confrontation.

He had a hard, angular face, barely fleshed, yet there was an austere and compelling beauty in its strong bone structure. His skin colour was a natural golden tan, complementing thick black hair and eyes so dark they were almost black, as well.

Tessa had never seen such penetrating inescapable eyes on anyone. They gleamed with a diamond-hard intelligence that would not allow release until he willed it. The moment they locked onto hers, a weird feeling of vulnerability crawled down Tessa's spine. They gave nothing away, expressed nothing. They simply imparted his dominance.

"Miss Stockton."

A short nod of the head by way of acceptance, or approval, or acknowledgement. Tessa had no idea which. His voice had a velvet purr that raised goose bumps on her skin. Somehow she made her tongue work.

"Yes, sir" was all she managed. Even that was a pure act of will.

He gestured an invitation to a chair in front of his desk. "Good of you to oblige at such short notice," he said pleasantly, then waited for her to sit down.

His eyes flicked over her in quick appraisal as she walked forward. Tessa had the nerve-quivering impression that nothing about her—absolutely nothing—escaped his notice. She almost slumped into the chair. Her legs were proving unreliable under pressure.

She forced herself to look at him inquiringly. His mouth moved into a little quirk that suggested some sensual satisfaction. His eyes stabbed briefly into hers, then he sat down and concentrated all his attention on the documents spread across his desk.

Tessa stared at him, waiting for him to give her instructions. She waited so long that her mind started to drift through all she knew about him. He was now a widower, but his wife, Candice, had been a famous model-turned-fashion designer. Her wild mane of red-gold curls had been her trademark, along with flashing green eyes, pearly skin and a tall, fabulous figure. An eminently suitable match for a man such as Blaize Callagan.

No doubt he was finding it difficult to replace her since her tragic death three years ago in a speedboat collision. But it wasn't for want of trying, according to the gossip that circulated about his affairs. Although whether or not the rumours were correct that he was bedding women right, left and centre, nothing—but absolutely nothing—distracted him from getting on with his business.

Everyone said he had a brilliant incisive mind, and certainly he couldn't operate an international company with such success if he wasn't shrewd at top-level decision-making. Tessa knew that it was Blaize Callagan who set all policies for CMA and saw that they were carried through, come hell or high water. Ruthless, he was, in getting his way. So it was rumoured. And reported by Jerry Fraine.

His head lifted.

Tessa snapped her mind to attention.

But his eyes didn't lift to hers. They seemed to study her legs, running a slow and very deliberate survey from the shape of her thighs—outlined by the narrow black skirt—to her knees, to her calves and ankles. He gave such concentrated attention to every detail that Tessa felt every bone and muscle had been mapped and committed to memory. The expression on his face said he liked the map. Very much. He gave a quick, short, decisive nod of his head, then pulled his gaze to the documents again.

He must have been thinking of something, Tessa reasoned, although it didn't make her feel less conscious of the prickling of her skin against her stockings. And when, a couple of minutes later, he stared at her breasts, which her suit jacket moulded to prominent effect, no reasoning Tessa could come up with stopped her nipples from doing what they shouldn't. He seemed to know, to place them exactly. Those X-ray eyes of his were very, very unsettling. She was intensely relieved when he gave another nod and they dropped to the documents again.

Tessa checked her watch. She had been here fifteen minutes. It seemed ridiculous that he didn't ask her to do something. Why had he demanded that she be in his office at ten-thirty if he didn't want to put her to work? Did he think she would be incompetent? That she couldn't possibly measure up to the perfect Rosemary?

Tessa's professional pride stirred. She was as good a secretary as anybody, and could run rings around most. It was an insult to leave her sitting like this. An insult to Jerry, as well. She couldn't let it go on. In fact, she wasn't sure that the way he had studied her legs and breasts in that disassociated manner wasn't an even worse insult. Blaize Callagan might be the big boss, but she *was* a fellow human being. And a damned good secretary!

Tessa worked some moisture into her mouth and mentally adopted a brisk professional manner. "Where do you want me to start, sir?" she asked.

"At the beginning," he muttered, without looking up.

A blaze of resentment glittered in her tawny gold eyes. Pride puffed through her mind. He wasn't going to patronise her as though she were some silly dumb cluck! She dragged in a deep breath and spoke with very cool precision.

"If you would be kind enough to spell out specifically what you want..."

Finally the dark eyes shot up and fastened on hers. "The usual," he said, "although everything will be happening much faster, I expect, than what you are normally used to. Although the sessions will be taped for future reference, you will take a note of everything that is said, not only as a check to the tapes but also for my easy reference. After the meetings, you will be required to word-process any memos, directives or queries. You will liaise with your opposite number. You will make sure that everyone has what they need. Apart from that, every important thing is to be reduced to writing," he said in rapid-fire delivery. "With exactness and precision. Can you manage that?"

"Yes, sir," she fired back.

"And, Miss Stockton..."

"Yes, sir?"

"There is nearly a hundred million dollars of joint project money at stake."

"Yes, sir."

"Please...try not to stuff up, Miss Stockton."

"Yes, sir."

"Everything that you do will be important, Miss Stockton. Please appreciate that."

"Yes, sir."

His eyes returned to his documents.

Tessa felt she'd just been put through the wringer—picked up, squeezed dry, then hung out on a washing line again.

"And is there anything you want me to do immediately, sir?" she grated, determined to prove that she wasn't the ninny he took her for.

He looked up, and this time he really looked at her, his eyes gathering a speculative interest as he examined hers. After several heart-stopping moments, he softly said, "I don't think you'd be able to oblige."

Tessa flushed at his mortifying judgement of her.

A gleam of some secret inner amusement danced into the dark eyes, and again his mouth moved into a sensual little quirk. "Perhaps some other time."

Tessa didn't know how to interpret that. But his private amusement was not at all mollifying to her injured pride.

"The Japanese delegation has been held up for an hour or so. That's the reason for the delay," he said more briskly. "In the meantime, arm yourself with your tools of trade, Miss Stockton. Rosemary left an attaché case full of documents and documentation on her desk if you would like to check through them. Anything you might think you need, you will find in her office. Through the door behind you," he directed.

Tessa almost leapt from her chair, eager to do something useful.

"And, Miss Stockton..."

"Yes, sir?"

"In this business, it is impossible to anticipate everything. If there is anything we need at any time, you have my authority behind you all the way. Over everyone."

"Thank you, sir," Tessa said in some dismay. She found absolute power a scary concept. The responsibility of it was positively frightening. But she reassured herself with the thought that Blaize Callagan had accepted the responsibility of backing her. Although if she stuffed up...

"Some problem, Miss Stockton?" he inquired, as she stood there furiously thinking.

"No, sir." She was *not* going to stuff up. "Thank you, sir," she added for good measure, then turned briskly towards the door he had indicated.

However, as she walked across the room to his secretary's adjoining office, she had the very strong sensation that Blaize Callagan's penetrating dark eyes were studying her bottom and every movement it made. No doubt it amused him.

Never in her life had Tessa felt more conscious of being a woman, or more conscious of a man being a man. The tension that tightened her nerves had nothing whatsoever to do with proving her competence as a secretary. It was the way Blaize Callagan kept looking at her!

CHAPTER TWO

AT PRECISELY eleven-thirty, Blaize Callagan collected Tessa from his secretary's office. They were driven to the helicopter in a stretch limousine. He read documents all the way.

Her awareness of him would lessen, Tessa told herself. However, she couldn't help noticing that his fingers were long and supple. Occasionally he rubbed his thumb over their inner pads as his hand was poised ready to turn another page. The soft tactile movement was somehow disturbing. So was the tangy scent of his after-shave lotion in the close confinement of the car.

He said nothing to her and Tessa felt constrained not to break his concentration. Once the conference started she would be busy enough, she decided, so she might as well relax while she could. Except that was proving utterly impossible.

The fine woollen fabric of his trousers was stretched tightly across his thighs. She wondered if he worked out at a gym. Powerful muscles weren't formed and maintained without some kind of exercise. Tessa knew that from her aerobics class. On the other hand, Blaize Callagan might get all the exercise he needed elsewhere. Although Grant—the two-timing fink—didn't have hard muscular thighs like that, so perhaps Blaize Callagan did work out at a gym.

Three other executives were standing by the helicopter when they arrived. One of them was Jerry Fraine. He stared at Tessa, his eyebrows shot up, his mouth twitched, he passed a hand across his face, then he quickly swung towards the helicopter. His big burly shoulders visibly shook.

Whether it was a result of prolonged nervous tension, Tessa didn't know, but she had to swallow an impetuous giggle herself. Jerry had never seen her look so prim and proper and professional. And the glasses, of course, had been a joke between them. She hoped, when he recovered his composure, he would appreciate the effort she had made on behalf of her image. After all, it was for Jerry Fraine's benefit as well as her own. Not that it seemed to be working very effectively. So far Blaize Callagan didn't seem to see her as a career professional. Only as a body. A female body.

The conference was being held at Peppers, a highly reputable country hotel in the Hunter River Valley. It was set amongst the famous vineyards that produced some of the best Australian wines. Although it was about two hundred kilometres from Sydney by road, it was little more than a twenty-minute flight by helicopter.

Tessa had never been to Peppers, and she had never been in a helicopter, either. As soon as she saw the executives climbing aboard, she knew she had a problem. No way in the world was she going to be able to take the high step into the cabin in her narrow skirt. She heaved a deep sigh and looked at Blaize Callagan. He met her glance with a wickedly knowing gleam in his dark eyes.

"I'll lift you," he said.

Tessa burned. "Thank you," she bit out.

The pilot had already taken their attaché cases from them to stow in the baggage area. Tessa expected Blaize Callagan to hoist her up from her waist. He didn't. Before she even approached the step to the cabin, he swooped and lifted her right off her feet and into his arms.

"Nice body weight, Miss Stockton," he remarked appreciatively.

"Thank you, sir," Tessa whispered as she tried to recapture her breath.

One arm was around her thighs. His other arm was around her shoulders, with a hand coming perilously close to curling under her arm to the outside swell of her breast. She was pressed against a broad and unrelenting chest.

"Look after yourself, do you, Stockton?"

She looked him straight in the eye, blazing gold meeting devilish black. "I try to keep in trim."

"Good work, Stockton. Try to keep it that way."

"Oh, I will, sir. I will."

His mouth wore that funny quirk as he carried her forward and lifted her into her cabin seat with all the ease in the world. He really had very sensual lips. Tessa felt he knew just what to do with them and used them accordingly. To taunt, tease, excite or provoke. Right at this moment, she felt very provoked. And teased. And taunted. And, if she was totally honest with herself, treacherously excited. He certainly was a very strong man.

He released her smoothly, without the slightest suggestion of taking any liberties, and Tessa was left wondering if he was playing games with her or not. She concentrated on fastening her seatbelt until he was settled in the seat in front of her, next to the pilot. She wished she had bought a trouser-suit. She was almost sure he had enjoyed touching her like that.

The helicopter lifted off. When the heat in her cheeks became slightly less painful, Tessa turned to look at Jerry, who was sitting next to her. Impossible to talk, but she would have liked a look of moral support from him. He had his gold-rimmed spectacles off. One hand was lifted to his eyes, finger and thumb squeezing the eyelids hard. His brow was furrowed. His head was bent. He looked as if he was fiercely concentrated in prayer...or something.

Tessa sighed. No help there. Maybe Jerry hated flying. Or maybe he was praying that she wouldn't stuff up. She beamed a hard thought at the back of Blaize Callagan's head. I am not here for your amusement, Blaize Callagan, she told him. And my body—fit or not—is no business of yours. You either take me seriously, or don't take me at all!

Except she was here in this helicopter, and on her way with him, and she couldn't exactly jump off in mid-air. In fact, there was very little she could do about it, so she turned her head to the view below and watched the city give way to country. At least she was getting away from other problems for a while.

There had to be someone down there, she thought. Someone a whole lot better than Grant Durham. Someone who would at least be faithful to the so-called love he talked about. Tessa wondered if Blaize Callagan had been faithful to his wife. Maybe men weren't faithful animals. But she certainly wasn't going to marry one who couldn't be faithful to her seven weeks before their wedding day!

Tessa heaved another sigh. How was she going to tell her mother the wedding was off? She could readily imagine the hysterics and the recriminations. "What will people think?" and, "All the arrangements are made!" and, "You've been wanting to marry Grant for four years, Tessa! You won't get anyone if you don't have him." Her mother was going to throw an absolute fit. Reason would have nothing to do with it.

At least her father would listen. He had never been all that keen on Grant. Besides, her father was about to be saved a lot of money on the wedding reception. He would appreciate that more than her mother did. Tessa had always found her father a sane, sensible man.

It seemed no time at all before they were over the Hunter River Valley. The rolling hills were lined with rows and rows of grapevines. The helicopter swooped in towards an impressive complex of colonial-styled buildings situated on the top of a small hill. Cream walls, green roof and verandahs all around. Nothing higher than two storeys. Landscaped gardens close in, and expanses of lawn rolling down the hill with lovely stands of native gum trees and a huge lake-like dam to add interest.

They landed on the lawn near the tennis court. Blaize Callagan lifted Tessa out of the helicopter as efficiently as he had lifted her into it. Apparently they were the last to arrive. The verandah above the slope of lawn was crowded with company people and a smattering of Japanese, all enjoying a pre-luncheon drink while they waited for the big guns to lead proceedings.

Tessa looked at the grassed slope to be traversed and regretted her spindly high heels. Blaize Callagan offered his arm.

"Please try not to fall flat on your face, Stockton. It wouldn't create a good impression," he murmured out of the corner of his mouth.

"I'll hang onto you like grim death, sir," she retorted.

"A lively way to meet your end, Stockton," he said with a totally impassive countenance. "Might I suggest a more forward pressure on your toes?"

"At your command, sir."

"Nice attitude, Stockton."

"Thank you, sir."

She made it up to the verandah without mishap. At which point, she became nothing but a cipher at Blaize Callagan's side until luncheon was over, although she was treated with impeccable courtesy by all the men present, Australian and Japanese. Her opposite number, with whom she would have to liaise, was a man. Who, she was pleased to note, was as short as she was, which made him a whole lot less intimidating than he might have been. She was the only woman from either side.

At two o'clock, they all trooped down to the conference centre and the nitty-gritty business began. Tessa had no time to admire the facilities provided, the fine proportions of the big conference room, the interesting paintings on the walls or the artistic floral arrangements. She concentrated hard on her shorthand notes, arranging them in a system for easy reference points—the names of the speakers, their contributions to the discussion, the proposals, the objections, the suggested compromises.

Jerry Fraine was good. She felt positively proud of her boss's negotiating skills. But Blaize Callagan was the pivot, without a doubt. Everything turned around him. It was an education to listen and watch as he swung an argument or worked around it, seizing advantages, defusing problems, plotting a winning course.

They broke briefly for afternoon tea, which was served in the reception room, allowing people to mill around and relax for a breathing space.

"Got all that, Stockton?" Blaize asked as he accompanied her out of the conference room.

"Yes, sir," she replied confidently.

"I hope so, Stockton. This is one tough nut to crack and I'm going to need every last bit of ammunition we can get," he said grimly.

Tessa held her tongue. She thought he had been doing extremely well. The majority of Japanese seemed to be in agreement with what he was pushing. Nevertheless, he obviously knew his business better than she did. When they returned for the last session of the day, Tessa made sure she didn't miss a beat. If any little thing was critical, she had it faithfully recorded.

At five o'clock they broke for the day. But it was far from the end of her working day. A hotel staff member was on hand to lead Blaize Callagan to his accommodation, and Tessa was taken along with him. They were led away from the main buildings of the hotel complex to a private cottage on the edge of the grounds.

A verandah led into a large living room. Office equipment had been set up for them here; a worktable holding an IBM computer and a laser printer with a pile of stationery for ready use. A marvellous fireplace opened to both the living room and the dining room. There was a well-equipped kitchen and four bedrooms. But only *one* bathroom. To be shared by the occupants. The staff member showed them through every room, pointing out all the facilities and assuring Blaize Callagan that anything he wanted, anything at all, was on call.

Tessa noticed that her suitcase had been put in one of the bedrooms. It had obviously been arranged that she was staying here, with *him*, alone with him!

She tried telling herself that this was where it had been planned for Rosemary Davies to stay, but it didn't help to calm her pulse. The truth of the matter was she didn't know if Blaize Callagan's relationship with Rosemary Davies was purely professional. She had never heard any rumours to the contrary, but this was certainly a more intimate arrangement than she had figured on. It was bad enough having to share a bathroom with him. How was she going to sleep tonight? Wasn't this situation at the very least compromising?

On the other hand, it was common practice these days for people of the opposite sex to share houses or apartments in the high rental climate of Sydney. Lots of women felt safer with a man in residence. No one raised eyebrows at it any more, or jumped to the conclusion that sharing accommodation meant sharing beds.

Tessa worked hard at assuring herself that her reputation was not about to be shot to pieces by staying under the same roof as Blaize Callagan. After all, this was part of the hotel and they did have separate bedrooms. Making any objection to the arrangement was completely out of the question.

But the moment the hotel staff member walked out the door and left her alone with Blaize Callagan in the living room, all the sane and sensible reasoning in the world could not dispel the feeling of danger—in capital letters.

"A ten-minute break for you to unpack or wash or whatever, Stockton," Blaize Callagan instructed. "Then I want transcripts of everything said by the Japanese speakers."

Tessa breathed a small sigh of relief. She could handle work. "Yes, sir."

"What would you like to drink?"

"Coffee, sir."

"White and one sugar, wasn't it?"

"Yes, sir."

She was surprised that he remembered such a trivial detail from the coffee she had had at lunch. It reminded her of a few other things he might have memorised about her, and she felt a surge of heat tingling outwards towards her skin. She turned away and headed for her bedroom fast before the blush became too obvious.

She even felt self-conscious about using the toilet with *him* wandering around nearby. Which was absolutely ridiculous! She ran cold water over her wrists for a few seconds, then dabbed it over her hot face. Stay cool, calm and collected, she fiercely instructed herself.

He might be the sexiest-looking man she had ever seen, but that didn't mean he found her sexy. Although he had taken an inordinate interest in her body. Nevertheless, he knew as well as she did that she was out of his class, and this accommodation had obviously been arranged for his convenience in a strictly business sense. He wanted her for work. That's all. And she had to oblige him as best she could.

Unpacking didn't take long. She hung up her new dresses, although both of them were in uncrushable fabrics, then set out her toilet things in the bathroom. She checked her appearance in the mirror—still tidy—then returned to the living room to work.

Blaize Callagan was stretched out in an armchair, suit coat off, tie loosened, top two buttons of his shirt undone. He was nursing a drink in his hand, something with ice, and he looked very relaxed. It did not make Tessa feel relaxed at all. It made her a lot more conscious of his body.

"Coffee by the computer," he said.

"Thank you, sir."

The computer and printer were already switched on, ready to go. Tessa opened her attaché case, which had been placed on the table beside them, removed her notebook and sat down. She sipped the coffee as she ran her fingers over the keyboard, setting up the word-processing program to suit her needs.

"Kick your shoes off, if you like, Stockton. Undo your jacket. Be comfortable."

"I'm comfortable as I am, thank you, sir," she said, keeping her eyes glued to the monitor screen. It was bad enough having him flaunting his body at her. She wasn't about to let her guard down.

"Put each speaker on separate pages and pass them to me as they're done," he instructed.

"Yes, sir."

Tessa worked at top speed for the next hour, transcribing her shorthand into neat sheets of printing. She did not pass them to Blaize Callagan. He was up and waiting for each sheet to emerge from the printer, taking it away, studying it, pacing around, pouncing on the next one, occasionally muttering to himself.

"What next, sir?" Tessa asked, when she had finished the last Japanese speaker.

He looked up from the page he had just snatched, frowned at her. "I've got to think. Go and have a bath or something, Stockton." He checked his watch. "Pre-dinner drinks in the bar at seven. Be ready."

"Yes, sir."

"There'll be no business over dinner. The Japanese don't work that way. So you can relax for a while, Stockton."

"Yes, sir. Thank you, sir."

She was already dismissed, his concentration back on the pages in his hand.

The way he could switch on and off was little short of incredible, Tessa thought, as the evening progressed. He was tense and silent, inwardly focused, until they reached the bar in the main building. In an instant he was emanating goodwill and fellowship. Over dinner he was a charming host, telling jokes, swapping stories, affable and interesting, controlling the conversation with enviable ease and mastery. The moment they walked out of the hotel, he closed into himself again, tense and silent.

They were halfway back to the cottage before he spoke, and that was only to use Tessa as a sounding board for his thoughts.

"We've got a real problem. The way things are shaping up, I can't see the Japanese getting *ringi*," he said abruptly.

"What's *ringi*, sir?" Tessa asked. She had never heard the term before.

"Their seal of approval. Every delegate has to give it before the project can go ahead. It's a symbol of their complete dedication and commitment to the project. A totally different system from ours. I can make a unilateral decision and force it through. Saves a lot of time and trouble. But they won't move without consensus."

The impatience and frustration in his voice told Tessa what he thought about *that* system. But then Blaize Callagan was obviously a born dictator. Tessa thought the *ringi* system was a lot fairer than orders from on high. Less open to abuse. But she kept her opinion to herself.

"Stockton, what happens when you run into an immovable object at full speed?"

"You get hurt, sir."

"Don't be a fool, Stockton. I'm talking about me."

This left Tessa feeling confused. Did Blaize Callagan think he was invulnerable to hurt? Was he? "I don't know, sir," she said. It seemed the safest comment.

"There are only two things to do, Stockton. Run into it and get hurt, as you suggest. No point in trying to shift it. That's impossible. The far better thing is—get around it."

"Yes, sir."

"I'm going to sidestep *ringi*," he said decisively.

"Yes, sir."

By this time they were walking up the steps to the cottage.

"Need to write a memo, Stockton."

"Yes, sir."

As soon as they entered the living room, Tessa went straight to the computer, switched it on and sat down, readying herself for his dictation. He paced up and down the room, gathering his thoughts.

His suit jacket came off. It was tossed onto a chair. His tie made its exit, as well. Four buttons on his shirt were flicked open, revealing a dark sprinkle of hair below his throat. Tessa was beginning to feel a bit tight around the throat herself.

He paused, frowned, then started to dictate, setting out the strategy he had decided upon in clear precise terms. Tessa's fingers flew to keep up with him. There was another long pause for more concentration. He removed his cufflinks and rolled his shirt sleeves up to his elbows. His forearms were indeed muscular. Tessa hoped the undressing was going to stop there. It was getting very, very distracting.

"There's a lot of nervous tension here, Stockton," he remarked.

"I've noticed that, sir."

The dark eyes stabbed at her with amused appreciation. "I'm glad you have more words in your vocabulary than 'yes, sir', Stockton. It comes as a relief."

"Yes, sir."

He dictated further points for the memo then came to stand behind her chair to read the monitor screen. "Turn it back to the beginning, Stockton," he directed.

"Would you like me to print it out, sir?"

"No. Just roll it through the monitor for me. I'll tell you what to add or delete as we go."

"Yes, sir."

How Tessa held her concentration together she didn't know. Several times he leaned over her to point out a place in the printing on the screen, thrusting his bare forearm right in front of her eyes, making her overwhelmingly aware of male flesh and muscle…and the long supple fingers…and the warmth of his breath near her ear…and the scent of his strong masculinity.

Several times her fingers fumbled and she had to correct her mistakes. He made no critical comment. He patiently waited until she was ready to go on. At last they came to the end of it. Then he asked her to turn it to the beginning and roll it through again.

"Very tense, Stockton," he commented. "I think we should do something about it."

Tessa had no suggestions. She didn't know if he was commenting on her or him or the memo. She couldn't even bring herself to say, "Yes, sir." She sat there in piano-wire tautness, waiting for his next instruction, hoping she could carry it out with some air of competence.

She felt a hairpin being drawn out of her topknot. Then another one. And another one. She stopped breathing. Her heart slammed around her chest. After several moments of blank shock—and the loss of several more hairpins—Tessa's mind dictated that she should start breathing again because her chest was getting very constricted and her heart was protesting quite painfully. Her mind added that she ought to say something, as well. But before she could find some appropriate words, he spoke.

"Nice hair, Stockton," he said as her ponytail fell down and his fingers drifted through the silky weight of the thick tresses. He leaned over her shoulder and placed a bundle of hairpins on the table. Then he went to work on the rubber band, gently untwining it to release her ponytail. "You'll feel a lot better with your hair down," he said.

"Mr. Callagan…" Tessa almost choked on his name. She decided it was best not to make an issue of her hair at this late point, but to get his mind—and hers—firmly directed onto business. "Would you like this memo printed out now?"

"No."

The rubber band was tossed on top of the pins. His fingers lifted her hair away from its former constraint, fanning the long tresses out in all their glossy glory before sliding through them to gently massage her scalp.

"Do you want to make more changes to the memo?" she asked, beginning to feel quite desperate about his absorption with her hair.

"Perhaps later. Needs thinking about. Feeling less tense now?"

"Yes. Thank you." It was a terrible lie, but what else could she say?

"A pleasure, Stockton," he purred in his velvet tone. And thankfully removed his hands from her hair. Then, just as she sucked in a much-needed scoop of oxygen, he said, "Let me help you off with your jacket." And he was bending over her again, his hands working on the buttons at her waist with swift effectiveness.

She froze. Her mind went into stasis for the few critical seconds that it took for him to have her jacket unbuttoned and opened wide.

"Just lean forward a bit and I'll slide it off your shoulders," he said.

Tessa's mind burst out of stasis and into frantic activity. It was only her jacket. He hadn't groped over her breasts or anything. She leaned forward and lifted her arms out of the sleeves as he smoothly pulled the jacket away from her.

"Smart suit, Stockton," he said, as he tossed the top half of it on a chair. "Does you credit."

"Thank you, sir," Tessa managed to croak.

Somehow, his approval of her choice of clothes didn't carry much weight at this moment. Some belated instinct of self-preservation urged her to stop sitting like a waiting dummy and take some positive initiative. She stood up and turned to face him. It wasn't easy meeting his eyes. First she had to drag her own up from his chest—there were more of his shirt buttons undone. Right to the waist!

"I think," she forced out, "since you don't need me..."

"Oh, but I do need you, Stockton," he said softly, the dark eyes locking onto hers in hot, purposeful intent. "I need you very much."

He moved. One hand slid around her waist, the other gently tilted her chin, keeping her eyes fastened to his as he drew her lower body against his, letting her know the shape and urgency of what he desired of her. "Very much," he repeated with slow deliberate emphasis.

CHAPTER THREE

THERE WAS ABSOLUTELY nothing unmistakable about what was going on now. The hardness pressing into her stomach had a rampant virility that left Tessa in no doubt whatsoever. Her mind was suddenly very clear, even though the rest of her was a melting mess.

In the clarity of her mind was one brightly burning thought. Blaize Callagan found her desirable. Urgently desirable. Her erstwhile fiancé had fancied someone else, but Blaize Callagan—this man amongst men—fancied *her!*

All the same, that sweet balm to her wounded soul was no reason to lose her head over him, Tessa swiftly reasoned. Her hands fluttered up to his chest. As a means of protest they were hopelessly ineffectual. One of her thumbs hit bare warm flesh and stuck there. She cleared her throat.

"I think…"

"Stockton, this is not the time for thinking," he advised kindly. He lifted his hand from her chin, took off her glasses and lobbed them onto the table behind her. His hand moved to her throat and began unbuttoning her blouse.

"Interesting thing about your eyes, Stockton," he said, looking into them with mesmerising intensity. "They don't look at all weak or vacant without your glasses on. In fact, they appear brighter…and infinitely more fascinating."

"Thank you, sir," Tessa said, swallowing hard. "I'd like to say, sir, that this isn't a good idea." At least her voice could register a protest, even though the rest of her was playing traitor to any sense of right or propriety.

"On the contrary, Stockton. It's the best release for tension I know. I've had a lot of experience."

"Yes, sir. I'm sure you have, sir." He was unbuttoning her blouse with such swift and smooth expertise that the buttons seemed to know they had to obey him without falter. "But it so happens, sir, that I don't go in for one-night stands."

"Perish the thought, Stockton. We have at least two nights."

Tessa took a deep breath, trying desperately to ignore what he was doing and act with as much dignity as she could. "Look, sir, just because your normal secretary performs this service for you, doesn't mean you can expect…"

"Stockton." He looked at her severely as his hand continued its unrelenting intent, parting her blouse and tracing soft sensual paths across the swell of her breasts with gentle fingertips. "I do not require or want this service—as you put it—from Rosemary Davies. I make it a practice of never mixing business with pleasure. It's a ruinous mistake."

Her skin trembled with excitement under his touch. "Then why are you doing it?" she argued with impeccable logic.

"One must adapt to extraordinary circumstances," he replied with commanding authority.

Extraordinary… The word spun around Tessa's mind, gathering a hypnotic power. It certainly fitted this situation. He was right about that. It was extraordinary that Blaize Callagan should *desire* her, and extraordinary that she was actually letting him take such liberties. Not only letting him, but liking what he was doing to her. I need to feel desired, she thought. And he was not just anybody! In the normal course of events, she would never again be with

Blaize Callagan like this. It was time out of time. Extraordinary circumstances. An encounter. For both of them.

Whether he took her silence as encouragement or assent, Tessa didn't know. Perhaps he saw the softening of vulnerability in her eyes, or was hell-bent on pressing his own will anyway. Whatever...

He found the front fastening of her bra and undid it without the slightest fumble or difficulty. Very softly, he grazed his fingers under the nylon lace, gradually peeling it away and replacing its cup with the warm palm of his hand. With exquisite delicacy his thumb began a sweeping caress over her breast. Not once did he glance down to look at the flesh he had bared, or see what he was doing. His eyes never left hers.

She didn't look down, either. She stared at him, her mind achurn with alien thoughts, but she was conscious of her body responding to his touch with wild spasms of nervous excitement.

Why not? she argued feverishly. The only man she had ever given herself to had been unfaithful to her last night. Why shouldn't she have this man? Why shouldn't she have this experience? Grant certainly hadn't nursed any scruples about sampling what he wanted. She was free to do anything she liked. With whomever she liked. And right now she was being offered the kind of fantasy that Blaize Callagan had always evoked. It would never come her way again. So why not grab it while she could? Wouldn't she regret it afterwards if she didn't?

"Don't be inflexible, Stockton. It's ruined more people than I care to name," Blaize said persuasively. "What we have here is an intensely desirable situation. And to be perfectly frank, there is a great deal of tension between us. Much more tension than can be summarily dismissed. Don't you agree?"

Desirable, desirable… The word beat around Tessa's brain, heightening the temptation. Where had all her fine standards of morality got her? Out in the cold while a big-boobed floozy took over her bed. Well, she needn't be cold tonight! Blaize Callagan wanted her. And, yes…she wanted to know what he was like as a lover, however brief the encounter.

"Agreed," she said, in a rush of heady recklessness.

"No regrets?" he asked.

If she had any regrets afterwards…well, she would live with them. At least they would make better memories than seeing Grant and that creature in her bed.

"No regrets," she said.

She felt the rise of his chest at his sharp intake of breath. His eyes were instantly hooded, but not before Tessa saw the flaring glitter of triumph in them. He had got his way, she thought, with ruthless disregard for anything but his own desire. Yet she didn't resent it. He had at least asked her, although he had certainly loaded the dice before rolling out that little nicety.

Perhaps it was that quality in him that made him so provocative, so exciting. The will to dare, to take the opportunity, to win. And the arrogance of the mind behind that will.

But she also had a will, and Tessa knew inside herself that she was not his conquest. She had made a choice, for better or for worse. And she did not intend to be a passive victim to his will.

She moved her hands, sliding them under his opened shirt. If she was going to do it, she might as well fulfil every fantasy she had ever had. No point in holding back.

He went completely still, perhaps surprised by her initiative, perhaps savouring her touch on his flesh. He was, Tessa thought, a very sensual man. He waited as she pulled his shirt apart, pushed it off his shoulders, but he didn't move his hold on her to let her drag it off his arms.

He was beautifully made, sleek and powerful, the muscles of his chest firmly delineated, his shoulders broad and strong, his upper arms… Tessa ran her fingernails down them, testing the tensile strength underneath his gleaming skin.

She heard his breath hiss through his teeth and looked at him through her thick lashes, the gleaming gold of her eyes smoky with a savage desire of her own. ''Not all your own way, sir,'' she taunted softly.

He smiled, and it was the smile of a predator about to take up the hunt. He lifted his hand from her breast, slid it under her hair, caressed the nape of her neck, tilted her head back, then, holding her firmly, brought his lips down on hers.

He kissed her hungrily, with quick shifting pressures, sensuality mixed with an aggression that barely allowed her to catch breath. She reached up to wind her arms around his neck. He curled his hand under her bottom and hoisted her into more intimate contact with his aroused state, scraping the softness of her breasts up his chest, crushing her against him as he turned and headed for the closest bedroom.

Tessa's shoes slipped off her dangling feet. He kicked them aside. He laughed a deep throaty laugh as he stood her on the bed and swiftly disposed of her blouse and bra. ''I knew you were beautiful,'' he said, and with his mouth he paid devastating homage to both her breasts as his hands worked to strip off her skirt.

It felt so good, so exultantly good that he didn't want her to have huge melons like that woman Grant had put in her bed. She moved herself with a fierce abandonment against his gloriously ravaging mouth, inviting, enticing, withdrawing, plunging forward, digging her fingers into his hair, making him work, shifting from one taut mound of pulsing flesh to the other, feeding a deep savage satisfaction that had very little to do with Blaize Callagan...except he was the perfect person to give her what she wanted.

Whether he sensed this or not, she didn't know. Suddenly he wrenched his head out of her grasp and lowered her down on the pillows. He pulled the rest of her clothes off her legs with swift efficiency but no delicacy at all. Tessa didn't care about that. She didn't care about anything except what might be coming next.

He was breathing hard, harder than she was. And there was a gleam of raw savagery about his face as he tore off his shirt and threw down his trousers. He was every bit as magnificent as she had imagined he would be. He sat beside her to remove his shoes and socks, and she ran her fingernails down his taut thigh. She had actually fancied doing that in the limousine this morning.

An animal growl rumbled from his throat. He twisted, caught her hands, pushed them above her head. Then with slow and very deliberate control he moved onto the bed, stretching out on his side next to her, leaning over her with dark simmering intent. *His way*...that was what was glittering in his eyes.

It stirred a strong ambivalence in Tessa, the desire to know his way and the desire to turn it into something different, unique both for him and herself. She did not want him to use her and forget her. Even though she could be nothing more than a memory to him in time to come, she wanted the memory to stick. As something special.

He held her hands inactive with one detaining arm so that he could use his free hand to touch her where he willed. He stroked her throat, the now wildly pulsating sensitivity of her breasts, her stomach, her thighs. He watched her face as her flesh quivered to his touch.

Tessa made no move, no sound. She watched him in silence, both loving and defying his sensual expertise. Take me when you want, but I'll take you, too, she promised him.

He bent and ran the tip of his tongue between her lips. She touched it with hers. He moved into a slow escalation of the kiss, teasing, tantalising, playing for maximum sensation. He slid his hand between her thighs, skilfully arousing her, slowly driving excitement and anticipation to breaking point.

She knew instinctively that it was what he wanted, to make her cry out, to plead, to make her want him beyond any thread of control. Every nerve end in her body screamed for release but she held on, grimly refusing to be easy for him.

She didn't know why it was so important to her. Maybe it was some dark deep unfathomable sense of revenge. The man she had loved had taken her for granted. Treated her with disrespect. Thought he could get away with anything. If ever there was an archetypal man, it was Blaize Callagan. And this time, this time with him, nothing about her was going to be taken for granted.

"Relax," he growled.

"Please let my hands go, sir."

He released a long shuddering sigh, which told her he was stretched fairly taut himself. "Try not to claw me to death, Stockton."

"It will only be a little blood, sir." A drop of life, that's all it would be, but he would share it with her. She would make him.

"Somehow I feel I can't count on that, Stockton."

He sensed the dark well of intensity in her, and it was getting to him. Tessa felt a thrill of power. "Trust me, sir."

"With those tigress eyes?"

She smiled. "He who rides a tiger takes his life in his own hands, sir." It was a challenge that a man such as Blaize Callagan would never back away from.

His eyes narrowed. "Very profound, Stockton."

"Thank you, sir."

He released her hands, then waited, tensely poised, to see what she would do with them. She curled one around his head and gently raked her fingers through his thick black hair, feeling the texture of it, enjoying its soft springiness. She lifted her other hand to his face, obeying an impulse to trace his beautiful bone structure with her fingertips; his brow, his cheeks, his nose, his jawline. It was a curiously exhilarating exploration, almost as though she was touching the inner man under his skin.

She wanted to touch his lips, the finer texture there, the sharp line of definition that outlined them. But he suddenly opened his mouth and sucked her fingers in, biting them a little before releasing them.

He bent and kissed her hard. She responded with a passion that fired even more passion from him. She ran her foot down his calf. He shuddered. She ran her fingernails down his back, very lightly, but he reared up, an inarticulate cry tearing from his throat.

He took her then, the need to smash her control so intense that his possession of her was explosive. Tessa's response was instant and aggressive, riding the storm of sensation with all the intoxicating elation of a surfer on a rip curl, balancing her body through every rhythmic change, every wild contortion, welding with him in a mad drive for more and more sensation that drove them both to excesses in their fierce desire to exhaust the other.

It ended in peaceful togetherness. She melted around him, he lost himself in her, and their sweat-slicked bodies slid finally to rest.

For a long time, neither moved. They were totally spent, floating mindlessly on a tide that had ebbed but still had them in its grip. Eventually Blaize summoned enough energy to lift himself away from her and roll onto his back. They lay side by side, not talking, not touching, not moving.

Tessa had no idea what he was thinking but the silence didn't worry her. She was busy with her own thoughts as she reviewed what had just happened with a sense of awe and wonder.

It had been a wild experience. In all her time with Grant, she had never been so...so— She searched for some way to express it, but there simply weren't words for what had happened with Blaize Callagan. Involved? Crazy? Uninhibited? Intensely focused? She couldn't even call what they'd done together lovemaking.

It had nothing to do with love. They hardly knew each other. Yet it had certainly been more intimate than any lovemaking she had experienced with Grant. More physically intimate. It left her feeling she had never really known herself. In hindsight, she was shocked that she was capable of that act of sexual aggression and totally primitive gratification. It was a revelation. A new dimension to herself that she had never suspected.

Even more disturbing—all she had ever felt for Grant Durham seemed weak and insubstantial, as if he wasn't reality at all. Blaize Callagan, whom she had always thought of as a fantasy, was the raw reality. Which was very confusing.

She wasn't emotionally involved with Blaize Callagan.

Except in a terribly mixed-up way. He certainly affected her emotions, her body, her way of thinking, everything.

She didn't think she affected him in the same way. Obviously he had only had one reason for doing what he'd done. He had wanted to get rid of the tensions stirred by the business of the day. Purely a loosening-up process. He hadn't pretended anything else. It had nothing to do with her personally. She was just a handy female body to him— a desirable body that he had wanted to use.

With beautiful breasts.

Tessa smiled smugly to herself. She was sure that Blaize Callagan was very discriminating in his taste when it came to women. There was no need for him to have said that unless he meant it. She could rightly hug the compliment he had given her for the rest of her life. It made up for a lot.

She heard him sigh. He turned his head towards hers. "There is more to you than meets the eye, Stockton," he said.

"I'm an ordinary person, sir. With very simple needs," Tessa replied. Like a man to love her and stay faithful to her, as she would with him. But, failing that, she at least had something exciting to remember.

In some perverse way—totally against all she had ever lived by—she was feeling an intensely primitive satisfaction in casting all her principles aside with Blaize Callagan. She wondered if there was an untamed beast in everyone underneath the skin of social strictures that ruled ordinary everyday life.

"Not at all, Stockton. I can't agree. You're complex," he said consideringly. "Very complex."

"If you say so, sir."

"Thank you for agreeing with me, Stockton." A touch of dry amusement there.

"My pleasure, sir," she answered sweetly.

His head turned away again and he lapsed into silence.

Tessa smiled. At least she had forced Blaize Callagan into a reassessment of her. She had surprised him. He hadn't expected her to be like that at all. She didn't imagine Blaize Callagan was presented with the unexpected very often. It had certainly got to him. He hadn't been able to switch his mind straight back to business. That was definitely a positive score for her. Not his way! Not *all* his way, anyhow.

However, no matter what had happened and how she felt, it behove her to keep things in perspective. When this conference was over, the parting of the ways would come. What she had just experienced with Blaize Callagan was memory material. No more than that. Something to tuck away in her mind and bring out with wonder occasionally. She mustn't get serious about it. The only serious thing to Blaize Callagan was business.

He heaved another sigh. "I don't know how you feel, Stockton, but I'm feeling very good. Very relaxed." His voice purred with satisfaction.

"Oh, limber, sir," she said airily. "I'm feeling very limber."

"Limber," he repeated appreciatively. "Your vocabulary is improving, Stockton."

"Thank you, sir."

"I think I'll go and look at that memo again."

Yes, it was back to business all right. Tessa resigned herself to the inevitable, glad that she hadn't started fooling herself into hoping for any more from him. "Do you require any help from me, sir?"

"A cup of coffee would go fine."

"Black and two sugars, wasn't it, sir?"

"Good memory, Stockton."

"I try, sir."

He rolled over and kissed her. Very thoroughly. "I like the way you try, Stockton," he said.

Then he heaved himself off the bed, picked up his clothes and walked out of the bedroom. Which was not the bedroom designated for either of them. Tessa recollected her wits, which had been shattered by his kiss, and told herself to get moving, as well. If he could wander off naked, she supposed she could, so she picked up her clothes and made her exit from the bedroom. She didn't see him on her way to her own room.

The hotel provided bathrobes, which was handy because she hadn't packed her dressing-gown. She put on the terry garment and went to the kitchen to make the coffee. Having done that, she found Blaize seated at the computer. In his bathrobe. He certainly had fantastic legs.

"Thank you, Stockton," he said as she placed the mug on the table. He didn't look at her. He was concentrating on the monitor screen. Totally switched to business, she thought wryly, now that he was nicely relaxed.

"You can go to bed if you wish," he said. "It's been a very tiring day."

"Thank you, sir. It certainly has been tiring!" she said, with truly marvellous aplomb, particularly since she had a maniacal urge to hit him over the head with the nearest blunt object.

She took a deep steadying breath instead. She knew this was how it was. There was no point in wanting anything different from him. It wasn't going to happen. That was raw reality! But at least he wasn't pretending anything different, like Grant Durham! With Blaize Callagan, what you got was what you got. However, she did have the satisfaction of knowing that he would be more careful about underestimating her from now on. She was not just a handy female body.

Tessa picked up her glasses, her hairpins and rubber band, collected her suit jacket from the chair and went to her bedroom. She hung up her clothes, washed her face and went to bed. All of a sudden, she was very tired. She was asleep within seconds of her head hitting the pillow. Either she was totally exhausted or her mind was at peace. Her sleep was deep, uninterrupted and dreamless.

CHAPTER FOUR

"TIME TO RISE AND SHINE, Stockton!"

Tessa's eyelids flew open. Blaize Callagan stood in the bedroom doorway, resplendently handsome in a navy pin-striped suit, emanating the air of command that she had come to associate with him. For one fuzzy moment Tessa thought it had to be a dream. Then memory slashed across her mind, sparking a tide of heat that clothed her bare skin in a rosy flush.

His lips moved into that quirk, which she could now identify as amusement laced with knowingness. "It's seven-fifteen," he said. "Eight o'clock breakfast. I let you sleep as late as seemed viable."

Tessa found her tongue. "Thank you."

He looked at her for a few moments longer, gave that small decisive nod of his head, then moved off towards the living room.

Tessa wondered if she had passed his standard for how a woman should look the morning after. She shot out of bed, wrapped herself in the towelling robe and raced to the bathroom. The vanity mirror reflected a wild mane of rich brown hair, a face that was ironed free of fatigue and blooming with colour, and eyes that looked brighter and larger than usual. But since she didn't know what Blaize Callagan's standard was, she couldn't make any meaningful judgement.

Besides, it was irrelevant anyway. It wasn't as if he had

any intention of making her a fixture in his life. Tessa told herself sternly that she mustn't lose sight of that. It was important to act accordingly. Pride and dignity and self-respect were all at stake here. Having never had an encounter before, Tessa wasn't too sure of the rules, but she suspected that one didn't refer to it unless the other party did.

Nevertheless, it was nice of him to let her sleep in, she thought, as she crammed her hair into a shower cap. It showed consideration. On the other hand, he probably hadn't needed her for anything. She mustn't fall into the trap of reading what she wanted to read into Blaize Callagan's actions or manner towards her. Any kind of emotional involvement was out.

She had had four years of emotional involvement with Grant Durham, and where had that got her? Betrayed, that's where! Betrayed and put down. She was going to keep her head around Blaize Callagan, no matter how lethally attractive she found him. She had only let him use her because she had wanted to use him. That was equality. She wasn't losing to him. She was finished with being a loser. From here on in, she was going to be a winner.

Tessa turned on the taps, tested the water temperature, then stepped under the stinging spray. A lot of very physical memories came flooding back as she soaped her body.

Two nights, Blaize had said.

Tessa had to admit to herself that she was now abandoned enough to want another experience with him. Totally shameless it might be, but a woman could be pardoned one encounter in a lifetime, couldn't she? So far she didn't have any regrets.

On the other hand, it was better not to take *two* nights for granted. He might have only said that to win his way last night. Be content with what you've had, Tessa admonished herself. Expect nothing. She who expecteth little is seldom disappointed. Much nicer to be surprised.

Satisfied that she had worked out the correct attitude to adopt for the day, Tessa turned off the taps, stepped out of the shower and set about producing a professional image.

Twenty minutes later she stepped into the living room, every hair wound into an immaculate topknot, make-up subtly perfect, glasses on, her three-hundred-dollar dark red business dress making the most of her figure with a simplicity of line that shrieked *class,* her black high heels freshly shined of every speck of dust.

"Ready, sir," she announced.

Blaize Callagan was standing in the doorway to the verandah, his back to her. He swung slowly around, a look of deep introspection lingering on his face before his eyes flicked into an acknowledgement of her presence.

"I trust you understand you are in a confidential position, Stockton," he said, the dark eyes boring into hers with commanding intensity.

Pride tightened her face and lifted her chin. Did he think she was going to blab to everyone that she had been to bed with him? Fiery indignation sparked a glittering resentment at him, but she disciplined her tongue to the terse little reply that gave him nothing to be critical about.

"Yes, sir," she said.

He nodded. "I've decided to play a lone hand today, Stockton. It's important that no one knows of the strategy suggested by that memo last night. The appearance of sincerity can best be maintained on our side by true belief. Therefore we let the cards fall where they will until only one play becomes possible. I've deleted the memo from the computer file. Delete it from your memory, Stockton."

"Yes, sir."

Tessa had to stifle a derisive laugh at herself. Business.

Strictly business. If she had stopped to think about it, she should have realised that Blaize Callagan wouldn't give a damn about anyone knowing he had "relaxed" with her. It simply wasn't important to him.

"And what I said to you about sidestepping *ringi*..."

"Deleted, sir," Tessa assured him.

He relaxed. His eyes drifted down to her ankles and back up again, having gathered a warm gleam of appreciation. "Nice dress, Stockton."

"Thank you, sir."

His mouth slowly curved into a dazzling smile that curled Tessa's toes and did a lot of chaotic damage on the way to reaching her extremities.

"You've got style, Stockton," he said approvingly.

Tessa sternly repressed the heady rush of pleasure in his compliment. "It's nice of you to say so, sir," she said offhandedly.

One eyebrow lifted in sardonic inquiry. "You think I'm nice?"

"Oh, don't go overboard, sir. Your niceness is only a very small percentage of your total self. Trivial, really."

He stared incredulously at her for a moment, then burst into a peal of laughter. He looked so devastatingly handsome that all Tessa could do was stare at him and try desperately to keep her body and soul in one piece. He finally sobered, but his eyes kept dancing with some deep inner delight.

"Stockton, your vocabulary and ideas increase in leaps and bounds. A lot of hidden depth there. However, it's time to fortify ourselves with a substantial breakfast. This day will not only be exhausting, but quite draining."

"Yes, sir," Tessa agreed, feeling very pleased with herself. She had surprised Blaize Callagan again. She mentally chalked up another positive score. He would be even more careful in future about underestimating her.

Breakfast was a buffet affair, although a hot breakfast could be ordered. Blaize Callagan, of course, sat down and ordered. Milling along a line of people was not his style. Tessa, however, was attracted to the wide selection of fruits and croissants. Jerry Fraine joined her in the queue.

"How's it going, Tessa?" he asked.

"Fine, Jerry," she assured him. After all, she hadn't done anything that would reflect badly on him.

"What's on the agenda for today?"

The question slid out naturally, his expression completely bland and open. Which meant he was very keenly interested. Tessa knew Jerry Fraine too well not to recognise his probing tactics. However, in this instance her first loyalty was to Blaize Callagan, and he had sworn her to absolute discretion. On the other hand, she would be going back to being Jerry's secretary, so tact was definitely called for.

She smiled. "Jerry, if it's anything like yesterday, I think we're in for a lot of surprises."

His eyebrows shot up in amused inquiry. "Like what?"

She leaned towards him conspiratorially. "If you can get Mr. Callagan to tell you, then I'd appreciate it if you'd tell me. He keeps a lot to himself. I never know what's going to happen next."

It was the right touch. He gave a dry little laugh. "I know what you mean. Just hang in there, Tessa. And don't—"

"Stuff up," she finished for him.

Jerry grinned at her. "Are the glasses working?"

Tessa frowned. "I think he suspects something, Jerry."

He started chuckling and quickly coughed to cover up. "Just hang in there, Tessa. Don't let your guard down.

Blaize Callagan is a great man, but...he could tear you apart."

It was friendly advice, she knew, and she appreciated his concern for her. "I can look after myself, Jerry," she assured him.

Jerry's eyes twinkled with some secret amusement. "I figured you could. Otherwise I wouldn't have..." He shrugged off whatever he had been going to say, then added, "He certainly didn't know what he was getting in you."

Tessa frowned at him. "Didn't you tell him?"

His face blanked out for a second, then projected wise experience. "Some things, Tessa, are better left for other people to find out for themselves," he said gravely.

That was true, she thought. It was no use telling anyone you could do things. It was better to show them you could. "Right," she agreed. "And thanks for recommending me, Jerry. I'm glad I got the chance to see how you people work."

They parted then and went to their separate tables. Blaize Callagan had a plate of eggs and bacon and sausages and tomato and mushrooms. He really meant "substantial," Tessa thought. She decided he would never bother saying what he didn't mean...unless it had a business purpose.

Tessa did not enjoy the morning conference. It was certainly an education to watch the subtle shifts in top-level negotiations, but she could not help feeling disappointed in one specific outcome. Blaize Callagan seemed to be admitting total defeat. Although his men fought hard to put across their points, he sat with his shoulders slumped forward, projecting a listlessness that seemed totally out of character. Even when the Japanese delegation advanced some counter-proposal, he would wearily shake his head.

By mid-afternoon, the business conference had come to

a premature conclusion. They were packing up, dejected, depressed, the usual courtesies hanging solemnly in the air like black thunderclouds.

Then Sokichi Nokumata, Blaize Callagan's chief opponent against *ringi,* made a suggestion about a project that was completely peripheral to the main deal. Tessa felt the instant tension flow in Blaize Callagan's body, saw the hard glitter come into his eyes. He gave the upward look of a man without any firm resolution, pondering the suggestion. Then suddenly negotiations were going full bore again.

The late afternoon session saw all Blaize Callagan's plans come to fruition. The Japanese delegates against *ringi* were all being siphoned off onto another project. Divide and conquer. This was a master deal maker at work. Tessa had never seen anything like it, not even from Jerry Fraine.

Only in hindsight did she begin to appreciate the tactics that had been outlined in the memo last night. And only now did she begin to appreciate the intricate and incisive mind that drove the man who had subtly engineered precisely what he wanted.

He had run into an immovable object, but he hadn't got hurt. Not Blaize Callagan. He had sidestepped it, waiting for all the cards to fall, until there was only one possible play left. The ultimate finesse was in bluffing his opposite number into laying down the losing card for Blaize Callagan to win.

Tessa had known he was the top gun, but now she knew why. She had known he was out of her league, and that knowledge was now confirmed beyond a shadow of a doubt. She might amuse him, surprise him on a very minor level and even stamp a pleasant memory into some tiny corner of his mind, but that was as far as it could ever go.

For a permanent relationship, Blaize Callagan would naturally choose a complementary top gun…like Candice. A secretary was just a secretary. But Tessa was glad she had had this encounter with him. A man like Blaize Callagan would certainly never come her way again. In a way, she felt privileged to have been given the opportunity to share a little drop of life with him.

And it wasn't over yet.

Maybe tonight…

Then again, maybe not.

He wasn't feeling tense any more. He had won.

He shared his victory with his colleagues, several of whom accompanied them to the cottage for further discussion on the new development. Tessa was not required to take notes. She fulfilled the role of hostess, seeing that drinks were refilled when required.

Dinner was a very relaxed affair, bonhomie flowing as freely as the wine. Blaize Callagan was riding a high. Tessa suspected that no woman—however close—could give him the charge he got from pulling off the kind of deal he had stage-managed today. It surprised her that he did not prolong their time at the dinner table beyond the serving of coffee. Nor did he invite anyone to the cottage with them. They set off alone.

He looked at the sky as though making an exhaustive study of it. "It's a fine night, Stockton," he remarked. "The stars shine more brightly here in this country than anywhere else in the world."

"Yes, sir. And congratulations on your success today, sir," she said with complete sincerity. "Your star is really in the ascendant at the present moment."

"Ah, there's many a slip 'twixt the cup and the lip, Stockton. It's not all tied up with pretty bows yet."

"You're well on your way, sir. And you do have some bows to tie."

"We got lucky, Stockton. That was all. We got lucky."

She slid him a mocking look. "Like being up half the night working on your strategy and ideas so you could get lucky?"

"It helps, Stockton. No more than that. Though as a general rule I've found that the harder you work, the luckier you get."

Silence. It felt like a companionable silence. The dim lights from the grounds, the moon above... It would be very easy to dream hopeless dreams, Tessa thought. A hand brushing hers, taking it, holding it firmly. It kicked her pulse into overtime and gave her the courage to ask what curiosity prompted.

"What does it feel like...?" She hesitated, searching for the right words.

"Well?" he prompted.

"When you bring off a coup like you did today, how do you feel?"

The pressure on her hand increased violently. He gave a derisive snort. His mouth curled with a savage irony she didn't understand. No answer was immediately forthcoming. He looked at the stars again, and his profile was sharply etched. Tessa had the impression of a man in angry defiance of the universe that beamed down on him. The silence went on. Tessa wished she hadn't asked. It had seemed a simple question, yet clearly he was having some difficulty in answering it.

When he did speak, his voice was low and husky. Tessa had to listen carefully to hear the words. "At first there is the elation and the triumph..."

"I can understand that," she encouraged.

"Which is quickly followed by a kind of flat feeling, hard to describe...perhaps emptiness."

That surprised Tessa. "Why?"

"I guess it's the journey that's important, not achieving

the goal.'' His sigh held a weary disillusionment. ''I've been to that particular well and drunk its waters so many times. Now it seems to be such a charade. What else is there left to do? Make deals bigger and bigger?''

He shrugged his shoulders. ''People think it important that I do it, but sometimes I wonder. I wonder if there isn't something more, something that I've left behind.''

Tessa pondered that. Had she been too hasty with Grant Durham? If the journey was more important than the goal, maybe she should consider forgiveness. Maybe what had happened was an expression of something gone wrong that needed to be put right. Perhaps it was all part of the learning curve between two people. They had come so far…

Then the image of that overblown floozy with her big melons billowed across Tessa's mind. No, that wasn't part of the learning curve, she decided savagely. No forgiveness. The end. *Finis!*

''What's wrong, Stockton?''

''Sir?''

''You're nearly twisting my fingers off.''

''Sorry, sir.''

She instantly relaxed her grip and would have pulled her hand away except that he held on. His fingers began stroking over hers in a soothing motion that didn't really soothe. It reminded her how sensual his fingers could be. However wicked and wanton it was, she couldn't help hoping that he would feel a need for her tonight.

''What's on your mind, Stockton?''

She couldn't tell him that. It was tantamount to asking. Definitely against the rules, Tessa decided. An encounter should just happen. One didn't ask for it.

''I was thinking about what you said.'' Which was certainly true.

''Well?''

"Well, what?" She had never really felt this kind of desire before. It was very distracting.

He slid her a sardonic look. "What's a man supposed to do with his life, Stockton? Give me the benefit of your wisdom and insight."

His voice was mocking and sarcastic. Tessa didn't like that. She might be a lightweight compared to Blaize Callagan, but her life was just as important to her as his was to him. "I doubt that you're ready for the answer yet, sir," she said loftily. "A few more years of preparation perhaps…"

"Don't be patronising, Stockton," he said irritably. "It doesn't become you."

It didn't become him, either, she thought with a jab of resentment. He might be godlike in a lot of respects, but that didn't mean other people shouldn't be given their share of worth and respect.

"Yes, sir," she said, not giving him any ammunition to criticise her.

"Look at the universe out there, Stockton. Open your mind to it. Doesn't it make you feel the need to achieve something?"

"No, sir." She didn't have any need whatsoever to prove anything to the universe. All she had ever wanted was a decent life with a man who loved her.

"Doesn't it make you feel small and insignificant and insubstantial?"

"No, sir."

"Why not, Stockton?" He sounded slightly puzzled, as though he couldn't comprehend such an attitude of mind.

"It takes something *really* big to make me feel small and insignificant and insubstantial." Like Grant Durham's floozy.

He gave a soft little laugh. "I like your style, Miss Stockton."

Tessa felt a ripple of deep satisfaction. He had granted her the respect of a title. Miss... She wondered if she would ever be a Mrs., and had a moment of black depression.

Only a moment, because they had reached the cottage and suddenly Blaize Callagan turned and lifted her onto the first step up to the verandah. Which put her face to face with him so to speak.

"I like your style very much," he purred as he took off her glasses, folded them and popped them into his breast pocket.

Then he kissed her. And the stars of the universe were completely blotted out as he explored the dark sweet cavern of her mouth. Tessa stopped thinking. Blaize Callagan's kiss didn't leave any space in her mind for thoughts. He filled it with a marauding host of sensations, and as he pressed her closer and closer to him her body wantonly responded to the hard evidence of a need that Blaize had no intention of denying.

He had meant *two* nights.

CHAPTER FIVE

NO SEDUCTIVE MOVES this time. No talking. No asking. Blaize swept Tessa off the verandah step and carried her straight to his bedroom, urgency in every stride, urgency in ridding both of them of clothes, pressing her naked body to the pulsating power of his, kissing her with hungry passion, hands working fast to free her hair from its constraint, burying his face in its luxuriant silkiness, arching her body into the hard muscularity of his, groaning a primitive satisfaction in the yielding softness of her femininity.

No holding back. No contest for control. He came with her as he lifted her onto the bed and took her as he kissed her, a swift urgent invasion, plunging for the hidden depths of her to fill them with him, to immerse himself in her.

It was a complete coupling. Whether it was a need in both of them to forget everything else, or whether their bodies were simply driven by age-old instincts, or whether there was some dark common chord of innate savagery that rose to meet and answer the demands they made on each other, Tessa neither knew nor cared.

There was an intense satisfaction in the way their bodies moved together, an exhilarating intimacy, a knowledge that went beyond reason, response and counter-response, a greed for every sensation possible, excitement exploding into more excitement, an ecstatic fulfilment in the climax that rushed upon both of them, a sense of bonding that was very real, however fleeting.

And it was fleeting.

Blaize separated himself from her. With gentleness. But decisively. He lay on his back, his body completely still except for the rise and fall of his chest as his breathing gradually slowed to a normal pace.

Tessa did not want to think tonight. She turned her head and watched him, wondering what thoughts were going through his mind. If he was thinking at all. Perhaps he simply let his mind go blank at such times as these.

Tessa knew she shouldn't resent his silence, or his absorption in himself. Yet it didn't feel right that they could be so close together one moment and so far apart the next. Perhaps it was against the rules of an encounter, but she wanted more from him. The kind of physical communion they had just shared screamed out for corresponding verbal communion.

"Does that help assuage the emptiness, sir?" she asked, careful to keep any emotional demand out of her voice.

"It helps, Stockton," he said quietly. "It helps a great deal."

He'd dropped the "miss" again. The message was crystal-clear. She was back to being a body. One that had given him what he wanted, but only a body, nevertheless.

He turned his head and looked quizzically at her. "What about you?"

"Oh, I had a good time, thank you very much," she said airily. Although her heart felt like lead, for some reason.

He rolled onto his side and scrutinised her face, as though searching for something. There was a slight crease between his brows, suggesting that she presented a puzzle to him that he hadn't yet solved, and he didn't like anything eluding his ability to pigeonhole it. Even a slight gap in his all-knowing mind could not be tolerated.

Good, she thought fiercely. If for no other reason, you

will remember me for that, Blaize Callagan, because I will not give you the satisfaction of pigeonholing me.

A gleam of purpose burned into the dark eyes. "I think what we need is a drink," he said.

"What a fine idea!" she said, but if he thought a drink would loosen her tongue he could think again.

"Stay here, Stockton," he instructed. "I'll bring it in."

"Thank you, sir."

He heard the derisive note in the "sir" and shot her a sharp glance as he rose from the bed.

She gave him her best smile.

His eyes glittered appreciation of the ploy, but there was also a threat or a warning in the glitter. Blaize Callagan did not give up on what he went after. She had become a curiosity to him, and he wanted his curiosity satisfied.

He left the bedroom without bothering to don his bathrobe, totally unselfconscious about his nakedness. Tessa decided she wasn't going to be self-conscious about hers, either. It did seem rather stupid to even consider it after all that had gone on between them.

He returned a few minutes later with an opened bottle of yellow-gold wine and a couple of glasses. Tessa sat up against the pillows. He smiled at her, obviously liking what he saw. Which was fine. Tessa liked what she saw of him, too. He poured the wine into the glasses and handed her one. Then he clinked her glass with his and smiled some more.

"A glass of wine and thou," he said.

"You forgot the loaf of bread," she answered drily.

He laughed and stretched out on the bed beside her, looking supremely content with his world. "Tell me about yourself, Stockton," he invited, idly stroking her skin with his free hand.

"I'm twenty-four years old, and not one of the years that I've lived would interest you, sir," she said dismissively.

"Let me be the judge of that," he retorted with silky-smooth persuasion.

Tessa took a sip of the wine. It was silky-smooth, too, sweet, heavy with the taste of fruit, caressing her throat like liquid velvet. She suspected it was very heavy in alcohol content because even a taste of it sent an intoxicating buzz to her head.

"I don't like being a bore, sir," she said firmly, then took a smaller sip of the wine, testing its strength again. Liquid dynamite, she thought. But very, very nice. The slight chill on it made it all the more inviting, but she wasn't going to fall into that trap.

"How do you like the wine?" Blaize asked.

She looked him straight in the eyes and said, "Oh, I'm managing to choke it down, sir."

A flicker of outrage crossed his face, quickly followed by a dry, barely hidden contempt. "I will concede this isn't the most expensive wine in the world. The 1801 Margaux does cost more. So, too, does the 1795 Madeira." He twirled the wine around in his glass. "This is a mere '29 d'Yquem."

"Is that a fact, sir?" Tessa said with arch interest.

He took a sip, rolling the wine around in his mouth before swallowing it. "That's a fact," he said with heavy irony.

"And does such an expensive wine help to fill the emptiness, sir?" she asked curiously.

His expression underwent a lightning change, wiped clear of any trace of irony or contempt. His eyes bored into hers with a piercing brightness that would not be denied anything he wanted to know.

"You are a tease, Miss Stockton," he said softly.

"No, I am not, Mr. Callagan," she returned, her eyes defying his judgement. Then she smiled. "Although I will concede it's no hardship to choke down this wine. And I thank you for the privilege of tasting its unique quality. Such a luxury is not part of my ordinary life."

She took another sip, her eyes still challenging his over the rim of her glass. He watched her for so long, she took another sip because his intense scrutiny had somehow made her mouth go dry. Quite unconsciously, her tongue flicked out to lick her lips.

His gaze dropped to her mouth, simmered there for several moments, then he took another swallow from his glass and placed it on the bedside table. He leaned over and took her glass out of her hand and placed it on her bedside table. Sheer unholy wickedness danced in his eyes as he slid her down on the pillows. Then his mouth mingled with hers, savouring the taste of the wine on her tongue, playing a slow erotic dance that was more intoxicating than the wine.

He dipped his fingers into her glass and anointed her breasts with the sweet sticky liquid. It didn't stay there. And it didn't stop there. He used the d'Yquem all over her body, making trails for his mouth to follow, filling her navel like a miniature cup for him to drink from, making the rich wine a scented aphrodisiac, which drew him on to taste all of her, and Tessa was totally lost in a world of incredible eroticism, inescapably enthralled by what he was doing to her. He wove a silken web of sensuality that held her totally captive, all the more so because it was done with such delicacy, tenderness, exquisite pleasure.

She closed her eyes and floated on a gentle sea of undulating sensation, feeling her body flow with different currents of excitement, some high, some low, but all mesmerising in their intensity. She was boneless, utterly limp when he finally slid inside her, and he moved her body gently around his, stirring even sweeter rivulets of pleasure.

"Open your eyes," he commanded softly.

Tessa obeyed without thought, completely drawn into his will, his desire, his way. She had no idea what he saw in her eyes as he took his possession of her in slow deliberate strokes. He felt very deep inside her. He felt part of her. A necessary part. And she knew she would feel bereft when he left her.

She didn't want it to end. When it did, the pleasure of feeling his life essence mingling with hers was shot through with the pain of knowing that it didn't mean what it should. Another drop, that's all it was...and she closed her eyes as tears welled into them and overflowed.

"No, no," he murmured thickly, and gathered her up in his arms, holding her tightly to him as he rolled onto his side, cradling her against him, stroking her hair, trailing soft kisses around her temples. "Don't cry. Don't," he pleaded.

But she couldn't stop the tears from coming. Somehow the caring gentleness of his embrace made it harder, but she valiantly tried to stem the flow, knowing she was breaking the unspoken pact of an encounter.

"I'm...I'm tired. That's all," she choked out, desperately trying to explain away the ungovernable flood of desolate emotion.

He would never understand how wrong this was to her. That he should make her feel so possessed by him when he didn't want to possess her, except for a few moments that might fill his emptiness. Somehow it was a worse betrayal than Grant's, although she couldn't accuse Blaize of dishonesty. Or infidelity. But it hurt. And she wished he hadn't taken her like that. Wished he hadn't made her feel so much. It wasn't fair. Not when he meant nothing by it, apart from some brief gratification.

"Hush…it's all right," he murmured, turning onto his back, taking her with him so that she lay half-sprawled across his body.

He kept stroking her hair and her back in soft soothing caresses, and gradually Tessa was able to blink the tears back. The effort exhausted her, and she could not find the strength to move away from him. He didn't seem to mind.

I mustn't think about this, Tessa told herself. Better to blank out her mind. Just let it be. It was over. Already the past. He was only a warm body, in comfortable contact with hers. Her cheek was pressed over his heart. She listened to the deep heavy thud of it, let it fill the empty spaces she forced into her mind, and slowly there was nothing else left but the hypnotic thud of Blaize Callagan's heart and the rhythmic strokes of soft fingertips on her back.

A deep languor seeped through her body. Drowsiness clouded her dulled mind. She fell asleep without any awareness of it descending upon her. She had no knowledge of Blaize Callagan gently shifting her onto a pillow, tucking bedclothes around her, softly smoothing her hair away from her face. No knowledge of him watching over her as he finished the bottle of d'Yquem alone. No knowledge that he walked out to the verandah of the cottage, looked up at the stars—cold taunting pinpoints of light in the bottomless pit of black sky—and in a fit of deep frustration hurled the empty bottle into the night.

She awoke to a soft caress on her cheek and found him sitting beside her in his bathrobe, smelling of cleanliness and his tangy-fresh after-shave lotion, his black hair slightly damp, his tanned skin shiny and stretched tautly over his beautiful facial bones, his dark eyes wary and watchful.

"It's time to get up," he said quietly. He nodded towards the bedside table. "I brought you coffee."

She was embarrassed to find herself still in his bedroom. Even more embarrassed by the memory of her weeping jag last night. "I'm sorry," she said, wrenching her eyes from his and struggling to rouse herself. "I didn't mean to... to..."

"It's okay. There's no great hurry. It's only just gone seven. I wanted time to talk to you before we go to breakfast."

Sheer panic coiled through Tessa's stomach. She wasn't ready to talk to him right now. She needed time to compose herself. "Yes, sir. When I'm dressed, sir, if you don't mind," she gabbled.

He frowned, impatience stabbing from his eyes. But he stood up, jammed his hands into the pockets of his bathrobe and paced away. "When you're ready, then." He tossed the words at her from the doorway, left her to make an exit from his bed by herself. For which she was extremely grateful.

She noticed her bathrobe on the bed. He had brought it in for her as well as the cup of coffee. Both were marks of consideration that she hadn't expected from Blaize Callagan. But then he probably knew the rules of an encounter a lot better than she did. All the same, she appreciated both gestures very deeply.

Tessa scrambled out of bed, wrapped herself in the bathrobe and looked around for the clothes discarded last night. They weren't anywhere to be seen. Nor were her hairpins. She grabbed the cup of coffee and hurtled along to her own room. She found everything neatly laid on her bed. She shook her head in wondering disbelief. She would never understand Blaize Callagan. He was a man full of contradictions. The arrogant taker...and the considerate giver.

She gulped down the coffee and headed for the bathroom. It was just as well today was the last day, she thought. She was getting in too deep with Blaize Callagan. Far too deep. And it couldn't lead anywhere. It was even more paramount now that she keep her head or she would end up a very bad loser. It was bad enough that he would remember her crying. What she had to do now was make a graceful dignified exit from his life. If she was to keep her self-respect.

The bitterly ironic part of this encounter was that she had embraced it for the memories it would give her, yet as she stood under the shower and soaped off the lingering smell of d'Yquem from her skin her mind sheered away from last night's experience. She knew it wasn't lovemaking, yet it had ended up feeling too much like lovemaking for her to take any comfort from the memory. It was too disturbing. Too close to the bone.

She hurried out of the shower and concentrated fiercely on getting herself under tight control. She brushed her hair hard, wishing she could brush the memory of his touch out of it. It had felt like a tender loving touch, but it couldn't have been. It was a relief to get it all twisted up into a topknot again.

The green dress, thank heaven, had a flared skirt. Blaize Callagan wouldn't have to lift her in and out of the helicopter. She couldn't have borne that casual intimacy after what she had shared with him. Her hand trembled so much it was difficult to apply her make-up with any real expertise, but she managed a fair job of it. She looked around for her glasses. Her heart sank when she remembered Blaize had put them in his coat pocket.

She couldn't go into his bedroom!

She stood frozen for several seconds, worrying how to deal with the problem. Then her distracted gaze caught them lying on her bedside table. Blaize had remembered them. Of course, she thought in savage recrimination. He remembered everything. He had a computer mind that she could never match. Never.

She snatched them up and put them on. Then she packed all her belongings and zipped up her suitcase. The end, she thought. Another chapter in her life finished. Two chapters in one week. It had been a very eventful week. But at least this chapter could be finished with some style. Blaize liked her style. She would not let herself down—or him—by going out on anything less than a stylish note.

She found him in the same place he had been the previous morning, standing in the doorway to the verandah, looking out over a valley lit by bright morning sunshine. He wore a light grey suit today, impeccably tailored to fit his powerful physique.

Tessa paused for a few moments, remembering how she had run her fingers through the thick black hair, how her arms had clung around the strong column of his neck, how he had shuddered when she had run her fingernails over his back, how she had clutched his taut buttocks when...

She shut her eyes and willed the memories away. It was over, she reminded herself. Over. She swallowed hard, composed herself into businesslike practicality and forced herself to speak.

"I'm ready, sir."

He swung around, his face alight with a warmth she had never seen before. The dark eyes gleamed with pleasure as they ran over her dress. "Green suits you," he said softly.

His voice felt like a caress on her skin. "Thank you, sir," she said stiltedly.

He smiled, amusement twinkling in his eyes. "I need some more help from you, Miss Stockton."

"Yes, sir?"

"I seem to have developed a bad case of emptiness. I don't think two nights are enough."

There was a rush of blood to her head as she realised he didn't want to be finished with her. Then it drained slowly away as the reality of what he was asking hit home. More of the same. And she couldn't take it. It was a losing play all the way.

"I'm sorry, sir, but enough is enough. You've had your emptiness quota from me, sir," she said firmly, determined not to let her voice shake. It was bad enough that she felt so weakly tremulous inside.

He gave her an appealing smile. "Stockton, you can't walk out on me like this."

The dropping of the "miss" hardened her resolve. Her tawny gold eyes glittered into metallic defiance. "Oh, yes, sir, I can. That's precisely what I'm doing."

His eyes narrowed. He shook his head. "I don't believe you mean that."

"In a very short space of time, you'll come to believe it, sir," she said.

He stared at her for several seconds, the dark eyes projecting the dominance of his will. Then very deliberately he dropped his gaze, running it slowly down her body, burning through the green dress to remind her of every intimacy she had allowed him to take.

Tessa could do nothing to prevent the melting heat that radiated through her in debilitating waves. He could take her again now, and she wouldn't want to stop him. But she could and would control her future. There was no place in her future for a man who only wanted to use her, particularly when that man could hurt her as Blaize Callagan could. Not that he knew it. And she didn't intend that he should know it. She simply knew that he would never give her the kind of loving permanent relationship she wanted with a man.

His eyes returned to hers in blazing challenge. "Miss

Stockton, are you seriously suggesting I'm not good enough as a lover for you?'' he asked silkily.

Tessa took a deep breath. ''Please don't feel put down, sir.'' She managed a dry little smile. ''If I were writing a book on the rich and famous, and giving point scores for lovers, you'd score very highly.''

''So?'' he shot at her, as though she had just proven his point.

Tessa shrugged. ''These things are interludes in life. It's run its course, sir. Better to accept that and get on with our real lives. I'm sure, if you stop to think about it, sir, you'll agree with me.''

''And what if I don't?'' he asked softly.

''Perhaps you should give it some more thought, sir. It would be best for both of us if you do agree.'' She pushed her lips into an appealing smile. ''I'd prefer to remember it ending well.''

He retracted the challenge from his eyes. It was replaced by a wry appreciation. He slowly returned her smile. ''I do like your style, Stockton.''

''Thank you, sir.''

He walked over to her, rested his hands lightly on her shoulders and pressed a warm kiss on her forehead. ''And thank you…for the interlude,'' he said softly.

''My pleasure, sir,'' Tessa managed huskily, desperately willing tears back from her eyes.

''So let's go tie up the Japanese,'' he said, a purposeful briskness in his voice.

Back to business, Tessa thought.

It helped.

No doubt about it. She had made the right decision.

But she didn't feel like a winner.

Tessa didn't know how she managed to walk to the hotel for breakfast. Her legs performed miracles. She ate some breakfast, but if anyone had asked her afterwards what she had had she wouldn't have been able to recollect any part of it. Fortunately the demands of the morning session with the Japanese forced her to concentrate on her shorthand. She was a good secretary and proud of it. And life would be back to normal tomorrow.

Lunch was devoted to wind-up pleasantries. Two deals had been tied up. Everyone was happy. The glow of a successful conclusion to the conference was on every face. Except Tessa's. However, she did manage to look cool, calm and collected.

At two o'clock the helicopters started arriving. A hotel porter took down a trolley of luggage. The pilots stowed it all away. Farewells were taken. The company men took off in their helicopters first. Blaize Callagan was the last to take leave of the Japanese delegation. He automatically took Tessa's arm to walk her down the slope of lawn. As soon as they were on the flat she disengaged herself and boarded the helicopter without Blaize's help. He took his seat by the pilot and they lifted off.

They might have been strangers, Tessa thought, for all the attention he had paid to her since leaving the cottage before breakfast. He had treated her with distant courtesy, no more, no less.

It was the same when they landed in Sydney. He helped her into the waiting limousine, sat beside her and studied documents from his attaché case. It reminded Tessa that she hadn't transcribed any of her notes from yesterday, and there were all those from this morning, as well.

She cleared her throat. "Mr. Callagan…"

"Mmm…yes, Stockton?" He belatedly lifted his head, as though dragged against his inclination to look inquiringly at her.

Tessa flushed in painful self-consciousness. "All the notes...shall I type them up when I get back to the office?"

"They're in Rosemary's attaché case, aren't they?"

"Yes, sir."

"They'll be put safely aside in case they're needed. Whoever's been appointed my temporary secretary can transcribe from the tapes. No need for you to do any more, Stockton, unless we run into some audio problem. In which case, my secretary will call on you," he said dismissively, and returned his attention to his documents.

Tessa turned her face to the window, trying her utmost to ignore him as thoroughly as he could ignore her. This was what she had insisted upon. Complete cut-off. She could have had him as a lover...

No regrets, she told herself savagely.

That was the main rule of an encounter.

She had made the right decision. The way Blaize had cut it all dead from this morning was convincing enough proof of that. So no regrets.

The car pulled up outside the CMA building in North Sydney. Blaize packed away his documents and looked inquiringly at Tessa again.

"Where do you live, Stockton?"

Heat raced into her cheeks again. Did this mean...?

"No point in you coming in to the office for these last couple of hours. I'll take Rosemary's case with me. As it is, you've worked overtime the last few days. I'll give the driver your address so he can take you home," he said pleasantly.

Fool! she berated herself. She bit out where she lived and watched him leave the car, aching for something more from him, even though she knew it couldn't be expected. He spoke to the driver, held up his hand in a last brief salute to her, then strode into the building without a backward glance.

Finis.

The car moved off, taking her to the apartment she had left on Sunday night, the apartment she had shared with Grant Durham. She dragged her mind back to her real life.

The interlude was over.

She had a wedding to call off.

CHAPTER SIX

TESSA'S APARTMENT was in Neutral Bay, very handy to her work place in North Sydney. It was only a ten-minute drive from the office, although the trip took longer by the bus route. The bad news was fairly evident as soon as she walked in to the living room. While Grant was not physically present, his belongings still remained. He hadn't heeded her ultimatum.

Tessa felt sick at the thought of having to face him. Worse still, it was obvious from the state of the apartment that Grant meant to try for a reconciliation. It was clean and tidy. For Grant Durham, unbelievably so, after three days' occupation by himself.

Grant hated housework. He tidied up and did a few household chores only when Tessa took a firm stance about it. Nothing was ever done without her asking. He never picked up her clothes or brought her morning coffee like... But there was no point in thinking about Blaize Callagan. The niceties of an encounter were one thing, the niceties of a relationship quite another. All the same, Blaize had been good to her in that respect.

The fact that Grant had gone to so much trouble, even to a vase of fresh flowers on the table, was a sure sign that he was angling for forgiveness. She noticed, with grim distaste, that the bed was made up with fresh sheets and pillow slips. It was a bit late for common decency, Tessa thought savagely. She wasn't sure she could ever sleep in that bed again without remembering that woman. She was absolutely certain she could never share any bed with Grant again.

There was only one thing to do, she decided. Pack all his things for him before he got back from work. She would present him with a fait accompli, which would leave him as little ground as possible to stand on. As far as she was concerned, he had no ground at all, and she would tell him that in a few well-chosen words.

The packing served to keep her mind off Blaize Callagan, but it evoked a lot of other memories that she could have well done without; clothes that she had lovingly bought for Grant, mementoes of good times they had shared together, books and music tapes they had both liked. Several times she paused and wondered if she was doing the right thing.

Then she remembered how Grant had kept her dangling at his convenience, blowing hot and cold over the years, not even buying her an engagement ring when he had finally come to the point of suggesting marriage. The good times had been good, but she had tolerated a lot of bad for the sake of the good.

There had been other women in the past, but Grant had sworn all that was behind him. For him to have had that woman in her bed seven weeks before the wedding! Tessa wondered what she would have done if she had found that happening seven weeks *after* she was married. She shuddered at the thought.

Besides, after her encounter with Blaize Callagan, to be absolutely honest with herself, Grant just didn't measure up. At least not in that particular way. Tessa wondered if anyone ever would. It was a singularly bleak thought.

Tessa was sitting at the table in the living room when Grant walked in. He saw the suitcases and boxes piled up in the small lobby first, so he was prepared for her decision before actually facing her. The strange part was, Tessa felt nothing when she saw him, no anger, no revulsion, no outrage, no regret, no love, not even a remnant of liking. He was almost a curiosity.

There he was, a well-made man of above average height, well-dressed in a fawn business suit, a successful insurance salesman, intelligent and street-smart, very presentable in any situation. His sun-streaked blond hair had a natural wave that lent his rough-handsome face a lot of charm. Not that he needed extra charm. Charm oozed from Grant Durham. As it did now. His hands lifted in a gesture of apologetic appeal, his green eyes begging Tessa to believe she was the only woman who was special to him.

She felt nothing.

Four years of single-minded devotion to this man wiped out by a brief encounter with Blaize Callagan. Her mind said it was wrong that it should have happened...but it was no use denying that it had. She looked at Grant and it was as if a curtain had been rung down between them. The show was over and there was only emptiness.

"What can I say?" he began.

"Nothing," she replied flatly.

He walked over to her, sat down at the table, struck a confidential pose. "Tessa, we can talk this through—"

"No, we can't, Grant," she cut in. "We're finished. Quite finally this time."

"Tessa, that woman...she meant nothing to me—"

"Then why take her to bed?"

"It was a strange encounter. Nothing to it. It just happened."

"In *my* bed? It just happened in *my* bed?"

He saw the battle light in her eyes and hastily retreated.

"Let me rub your shoulders and back. You've been under a lot of tension."

"NO!" Tessa said it in capital letters.

"There's an explanation for this…"

"I don't want to hear it. I simply don't care any more. Nothing you say will make any difference to me. You'll be wasting your breath."

He shook his head in pained protest. "I can't believe you would change like this."

"It's because I believe you *won't* change that I'm like this," she replied stonily.

"Unbelievable."

"Believe it!" she said harshly.

Why did men have trouble believing anything they didn't want to hear from a woman? Blaize had been the same this morning. Didn't they think a woman could know her own mind?

Grant composed his face into an appeal for reason. "Look, I've gone and had some therapy over this."

"You've what?" Tessa looked at him in astonishment. Was he serious? Doubts sliced into her mind again. Perhaps she was being too hasty in condemning him. Four years of her life…and encounters did happen, as she had just experienced herself. But not if you were happy with someone else. Or committed to someone else, as Grant had supposedly been committed to her.

"I wanted to make amends," he said. "So I've had therapy."

The words slid out a bit too glibly to Tessa's mind. She looked at Grant suspiciously. "What did the therapist say?"

"Well, she said that what we've got to do is start touching again—"

Instant recoil. "NO!"

"—physically, so that our minds can meet," he added persuasively.

Revulsion at the very thought. "NO!"

"And that will help you get over your bitter black jealousy."

Tessa stared incredulously at him. Suspicion gradually hardened into bleak cynicism. "Your therapist," she said sarcastically, "told you that it's all my fault?"

"Well, in a way it is," he said, looking at her with soft sympathetic eyes. "I mean, I'm not jealous of you, Tessa. You're the one who's jealous of me."

No contrition. Not even a guilty conscience, let alone repentance.

"My black jealousy," she said softly, the anger beginning to seethe again.

Grant nodded. "Your black jealousy. It's a character defect in many people—"

"I'm not jealous!" It was the breaking point.

"Yes, you are."

"That's the last straw, Grant!" she yelled at him, leaping up from the table and storming around the room in fulminating rage, her hands gesticulating her furious rejection of him. "What we had is broken and can't be fixed. Ever again. I'll cancel all the wedding arrangements. There's nothing you need do except go. You're free again, to do whatever you want, to whomever you want, wherever you want."

"I want you, Tessa. You know I've always come back to you. I always will come back to you. You're the one…"

He rose from his chair and tried to catch her arms. Tessa beat him away.

"No! No more! Leave me alone. Find someone else to come back to. I don't want to talk about it. Go screw some other floozy. But not in *my* bed! Not ever again!"

"Tessa…come on, now…change your mind."

The indulgence in his voice only inflamed her rage. "I'm not going to!"

"Why not?"

She flung it at him recklessly. "Because I've started an affair with someone else!"

His face went white. "You slut!" And he hit her a ringing blow across the side of her face.

She stood still, her chest heaving, her eyes dilating as she fought for control. "Black jealousy, Grant," she taunted him bitterly. "You'd better get some more therapy."

He ranted. He raved. He tried tears. Crocodile tears, since they were soon blinked back when they didn't win any softening from her. Tessa stared at him stony-faced, giving him no encouragement whatsoever, projecting total indifference. It wasn't hard. It was precisely what she felt. Eventually Grant realised he was faced with a brick wall and he hadn't made the slightest crack in it.

"You're a bitch, Tessa," he said resentfully.

"I wonder why?" she mocked. "You'll find no more joy here, Grant. This is what's called irretrievable breakdown. Quit while the going's easy. The longer you stay, the harder I'll get. I'll even call the police to get you out of my life."

"No need for that," he snarled at her.

He went.

It wasn't a gracious exit.

Tessa didn't care. He was gone. That was all that mattered. There was still the unpleasant task of calling off the wedding, but, apart from weathering her mother's recriminations, that was just mechanics. The truth of the matter was, she had had a lucky escape from being tied to a man who wasn't worth being tied to. She was glad Grant was gone, glad that she wasn't going to be his wife. But she wasn't glad to be free. She wanted to be loved. Truly loved.

Tessa did sleep in her bed that night. It didn't seem to matter any more. Somehow seeing Grant again—feeling nothing for him—made last Sunday's infidelity completely meaningless. It had simply been the straw that had broken the camel's back, her back. The burden that Grant Durham had placed upon her had become too great to carry.

She lay in the darkness wondering if that meant she had fickle emotions. For the first time she felt unsure and insecure about the future. Not with the decision she had made about Grant Durham. That was inevitable, given the way she felt. The path into the future, though, was very dark, very obscure and very unnerving. Or was that what encounters did to people—rearranging their perspectives and making everything look different and feel different?

It was not the same for men, Tessa decided. They seemed able to go from woman to woman without getting at all emotionally affected by it. Just sex. Blaize Callagan had obviously liked the sex he'd had with her and wanted more of it. To say he wanted to be her lover…that was a misnomer if ever she'd heard one. He wasn't offering love. He simply found her body's response to his very satisfying. Enough to prolong the experience for a while.

Tessa stifled her stupid desire for more of him with the thought that he would soon find someone else to satisfy him. He probably had someone else all the time. A lot of someone elses. A man like Blaize would never have to look far for that kind of satisfaction.

He hadn't cared about her as a person. She was just the nonentity called Stockton. The person whose vocabulary was limited to "yes, sir", so that she wouldn't get into trouble. Stockton. Hardly a person. Just a thing. The darkness of the future loomed even larger.

Tears welled into her eyes and she turned her face into the pillow and cried. It didn't matter if she shed tears tonight. There was no one to see her. No one to hear her. No one to comfort her. She was alone, and felt more alone than she had in her whole life.

The lesson was clear, she told herself. Encounters were not her style. She had been mad to think she could handle such an interlude. If it hadn't been for Grant's infidelity...

No. She couldn't justify her behaviour on that alone. Although if Grant hadn't done what he had, she would never have responded to Blaize Callagan, no matter how attractive she found him. One thing led to another with the strangest results.

In the end she didn't regret what had happened. Blaize Callagan had got to her. In a way that no other man had. She didn't regret having known him. She regretted that she was not the right kind of woman to suit him. Like Candice. Full of flair, sophistication and bright red waves of tossing, tempestuous hair.

The next morning Tessa made no attempt to create a professional image. She was herself again. Back to square one, back to go, back to her real life, and the sooner she started getting on with it the better, she told herself sternly.

The first thing would be an exotic holiday somewhere as soon as she had cancelled the wedding. Time to form new memories. Time to heal. Time to forget. Perhaps a cruise around the Pacific islands. Or anything else. It didn't matter what she chose. She had four weeks' leave coming up— for the honeymoon she wouldn't have—and she certainly wasn't going to spend it moping around alone at home, thinking of what might have been, or what should have been happening.

Tessa mentally squared her shoulders and prepared to face the new day. As she entered the CMA building she refused to think Blaize Callagan was also on the premises. He had nothing to do with her real life.

Jerry Fraine looked surprised to see her at her desk when he arrived at the office. He raised his eyebrows in quizzical fashion. "I thought I'd have to manage without you until Rosemary Davies returned," he remarked.

Tessa returned her own surprise. "You did say I was only needed for the conference, Jerry."

He gave a quirky little smile that seemed to express some inner satisfaction. "Well, I'm glad you're back with me. I don't suppose the conference went quite the way Blaize Callagan expected," he added musingly, "but in the end we managed."

"I think he was pleased with the result," Tessa said.

"So he should be. We got lucky this time. Real lucky. Not even Blaize Callagan could have anticipated this result."

He went into his office, and Tessa thought that if she told Jerry Fraine what had really happened he would get the shock of his life. But Blaize Callagan wanted that kept confidential and that was the way it was going to be.

She idly wondered if Blaize might have been briefly piqued by her rejection of him as a lover. Decided against it. He had succeeded in getting what he wanted from the Japanese delegation. That was the important thing to him.

Although he had seemed to have some doubts about its importance on the second night. But by that time, Tessa thought cynically, he'd already achieved what he had set out to achieve. What was the phrase for it? Post coitus tristesse? After sex the sadness. She figured that all great men probably had the occasional doubts about what they were doing, but it didn't stop their will to achieve.

Jerry poked his head around the door between their offices. "I wonder..." He gave a funny little laugh. "I wonder about a lot of things. As you so aptly remarked, Blaize Callagan keeps a lot to himself. Very difficult to know what he's thinking. Or what he's doing. Or what he's done.''

"Yes," Tessa agreed.

"Any comment?"

"No."

"That's what I thought." He seemed to be pleased with himself. "So he did get up to tricks."

"Jerry, you mustn't make inferences like that."

He immediately changed the subject. "Is the wedding on again?" he asked curiously.

"No." She gave him a mocking smile. "It was a full-scale rift, Jerry. Not a tiff. We said our final goodbyes last night."

"Oh!" His face softened into sympathy. "Sorry about that. I guess this has been a bad time for you."

"I'll survive," she said airily. "There's a lot more fish in the sea. That's what people always say to you at a time like this. I've decided to go on a Pacific cruise and look them over. See if there's one waiting with its mouth open to be caught."

He relaxed into an approving grin. "Good for you, Tessa!"

Jerry was in excellent humour all day. He had figured out what really happened at the conference, and he made Tessa feel valued and appreciated with extra little courtesies. It helped.

That night she rang her sister. Sue was seven years older than Tessa, happily married with a husband who adored her and two beautiful children. Because of the age difference, Tessa had been deprived of any real sisterly companionship while growing up, but in recent years she'd forged a closer understanding with Sue.

That was why she had gone to her place on Sunday night

to take refuge from Grant's occupation of her apartment. At this stage, Sue represented a more sympathetic person to talk to than her mother would be. There was not so much of the generation gap that seemed totally unbridgeable with her mother.

"I'm calling the wedding off," she told her sister bluntly.

"Thank God you've come to your senses at last!" came the approving reply. "You should have called it off with Grant years ago."

"You didn't like him?" Tessa asked weakly. She hadn't known.

"He never appreciated you, Tessa. For heaven's sake, having made the decision, don't backslide now. Don't let him talk or pressure you into going back to him."

"You never said anything like this before."

"You wouldn't have listened. No point in saying anything. People never take advice about their love life. I can say it now because it's not advice. I'm glad you've woken up in time. Never thought you would. Grant Durham wasn't husband material, Tessa."

"No. I guess he wasn't. It still hurts a bit, though."

"Better to hurt now than to cost you later."

"I suppose so. Will you back me up when I tell Mum? I'm not looking forward to that."

"Mum wears rose-tinted spectacles. She is incapable of seeing harm in any handsome man. Lack of judgement. If she calls me, I'm all on your side."

"Thanks, Sue."

"Pleasure. And if you're feeling miserable, pop over. You're welcome any time."

"Mum's going to be upset about this. There's no way of avoiding it."

"Mum wasn't going to marry the jerk. You were."

Tessa recoiled from that description of Grant. It was wounding to her pride, if nothing else. "I didn't know that you thought Grant was a jerk."

"He was."

Tessa sighed. "Oh, well, with my luck with Mum…"

"If she throws a tantrum, remember one thing."

"What?"

"You would have copped the consequences. She wouldn't."

"Thanks, Sue."

"My pleasure."

They ended the call on this note of mutual understanding.

For the rest of the evening Tessa managed to keep Blaize Callagan out of her mind by reviewing her relationship with her mother. Which wasn't good. Her mother criticised everything she did, and always had. Nothing was ever right or proper. Her mother was sixty years old—Tessa had been a late child—and the world had changed a lot since she was young. Tessa's father had kept up with it, more or less, but her mother…there just didn't seem to be a meeting place between them.

Tessa tried. She loved her mother. It wasn't that she deliberately courted her disapproval. Basically she wanted what her mother had. A good marriage. The manner in which this purpose could be accomplished had altered so dramatically in the last forty years that the rules applicable then were no longer applicable now.

Her mother didn't seem to understand. Women did have to work, did have to have a job to help pay off the mortgage. Men couldn't survive financially without their women to help. And men had to respond by looking after their women differently. Her mother didn't understand that, or a lot of other things, either, like sex. Disapproval of Tessa's live-in relationship with Grant had soured many things between her mother and herself. At least, now, that was at an end.

Tessa wished it was as simple as it seemed to have been in her mother's day, but the clock couldn't be turned back. Fashions were different, hairstyles were different, music was different, the kind of social life people enjoyed now was different...all different. Women earned good enough wages to afford choices that hadn't been available forty years ago. Tessa didn't need a man to support her, not financially. But she wanted one to stand by her side and share her life, just as her mother had. That was one common ground between them.

The next morning Tessa packed her bag for the weekend. She would catch the commuter train to Gosford after work. Her parents were expecting her because it had been arranged that the invitations to the wedding were to be written out. They were expecting Grant to come with her, as well, and in that respect they were in for a major surprise. They certainly wouldn't be expecting the announcement she had to make, but she resolved to be very patient with her mother and try to reach a better understanding.

The day passed quite pleasantly at the office. Tessa liked being busy and Jerry had a lot of work for her to do. She was with him in his office, taking notes for a memo, when a call came through from Blaize Callagan's office, demanding Tessa's presence forthwith. It was four o'clock, only one hour left in the working week.

Jerry looked at her speculatively.

"They must want me to translate some of my shorthand notes," she said, doing her best to ignore the ebb and flow of colour in her cheeks.

It couldn't possibly mean anything else, she argued fiercely to herself. It was utterly absurd for her heart to be pounding like a jackhammer. She would only be seeing his secretary, not *him*. Even if she did see *him*, he would only treat her in the same offhand manner as he had before. Their intimate interlude would not be referred to in any way, shape or form.

Jerry gave her a dry little smile. "Got your glasses, Tessa?"

She groaned as she realised her present appearance fell far short of the professional image she had created for Blaize Callagan. "I left them at home, Jerry."

Not only that, she was wearing a black miniskirt and a red T-shirt, which was bunched around her waist, pulled in by a dark burgundy leather belt. Having been in a hurry because of having to pack a bag this morning, she had simply slid side combs into her hair above her ears, and her only make-up was a dash of lipstick, which was probably eaten off by now.

"What am I going to do?" she cried in dismay.

Jerry chuckled. "Oh, I daresay you can carry it off, Tessa. No doubt you've already given Blaize Callagan a surprise or two. He's got a strong heart. He'll survive one more."

"You don't mind him seeing me like this?"

"Why should I?"

"Because I'm your secretary. I thought you didn't want me to let you down."

He laughed outright. "Not over how you look, Tessa. No man in his right mind could possibly object to how you look. Don't worry about it. Just go. Blaize Callagan doesn't like to be kept waiting."

She went.

Anyone who worked for CMA did not say no to a summons from Blaize Callagan. Tessa had no choice but to go. But there were some things that she could say no to. And she would. If she had to.

Not that it could be about that, Tessa told herself. It was silly to even think about it. In fact, she mustn't think about it. Not if she was to carry off this unexpected meeting with any style.

CHAPTER SEVEN

ON THE WAY UP in the lift she rearranged her T-shirt around her belt, making sure it was at least evenly pouched. It wasn't a raggy T-shirt, she consoled herself. It was top quality. She wished her skirt wasn't quite so short, but there wasn't anything she could do about that. Besides, she did have good legs. Which was why she favoured mini-skirts. Although this one wasn't as short as some. Only a few inches above the knee. It wasn't as if it was indecent.

She licked her lips, hoping that if there was any lipstick left a bit of moisture might help heighten the colour. She didn't think Blaize had been fooled about the glasses, anyway. Besides which, Jerry didn't mind about her appearance, and she had told Blaize she was going back to her real life. This was her real-life image. He could take it or leave it.

Undoubtedly he would leave it.

She was crazy even to be thinking like this. Blaize Callagan had already put aside his interest in her. She didn't want what he had offered her anyway.

She wished her heart would stop beating so fast. Her skin was beginning to feel clammy. She wiped her hands on her skirt as the lift doors opened onto his floor. Cool, calm and collected, she told herself, then tilted her head high, squared her shoulders and stepped out.

Two women were in the outer reception area, obviously packed up and ready to go home, their handbags slung over their shoulders. One was the receptionist Tessa had met briefly on Monday morning. The other was probably the temporary secretary replacing Rosemary Davies. They both looked at Tessa with sharp curiosity.

"I'm Tessa Stockton," she forced out. "Mr. Callagan…"

"Go straight in," the receptionist invited. "Mr. Callagan is waiting for you, Miss Stockton."

Tessa was well aware of their eyes boring after her as she went in to the managing director's office. It was clear now that she hadn't been asked up here to transcribe her notes. Which meant…what?

Blaize Callagan was standing at the picture window, which gave him a view over Sydney Harbour. The afternoon sunshine struck his face in a way that highlighted the spare purity of his bone structure, like a perfect Greek sculpture. His eyes, however, were not the lifeless eyes of marble or wood or stone. The moment Tessa shut the door behind her they were burning over her, devouring her with such vibrant intensity that her insides turned instantly to jelly.

Her clothes were totally irrelevant. She knew he wasn't seeing her clothes. He was stripping her naked. Remembering. Heat scorched over her skin in prickling waves. Pride insisted that she stop him from reducing her to a body like this. She swallowed hard then forced her tongue to work.

"You wanted me, sir?"

It was a most unfortunate choice of words. As soon as they were out Tessa would have given anything to retract them. They hung in the air between them, gathering sizzling overtones and undertones while Tessa squirmed in agonised mortification. To give him such a lead-in was tantamount to an invitation, and that wasn't what she had meant at all.

"Yes," he said, his lips moving into that sensual quirk that knew too much. "Yes, I do want you," he added slowly.

He would have her here, right here in this office, if she let him. His suit jacket was off. His tie was loosened. The top two buttons of his shirt were undone. His stance was all aggressive male, confident of his power to attract her, to stir the same desire he felt, to command her response.

His strong sexuality was reaching her in waves, determined on drawing her to him. That was why he had dismissed his closest ancillary staff. He wanted to be alone with her, without fear of interruption. Any second now he would say he needed her. Needed her very much.

He lifted a hand.

Tessa stiffened. The door was just behind her. She didn't have to stay—wouldn't stay—if he started approaching her. She was not going to be used like that, not by anybody.

He waved an invitation towards the chair in front of his desk. "I want to talk to you," he said quietly. Soothingly. As though he could read what she was thinking and was subtly backing off.

Tessa hesitated. She didn't like the idea of sitting down while he was standing up. The last time they were in that situation he had taken advantage of it. No, it was better if she remained on her feet and near the door. Besides which, she wasn't sure her legs would carry her over to the chair with the dignity she was determined on maintaining.

Her eyes challenged his. "What would you like to talk about, sir?"

He sighed and turned away from her, walking to the front of his huge executive desk. He swung slowly around to face her again, then propped himself against the desk and folded his arms, deliberately adopting a relaxed and non-threatening pose.

"We have a problem, Stockton," he said. "If you'd be so obliging as to sit down, I'd like to discuss it with you."

She remembered how he had used body language to great effect with the Japanese delegation. Blaize Callagan was a master of it. What was in his mind was not necessarily what he portrayed at all. Yet she was also aware of his ability to switch on and off. Perhaps he had stopped remembering and actually did have some business to discuss with her. In an ultimate sense, he was her boss.

Tessa sent a shot of will-power to her shaky legs and moved to the chair. She sat down, extremely conscious of her short skirt and the amount of thigh she was showing. However, Blaize Callagan kept his gaze fixed on hers. Which reassured her. Slightly.

"Yes, sir?" she said, inviting him to state the problem.

The dark eyes bored into hers, commanding her full attention. "It's not working, Stockton," he stated softly.

"What's not working, sir?"

"Parting the way we did. I have given it more thought, and I can't agree."

Tessa's heart leapt. "Can't agree with what, sir?"

"We haven't run our course, Stockton. As far as I'm concerned, we've barely started running our course. I want you to spend the weekend with me. I have a boat moored at Akuna Bay. I'll take you cruising around the Hawkesbury River. Just the two of us together. For the whole weekend. Agreed?"

Tessa was torn by temptation. A whole weekend with Blaize Callagan. No business. Just the two of them getting to know each other. Except he only wanted to know her in the biblical sense. A weekend of saturation sex. That's what it would be. Another interlude. And this was one weekend when she had to face real life.

"I'm sorry, sir. I have other plans for this weekend,"

she said, her tawny gold eyes mocking his disinterest in her real life. He hadn't asked if she was available. He arrogantly assumed that his time was more important than hers and she would fall in with his plans.

"Cancel them, Stockton."

The command in his eyes riled resentment. "Oh, I am cancelling them, sir. All the plans I've made for years. I realise you don't know about them. I realise you don't care about them. But other people do. Particularly my parents."

She smiled sweetly. "You see, sir, I'm going home to cancel my wedding. I can't leave it any later. Six weeks is the cut-off point. The obligatory notice one has to give or pay the penalty of financial loss on the arrangements. I don't want to put that on my parents, as well as the costs they've already incurred on my behalf. So, quite simply, I'm not free this weekend."

Shock tightened his face. His eyes sharpened, drilling into hers with urgent intensity. "This wedding, Stockton. Is it being put off because of me?" he asked quietly.

Tessa assumed a carefree expression. "Oh, no, sir. Nothing to do with you, sir. How could it possibly have anything to do with you?"

There was a further tightening of his facial muscles, a fleeting look of puzzlement—or irritation—jetting across his brow. "I don't understand you at all, Stockton. When did you make the decision to cancel?" he shot at her.

"Last Sunday night. Before I—"

"Why?"

Tessa shrugged. "Well, if you must know, sir, I found my fiancé in bed with another woman."

"Hell!" he said, astonished.

"That was, to put it mildly, the beginning of the end," Tessa said.

He made a contemptuous sound, straightened up and

strolled to the window. Tessa turned in her chair to look at him. There was an angry cast to his face. His mouth had thinned. The view was giving him no pleasure. He was probably vexed because she had put a spoke in his cosy little plan for the weekend.

Goaded by his dismissal of all the pain she had felt over a man to whom she had devoted four years of her life, however foolishly, Tessa cynically asked, "Are you feeling any better now, sir?"

"Worse," he bit out, not looking at her.

"There are always other women," Tessa said derisively. "There seem to be plenty of them around, willing to take their chances."

He gave her a sharply mocking look. "Never the right ones."

It hurt. Even though she knew she wasn't the right woman for him, it still hurt. "Sorry I failed you, sir," she said flippantly.

"You didn't fail, Stockton." His mouth curved into an ironic smile. "You were very good for me."

It was some balm to her wounded soul. "Thank you, sir."

The memories were back in his eyes, burning into her again. Tessa's pulse started to act erratically. She was beginning to have trouble breathing. Her mind dictated that she had to get away from him. Fast. She pushed herself up from the chair before her legs went all watery on her.

"I'll go now, sir."

"Stockton..."

She wrenched her eyes from the simmering seduction in his and turned towards the door.

"Miss Stockton..."

"Goodbye, sir." She sliced the words quickly at him, and forced herself to walk, one foot in front of the other.

"Tessa..."

The soft caress of her name curled around her, holding her still.

"I'm asking you, very nicely...please, would you reconsider our, er, arrangement?"

Tessa did not look back. She took a deep breath, stiffened her spine and held fast to a sane sensible course. She was not going to be anybody's floozy on the side. Not even Blaize Callagan's. "No, sir," she said firmly.

"Let's get straight to the point. Why not?"

"I'm not interested in casual sex. Nor affairs. Not on a long-term basis," she stated decisively.

"I see."

She gathered her nerve to face him and turned, chin high, a fierce pride blazing from her tawny gold eyes. "I hope so, sir."

He looked at her speculatively, as though she was something entirely new to him...interesting. "So, you're leaving me to my own devices," he softly drawled.

"I'm afraid so, sir," Tessa answered loftily.

He raised an appealing eyebrow. "Nothing I can do?"

"No, sir."

His mouth moved into its sensual quirk. "You don't like me much, do you?"

She gave him a mocking smile. "I guess I'm cautious, sir."

"You think I'm not to be trusted."

Tessa tilted her head to one side consideringly. "I must confess...I wondered, when you were married..."

"If you're asking was I faithful to my wife, yes, I was. I had affairs before I married, and I've had affairs since. I'm a man who likes sex. And a lot of it. But I've never made a practice of mixing women. And I'm very careful about whom I mix with."

"I've noticed, sir."

He winced at the derision in her voice. "You were the exception to the rule."

"I guess I should feel flattered."

His mouth twisted sardonically. "Regardless of what you think of me, I do have a few principles that I live by."

She returned an ironic smile. "Oddly enough, sir, although you may not believe it, so do I."

His eyes gleamed a rueful appreciation as he walked slowly towards her. "I caught you at a vulnerable time, didn't I?"

She tensed, her eyes glinting a hard warning at him. "Yes, sir, you did," she said flatly.

"On the rebound."

"More or less."

He kept coming. "I won't say I'm sorry, Tessa."

It seemed important to hold her ground and stand up to him...no matter what! "It was my decision as well as yours, sir."

"That's why you cried," he said softly.

Tessa flushed. Her eyes burnt with a bright defiance as she replied, "Not precisely, sir. I guess you could say a few things caught up with me."

"No regrets, Tessa?"

"I am sorry if I disappointed you, sir."

His eyes mocked her as he slid his arms around her waist and drew her into a loose embrace. "You know damned well you didn't disappoint me. And I won't accept that you don't want anything more to do with me. We're good together."

"In bed, sir. That's all."

"That's a start." He pulled her closer to him, bringing her body into electric contact with his.

Little quivers ran down her thighs, but Tessa found the

presence of mind to press her hands against his chest and push herself back, putting some space between them. "More like a finish, sir."

"Not for me it isn't."

Her eyes flashed fierce determination. "I happen to want more than sex from a man, Mr. Callagan."

"Are you implying I can't give you more?"

"You only want my body."

"All weekend?" His slow smile taunted her. "True, I do want it. I'm also impressed by your belief in my virility. But every man needs a breather now and then. Apart from which, I enjoy other pastimes as well, and I'm inviting you to share them with me."

"Like what?" she scoffed.

"Fishing. Swimming. Eating. The occasional word passed in companionship. Basking in the sun. I definitely, most definitely do not want to use your body any more than I want you to use mine."

"Yes, you do."

"Not at all. I concede only that I want to make love to you from time to time, beguile our senses..."

"I'm going home. I have a wedding to cancel."

"I'll cancel it for you."

"It's something I have to do myself."

"All right. Do it tonight. It can't take all weekend. I'll pick you up in the morning."

"I'm going to Gosford. That's where my parents live. And this is something I can't rush. I owe it to them."

He heaved a deep sigh and contemplated the stubborn pride on her face. "I want to kiss you senseless, but I have a feeling you wouldn't like it this time. It's a losing tactic, isn't it?"

"I wouldn't advise it, sir."

One eyebrow rose in appeal. "Definitely a losing play?"

"Yes, sir. Let's just keep the good memories."

"Stockton, I have a terrible weakness for challenges."

"You might get hurt, sir."

"Ah! What do you do when you run into an immovable object and you don't want to get hurt, Stockton?"

"You sidestep it, sir."

"Good memory, Stockton."

"Yes, sir."

"Excuse me while I sidestep."

He dropped the embrace—much to Tessa's relief. If he had kissed her she wasn't at all sure she wouldn't have weakened in her resolve. She watched him shakily as he stepped to the desk, scribbled something on a card, then came back to her and handed her the card.

"My telephone number. Ring me when you've finished cancelling the wedding. What is left of the weekend we will spend together."

Tessa looked at him sternly. "Don't hold your breath, sir."

"Something I ought to tell you, Stockton." The dark eyes gleamed with ruthless purpose. "I never give up on something I want."

"Funny you should say that, sir," she retorted. "Neither do I."

She swung on her heel and marched towards the door.

"Nice legs, Stockton," he said appreciatively.

She opened the door before sending him a derisive look. "Thank you, sir. And may I say…?"

She paused deliberately. It gave her a thrill of real pleasure to see the look of hope flash into his eyes.

"Yes, Stockton?"

"Your legs aren't too bad, either."

She grinned at his surprise, then made a fast exit on her note of triumph.

It occurred to her, on the way down in the lift, when her wild exultation calmed down to a mere simmer of excitement, that maybe her mother was right in some circumstances. Maybe saying no did draw a man on. If the man was like Blaize Callagan.

The card he had given her was burning a hole in her hand.

CHAPTER EIGHT

TESSA'S PARENTS lived at Green Point, on the outskirts of Gosford. Fortunately Tessa had caught an express train so the journey had only been a little over an hour. She caught a taxi from the railway station. The sense of impatience, almost urgency to get the issue of Grant Durham over and done with had a lot to do with Blaize Callagan's card in her handbag, but Tessa kept telling herself she would only be jumping out of the frying pan and into the fire if she let herself get involved with *him*.

No future there.

Nothing but bed and possibly breakfast. Occasionally. When it suited him.

She had to be absolutely off her brain to even hope that there was a chance of a real commitment between them. Just because he made her blood sing and she had got the better of him a few times didn't mean his interest would stick beyond the gratification he found with her.

It was a pipe dream.

Sheer pie in the sky.

She was brought sharply down to earth when the taxi pulled up outside her parents' home. It was a well-presented home with neat lawns and gardens, comfortable and solidly middle class.

Tessa was proud of what her parents had achieved, and proud of the independence she herself had achieved. She simply wasn't a match for a high flyer like Blaize Callagan.

That was reality, and there wasn't any future in indulging fantasies.

She paid off the taxi driver with a heavy heart and walked down the path to the front door with a dirge-like tread, knowing that the music she had to face was going to be unpleasant. She rang the doorbell and waited, resigning herself to the inevitable in more ways than one.

The door was opened by her mother. She was, as always, neatly dressed in conventional clothes, her hair conventionally permed into rigid waves and curls, lipstick in place, a strand of pearls around her throat, and absolutely everything about her appearance just so. She looked at Tessa, looked past her, then asked, "Where's Grant?"

It had taken Joan Stockton only a few seconds to assess the undeniable fact that Tessa had arrived at her parents' door alone. Grant's car was not in the driveway. Grant was not beside Tessa. Hence, Grant was not here. Her expression instantly became disapproving. Joan Stockton never reacted well to anything that didn't match up to her sense of what was right and proper.

"He won't be coming," Tessa said bluntly.

Chagrin mixed with the disapproval. "I cooked that lasagne he likes especially for him."

Typical, Tessa thought. Her mother's outlook was that men had to be indulged to keep them firmly caught. Except the indulgence didn't run to free sex. "I like it, too, Mum," she said. "It won't go to waste." She kissed her mother's cheek and pushed through the hallway to greet her father.

He wrapped her in his arms with his usual bear hug. He was an affectionate father, and an indulgent one. Tessa hugged him back fiercely, wishing she could find a man like him.

Grant had decided not to come last weekend, supposedly because Tessa was working on the wedding arrangements with her mother. Although it was plain now that he had had an ulterior motive for staying in Sydney. However, there was absolutely no excuse for his absence this weekend, as Tessa knew. And her parents knew that, as well.

Her father drew back, a look of concern on his weatherbeaten face. He was still a strong man at sixty-five, but his face was deeply lined. He looked his age, although Tessa maintained he had worn well. His iron-grey hair was as thick as ever, and his warm sherry-brown eyes always looked young to her.

"Anything wrong, sweetheart?" he asked perceptively.

"A long hard week, Dad. I had to go to a conference," she said brightly, and proceeded to regale her parents with censored details of the three days she had spent at Peppers.

This lasted her through dinner. After the washing-up was done, her mother cleared the dining-room table and brought out the wedding invitations. Tessa looked at them glumly, knew that prevarication could not be prolonged, sat down at the table and plunged to the heart of the matter.

"Mum... Dad..." She looked at both of them in desperate appeal. "I've got something to tell you. I'm sorry, but there isn't going to be a wedding. I've told Grant, and we've broken up. I won't be seeing him any more."

Her father reached over and squeezed her hand. "I'm sure it's for the best," he said softly.

Her mother gaped. Her face coloured. She glared at her husband. "Mortimer, how can you say that? How do you know it's for the best? How do you know anything?"

Mortimer Stockton had worked as a carpenter all his life, a plain simple man with a very loving heart. From the moment he had set eyes on Joan Stockton he had adored her, and his philosophy was very simple. His wife knew best, and she was always right. He never argued with her, and agreed with all her opinions. Over the years, this had led to a very one-sided relationship. That didn't save Mortimer from frequently being wrong about things.

He shifted uneasily in his seat. He had been on the receiving end of his wife's diatribes many times in his life, and now lived by the motto, "Peace at all costs." But his youngest daughter was very dear to his heart, so he made one very cautious statement in her defence.

"Joan...I never thought Grant Durham was good enough for Tessa. He didn't treat her right. I'm glad she's decided not to marry him," he said quietly.

"Not good enough!" her mother shrieked. "At least he was good enough to want to marry her when he didn't have to! Who's going to have her now? She's ruined herself..."

It went on and on. A torrent of recriminations was heaped onto Tessa's head: all her past sins, all her shortcomings as a daughter and as a woman. No decent man would want to marry her. She was wilful and wayward and she had made herself cheap. And now she had thrown away her only chance of redemption.

For once, Tessa felt no inclination to fight back. She didn't try to express a contrary point of view. She sat numbly through it all. She was grateful for her father's efforts to calm his wife down and mitigate the things she was saying, but it didn't really help. It only set her mother off on new tangents. As far as Joan Stockton was concerned, this was the final straw, the ultimate let-down. Tessa was a total write-off. Her only saving grace was the fact that she wasn't pregnant. Or was she?

The negative reply fuelled another barrage on Tessa's attitudes and loose living habits. She could only come to a bad end. No one would ever care about her or for her. A dark future, Tessa thought, her mother's words adding their weight to the sense of empty desolation inside her.

Eventually her mother declared it was impossible to talk

to her. Intransigently unreachable. A lost cause. If Tessa had any sense in her head she should call Grant Durham and beg him to take her back. It was her only chance of leading a decent life.

Then she stormed off to bed.

Tessa sat on at the table, white-faced and tight-lipped. Her father sat on with her, his kindly face creased in deep concern, his eyes begging forbearance.

"Your mother doesn't mean those things, Tessa," he said quietly. "She's upset. That's all. The wedding meant a lot to her."

Tessa shook her head. "I've always been a disappointment to her, Dad. I guess I always will be."

He squeezed her hand. "Not to me, sweetheart."

He had always called her his little sweetheart princess, and somehow the affectionate term meant a lot just now. "Thanks, Dad," she said, choking.

"There, there, sweetheart. It's going to be all right. You'll see," he soothed. "You mother means well. Sometimes she just gets a little bit upset. But you're a grand girl. There'll be many a man who'll want to marry my little princess."

"I don't know. I don't think I know anything anymore, Dad. All these years...maybe Mum's right...and all I've done is mess up."

"No, Tessa. Don't think that, sweetheart." He coughed apologetically as he made the most defiant statement of his married life. "Things aren't sometimes as straight and as narrow as your mother would like to have them."

"Mum didn't even ask me why I'd changed my mind."

"Don't you worry. Everything will be all right," Mortimer said vaguely. There were limits to how far he could go in opposing his wife. He could see a lot of storm clouds gathering.

"I guess I shouldn't come home for a while," Tessa said despondently. "Let the dust settle."

"I love seeing you." His eyes were troubled. His was a terrible dilemma.

"Maybe if I got engaged to someone else..." Tessa sighed. It was the only redemption her mother might accept. Unfortunately it could be a long time coming, if ever.

"Don't go running from the frying pan into the fire," her father warned anxiously. Things could get very black if Tessa made another mistake.

Her eyes searched his in desperate appeal. "You don't think I'm bad, do you, Dad?"

"No, Tessa. You're definitely not bad." He shook his head. Why did these things happen?

"What do you think I should do?"

"About Mum?"

"Yes."

Mortimer pondered the matter. "It might be a good idea for you to go back to Sydney in the morning. Give it time for all this to blow over. Your mother will come around. Just a matter of time, sweetheart."

She nodded. The lump in her throat was too large to circumvent.

"You go to bed now," her father urged kindly. "You're worn out. A good sleep. Things always look better in the morning."

Tessa stumbled from her chair, threw her arms around her father's neck and kissed his forehead hard. "I love you, Dad," she choked out huskily.

"There, there, now. It'll be all right. You'll see," he soothed, his voice gruff with emotion.

Tessa went to bed but she didn't go to sleep. She felt very mixed up in her mind, emotionally drained, and as close to complete despair as she had ever come. She had been blindly infatuated with a man for four years. Both her sister and her father had seen him far more clearly than she had. Grant had not treated her right, and she had taken it from him and come back again and again for more, even to the point of marrying him. How could she ever trust her judgement again?

And Blaize Callagan had to be another wrong choice.

Yet he had a lot of qualities that Grant hadn't had. He was honest, for a start. She had no delusions about what he wanted. He had spelled it out. No frills. But he had implied that he hadn't found anyone else who gave him what she did. Which put her ahead of a lot of other women.

Maybe there was a chance with him. Or more likely that was just a delusion because she wanted so desperately to be loved. Perhaps she was one of those foolish women destined always to choose the wrong man.

Nevertheless, despite the high tension between them this afternoon, she had enjoyed sparring with him. He had enjoyed it, too. He hadn't found her ordinary at all. She had piqued his interest. Got under his skin. Maybe she wasn't foolish.

Blaize had made his own luck with the Japanese deal. Wasn't it possible that she could make her own luck with him? Her father was right. Life wasn't as straight and narrow as her mother wanted it to be. Tessa wished it was. There was certainly nothing straight and narrow about Blaize Callagan. He was a very complex man. Then she remembered that he had said she was complex, too. It brought a smile to her face, the first smile since she had left him this afternoon.

Why not? she thought. As far as her mother was concerned, she was a ruined woman anyway. A weekend with Blaize Callagan was hardly going to ruin her much further. If she was as badly ruined as her mother thought, she couldn't actually be ruined any further. She had already achieved a hundred per cent ruination.

Besides, she should know by the end of the weekend if any future was feasible with Blaize Callagan or not. Better than closing the door without giving it a chance.

What was the alternative? Wallowing in dark emptiness for a long miserable lonely weekend until she could get back to work Monday. It might be stupid, but suddenly a weekend cruising down the Hawkesbury River seemed a lot better idea. It might lead somewhere, and then again it might not. If she didn't go she would never know.

A bad end, her mother had said.

She was probably right, Tessa thought.

Even so, for better or for worse, it was her life to do with as she chose.

She switched on the bedside lamp, got out of bed, picked up her handbag, extracted Blaize Callagan's card and went to the living room with a purposeful tread. The house was in darkness. She switched on the light. It was almost midnight.

A heady recklessness was upon her. So what if she woke Blaize Callagan up? If he wanted her, he wanted her. Let him suffer for it. She was through with suffering for a man. This time she would dictate the terms.

She picked up the telephone and dialled the number he had written down. It rang three times before the receiver was picked up at the other end of the line. His voice was not at all sleepy. "Blaize Callagan," he said crisply.

"Not in bed?" she asked.

"Stockton?"

"My name is Tessa," she said with pointed emphasis. No more Stockton. If Blaize Callagan wanted her, he could toe the line she set.

He laughed. It was a soft laugh with a warm ring of

pleasure in it. "Yes, of course," he murmured. "Definitely Tessa."

Her heart leapt in exultation. Another point won. "I trust you have a good memory."

"Excellent."

"I wouldn't like you to forget what my name really is."

"Trust me."

That was a tall order. On second thoughts, he hadn't said anything he hadn't meant so far, Tessa reminded herself. "I'm coming back to Sydney in the morning."

"It will save time if we meet at Akuna Bay."

"I don't know how to get there."

"I'll send a car to pick you up and bring you to the marina. What's your parents' address?"

She told him. There was a pause while he wrote it down. "It's always good to get an early start. Will eight o'clock suit?" he asked.

"Fine," she said, smugly pleased that he had asked her instead of telling her.

"Mmm...I guess I can attribute this change of mind to my not-too-bad legs."

"You may have a few other good points," she said airily.

"Like what?"

"I'll think about it, see what I can come up with."

Again he laughed. "Tessa...you have just made my weekend."

"Don't be too sure of that...Blaize," she said daringly. "There's many a slip 'twixt the cup and the lip."

"I'll try to please."

"I wouldn't like to be riding at anchor the whole weekend."

"Rest assured you shall have everything."

"I do have a mind, as well," she said drily.

"We'll explore it together—" a slight pause "—darling."

"Do you get onto such intimate terms with all your women so quickly—" a sense of wickedness made her add sweetly "—darling?"

"I swear this is the first time it's ever happened in my life. Are you in bed?"

"No. Are you?"

"Yes. I was thinking of you. A very bad case of emptiness. Worst I've ever seen."

"Willing me to call?"

"Yes. It worked, too," he said smugly.

"Oh, I wouldn't bet on that, darling Blaize. Maybe I just feel like some distraction."

Silence. Then… "Been having a hard time of it, Tessa?" he asked softly.

"Not easy," she admitted.

"You want another interlude."

"Perhaps." She didn't want him too certain of her. She didn't want to be taken for granted ever again.

"Am I being used?" he asked musingly.

"Yes," she retorted.

"We'll go on a journey of discovery together."

"Sounds reasonable."

"We are in agreement, then. Goodnight, Tessa. I'm looking forward to tomorrow."

"So am I."

"Don't change your mind."

"There's no one else in my life to change it over."

"Keep it that way."

"I'll try." He had better try, too, she thought, or they would reach the end in very quick time. She didn't have another four years to waste on a man who didn't give her what she wanted.

"Sweet dreams," he said softly, seductively.

"Goodnight," Tessa said offhandedly.

She set the radio alarm by her bed for seven o'clock. She lay awake for quite some time, imagining Blaize in his bed. It made her body tingle. Her mother was undoubtedly right. She was wayward, wilful and wanton, as well, but she was going to try her luck with Blaize Callagan. If it came to a bad end, it did. If she could waste four years with Grant Durham, she could waste a weekend on Blaize Callagan.

Eventually she fell asleep. She woke to music on the radio. Her parents were already up. She could hear them talking in the kitchen when she dashed into the bathroom for a quick shower. Her mother's voice didn't sound quite so strident this morning. She hoped she wasn't going to be subjected to another scene over breakfast.

Tessa dressed in white jeans and a yellow T-shirt. She put her hair up in a ponytail. She didn't want it blowing everywhere once they were on the water. She didn't bother with any make-up at all. If Blaize Callagan wanted to be part of her real life, he could accept her as she was. Without frills. Fortunately she kept an old bikini at her parents' home so she stuffed that into her bag, zipped it up, then carried it out to the hallway near the front door.

She braced herself for another possible onslaught, then went out to the kitchen to face her parents. "Morning, Mum…Dad," she said breezily, heading straight for the cupboard that held the breakfast muesli.

"Good morning, Tessa," her father replied, looking up from his newspaper and giving her a smile.

"Good morning, Tessa," her mother said stiffly. "Do you want coffee?"

"No, thanks, Mum. I'll just have a plate of cereal and then I'll be going." She quickly poured some muesli into a porridge plate and headed for the refrigerator to get the milk.

"Going?"

"Yes." She flashed her father a look of appeal. "Dad said he'd do the necessary cancellations. And since I'm only upsetting you further…"

"I have every reason to be upset, Tessa."

"Yes, I know, Mum. I'm sorry. Truly I am. But I can't marry Grant." She poured the milk over the breakfast cereal and returned it to the refrigerator.

"Why not?" her mother demanded.

Tessa looked at her mother and knew she would never understand. Grant's infidelity was beyond her comprehension. In fact, even if she accepted it as truth, she would probably blame Tessa for it anyway. But she was not going to be satisfied without a reason, so Tessa gave her one.

"Because I'm in love with someone else, Mum," she said quietly. It was probably a stupid thing to say, but she just couldn't stand any more recriminations.

Her mother's jaw dropped open.

Her father looked up from his newspaper, eyes sparking with keen interest.

"You've got someone else?" her mother squawked.

Tessa shrugged and sat down at the kitchen table, opposite her father. "It might not come to anything, Mum. But I'm going out with him today. In fact, he's sending a car for me at eight o'clock so I'll have to hurry with breakfast."

She quickly scooped up a spoonful and started eating.

"Sending a car? What do you mean, sending a car?" her mother demanded.

"That's what he said. So I expect a car will turn up for me at eight o'clock," Tessa said offhandedly.

"Who is *he?*" her father asked.

"The boss of CMA, Dad. Blaize Callagan. I filled in as his secretary at the conference," she explained.

"Ah!" he said. "Taken a shine to you, has he?"

"It seems that way, Dad."

"How could you fall in love with him?" her mother accused more than asked.

Love? Tessa paused for a moment to consider that question. Was she in love with Blaize Callagan? The thought hadn't occurred to her before. Perhaps she was. And that was why her body reacted to him…and her mind. Certainly she was very strongly attracted to him in every sense there was. But her mother would never understand that. Better to say something that she could relate to.

"Well…he's the most handsome man I've ever seen. And the smartest." Tessa refrained from saying the sexiest. And that in some ways he appeared to be caring and nice. Apart from being a challenge and…

"How old is he?"

"Thirty-six."

"Is he married?" Suspicious. Expecting the worst.

"Widowed."

Visible relaxation. "How serious is he about you?"

"I don't know."

"Why not?"

"He's never told me."

"Tessa, you can't play fast and loose forever."

"No, Mum. I'm not going to. Cross my heart."

Her mother relaxed a little bit more. "Where are you going?"

"He's taking me out on his boat."

"Alone?"

"Yes, Mum. Alone. He wants to get to know my mind. We're going to explore it together."

"Well, you make sure he doesn't get to know anything else, Tessa," her mother said with a hard look.

"Yes, Mum." After all, he could hardly get to know what he already knew.

Tessa absorbed a barrage of advice. It was better than a barrage of abuse. Her father just smiled. Tessa ate her cereal. At five minutes to eight, her mother took up a vigil at the front door to see what kind of car would arrive for her hopelessly wayward daughter. At precisely eight o'clock, she almost had an apoplectic fit.

"Good heavens!" she choked. "It's a limousine. A white stretch limousine." She recovered fast. "Tessa, are you sure you can trust this man?"

"I hope so, Mum," Tessa said, grabbing her bag for a quick exit. She had to say one thing for Blaize Callagan. He had a lot of style. Almost enough to silence her mother. Except it probably wouldn't last.

Her father came to have a look at the car, as well. Not many white stretch limousines were seen at Green Point. A chauffeur alighted from the driver's side and headed down the driveway.

"Well, 'bye, Dad," Tessa said, giving him a quick hug. "Thanks for everything. Thanks for listening."

"Take care of yourself, Tessa," he said, his forehead creased with concern.

"Not to worry. Everything will work out okay," Tessa assured him.

She gave her mother a quick peck on the cheek. "Sorry about everything, Mum."

"Be a good girl," her mother called after her, more in hope than belief.

The chauffeur took her bag and saw her into the limousine with deferential courtesy. Tessa sat back in the plush leather seat and wondered about the wages of sin. Nevertheless, if Blaize Callagan thought he could seduce her with his wealth, he had another think coming!

All or nothing, she decided.

No compromises.

No half-measures.

The weekend would settle what they wanted from each other, and how much they wanted it. If it wasn't enough to get serious, then there'd be no more. If it was enough to get serious, Blaize Callagan would have to rethink his future, because Tessa was finished with grey areas.

White or black.

White, in Tessa's opinion, was for brides.

Black was for emptiness.

And she wouldn't be filling Blaize Callagan's emptiness for long if he didn't want white. The issue was cut and dried in Tessa's mind. Her mother wasn't wrong about everything. It was just that Tessa had to take a slightly crooked path to get to the straight and narrow with Blaize Callagan.

CHAPTER NINE

TESSA HAD NEVER CRUISED the Hawkesbury River. She had
passed over it thousands of times in the train, or on the
expressway, travelling between Gosford and Sydney. She
had always thought it awesome. Wooded hills and stone
cliffs rose almost perpendicularly out of the water, the rem-
nants of a river valley that had been submerged by the sea
aeons ago.

It had a primeval feel to it, a timelessness that man could
never make any real impression on. In some places houses
clung precariously at water's edge, but no one could ever
tame this wilderness. Boats scythed through the waterways.
But the majesty of the fiords made everything else seem
unchanging, puny and irrelevant. Even Blaize Callagan's
magnificent motor cruiser.

The white stretch limousine had prepared Tessa to expect
luxury on the water, and that was a fair description of
Blaize's boat. Sheer extravagance from stem to stern. All
the latest technology combined with streamlined comfort.
Blaize hadn't yet shown her the stateroom, but Tessa knew
that was only a matter of time. She had no doubt it accom-
modated his every material need, as did the galley and the
saloon.

He was able to drive the boat from the sun deck on top,
and that's where they were, the wind blowing on their
faces, sun shining its summer warmth on them, the light

glittering off the small waves coming in from the sea. Tessa had a delightful sense of freedom from all care.

"It seems as though you could lose yourself here forever," she remarked musingly.

Blaize smiled at her. "Great idea! They could make a movie about us. *The Man Who Never Came Back.*"

Their eyes clung for a few moments—wary, searching, wanting—then looked away. Tessa wondered what kind of game Blaize was playing with her. He seemed subdued, but Tessa wasn't sure if he was being artful or genuine.

He hadn't placed any pressure on her at all. When he touched her it was only for fleeting moments, nothing she could object to. A touch on her shoulder, her waist, her arm—innocuous really, but it made her shiver.

She knew as well as he did why he wanted to spend the weekend with her. For the moment, it apparently pleased Blaize Callagan to pretend otherwise. He seemed to accept her need to feel free. But Tessa had seen his body language in action before, and she knew how crafty he could be.

He wore well-fitting white shorts, his legs very much on show. His navy and white sport shirt had a collarless V neck and short sleeves. Tessa was very conscious of his body and all its latent virility. It made her very conscious of her own body and every feminine part of her.

"I'm glad you're not a chatterer," he said.

She slid him a mocking look. "I thought you wanted to explore my mind."

Again the dark eyes fastened onto hers, holding them in a sharp passage of intimacy. "I am. Silence can be just as effective a form of communication as speech. You are enjoying yourself, aren't you?"

"Yes."

"You don't need to talk if you don't want to."

"Fine."

He nodded and turned away, picking up his mug of beer to take a sip of it. He hadn't drunk much. Neither had Tessa. He had made her a gin and tonic before coming up to the sun deck and she had barely touched it. Not through any sense of caution. She simply hadn't thought about it. The pleasure of the boat trip, being with him, was quite heady enough for Tessa.

They cruised idly through the jigsaw puzzle of waterways, finding a remote bay, which looked as though no man had visited it in the last two hundred years—a small beach, stands of angophoras, iron barks and the odd blue spotted gum lending their shade to the hot sand.

They had a picnic lunch, drank a bottle of wine, and in the stillness of the afternoon they lay on a blanket underneath the trees, replete, relaxed and drowsy in the softly dappled sunshine. Blaize played idly with her hand, his long supple fingers stroking through hers, interlacing, interlocking.

"You have delicate hands," he said. "Quite dainty."

"Yes," she agreed. They *were* fine-boned, small. Like the rest of her. A sharp contrast to the tall model he had married.

"Very feminine," he said.

"Thank you." She was glad he liked them.

He rolled onto his side, looking down at her face as he lifted her hand to his mouth and ran her fingers slowly over his lips.

This is it, Tessa thought. Am I in love with him? How did one define love? Where was the dividing line between being in love and not being in love? Or was it possible to be partly in love and partly out of love?

She could feel her tension rising as he began to caress her, her temples, ears, throat. His lips followed his fingertips, softly seductive, knowingly erotic. She forced herself to relax, but her heart wasn't in it. Where did it lead? Did she love Blaize Callagan?

It was a strange thing, life. When it hadn't mattered what Blaize Callagan thought of her, she had been free of all inhibitions. Now it meant something to her...

He lifted his head sharply, the dark eyes seriously questioning. "You're not responding."

Her throat was tight but she forced herself to speak lightly. "Perhaps I ate too much for lunch."

"And the real reason?"

Relentless, ruthlessly demanding, slicing through any prevarication. Honest.

"Perhaps I like you making love to me too much, Blaize," she said softly.

"So?"

"It makes it hard to turn away."

He frowned, the dark eyes boring into hers with more intensity. "If I make love to you, you want it to be permanent?"

"Something like that. I guess I don't want to become involved in a situation where I can't win."

He nodded. "I can understand that."

His gaze dropped to her mouth, seemed to study the line and shape of it. Then he bent his head and brushed his lips gently over hers in tingling, tantalising sweeps. Tessa put her arms around his neck. Maybe, if she wasn't already in love, she was rapidly falling.

She let him persuade her lips apart. Or maybe they parted of their own accord. He kissed her, sensuality giving way to hungry passion. Tessa could feel her defences melting as desire surged through her, making her feel utterly helpless. How did one resist an irresistible force? Once in the grip of it...impossible not to be swept away. The only answer was to avoid it. Which wasn't possible this weekend.

"I want to make love to you," he said huskily.

No future promise...just now. "You can if you want to," she whispered.

She could feel his strong desire, the electric tension in him. All her nerve ends were tingling in response to it, strung tight, waiting, wanting.

His eyes burned into hers, their command oddly blurred by a need she couldn't define. He drew in a deep breath and slowly released it.

"I don't think I will," he muttered, more to himself than to her.

"Why not?" she asked curiously. It was why he had brought her here. She had given her consent. What was stopping him?

His mouth curled sardonically. "Do you want the smart answer or the serious answer?"

"What's the smart answer?"

His eyes mocked the curiosity of hers. "Time's on my side."

Relentless, she thought again. Relentless and ruthless in going after what he wanted. He had warned her. But she had meant what she had said, too. He could have this weekend *his* way. But no more after that.

"And the serious answer?" she asked.

His expression slowly changed to one of rueful self-mockery. He lifted his hand and stroked her cheek with a tenderness that seemed at odds with his character. "I don't want to hurt you," he said softly.

Her heart turned over. She was in love. Stupid, really, but irreversible. She wished that, just for once, fate would be kind to her, but it was almost certainly a vain wish. Yet maybe there was a slim chance...if Blaize Callagan didn't want to hurt her. That meant he cared, didn't it?

He hadn't cared about hurting her that first night at the

conference. It had been all take then. With a nominal bit of asking. But he hadn't known about her cancelled wedding then. He had thought it was simply a case of mutual desire.

Tessa remembered his vexation yesterday. He hadn't liked thinking it was a rebound effect instead of something strictly between them. And he hadn't liked her crying.

She suddenly realised why he had been stand-offish this morning, treading cautiously, waiting. He wanted her to respond to him. Only him. He didn't want her remembering any other man. And he didn't want her to cry afterwards. He wanted her to be happy with him.

Which did show consideration. Certainly it was tied up with his wants, but he was not the taker she had thought him to be. He genuinely wanted to give her pleasure. He had definitely been considering her feelings. Unlike Grant Durham.

"Come on," he said, heaving himself onto his feet. "Let's clean up here and go cruising."

They went to the boat and packed their lunch things away in the galley. Tessa didn't mean to be provocative. She didn't quite know how it happened. She was thinking how nice it was to be with a man who didn't mind cleaning up things and putting them away, who didn't expect her to do everything. The easy companionable way he shared the chore was so natural, as though they had been doing things like this together all their lives. And somehow her eyes couldn't help feasting on him, the lithe economical way he moved, the male beauty of his face, the perfect proportions of his body so powerfully filled out...

"Stockton."

She looked up, surprised by the harsh rasp in his voice. "Yes, sir?" she replied automatically, forgetting that he wasn't supposed to call her that.

The dark eyes blazed raw desire at her. "I do not have a strong nobility streak," he grated. "If you keep looking at me like that... Oh, to hell with it! I want you!"

He tipped the glass he'd been washing in the sink. He tore the towel out of her hands and tossed it away. He scooped her hard against him and plundered her mouth with an urgency that ran through Tessa like an electric shock, igniting a response that shattered all inhibitions. She wanted him just as fiercely...wanted him with a desperation fed by all her unanswered needs.

He leaned against the sink, drawing her with him, moving her in between his legs so that she was trapped by his powerful thighs, so that she was intensely aware of his arousal as he kissed her mouth, her face, her throat, with a fast feverish passion that allowed her no respite for thought. When he paused for a moment to lift off her T-shirt, his face was dark and brooding, his eyes glittering a searing challenge into hers as he tossed the garment away.

"Stop me if you want to," they said, "but you'll be lying if you deny me."

Tessa was not about to deny him. Her excitement was far too high to be doused, and the intensity of his need for her was like a wild intoxicant coursing through her blood.

He unfastened her bra and tossed it away. Lifted off his shirt and tossed it away. The muscles of his chest pulsed to his harsh shallow breathing as he cupped her breasts in his hands, moulding the soft flesh to his touch. His thumbs dropped to the underswell, his fingers splaying out beneath her arms as he slowly drew her to him, brushing her aroused nipples over his chest, easing her more and more against him, savouring the feel of her warm flesh giving, spreading over the firmness of his.

He threw back his head and a raw groan tore from his throat. His arms wrapped tightly around her, crushing her to him. He tipped her head back and once again his mouth ravished hers, stoking his desire and hers to screaming point.

She was barely conscious of their move to the stateroom. They fell onto the bed in a tangle, their bodies rolling. Her hands scrabbled through his hair, kneaded his shoulders, scraped over his back as his mouth worked its sweet devastation on her breasts, every movement a pulse of sharp pleasure. They squirmed out of the rest of their clothes, loath to lose any body contact, revelling in every touch of their heated flesh, sensitising each other to fever pitch.

Their coming together was another soaring into exquisite satisfaction, need chasing need, higher and higher, deeper and deeper, the spiralling turbulence finally exploding into ecstatic fulfilment. But best of all, for Tessa, was holding him afterwards, hugging him to her, stroking his hair, his back, indulging herself in sweet pretence, letting the need she felt flow through her and express itself in tenderness, while he was too drained of strength to move. She didn't think of the future. Or where this was leading to. It was enough to hold him clasped to her, to feel his heart thudding against hers, to own him…a little.

Eventually he stirred and levered himself up to look into her dreamy golden eyes. He won't recognise what I'm feeling, she thought. He won't see what he doesn't feel himself. So she stared at him without any attempt to disguise the deep well of emotion he had tapped.

He brushed his fingertips around her temple while his eyes studied hers as though they were strangely foreign to him. Then he bent and kissed her softly before moving away. Tessa did not try to hold him. Nor follow him. She knew instinctively that clinging would be anathema to him. He was a man who made his own decisions, who went his own way.

But he did not lie on his back, separate and apart from her. He propped himself on his side and idly trailed his fingers over her stomach as he studied her face some more. There was no tension in their silence, more a peaceful stock-taking of where they were now.

"Would you consider coming to live with me, Tessa?" he asked.

It surprised her that he had made the leap from casual lover to a live-in situation. It meant that he wanted more of her than he had first indicated. But she wasn't going to fall into the grey area again. Once was enough.

"No," she said firmly.

There was no reaction on his face. Blaize Callagan gave very little of his inner thoughts away. He simply watched her intently, assessingly. "Any particular reason?" he asked after a short pause.

Tessa shrugged her shoulders. "You…living with one of your secretaries? You'd want to hide it, Blaize. Downplay it. Degrade it. I don't blame you for that. It would only be natural. But it's not for me. I'm not good at playing second fiddle to anyone. Not even you."

He nodded his head. His brow creased in thought. "So we keep meeting like this."

"I don't think so."

Again a cautious pause. Then lightly, "Any particular reason?"

"I don't want to spend my life waiting for you to fit me into yours from time to time."

"I'd make them good times, Tessa."

She shook her head. "A string of fantasies, Blaize. I want real life. And I want a man who'll share that real life with me. What you're suggesting would only put me on hold from what I'm looking for."

He gave that quite long consideration before he spoke again. "So this is our first weekend together, and our last."

Tessa bravely hid the painful stab of disappointment she felt. No chance with him...ever. Of course, she had been foolish to think there might be. Men like Blaize Callagan simply did not get serious about women like her. Pie in the sky.

At least she had stuck to her guns and not crumbled into compromises and half measures. She could be proud of herself on that score. She had faced up to the future and not made a foolish choice. Which left her only this weekend with him. One night and another day to indulge what could be the love of her life.

She knew what he wanted from her—to be happy with him—and she wanted that, too, for the short time she would have him. She smiled, her golden eyes lit with hopeful appeal. "Let's make it beautiful, Blaize. Happy and beautiful."

For a fraction of a second he looked puzzled. Then he smiled at her. "Agreed. Happy and beautiful."

And it was happy and beautiful. It seemed that, the decision having been made, they both relaxed their private guards and did precisely as they pleased, making the most of the brief time they had together. If Tessa felt like touching him she did, and Blaize enjoyed the same freedom, neither one rebuffing the other at any time. Tessa found it intensely pleasurable to just follow whatever whim took her, often teasing Blaize into surprised laughter. The sense of sharing grew more and more intimate as all inhibitions fell away between them.

When they made love that night, Tessa asked Blaize to hold her afterwards. She told him she liked being cuddled. He seemed to enjoy obliging her. He cuddled her until she went to sleep, and when she woke up in the morning his

arm was still around her waist, her body snuggled spoon
fashion against his. The moment she moved, his arm tightened around her, and they made love again before getting
up.

Sunday was a perfectly glorious summer's day. They had
a swim before breakfast—skinny-dipping, which was something Tessa had always wanted to do but never done. It was
a deliciously sensual experience, made even more so by
being with Blaize. He was an incredibly exciting lover, unpredictable and very erotic. He certainly hadn't lied about
being a man who liked a lot of sex. But Tessa didn't mind.
She found she liked it, too. A lot. With him.

After breakfast they did some fishing for a while, with
no success. Tessa thought they probably weren't concentrating on their lines enough. Occasionally she caught
Blaize looking at her in a wondering fashion, as though he
didn't understand what was happening or why, but he liked
it. He definitely liked it. The warm pleasure in his eyes was
not feigned. Nor was the amusement. He enjoyed being
with her.

By mutual consent they spent the last of the afternoon
in bed. They made love to each other, and Blaize held her
for a long, long time, not moving apart, lying joined together even when his aroused state was gone. It was beautiful. She felt happy and sad…happy for what she had had
with him, sad for the inevitable end to it. She snuggled
closer, kissed his throat.

"Thank you, Blaize," she murmured huskily. "Thank
you for being good to me."

He made no reply. The fingers threaded through her hair
tightened their grip for a few seconds, then slowly relaxed.
He sighed. "It will be dark soon. I guess we'd better start
moving."

They cruised slowly towards Akuna Bay. Blaize had the

Here's a **HOT** offer for you!

Get set for a sizzling summer read...

with **2 FREE ROMANCE BOOKS** and a **FREE MYSTERY GIFT!**

NO CATCH! NO OBLIGATION TO BUY!

Simply complete and return this card and you'll get **FREE BOOKS, A FREE GIFT** and much more!

- The first shipment is yours to keep, **absolutely free!**
- Enjoy the convenience of romance books, delivered right to your door, before they're available in the stores!
- Take advantage of special low pricing for **Reader Service Members only!**
- After receiving your free books we hope you'll want to remain a subscriber. But the choice is always yours—to continue or cancel anytime at all! So why not take us up on this fabulous invitation with no risk of any kind. You'll be glad you did!

326 SDL CPSW

**225 SDL CPSP
S-BR-05/99**

Name: _____
(Please Print)

Address: _____ Apt.#: _____

City: _____

State/Prov.: _____ Zip/
Postal Code: _____

▼ DETACH HERE AND MAIL CARD TODAY! ▼

The Silhouette Reader Service™ —Here's How it Works:

Accepting your 2 free books and mystery gift places you under no obligation to buy anything. You may keep the books and gift and return the shipping statement marked "cancel." If you do not cancel, about a month later we'll send you 6 additional novels and bill you just $3.12 each in the U.S., or $3.49 each in Canada, plus 25¢ delivery per book and applicable taxes if any.* That's the complete price and — compared to the cover price of $3.75 in the U.S. and $4.25 in Canada — it's quite a bargain! You may cancel at any time, but if you choose to continue, every month we'll send you 6 more books, which you may either purchase at the discount price or return to us and cancel your subscription.

*Terms and prices subject to change without notice. Sales tax applicable in N.Y. Canadian residents will be charged applicable provincial taxes and GST.

If offer card is missing write to: Silhouette Reader Service, 3010 Walden Ave., P.O. Box 1867, Buffalo, NY 14240-1867

BUSINESS REPLY MAIL
FIRST-CLASS MAIL   PERMIT NO. 717   BUFFALO, NY

POSTAGE WILL BE PAID BY ADDRESSEE

SILHOUETTE READER SERVICE
3010 WALDEN AVE
PO BOX 1867
BUFFALO NY 14240-9952

NO POSTAGE
NECESSARY
IF MAILED
IN THE
UNITED STATES

motors barely turning over. The shadows lengthened as the sun started to sink behind the mountains. The flaming clouds changed to a deep purple. Blaize didn't seem to be concerned about the gathering darkness. The boat puttered on.

"We'll take forever to get back there at this rate," Tessa commented drily. They could have spent longer in bed together, she thought regretfully.

He reached out and curled his hand around hers. "Do you mind?"

"No." She wasn't going to mind anything. Happy and beautiful to the end, she decided.

"Neither do I." His dark eyes seemed fathomless in the twilight, but she had the impression they were filled with good memories. "I like this speed," he murmured.

It was nice that he felt reluctant to part with her, Tessa thought. She laid her head on his shoulder. His arm slid around her waist, pressing her closer to him. A mood of melancholy wrapped them in silence. Twilight had fallen. The birds had gone to bed. There was a pale moon rising, a week older than when she had last seen it at Peppers. She wondered what Blaize was thinking.

He cleared his throat.

"Stockton…"

Ah! It was over. Back to business, Tessa thought with resignation. Time for the switch-off. She didn't know how Blaize did it. Although she guessed it was relatively easy when one's emotions weren't deeply involved. She was glad she had decided against any further "weekends" with him. They would have killed her.

"Yes, sir?" she drawled mockingly.

A long pause. She had the impression of furious mental activity. There was definitely a rise of tension in his body. His chest rose and fell on a long-drawn-out breath.

"Stockton, I'm not in the habit of making hasty decisions."

"No, sir," she recited flatly.

"So this decision—you'd better believe it—is not
hasty."

"Yes, sir."

"Stockton, I'm going to marry you."

Tessa's mind went totally blank with shock. She had
given up any hope of that remote possibility. She was resigned to the inevitable parting. She couldn't take it in.

"Why, sir?" she asked, unable to believe it.

"Because I want you, Stockton."

Good heavens! Tessa thought. I really did force him into
black or white by refusing all the grey areas. But she had
never really anticipated he would want her that much. With
the prospect in front of her, she suddenly thought of all the
reasons he shouldn't marry her. She was not another Candice. She would probably be a total misfit in his world.
And after he had been satisfied with the pleasure he obviously got from her, where would they be then? He would
begin to look critically at her. He would start thinking she
didn't measure up. And that would be dreadful. Dreadful!

"No, sir," she said in a very small voice.

"Stockton, did I hear you correctly?"

"Yes, sir."

"Give me one good reason we shouldn't get married,"
he demanded tersely. He was even more tense now.

Tessa was feeling very tense herself. "We wouldn't be
happy together, sir."

"Don't be a fool, Stockton. Marriage has got nothing to
do with happiness."

She gaped at him. He looked steadfastly ahead, grim-
faced with determination.

"Then what has marriage got to do with, sir?"

He switched off the motors. The cruiser drifted idly along the middle of the Hawkesbury River. He turned to her, lifted his hands onto her shoulders. He had a weary look on his face. He spoke in a tone of infinite patience.

"Tessa, marriage is about *need*. It's about two people needing each other. You recognise that. You need me. I need you. To the exclusion of everyone else. It's really that simple."

Tessa looked at him blankly. She had never thought of it like that before. In a way he was right. Grant had said he loved her, but he had never *needed* her. Not exclusively. And then there were her parents. Poles apart, but each leaning on the other for their needs. Sue and her husband... There were others. A long list of them. And this new perspective fitted them all.

"Perhaps you're right, sir," she said.

"Of course I'm right. We need each other. Exclusively. We get married. Simple." There was a ring of deep satisfaction in his voice. Problem solved.

No, it wasn't, Tessa thought. For one thing, she didn't like his switch-on switch-off inner mechanism. That had to stop if she was going to marry him. He had given her what she wanted this weekend. Having experienced that, she wasn't going to accept anything less. Why should she? Surely a wife was more important than a weekend lover.

She looked up at him defiantly. "I don't think you would like my conditions, sir."

"Like what?"

"You will treat me lovingly all the time," she stipulated firmly.

One eyebrow rose. "Regardless of how I feel?"

"Regardless of how you feel. Lovingly. All the time."

"What kind of deal is that? Where's the compromise?" he demanded.

If he thought he could make their marriage a business deal, he could think again, Tessa thought furiously. How could she have fallen in love with such an impossible man?

"There's no compromise, sir. That's the deal!"

He frowned. He turned dark brooding eyes to the shoreline. It was obvious that he didn't like being cornered. He was probably weighing up how much he wanted her against how much he didn't want to put himself out, Tessa thought cynically.

He seemed to brace himself as he turned to her. "I can do it," he said decisively. "I can do anything I set my mind to. Of course I can do it."

His hands fell to her waist and he started kissing her forehead, trailing his lips around her temples as he drew her closer to him.

"There are a few other minor problems," Tessa said.

"I'm showing you how loving I can be," he murmured, planting warm kisses on her hair.

"You're arrogant and overbearing..."

"Trivial," he scoffed, nuzzling her ear.

"Demanding and impatient..."

"What does that matter?" He transferred attention to her nose, kissing the tilted end of it.

"Thoughtless and self-centred..."

"Details," he said. "Mere details." And closed her eyes with more gentle kisses.

"Uncaring of what others think and feel..."

His head jerked back. "Now you've gone too far," he said sternly. "That is not *true*."

"Isn't it?"

"No." His gaze dropped to her mouth. "I care a lot about how you feel when I do this." He tilted her head so he could kiss her on the lips. It seemed to last forever. Not just sensual, although it was certainly that. Loving. He had to want her an awful lot, Tessa thought with a deep thrill of pleasure.

Was she in love? Well on the way, she thought. Just the slightest bit more encouragement and she could be head over heels. She kissed him with all the fervour swelling from her heart.

He leaned into her, moaning his desire.

"We could go below," she suggested.

He took a very deep breath. His eyes glittered with triumphant satisfaction. "And leave this boat floating around the river? That's irresponsible. You'll have to learn to control your desires, my girl."

Tessa laughed at the payback for making him control his desires. "Yes, sir," she said mockingly.

"And stop calling me 'sir'. Use your memory bank, Stockton."

"Yes, darling Blaize."

"Say you're going to marry me."

"Are you going to stop calling me Stockton?"

"I only did that to concentrate your mind along the right path. You've been saying quite a lot of nos that I haven't liked. When you say you'll marry me I'll call you Tessa darling. So are you or aren't you? Be damned if I'll ask you again!"

She took a deep breath. Her mind was singing silly exultant songs. Her heart was pitter-pattering all over the place. "I think I must be crazy," she said slowly, "but yes, I think I will."

"Right!" he said grimly. "And don't think I'm going to let you slide out of it. When I want something, Tessa darling, I get it. One way or another."

He kissed her once more as a firm promise of that, then turned aside and switched the motors to full throttle. They roared to the marina. Tessa wondered if he was impatient to take her to bed again, but once they were docked he hurried her off the boat and over to the car park where he quickly bundled her into a streamlined white Lamborghini.

''Where are we going?'' she asked as he climbed in beside her.

He grinned. Jubilantly smug. ''To your parents' place. We are going to uncancel a wedding. A six-week engagement will suit me just fine. And naturally I intend to get your parents' blessing.''

Tying her up. With bows, Tessa thought. She suddenly had a sinking feeling their marriage wouldn't last very long. Blaize probably had no scruples about divorce. Relentless and ruthless, she reminded herself. He would have what he wanted from her for as long as he needed it...and then what?

Tessa heaved a deep sigh.

She would just have to take her chances and make the most of them.

At least, for a while, she would be redeemed in her mother's eyes.

CHAPTER TEN

BLAIZE MADE NO COMMENT on her parents' home. He helped her out of his car. The gull-wing doors were somewhat startling—not what Tessa was used to—but she hastily reminded herself that she was plunging into a lot of things she wasn't used to in marrying Blaize Callagan.

Was she really going to marry him?

The determined look on Blaize's face said he knew what he was doing. Tessa wondered if she knew what she was doing.

She realised, as Blaize hurried her down the path to the front door, that where and how her parents lived were totally irrelevant to him. They could have occupied a shack in the outback for all he cared. Probably her parents were irrelevant to him as well. Only one thing was relevant. Getting what he wanted. Signed, sealed and delivered. And tied up with pretty bows.

Her mother answered the doorbell, undoubtedly puzzled over who might be calling at such a dreadfully late hour. It was almost ten o'clock. She saw her wayward daughter first and instantly froze. "Tessa," she said. "What have you done?"

Then she saw Blaize. Her mouth remained open but no words came out. After all, Tessa reasoned, her mother liked men to be handsome. Blaize Callagan was probably the most handsome man she had ever seen. He did have this effect on women.

Tessa herself was still being strongly affected by him. Very strongly. He claimed he was faithful to one woman at a time, and he had better stay that way, she thought grimly. She had a few ideas of her own on how that could be accomplished.

Tessa took a deep breath and got on with introductions. "Sorry it's so late, Mum, but this is Blaize Callagan, and he doesn't work by the clock. He wanted to meet you and Dad. He thinks now is as good a time as any. In fact, he wouldn't consider any other time, so it's not my fault. Blaize, this is my mother, Joan Stockton."

"My pleasure, Mrs. Stockton," Blaize said, flashing his dazzling smile as he offered his hand.

Joan swam slowly out of shock. "Oh, dear, oh, dear, oh, dear," she gasped. Her hands went to her hair to primp, in case the permanent wave was not just so. Then she touched her lips in horror at the thought her lipstick might have faded. Her hand dropped to her throat. "And to think I've already taken off my pearls."

"You look fine, Mum," Tessa assured her, knowing how much it meant to her mother to always look her best.

Tessa was distracted by an oddly grateful glance from her mother. With a bit more firmness in her manner, Joan managed at last to take Blaize's hand. "Well, uh, you'd better come in, Mr. Callagan."

At least her mother hadn't quite melted on the spot, Tessa thought. Of course, that wouldn't have been right or proper. Joan Stockton fluttered, waving an invitation, and Blaize instantly got Tessa moving into the house.

She gave her mother a quick hug on the way to the living room. "It's okay, Mum," she whispered. "You're looking good. You always do."

"Thank you, Tessa." She sounded truly grateful.

Her father was in his favourite armchair, watching a Sunday night movie on the television. "Mortimer..." her mother warned stridently. "You won't believe this, but we have a visitor."

He looked up, saw Tessa and Blaize, and hurriedly rose to his feet. "If you like," he suggested brightly, "I could turn the television off."

His wife confirmed that the idea was a good one. "Yes, Mortimer, do that."

He stabbed his finger at the remote-control device on the armrest of his chair, straightened up then looked questioningly at his youngest daughter.

"Dad," Tessa began again. "This is Blaize Callagan. My father, Mortimer Stockton."

Her father looked Tessa's new man up and down as Blaize stepped forward to offer his hand. Her father wasn't the same with other men or women as he was with his wife. From a man he would never take a backward step. Only his adored wife had any right over the way he thought and how he thought it.

Tessa was proud of her father. He might have been a carpenter all his life, but he was a true craftsman with all the confidence and dignity that being a master of his job gave him. He took Blaize's hand strongly, but he did look somewhat overwhelmed by the presence of the man who had come among them.

But she had won today, Tessa reminded herself with deep satisfaction. She had set the terms and Blaize had gone for the white.

"Mr. Stockton," he said warmly. "I realise this is a rather late hour to be calling on you..."

"It is a bit," her father managed. "But where Tessa is concerned...well, that's fine."

"Very well said, Mr. Stockton. It's what I expected of you." Blaize was putting on his most genial soothing manner. Tessa had seen it at work during the mealtimes at the conference. "Tessa has to come first," he said. "That's precisely what I thought. I'm glad we agree about that."

Which surprised her mother and father no end.

"Well..." said Joan Stockton uncertainly. She had never thought like that and she couldn't see where it was leading to.

Blaize took over. "I understand from Tessa that you've had an upsetting weekend. With the cancellation of the wedding." He shot a sympathetic look at Joan Stockton. "That was too bad."

"Oh, very bad," said Joan.

"So I thought it best not to waste any time correcting such a distasteful situation," Blaize said helpfully.

Joan Stockton looked confused. "What can be done?" She slid into one of her nervous anxiety moods. "There is nothing that can be done," she answered herself rhetorically.

"Oh, yes, there is, Mrs. Stockton," Blaize assured her. He turned to her husband. "Mr. Stockton, there are a lot of fools in this world, but I'm not one of them. I want to marry Tessa. I've come to ask for your permission. Tessa has consented to marry me, and I'd like your blessing on that. And yours, too, Mrs. Stockton. I want to get this right, straight from the start."

He flashed his dazzling smile.

Tessa saw her mother go weak at the knees.

"Oh, dear, oh, dear, oh, dear." She fanned herself. She was definitely suffering a hot flush.

Mortimer glanced at his wife for help. Joan Stockton was beyond giving it. She was totally bewildered. All her sacredly held principles on how a woman should act had been shattered by Tessa. She didn't know whether this new marriage proposal was the work of the devil. Mortimer Stockton got no help from his wife.

He took a momentous decision. For the first time since he was married, he took an independent stance. He looked hard at Tessa, refusing to be swayed by the man at her side. "Well, sweetheart, do you want this man, or are you being railroaded into marriage?"

Tessa had to tell the truth. It meant too much to her father. "I guess it's a bit like you and Mum, Dad. I *need* him."

Mortimer Stockton nodded sagely. He understood that. His eyes lifted to the man his daughter needed. "Then, Mr. Callagan…Blaize…it's fine by me," he said firmly.

"Thank you, sir," Blaize said respectfully.

Mortimer Stockton relaxed. "Tessa's a good girl," he said.

Tessa smiled. She loved her father dearly.

"I appreciate that, Mr. Stockton," Blaize said, "and she's the right one for me." He drew her forward into the crook of his arm, taking up the stance of a man in firm possession. "Tessa and I are agreed that the wedding should go ahead in six weeks' time. The only difference will be that I'm the groom. If we have your approval."

Mortimer looked hard at his wife. It had been a hard struggle but Joan Stockton had come to a decision. "Yes," she said, and looked commandingly at her husband. This was certainly for the best. It saved Tessa from a bad end.

Mortimer Stockton gave his approval. "That's fine by my wife and me."

Joan Stockton looked as though she couldn't believe Tessa's luck. Tessa resolved never to tell her how that luck had come about.

"Well," she said, her face suddenly beaming with approval. "Let's all sit down. I'll make a pot of tea. Or would you rather have coffee, Mr. Callagan? Or perhaps a drink of some kind? I don't know what we've got," she added nervously. "What have you got, Mortimer—?"

"I'm driving, Mrs. Stockton," Blaize cut in smoothly. "Coffee will be fine. Thank you."

They settled around the dining-room table. Blaize took a keen interest in all the arrangements Joan Stockton had made for the wedding. They had already been to so much expense…what could he contribute? He, of course, would supply all the wines and drinks, and he was sure that Mr. Stockton would understand that, in this day and age, the groom's family should and would pay half the wedding costs. Did they think that fair? Tessa's father heartily approved this sentiment. Grant hadn't offered to pay for anything.

At Blaize's encouragement, Joan Stockton took a deeper and deeper interest in the new wedding by the minute. It would be nice to add this or that…

Of course, there was a great difficulty in explaining to her family and friends why Tessa would have a new partner for her wedding, but, considering all the difficulties of the situation in explaining previously why Tessa had no partner at all, this was most definitely the lesser of two evils. And if the wedding was grander than the original plan…well, who was going to think critically at all, particularly when they saw the groom?

Tessa looked on in amazement as Blaize Callagan turned his full charm on her mother, who was reduced to malleable putty in no time flat. By the use of judicious flattery, and the force of his personality and position, he had Joan Stockton eating out of his hand.

The devil, Tessa thought. He can not only charm, but bewitch a woman who is old enough to be *his* mother!

She felt a stirring of resentment. Blaize hadn't wooed

her like this. He hadn't used any charm on her at all. Then Tessa remembered Grant Durham's charm and decided she didn't want any more of that. She preferred things the way they were between her and Blaize. Honest and straightforward. She knew where she was with him. She wasn't being fooled into believing that he loved her, so she wasn't going to be let down on that score. He needed her. She needed him. Simple.

But she couldn't help wishing that things were just a little bit different.

"You're so knowledgeable about weddings, Mr. Callagan," her mother gushed. She hadn't yet gained sufficient confidence in the situation to be certain enough in her own mind to call him by his first name.

"I have had one before," Blaize said drily.

Which reminded Tessa…how would she stand up against Candice? What on earth was she taking on?

"Oh! Of course," her mother said. "I forgot." That nonplussed her.

"At this time we don't want to remember it," Blaize soothed. "This is a time to look forward to something happy and beautiful."

"Yes. You're right," her mother quickly agreed, her whole face glowing with approval at this obviously correct attitude.

Blaize asked for one of the wedding invitations, said he would have them all reprinted with his name on them. After all, it was all his fault the arrangements had been altered. He should pay the penalty. He would get them to Mrs. Stockton by Tuesday, along with his list of guests and a social secretary to write them all out under Mrs. Stockton's personal supervision. The secretary could get them posted without delay. It was a pity Tessa wouldn't be able to help but he needed her in Sydney with him. Urgent and pressing business, he called it, without so much as cracking a smile.

But he did look lovingly at her. In fact, he had peppered the whole discussion with a lot of loving touches and glances for Tessa. Blaize had very decisively set his mind on treating her lovingly. I hope this keeps up, Tessa thought.

Her father was most impressed. Her mother was over the moon with approval. Although every time she looked at Tessa there was a sort of glazed look of wondering disbelief in her eyes.

Tessa knew what she was thinking. "How did Tessa get a man like this?" To her mother's mind, Blaize Callagan was, without a doubt, the finest redemption Tessa could have come up with. She was almost saved. In fact, Joan Stockton was beginning to look at Blaize as though he were some kind of Ultimate Being—or at least a special messenger therefrom—because miracles were just pouring out of him.

Tessa wasn't too sure that she wasn't still heading for a bad end. However, only time would tell her that. At least she was on the straight and narrow for a while. She was actually being pushed along it at a rate of knots by the man who was intent on having her, one way or another.

Her parents accompanied them out to the white Lamborghini. Joan Stockton's eyes were like flying saucers. Perhaps she wondered if she was seeing a UFO—or having a special encounter of the third kind. As far as Mortimer Stockton was concerned, any car would have looked like a silver lining. The black clouds were drifting away. His wife would be happy…his little sweetheart princess would be happy… Cars didn't matter at all.

Joan was flustered into silence when Blaize pressed a

warm goodbye kiss on her cheek. He took Mortimer's hand again and squeezed it man to man.

"You look after our Tessa now," her father said. Then, as a last word on the subject, he added, "Treat her right."

"Like a princess, Mr. Stockton," Blaize shot back at him with fervour.

He couldn't have picked a better phrase. Tessa wondered if Blaize was psychic. It was uncanny how he could read minds. Although he hadn't been able to read hers. Not completely. She reminded herself to keep being somewhat unpredictable. She had to hold his interest somehow.

Her father gave her an extra-big hug. "He's all right, sweetheart. No mistake about him," he murmured.

Tessa hoped so.

The die was certainly cast now with her parents brought on side. No way were they going to countenance the cancellation of *this* wedding. That would be complete damnation. Her mother would never speak to her again.

"Happy now, Mum?" Tessa couldn't resist asking as she kissed her mother's cheek.

"For goodness' sake, Tessa," her mother whispered urgently. "We can't talk about that *now*. Keep being a good girl. At least until the wedding."

Tessa was happy to see her father looking very content as she and Blaize drove off together. Her mother's approval, unfortunately, had sunk into anxiety again. Tessa could read her expression loud and clear. "Don't stuff up." Except her mother would never say such words. They weren't at all proper.

The Lamborghini began eating up the expressway to Sydney.

"Nice parents," Blaize remarked smugly.

Tessa shook her head. She couldn't imagine any parents in the world looking down their noses at Blaize Callagan.

Apart from his natural qualities and his obvious wealth, his performance could not have been faulted. Courtesy, sensitivity, consideration, generosity—and very loving.

She, however, had a little problem. "What about your parents?" she asked, quailing at the thought. Would they accept her as easily as her parents had accepted Blaize?

"I'll take you to meet them tomorrow night," he said, shooting her an appealing look. "Best if it's done before the announcement's printed in the *Herald*."

"You're going to put an announcement in the newspaper?"

He looked sternly at her. "I'm very old-fashioned, and I have old-fashioned values."

Liar, Tessa thought. But he looked so smug and self-satisfied that she didn't argue with him at all. It really was amazing he had taken everything she had said to heart. Mind like a computer, she reminded herself.

"What should I wear to meet your parents?" she asked, hoping they wouldn't compare her too badly against whatever standard Candice had set as a daughter-in-law. Tessa had a sinking feeling that it was an awfully high standard.

Blaize's mouth quirked into that knowing little curve. "I thought that black suit you wore last Monday was very fetching." The dark eyes gleamed briefly at her. "But I prefer your hair down."

"Okay," she agreed. He ought to know best, she thought. Her hair wasn't red-gold, but it did have nice honey tones through the brown. Maybe his parents might like someone quieter looking than the flamboyant Candice.

"You will need a change in status, Tessa," he said thoughtfully. "You can't stay on as Jerry Fraine's secretary."

Good, she thought. She could keep a better eye on Blaize if she was *his* secretary. Make sure his eyes didn't drift anywhere they shouldn't. "What do you suggest?" she asked lightly.

"Oh...give up working."

And lose her independence? Tessa brooded on the implications of that for several moments. She didn't like the idea at all. It made her feel too vulnerable.

"Are you going to give up working?" she asked.

"No."

"Neither am I," she said firmly.

Blaize frowned at her. "I certainly don't want you working for Jerry Fraine. The status is all wrong, Tessa."

"I could work for you," she suggested.

"No. Definitely not."

"You need looking after," she argued.

He slid her a mocking look. "We wouldn't get any business done."

"I'll wear my glasses."

"No. No. No. Not those rotten ghastly glasses."

"And I'll put my hair up."

"No." He groaned. "Not that either."

"I'm a good secretary."

"The best I've ever had." He smiled.

"Then why don't you want me?" Tessa demanded.

"I do," he said feelingly. "That's the problem."

"Then I'll get a job with some other firm," Tessa declared determinedly. He wasn't going to dominate her life if she couldn't dominate his!

"I'll think of a way," he said grimly. "But in the meantime you finish with Jerry Fraine tomorrow."

"Sounds like being fired," she said resentfully.

"Something like that," he agreed, refusing to give an inch on that issue.

Tessa sighed in resignation. He did have a point. Big companies like CMA had clearly defined status levels...even to the point of who got into which helicopter. Although Jerry Fraine was a top-level executive, it wouldn't be right for Blaize Callagan's fiancée to be working for him.

In fact, she could see that Blaize would not like to have his wife working in any lowly position. Candice, of course, had run her own business—a very successful high-status one at that—which had been perfectly acceptable. This thought made Tessa feel miserable.

But she was a good secretary.

Tessa was not given to putting herself down, and stubbornly fought the sense of inferiority that Candice's image kept pressing onto her. The only solution that Tessa could see to the dilemma was to be Blaize's secretary. Or personal assistant. That sounded even better. She decided to work that angle when a suitable time came up. Which was not right now.

They arrived at her apartment block and Blaize escorted Tessa up to her door. She wasn't sure, at this point, if she was supposed to ask him in or whether that might contravene the white decision. Her mother had advised being a good girl. But when she opened her door and turned to kiss Blaize goodnight, he decided the matter for her.

"You know I'm going to marry you, Tessa," he said, taking her into his arms and pressing her body to his with deliberate suggestiveness. "Very soon," he added persuasively.

Don't hold him back?

Tessa struggled with the quandary.

"Are you frightened?" he asked softly, the dark eyes instantly picking up the confused vulnerability in hers.

"A bit," she admitted.

"I'm not."

"You're a man," she said. Nothing much changed for a

man with marriage. His life went on along the same course. It was the woman who got forced into giving up things.

"Is there a difference?" he asked.

"Haven't you noticed?" A thread of hard cynicism there.

He sighed. "Do you want me to hold back?"

"Maybe a little bit. Until we're married."

"Okay," he said, then scooped her up in his arms, strode into her apartment, kicked the door shut behind them and found his way to her bedroom as though he had a homing device.

"Do you call this holding back, Blaize?" She meant to sound critical, but her voice came out all husky bemusement as he started undressing her with swift efficiency.

"I won't stay all night," he said.

"Oh. That's all right, then," she murmured vaguely as he started kissing her throat on a blissfully exciting downward trail.

Some considerable time later, when Tessa lay peacefully in Blaize's arms, happy and content and tired, she wondered if it was possible to be ruined and saved concurrently. She decided that it probably didn't do any harm to keep Blaize's need for her at the forefront of his mind. Although he had an excellent memory, she didn't want to take any risk of it dimming. And after all, they were now committed to marrying each other. Which did save her from being ruined.

"What will I say to Jerry?" she asked, idly planting little kisses around Blaize's beautiful face.

He looked surprised. "You tell him the truth, of course."

"He's going to be disappointed about losing me as his secretary."

"He'll take it on the chin. He has too much sense to give you any argument about it."

She didn't like to admit she felt nervous about telling Jerry the truth, so she let the subject drop. Apart from which, Blaize decided it was time to distract her again. He had a very high success rate. Tessa wondered how he gathered the energy to leave her, but he did eventually do so, in the early hours of the morning.

"You're a hard bargainer, Tessa darling," he muttered as he got into his clothes.

She had a moment of weakness when she almost said he could stay, but she wanted Blaize to keep respecting her, so she held her tongue. She waited until he was dressed then gave him a long lingering kiss.

"Goodnight, darling Blaize," she whispered.

"Six weeks is a hell of a long time," he growled, taking his leave darkly.

So is a lifetime, Tessa thought unrelentingly.

She could see a lot of problems ahead.

How she was going to solve them, Tessa didn't know, but she was going to work hard at it. One thing she didn't want was a failed marriage.

CHAPTER ELEVEN

TESSA FELT AT ODDS with herself the next morning when she went in to the office. She regretted having to leave her job. Nevertheless, she had no choice. It was an unavoidable consequence of marrying Blaize.

She liked Jerry Fraine. He had been good to her, and she wanted him to think well of her. It was such an unbelievable announcement that Tessa still felt nervous about it. She hoped they could part on a friendly note.

She started packing up her personal things while she waited for him to arrive. He breezed in at nine o'clock, wishing her the top of the morning from his doorway.

"Uh, Jerry, I need to tell you something." Tessa rushed the words out before he retreated into his office.

"Sure. Come on in, my girl. Bare your breast. Not literally, of course."

Tessa breathed a sigh of relief. He must have had a happy weekend, she thought. He was in a good mood. Which had to help. She followed him in to his office. He sat down behind his desk and lifted his eyebrows expectantly.

Tessa plunged in. "I'm getting married, Jerry."

"Ah!" he said. "Rift healed."

"No." Tessa shook her head. "Not to Grant Durham. I told you that was finished, Jerry." She took a deep breath and spilled it out. "I know this will probably come as a shock to you. Blaize Callagan has asked me to marry him.

I'm going to do just that. In six weeks' time. He insists I have to resign. Today, in fact. Otherwise he'll fire me.''

Jerry's jaw dropped. He stared blindly at her for several unnerving seconds, then the strangest mixture of expressions flitted over his face—bemused wonderment, rueful appreciation, self-mockery. Finally the faint curl of his lips grew into a broad smile, and a soft chuckle issued from his throat. His eyes started dancing with some unholy joy.

"Jerry," Tessa reproached him. "It's not a joke. I'm completely serious." She lifted her hands in an appeal for his belief. "Blaize has already reorganised the wedding. He really is marrying me. And I'm marrying him."

"I'm sorry, Tessa." He made a valiant effort to clear his throat. "I'm sure it's serious," he affirmed, but although his mouth tried to maintain a serious line his lips kept twitching into an irrepressible grin.

"Then what's so funny?" she demanded tersely, feeling hurt by his reaction. Perhaps Jerry Fraine didn't think she was good enough for his boss.

"Nothing! Nothing at all!" he replied dismissively.

Her tawny gold eyes glinted with hard accusation. "You laughed."

A flicker of discomfort was instantly followed by the adoption of Jerry's best bargaining face. "I've been a good boss to you, haven't I, Tessa? Tried to keep everything pleasant for you?"

"Yes," Tessa acknowledged. "I'm sorry I have to leave you in the lurch like this."

"That's okay! That's fine!" He made a dismissive gesture. "As a last favour to me, don't tell Blaize Callagan that I laughed when you told me the good news."

"Why not?" Tessa bored in, not at all satisfied with the situation. Jerry Fraine was definitely hiding something.

He grimaced an appeal. "Please, Tessa, just forget it. Impulse of the moment."

"I want to know why you laughed," Tessa said with determination. He had aroused a lot of uneasy suspicions with his laughter, suspicions she needed settled.

Jerry Fraine looked at her eyes, the stubborn tilt of her chin, assessed the damage he had done to himself and knew he was fair and square on the horns of a dilemma. Another look at Tessa's eyes and he made his decision. Tessa Stockton had always proven trustworthy, and his best option was to trust her again.

"If I tell you, and you tell Blaize Callagan, it'll be the end of me for sure. You wouldn't do that to me, would you, Tessa? I've got a wife and kids to support," he pleaded.

She heaved an impatient sigh. "All right. I won't tell him anything. But you'd better spill the truth, Jerry. Tit for tat."

"Okay." He took a deep breath, grimaced again, then chose his words with extreme care. "Well, the fact is Blaize Callagan has been, uh, interested in you for quite some time. Months—"

"You've got to be joking!" Tessa scoffed.

"I'm not joking."

She looked searchingly at him. "How do you know that?"

"Because he's been picking my brains about you. What you thought, what you did, how you reacted to things. Everything. He wanted to know everything about you. It was never overt, always subtle, but always there. I knew what was going on. I knew he was going to pursue you...when the time was right."

"But..." When had Blaize ever noticed her? "He didn't know me," she remarked in puzzlement.

Jerry gave her a wise look. "He knows more about you than you can possibly imagine."

"Then why didn't he do something about it? If he was so interested in me…"

"Oh, Blaize Callagan is a master of strategy," Jerry said bitterly. "He would wait until the time was right for him."

Tessa frowned over that remark, aware Blaize did calculate everything to his best advantage. He certainly liked time to be on his side.

Jerry quickly recollected himself and projected an earnest look. "I did my best to protect you, Tessa. I never realised something serious might come of his, uh, interest. So I tried to put the lid on it. I told him you were getting married. Wouldn't even look at another man. But that, quite obviously, was no deterrent to Blaize Callagan."

"Oh!" Tessa did not know whether she was shocked or flattered by Blaize's ruthless disregard for her attachment to another man.

"When the accident happened to Rosemary, he saw his chance. And took it. No doubt if that hadn't happened he would have made some other chance to open the way," Jerry said musingly. "Once that guy makes up his mind, nothing stands in his way."

If it does, he steps around it, Tessa thought.

Jerry paused to project apologetic appeal. "I was called to choose a substitute secretary for the conference. But it was…made clear to me that you were the only suitable choice. Not spelled out exactly. But the message was quite unmistakable. I am not known to be slow at picking up inferences. I got the message. After all, I've got a wife and kids to support."

He heaved a rueful sigh. "I regret to say that, although it weighed heavily on my mind, I did put my livelihood ahead of your welfare, Tessa. I hasten to add that, knowing

your particular circumstances and your character, I felt if
any woman could stand up to Blaize Callagan you were
the one. And I prayed very hard that everything would go
right.''

Tessa remembered Jerry had looked as though he was
praying in the helicopter. After Blaize had lifted her bodily
into her seat. And he had advised her, too late, on Tuesday
morning to keep her guard up with Blaize or she might get
torn apart.

''I have always thought you were a grand girl, Tessa,''
Jerry went on with gathering fervour. ''Taken a personal
and paternal interest in you. I hope you appreciate—I'm
sure you do—that Blaize Callagan is a very hard man to
say no to. I just couldn't.''

''I see.'' She gave him a stern look. ''You let me walk
into the lion's den without so much as a word of warning,
Jerry Fraine.''

He lifted his hands higher. ''Tessa, I swear, I didn't
know for certain. I could have been putting two and two
together and making five. But the fact is…well, to put it
bluntly, you do have a lot of femininity…and…''

''I do?''

Jerry nodded knowingly. ''The cutest bottom in the
building.''

Tessa huffed. ''I'm more than just a bottom, Jerry
Fraine.''

''I know. I know,'' he said hastily. ''And I figured Blaize
Callagan would find that out in very short order. At least,
I hoped so. I prayed for it.''

Tessa now understood why Blaize had looked at her as
he had in his office last Monday morning—studying her
and giving those little nods of satisfaction. He had noticed
her, and wanted her, and when extraordinary circumstances

had presented him with a handy opportunity he had gone for what he wanted. Totally ruthless.

He had known she was getting married. And he hadn't known the wedding had been called off. Was he a complete cad? Well, she was going to find out about that when a suitable moment came.

Jerry grinned. "Obviously you got to him, Tessa. And good for you! I couldn't be more delighted. Thrilled. Without a doubt, what Blaize Callagan needs is a wife like you."

Tessa frowned. Why did Jerry think Blaize needed a wife like her? On the surface of it, she wasn't suitable for Blaize at all.

Jerry suddenly cracked up, peals of mirth spilling from him in uncontrollable bursts. "I just think it's glorious justice that everything's turned out the way it has. The biter got bitten. Well and truly. Not even Mr. God Almighty Callagan could have anticipated that it would all turn out like this."

He took his spectacles off and wiped tears from his eyes. "Or maybe he did. Forget what I just said, Tessa. Maybe he always meant it to. God knows, I've never been able to read him right. Not completely right."

Blaize had meant to have her, Tessa thought. That was absolutely right. However, she was only too aware that it was she who had forced the marriage decision onto him. If she hadn't, would Blaize have ever come to it?

Jerry shook his head. "I was wrong to laugh. It was the surprise of it. That's all. Apart from my wife, you're the most marvellous girl it's been my privilege to know, Tessa. And I congratulate you. With all my heart and mind and soul, I do most fervently congratulate you. You're the only person I know who's beaten Blaize Callagan on a deal and come out winning. A pity you can't stay on. You could have given me lessons.''

Tessa couldn't help smiling at him. Whether the winning would go on was a big question mark. She had no idea what the future held. "Why do you think Blaize needs a wife like me, Jerry?" she asked bluntly.

Jerry Fraine was a very shrewd and a very smart man. He paused, instantly sensing it was a serious question, and he gave her the respect of giving it serious thought. "Don't repeat this, Tessa. This is between us. But I think Blaize Callagan needs humanising. I do believe you're possibly the one person who can do it. And, Tessa…"

"Yes?"

He smiled in his kindly fashion. "I hope he makes you happy. I don't know if you will be, but I wish you all the best…always.''

"Thanks, Jerry.''

They parted with mutual regret. They had shared a good working relationship. Tessa thought if she had any influence over Blaize, Jerry Fraine would eventually be promoted. She had no concern at all over Jerry repeating this story to anyone, except possibly his wife. Jerry was the soul of discretion when it came to his business life. After all, he had a wife and kids to support.

Humanising…

The idea lingered long in Tessa's mind. She thought over the weekend she had shared with Blaize, remembering how he had relaxed more and more with her. No pressures. No superficialities. No pretences. Just being their true selves. She wondered if it was what had influenced Blaize into asking her to marry him. Maybe his need for her wasn't just man-and-woman attraction after all. He had spoken of need. Two people needing each other. Exclusively. If that was the case, she did have a chance of making this marriage work. Permanently.

She decided to ring up Sue and ask her advice. As far as Tessa could see Sue had a very good marriage, so her sister ought to have a few clues on how to keep a husband happy.

However, when she called Sue she found her mother had already been on the telephone to her older daughter most of the morning, regaling her with the unbelievable news. So Tessa had to give her version of the latest development in her love life before she could get to the point. Eventually the moment came.

"How do you keep a man happy, Sue?" This was most important to her.

"Simple," Sue replied. "No difficulty there. Stay happy yourself. If you're happy, he'll be happy. He won't know why he's happy, but he will be. That's a fact."

It certainly seemed to fit yesterday's experience. She remembered Blaize looked at her as though he didn't know why he was feeling good. Nevertheless, it seemed too easy. Tessa was doubtful.

"Are you sure that works, Sue?"

"Positive."

That was reassuring. "Then thanks for the advice, Sue," Tessa said with sincere appreciation.

"Not advice. Never give it. Statement of fact."

"Thanks all the same."

"Pleasure."

Sue had a lot going for her, Tessa thought. A lot of wisdom. It could be handy for the future. She decided to consult her older sister more frequently.

Tessa put Sue's policy into immediate practice. That night Blaize took her to meet his parents. Tessa did not let herself become nervous and inhibited. She did not let their

obvious wealth intimidate her. She was happy to be with
Blaize, happy about their forthcoming marriage, happy to
meet his parents—who started looking indulgently at her
after a while—and happy that Blaize treated her so lovingly. She was, after all, head over heels in love with him,
and she didn't care who knew it.

It seemed to have a disastrous effect on Blaize's control.
After they made their farewells he drove around the block
and made love to her in the car. As always, with Blaize, it
was a very interesting and exciting experience. Then he
took her to her apartment and made love to her again. Less
frantically but with no diminishment of passion.

He was obviously reluctant to leave her, but he forced
himself to do so with good grace, merely commenting with
heavy irony that he had made a mistake about the wedding.
He should have got a special licence. Which assured Tessa
that he was still keen about marrying her. Keener than ever.

He took time off on Tuesday morning to take Tessa to
his favourite jeweller. None of the rings they were shown
satisfied his demanding taste. He commissioned one to be
specially designed for Tessa's hand. It had to be dainty, he
said. In the end, he settled for a spray of diamonds in a
delicate gold setting. Tessa would have been happy to have
any engagement ring, but she was delighted Blaize wanted
to give her something that would be uniquely hers. It made
her feel she belonged to him and that she was unique to
him.

"I'll take you to my accountant now," Blaize announced. "He'll fix up a few things for you."

"Like what?" Tessa asked.

Blaize looked uncomfortable. "It's a pro tempore solution. Because I put you out of your job. You'll need
money."

Tessa frowned at him. "I don't want your money, Blaize.

A good secretary can always get a job. If you don't want me as your secretary—"

"Tessa..." The dark eyes pleaded for forbearance. "Apart from anything else, there is Rosemary to consider."

"You could pass her on to Jerry Fraine."

"That would be a demotion."

"Promote Jerry, then."

His eyes hardened. "Are you trying to tell me how to run my business?"

She stared back stubbornly. "I want to be your secretary, Blaize."

He sighed. "I'll work something out. Meanwhile..."

He left her with his accountant, who took her to a bank, and very shortly Tessa was financially richer than she had ever been in her life. She had a personal account and a housekeeping account and was signed up for a stack of credit cards.

She suddenly had access to an enormous sum of money, more than Tessa had earned in all her working years. Somehow she couldn't bring herself to argue with the accountant, which was probably why Blaize had left her with him. But she did feel uncomfortable about it. She suspected Blaize was simply determined on getting his own way again.

Her parents, his parents, her resignation from her job, the announcement in the newspaper, the ring, the money... Blaize was tying a lot of bows fast and furiously.

Tessa remembered what Jerry had told her, and how Blaize had gone ahead and taken her anyway, despite the fact she was supposed to be marrying someone else. Maybe Blaize wasn't as honest as she thought him. Maybe he did whatever was expedient to get his own way. Maybe he was a cad. She recalled his smart answer, "Time's on my side."

Blaize Callagan was a complex man.

Tessa needed to get some straight answers.

Sue had invited them to dinner that night—to look Blaize Callagan over for herself—and Blaize called at Tessa's apartment at six o'clock. He was early, but he said he had nothing else to do. He stretched out on her bed and watched her get ready. He seemed to enjoy watching her, making the odd desultory comment.

It seemed as good a time as any to do a little probing, so Tessa casually asked, "Remember the first time we made love, Blaize?"

He flashed her his dazzling smile. "Vividly."

For a few moments, Tessa thought nothing else really mattered, as long as she had him. But then the question arose again—how long would she have him for? She wanted answers.

"At the time..." She pushed on, then hesitated, wondering how best to word the question without giving Jerry away.

"Yes?" Blaize prompted.

She projected curiosity into her voice. "Did you know I was going to be married?"

He didn't lie. "Yes."

She looked at him, her golden eyes troubled as doubts about his integrity flooded through her mind. "Why did you do it, Blaize?" she asked quietly.

He went very still, the dark eyes scouring hers. "Does it upset you?"

She turned away and went on brushing her hair, not wanting to lie to him. It did upset her. Yet, in another sense, if he hadn't done it, they wouldn't be where they were now. The problem was, she wasn't sure if that was a good thing or a bad thing.

In a fast fluid movement, Blaize was off the bed and taking the brush from her hand. He dropped it on the dressing table and turned her towards him, drawing her into a gentle embrace. The dark eyes burned into hers, demanding that she listen, demanding belief.

"Tessa, you weren't married to him," he said softly. "I wanted you with me, not with some other man." He grimaced in rueful self-mockery. "I wanted to be with you...to know what it was like to be close to you. That first night I wasn't playing around. I hadn't planned it. It...just happened."

He frowned. "Tension. It was the tension that decided it. And you didn't reject me. I'm sensitive to people...to vibrations. You may not think so, but I am. That's why I'm successful at doing what I do. But if you had made one move to stop me, Tessa, I would have stopped."

Would he have stopped? The doubt still lingered in her mind. Blaize went after what he wanted. He had told her so. What the truth of this was, she couldn't tell. "So it was all my fault?" she asked, trying to read his mind.

"No, my darling." He sighed, his eyes appealing for her understanding. "It was my need. I made all the moves. The fault was...is all mine. When I felt there was a chance for me, no way was I going to pass it up without trying. I wanted you, Tessa. And I knew, you see, that the tension wasn't all mine."

"No. It wasn't all yours," Tessa conceded. "The intimacy of the cottage...it was unnerving. And you..."

"What about me?" he asked, his eyes sharpening, probing with urgent intensity.

She felt the sudden rise in his tension but didn't understand the cause of it. She smiled to take it away. "Well, I don't want to boost your ego, but the plain truth is, you are my fantasy-lover material, Blaize."

For some reason her reply increased his tension instead of abating it. His face tightened into a grim expression.

However, before he made any response to her explanatory comment, the doorbell rang.

"Are you expecting someone?" he asked tersely.

Tessa shrugged ignorance. "Might be a neighbour wanting to borrow something," she said, and went to answer the summons, quite relieved to have a breathing space to sort through what was happening with Blaize.

It wasn't a neighbour.

It was Grant Durham.

He pushed past her, thrust a page of newspaper in her face and burst into outraged speech. "Is this some horrible joke?" he demanded furiously, eyes glaring suspicion and accusation. "I give you time to cool down and come to your senses, and—"

"Who is this man, Tessa?"

Blaize Callagan's voice whipped down the living room and curled Grant Durham around to face him. Grant gaped at him. As well he might. If looks could kill, Grant would have been slain on the spot.

"My ex-fiancé," Tessa said briefly, extremely conscious of the explosive tension emanating from her new fiancé.

"Tessa is mine!" Grant burst out belligerently. "She's been mine for years!"

Blaize started walking towards him, deadly intent in every step. He was bigger, taller, more robust and powerful than Grant.

"She is not yours anymore," Blaize said very quietly. "You treated her badly. Beyond contempt. You don't deserve her, you filthy gutter scum. You denigrated her. You upset her. You despised what you had."

Grant lifted a hand in protest. "Now hold on a—"

Blaize grabbed the lapels of Grant's suit coat and lifted him off his feet. "If you ever come near her again, I'll smash your head in. And a few other parts, as well. Do you understand that, you slime bucket?''

''Look! You don't understand!'' Grant squawked. ''I've got a new therapist—''

The expression on Blaize's face, the violence emanating from him in black waves was frightening enough to Tessa, let alone his target. ''You worm,'' he raged. ''You heap of green-tinged garbage. I'm going to—''

Tessa had to do something to stop it. There was no doubt what Blaize was going to do, and it was going to hurt Grant a great deal.

''Put him down, Blaize,'' she appealed hastily.

''Why?'' he growled.

''I don't want you to hurt him.''

He stabbed a sharp look at her, saw her anxious concern, then with great reluctance set Grant on his feet.

''That's better,'' said Grant, pretending not to be more than ruffled. ''Much more natural…''

''Please go, Grant,'' Tessa slid in quickly. It was plain stupid of Grant to think he could twig a tiger by the tail. She could feel the coiled tension in Blaize. He was all set to pounce again. The dark eyes were black with barely repressed passions.

Grant perversely tried his luck again, his green eyes projecting the full blast of his lying charm. ''I love you, Tessa.''

''Truly?'' she tested coldly.

''Yes. Above everything else…I'd do anything for you.''

''Do you want me to be happy, Grant?''

''Yes. Of course I do, Tessa,'' he said with vehement fervour.

''Then I'm sorry, Grant, but I don't love you. And I'm happy with this man. I'm going to marry him. So if you truly want me to be happy…''

"But we've been together so long," Grant argued passionately. "How can you be happy with someone else?"

Blaize growled a warning.

Grant threw a wary glance at him then quickly concentrated on Tessa again. "What am I going to do?"

"See your new therapist," she advised.

"You're going to need a lot of therapy if you don't start moving," Blaize promised him threateningly.

"Yes. I suppose that is the best thing," Grant said nervously. He moved away from Blaize, reached the door, then looked at Tessa, pained bewilderment on his face. "You're really going to be happy with him, Tessa?"

"I'm happy now, Grant," she stated pointedly.

"I'm sorry. Sorry for what I did, Tessa. Sorry I failed you…" For the first time ever Grant looked vulnerable, totally at a loss.

"It's too late, Grant," Tessa said softly. The four years hadn't been all bad. But they were over. "This is goodbye," she said firmly.

He left on a muted half-sob.

Weak, Tessa thought. And turned to the man who was strong in every way.

Blaize's eyes were glowing furiously. "You should have let me finish him off."

If anything, his tension was even more pronounced. Tessa sighed to relieve some of her own. The situation had been awkward, to say the least, with her old lover and her new lover confronting each other. "I'm sorry you had to be here," she muttered self-consciously.

"I'm sorry I didn't throw him out the door," Blaize grated.

She lifted appealing eyes to him. "It's over now, Blaize."

His eyes bored into her, wary and watchful. "You did say permanent, Tessa," he reminded her sternly.

"Yes, I did," she affirmed.

"I told you I meant to have you," he said.

"Yes, you did."

"You don't need him."

"That's why I told him to go."

"You need me."

"Yes," she said fervently, realising Blaize was feeling uncertain of her.

"He might come back."

"Blaize, I don't want him back. If he comes, I'll tell him to go again," she assured him.

Still he was disturbed. "Fidelity works both ways, Tessa."

"Yes, it does."

"No changing your mind."

"No."

"I think you'd better come and live with me."

"Are you still going to marry me?"

"Yes," he said vehemently.

"I don't like you not trusting me."

He paused. Frowned. "I do trust you. I just want to protect you."

"Am I going to be your secretary?"

He grimaced. "Tessa…"

"I just want to protect you, Blaize."

He heaved a deep sigh. "Well, if you're living with me, I guess I might be able to get some business done during the day. All right. You can be my secretary."

"All right. I'll come and live with you. But you still have to marry me."

"The wedding's set," he reminded her. "If you want, I'll marry you tomorrow and to hell with the wedding."

"No. Six weeks is fine." She couldn't possibly upset her mother again.

"We're agreed, then."

She smiled. "I think we have *ringi*, sir."

He relaxed. He smiled. Then began to chuckle. Then to laugh. A look of intense happiness lit his face. He scooped Tessa up in his arms, twirled her around, then paused, his eyes burning into hers. "Just remember the Japanese don't sidestep. It's consensus all the way."

"That's fine by me, Blaize darling." Her eyes danced teasingly. "I've never liked dictatorships."

He growled and kissed her. Tessa wound her arms around his neck and kissed him back. She felt very secure. Maybe it was just male possessiveness on Blaize's part, but it seemed to her that his emotions had been very involved a few moments ago. Although it only took a few moments more before he got very physically involved.

He certainly was a complex man.

Maybe, after they were married, she would be able to get him all sorted out. In the meantime, living with him and being his secretary would surely help her in this task. Except she mustn't tell her mother what she was doing. It would upset her mother terribly.

CHAPTER TWELVE

THE SIX WEEKS seemed to fly by for Tessa. Living with Blaize was vastly different from living with Grant. Blaize owned a penthouse apartment at Milson's Point, which was not far from where she had lived. Not only was the place sheer luxury to Tessa, but there was also the service of a daily maid who came in to do the housework, the washing and ironing, and whatever food shopping Blaize required. Blaize cooked his own breakfast—and Tessa's—and more times than not they ate out in the evening.

Most weekends they were engaged in a whirl of social activities. Blaize insisted she use *his* money for the extra clothes she needed to fulfil these engagements, and even came shopping with her to make sure she didn't stint on anything. Tessa simply wasn't used to having enough money to buy *anything*. She found it difficult not to keep checking price tags. Blaize didn't so much as blink an eyelid at the cost.

She was deliriously happy with him, and Blaize showed every sign of being absolutely content with her. To Tessa's amazement his friends seemed to accept her without reservation. She decided it was probably because no one had the temerity to criticise Blaize Callagan's choice of wife, particularly since he always treated her lovingly. He was exceptionally good at that. Which just went to prove that when Blaize set his mind on something he carried through with complete dedication.

He found a position for Rosemary Davies as personal assistant to one of his high-powered friends. The beautiful blonde made no waves about being asked to resign. Tessa was established as Blaize's executive secretary, and she did her best to keep his mind on business.

There were times when he got very tense. Luckily his apartment was only five minutes away from the CMA building. They often took work home with them. Tessa liked sharing everything with Blaize, and he very quickly became used to it. He even went so far as to express the view that it was a good system. Efficient and relaxing.

A week before the wedding there was a meeting of executives in the boardroom. Jerry Fraine remarked that she looked happy. Tessa replied that she was. Jerry smiled at her and slyly added that Mr. Blaize Callagan seemed to be getting more and more human.

The day before the wedding, Tessa went home to her parents' house. Her mother expected it. Besides, Tessa wanted to have one last night with her parents before the final commitment to a new life as a married woman.

Blaize was reluctant to let her go. It almost sounded as though he nursed some suspicion she would get cold feet about their marriage at the last moment if he let her out of his sight. Which was too absurd to credit. Nevertheless, he informed her, before she left him, that if she wasn't at the church on time there would be dire consequences.

Joan Stockton was in a flutter, checking and rechecking everything, wanting everything to be right and proper and perfect for the big day. Tessa and her father did their best to calm her down. Joan insisted that they each take a sleeping pill so that they would get a proper beauty sleep. Mortimer remarked that he didn't think it would help his beauty, but he took the pill from his wife without any argument. After all, she knew best.

Tessa woke to a stream of beautiful morning sunshine spilling through her bedroom window. A zing of nervous excitement instantly raced through her veins. This was it— her wedding day. By tonight she would be Mrs. Blaize Callagan.

"Happy the bride the sun shines on," she sang in her heart. Her eyes lingered exultantly on the beautiful wedding dress hanging on the door of her wardrobe. The beading on the high collar and on the lace bodice sparkled through the plastic covering. This afternoon she would walk down the aisle in that dress, and Blaize would be waiting for her in front of the altar, and they would be married... *To have and to hold unto death do us part.*

Her wedding day. Tessa could hardly believe it. After all these years this was the day she would marry the man she loved.

A light tap on the bedroom door drew her attention. It was bound to be her mother, Tessa thought, and hitched herself up on the pillows, a smile of greeting already lighting her face as the door opened and her mother's head poked around.

"Ah! You're awake!" Joan said with satisfaction. She bore a tea tray into the room. "It's a beautiful morning. Not a cloud in the sky. Did you sleep well, dear?"

"Like the proverbial log, Mum." She grinned at the tray, which held considerably more than a pot of tea—a plate of bacon and eggs and a pile of toast, all freshly prepared. "Am I being spoiled with breakfast in bed?"

"I thought you might like it," her mother said indulgently. She sat on the bed, her hand automatically lifting to her daughter's face to tuck some wayward strands of hair behind her ear—a small dainty ear, as delicately feminine as her hands and feet. She heaved a sigh and looked at Tessa with troubled eyes. "I just want to say...I've only ever wanted the best for you, Tessa. If sometimes…well, we haven't seen eye to eye about a lot of things…but all's well that ends well. And I hope you'll be very happy with Blaize."

"Thanks, Mum. I'm sorry I've been such a worry to you. I promise you I'll be the best wife I can be, so you won't have to worry anymore," Tessa said with deep sincerity. Then she threw her arms around her mother's neck and kissed her. "I do love you, Mum. And thanks for cooking a wedding day breakfast for me. I really appreciate it."

"There, there… You're a good girl, Tessa," her mother said. Which was the equivalent of, "I love you very much and thank heaven you're now saved." She was always flustered by any show of emotion. "Eat up now before it gets cold," she commanded, but there was a blur of tears in her eyes as she quickly withdrew.

It was a happy day. Sue and her family arrived soon after breakfast. Sue was to be matron of honour, and her four-year-old daughter, Jessica, was to be bridesmaid. The three of them spent most of the morning at a hairdressing salon. In the meantime, Tessa's two older brothers and their families turned up. There was a boisterous family luncheon where her brothers jokingly gave her a lot of advice about how to please a husband, and their wives did quite a bit of correcting them on their opinions.

Sue advised Tessa on her make-up—a touch of blusher to lend an interesting contour to her cheeks, two shades of lipstick to give her lips more definition, a delicate application of subtle eye shadow and a dusting of a very expensive powder that gave her skin a pearly sheen. Tessa was delighted with the result.

The flowers arrived promptly at two-thirty, as arranged. Tessa's bouquet was a long spray of stephanotis that smelled divine. Sue's was a mixture of pink carnations and white roses, while Jessica was to carry the white basket of miniature pink roses.

It was then time to dress. Jessica could barely contain her excitement as Sue zipped her into the sky-blue silk gown with its flounces of lace and threaded ribbons. She looked like a beautiful little doll with the circlet of flowers around her curly fair hair. She raced off to show Grandma and Grandpa, leaving her mother and aunt to their final toilettes.

"I hope she's going to behave herself in the church," Sue said with a rueful smile as she closed the door after her.

Tessa laughed. "She's going to love every minute of it." Then she set about fastening the diamond earrings into her lobes. They were a wedding present from Blaize and matched the design of her engagement ring, five diamonds on a delicate curve of gold.

"They're fabulous, Tessa," Sue said with warm delight. "You sure came up with a prize in Blaize. Perfect husband material."

"You think so?" Tessa was still a little doubtful about that, although nothing was going to stop her from marrying him.

Sue laughed. "Tessa, he adores you. He would die for you."

"I don't know that he'd go that far." Sue didn't understand about how Blaize could set his mind on something and do it.

Her sister raised a challenging eyebrow. "Want to bet?"

Tessa shrugged off the subject with a smile. "No bets." She didn't want to tell Sue that Blaize had never once spoken of love. Not that it mattered all that much. She loved him enough for both of them. She hoped.

She handed Sue a small gift box. "Blaize bought these for you. In appreciation for being my matron of honour."

Sue exclaimed delightedly over the beautiful pearl earrings. "A prize of a man," she insisted again. "He's got taste and generosity."

Sue looked lovely in her sky-blue silk with fitted lace bodice and full skirt. With her blonde-streaked hair and artful make-up, she didn't look a day older than Tessa, let alone seven years.

She helped Tessa lift off the plastic covering from the wedding dress, and then held the heavy gown for her to step into it. Tessa carefully fitted her arms through the high puffed sleeves that narrowed to a band at her elbows. She held her hair up while Sue did the zip and fastened the high band around her neck.

Tessa had a long neck and the style suited her, making her look taller and elegant. The top half of the bodice was a fine transparent organza, throwing the rich silk of the puffed sleeves and the beaded collar into sharp relief. The rest of the tightly fitted bodice was beaded lace that curved over her breasts and dipped to a low V below her waist, accentuating every curve of her body. The full skirt was lined with tulle petticoats to make it stand out in a graceful line extending into a flowing train.

Her waist-length veil was short and frothy. It clipped in behind the narrow plait the hairdresser had woven across the top of her head to hold the rest of her thick hair back. Tessa pulled some long tresses forward to curl over her shoulders.

"Perfect!" Sue approved.

Tessa thought so, too. There was a deep special joy sparkling in her eyes. Her wedding day... It was like a dream come true.

There was a tap on the door. "The cars are here," her mother called out. "Are you ready? May I come in now?"

"Yes," both women chorused in eager anticipation.

The door opened. Joan Stockton looked smart and elegant in a tailored suit of shell-pink silk. An orchid corsage dressed one lapel, proclaiming her mother of the bride. Her face was carefully made up to complement her clothes, but her poise was instantly crumpled by a well of tears.

"Oh, my dear!" She came forward and took Tessa's hands, squeezing them lovingly as she shook her head in wonderment and blinked hard. "Is this the baby I held twenty-four years ago?"

"She makes a beautiful bride, doesn't she, Mum?" Sue said with warm pleasure.

"Very, very beautiful…" Joan drew in a deep breath and let it out on a shuddering sigh, then at last managed a smile. "I've never felt prouder of you, Tessa."

"Thanks, Mum." Her voice came out huskily. It had to fight past a lump of emotion in her throat.

"Time to go. Your father is waiting at the front door with Jessica."

Sue picked up the bouquets, handed Tessa hers, then fell back to pick up the train of the wedding dress.

Ten minutes later, Tessa was settled beside her father in the back of a white limousine, heading for the church…and her marriage to Blaize Callagan.

"I'm not sure I'm ready to give my little princess away," Mortimer Stockton said gruffly, a film of moisture in his sherry-brown eyes as he looked at his daughter in her wedding finery.

"Sure you are, Dad. That's why you're all dressed up," Tessa teased, struggling to hold on to her composure. She tweaked the pink carnation in his lapel. He was looking distinguished in his light grey suit and pink silk tie, perfectly matched to her mother's outfit, and she loved him very dearly. Her father...about to hand her over to her husband-to-be.

He sighed. "Well, I've got to admit, if I have to give you away, I'm pleased that it's to a man like Blaize, sweetheart. I'm sure he'll look after you and treat you right."

"He's been very good to me, Dad," she said truthfully. In fact, when she thought about it, Blaize had done everything she had asked of him. Could Sue be right? Would Blaize do anything for her? Did he adore her? Did adore mean love?

They arrived at the church in good time. A photographer took a spate of photographs. They moved up the steps to the vestibule of the church. Sue made sure the forward section of Tessa's veil was arranged correctly over her face, then fixed the long train so that it would flow perfectly up the aisle. Her father tucked her arm around his. "Ready, sweetheart?" he asked softly.

"Ready, Dad," Tessa assured him with a glowing smile.

The organ inside the church stopped playing a hymn and began Mendelssohn's "Wedding March." Sue raised an eyebrow at Tessa, received a nod, then gave Jessica a gentle push to start her walking up the aisle. The little girl performed as though she was born to it. Sue followed at a stately pace.

Her father gave Tessa's arm a reassuring squeeze. "Now?" he whispered.

"Yes," she whispered, suddenly having an attack of nerves. Her mind frantically dictated instructions. Eyes straight ahead. Smile. Blaize is waiting for you. He chose white. White is for brides. This is your wedding. You can't stuff up now.

But was it right? What if she was making a terrible mistake? What if Blaize never came to love her as she wanted him to?

Her heart seemed to thud heavily in time with the music as they started out. One foot...pause...other foot...pause. Her legs felt very shaky.

Then the man waiting in front of the altar turned to watch her coming to him, and the dark eyes slashed a straight tunnel between them, blocking out everything else. They fastened on her with intense command, driving her heart faster, pouring strength into her legs, drawing her towards him, step by inevitable step.

No release.

For better or for worse, she was Blaize Callagan's bride. And when Mortimer Stockton handed his little princess to the man who had claimed her, Blaize's fingers curled so warmly around Tessa's that it felt as though they were curling around her heart. *To have and to hold from this day forth.*

The ceremony started. Blaize made his responses in a quiet firm voice. Tessa's voice quavered a little over hers, not because she was nervous or panicky any more, but because she felt so much. And the look in Blaize's eyes when he lifted her veil to kiss his new wife...it had to be love, or something very close to it. His kiss was gentle, tender, very loving.

The reception was a triumph for Joan Stockton. The best of everything, everything perfect. Nothing could have been more right and proper. Particularly the bride and groom, who behaved as though the sun and the stars shone out of each other. Joan even allowed herself a little weep when they departed. That was perfectly permissible for the bride's mother, and, of course, Mortimer was at her side to comfort her.

Blaize and Tessa drove to Sydney...man and wife. Tomorrow they would fly to Tahiti for a two-week honeymoon on Bora Bora. Tonight they would spend at the apartment. Neither of them had wanted to go to a hotel.

"Happy?" Blaize asked softly as they sped along the expressway.

"Yes," she answered. "It was a lovely wedding, wasn't it?"

He smiled at her. "Happy and beautiful."

Tessa privately wished he hadn't said those particular words. It recalled that first weekend they had spent together—a fantasy weekend outside of real life. She wondered if that was how he thought of today's ceremony, a white fantasy. He had her now, all his, for as long as he wanted her. The last pretty bow tied.

No regrets, she told herself.

This was what she wanted, too. Only probably more than Blaize did.

As if to complete the fantasy for her, when they arrived at their apartment, Blaize scooped Tessa up in his arms and carried her over the threshold.

"You didn't have to do that," she half protested.

The dark eyes glowed at her, a warm mixture of deep satisfaction and contentment. "I really do have old-fashioned values," he said, then smiled as he kept carrying her straight into the master bedroom.

"Be a little patient, Blaize," Tessa chided him. "I've got a wedding present for you."

"For me?" He seemed surprised.

"I bought it with my money. All the money I'd saved before I met you." Somehow it was important that he know that.

He set her on her feet but still held her in his embrace, the dark eyes looking quizzically at her. "Tessa, I have everything I want. You shouldn't have spent your money on me.''

''I wanted to, Blaize. Wait here, I'll bring it to you.''

She hurried to the second bedroom where she had hidden his gift in a cupboard. She had had it boxed so he wouldn't immediately know what it was. He had shed his jacket and tie by the time she returned. He shook his head bemusedly as she handed him the gift-wrapped box, all tied up with pretty bows. Tessa waited impatiently for him to open it, hoping he would appreciate the thought.

But he didn't smile when her gift was revealed to him. He stared at the two bottles of yellow-gold wine, a dark frown creasing his brow.

''I couldn't get the '29 d'Yquem,'' she hastily explained. ''It was too expensive. The best I could do was the '45. I thought two bottles...''

She faltered as his gaze lifted to hers, dark torment in his eyes.

''Did I do wrong?'' she whispered, distressed by a reaction that was not what she had anticipated at all.

''Why? Why would you want to remember that night, Tessa?'' he rasped. ''To give me this tonight...''

He shook his head as though in some dreadful inner anguish. ''I've tried so hard to make up for it. I've tried all I could to make you happy with me. I thought...''

The dark eyes searched hers with pained urgency. ''I thought today...it was all right. That I'd made the right decision for you as well as for me. Was I wrong, Tessa?''

''No. No... It was right for me,'' she rushed out with vehement conviction. Her eyes begged a frantic appeal at him. ''I don't understand, Blaize. I thought you liked this wine. I wanted to give you something special that you liked.''

She felt the relief surge through him even before it hit

his face. He stepped forward and swept her into a crushing embrace. His hands ran over her in feverish possession as he rained passionate kisses over her hair. She slid her arms around his neck and pushed her head away enough to look at him.

"Blaize, tell me why you were upset," she pleaded.

His mouth twisted into bitter irony. "Tessa, for me making love with you that night...somehow it went very deep...and when you cried, it made me feel like all kinds of a heel for doing what I'd done. It was only then I remembered about the other man in your life...but I wanted you so much..."

He expelled a long heavy sigh. "When you said you wanted it ended the next morning, I tried to do the decent thing, Tessa, and step out of your life. But I couldn't forget how you'd responded to me. I kept thinking I must have a chance with you...that you couldn't be very deeply in love with your fiancé if you could respond to me like that...even though you cried."

"So you called me up to your office."

He nodded. "And then I realised why you'd let me make love to you. It felt like having my gut kicked in."

"I'm sorry, Blaize. I didn't think you cared about me," Tessa said softly, beginning to realise that his feelings for her ran a lot deeper than she had ever imagined. She reached up and stroked his cheek. "I thought you just wanted a bit of sex on the side."

"I wanted *you*," he said gruffly. "Any part of you that you'd let me have. I thought if I could just stay in your life, given time enough, I could make you mine."

"I am yours," she assured him. "I'll always be yours, Blaize. I love you very much. More than I've ever loved anyone. More than I could ever imagine loving anyone."

It wasn't at all difficult to say those words with his dark

eyes burning with his need for her. Not just need for her body. *Her*...the person she was. Why it was so, or how it was so, didn't matter. She *was* the right one for him. Tessa truly believed that now.

"You love me, Tessa?" he said, half incredulously.

"That's why I accepted your proposal, Blaize. I fell in love with you that weekend on the boat."

He gave a funny little laugh. "As far back as then? You loved me then?"

She nodded.

"You mean I've been sweating blood to get you married to me, and you actually wanted to marry me all along?" he demanded, his arrogant confidence returning in a burst that blew aside all uncertainties.

"Well, I wouldn't precisely say that." Tessa backtracked. After all, it wasn't good for their relationship for Blaize to be too arrogantly confident of her. He might start taking her for granted. "I wasn't sure that a marriage between us would work. I thought I was taking an awful gamble saying yes."

"You thought you were taking a gamble!" He threw back his head and laughed. Then he picked her up and whirled her onto the bed, pinning her down when she teasingly tried to escape him. "I've got you!" he said. "And I'm not letting you go, so you might as well resign yourself to your fate, Stockton," he said with mock severity.

"I'm resigned, sir. Very happily resigned," she returned cheekily. "But you have to call me Callagan, sir. I got married today."

"Yes. You did." He kissed her. "And don't you forget it."

She kissed him back. "I have an excellent memory, sir."

"Tessa darling, you have a lot to make up for."

"I do?"

"Yes, you do. I worked harder than I've ever worked in my life, thinking of a way to put a proposal of marriage to you. I spent the whole of that Sunday convincing myself I had a chance. I was almost sure you hadn't just been pretending to be happy with me that weekend—"

"I wasn't."

"—and I couldn't believe that your responses to me weren't genuine."

"They were."

"But when it came to the point—make or break time—it was still the most terrifying moment of my life."

"You? Terrified?"

"Oh, it was all very fine for you, my darling. I wasn't using you as some kind of fantasy lover who couldn't be accepted into real life. You put me through hell!"

"Would a little taste of heaven help you forget, darling Blaize?" she asked, sliding her hands over him in deliberate provocation.

He growled.

She started to unbutton his shirt.

"You're a witch. You know that?" he accused, busying his hands on a similar exercise. "A provocative little witch who cast a spell on me months ago."

She slid her hands over his bare chest and ran her fingernails over his strongly muscled shoulders. He shuddered. His eyes narrowed threateningly.

"I think I might use one of those bottles of d'Yquem."

"Well, we'd still have one left," Tessa consoled him.

"On the other hand, I don't like to repeat myself."

"Surprise me, then."

He did. In many and glorious ways. Tessa secretly thought to herself that he really was a fantasy lover, but he made it all beautifully real. Ecstatically real. Afterwards, she even felt brave enough to ask him about his marriage to Candice.

"It was good for its time," he replied. "It was what I wanted then. A very active social scene. Riding high. Maybe we would have grown together."

He fanned Tessa's long hair out on the pillow as he thought about it. "I can't imagine I would ever have had with Candice what I have with you."

"And what's that?" she asked.

"We don't need anyone else," he answered simply. "Like that weekend we had on the boat. It was great...just being with each other. And now it's like that all the time for me."

"For me, too," Tessa said softly.

He trailed butterfly kisses around her face. "When did you know that you loved me, Blaize?" Tessa asked curiously.

He gave her a rueful little smile. "Oh, about the time I picked you up to put you in the helicopter. That felt very right to me. This is my woman, I thought. But, of course, I knew you weren't mine. Then the situation changed and I thought I could make you mine. Until you cried that second night...and I couldn't comfort you. Because I was the wrong man—"

"You weren't the wrong man, Blaize." She held his face between her hands, and her eyes glowed all her love for him. "I cried because you made me feel so much, and I didn't think you cared for me at all. It seemed so wrong. But it wasn't wrong at all. It was right, wasn't it?"

"Yes. It was right."

He kissed her deeply in the full knowledge of their love and need for each other.

It was their wedding day.

Dear Reader,

When Sherye opened her eyes and discovered the sexy man in her room was her husband, she considered herself fortunate to be married to such a hunk. Too bad she didn't remember anything about him. Her accident had wiped her memory clean.

Marriage is a serious commitment, as we know. We're committing ourselves to a future with another person without fully knowing them or understanding how they will react in different situations. We can only rely on our judgment of their character.

It helps to know that a man has the same concerns when he goes into a committed relationship. Sometimes it helps to put ourselves in the other's shoes, or as a writer would say, look at it from another point of view.

Writing books about relationships has been such a learning experience for me. It has helped me to detach from my single vision and look at each situation from the other's viewpoint. I've discovered the process to be a very enlightening one.

In this story, Sherye soon discovers that she's not a very likable person. You can understand her confusion as to why she would have behaved in ways that seem so foreign to her own sense of who she is.

I thoroughly enjoyed putting all the parts of this story together and hope that you enjoy it, as well.

Sincerely,

Annette Broadrick

MYSTERY WIFE

Annette Broadrick

This book is dedicated to Tara Hughes Gavin, my editor for eight of the ten years I've been published, for allowing and encouraging me to tell the kind of stories I want to tell in the way I want to tell them. I wouldn't have made it this far without your support.

Thank you, Tara.

Chapter One

She fought her way to the surface, frantically struggling to escape the swirling darkness filled with demons that grabbed and pulled at her, battering her until she thought her skull would burst with the pain. Whimpering from the effort exerted, she forced herself to continue, her terror giving her the necessary strength.

Exhausted from her labors, she managed to open her eyes.

She flinched at the brightness, squinting her eyes.

Diffused sunlight poured through a tall, narrow window draped with sheer curtains, dappling the glistening sheen of highly polished flooring with an abstract pattern of shifting leaves and fingerlike branches.

The pain in her head did its best to consume her, eager to blind her to her surroundings, but she valiantly fought to ignore the invader threatening to suck her back into the nightmare.

She stirred in an attempt to shift her weight, but her body ignored her signals.

Where was she?

Once again she peered around the room, her eyelids heavy and painful, searching for something familiar to give her a clue.

Nothing looked familiar. Nothing at all.

The walls glowed with a soft peach tint. A delicate watercolor hung on one of the walls. A pair of burgundy oversize leather chairs sat on either side of a finely crafted table. An elegant lamp graced the table.

With great care she turned her head, nevertheless paying the price for movement. Wincing, she closed her eyes and rested, wondering if appeasing her curiosity was worth the accompanying pain.

Eventually she opened her eyes once more in order to study the room from her new perspective. The bed where she lay looked wholly out of place with the exquisite furnishings. There was no disguising its utilitarian design. Only then did her gaze move past the end of the bed and focus on the door, its heavy wooden surface broken by a small glass window in its center.

At last she had found something identifiable, which was comfortingly close to familiar. She was in a hospital.

Pleased with her discovery, she allowed her eyes to close as a reward, welcoming the dark relief from the glare of the sunshine. Instead of easing, however, the pounding, clanging beat in her head seemed to escalate.

She forced herself to concentrate on something other than the persistent, mind-crippling pain. *A hospital. I'm in a hospital.*

She began to identify the different areas of her body. Her legs were heavy but otherwise did not ache. She was able to breathe without hindrance. Her arms lay on either side of her body...her right hand felt weighted down. She peeked at her hand and saw the obvious signs of her stay—a drip stand with a tube running down to the back of her hand where it disappeared beneath a gauze bandage. A black machine with a video screen beeped its scrawling message in a steady, monotonous tone not far from her right shoulder.

With her left hand she touched her face and discovered a thick bandage wrapped around her forehead. She must have suffered some kind of head injury, which certainly explained the throbbing, pounding pain that seemed so real she could almost see it bouncing in front of her eyes.

What had happened to her? Where was she?

Voices impinged on her consciousness for the first time since she'd awakened, and she forced herself to listen, hoping to have some of her questions answered. The voices were hushed and feminine, speaking Parisian French. She attempted to focus on what they were saying, but her head hurt too much for her to concentrate. She caught a word here, a phrase there, but she couldn't catch enough to make sense of their conversation. They spoke the language like natives, rapid-fire and sure of their phrases.

She smiled to herself, impressed with their ability, and wondered where they had learned to speak so well. She'd like to commend their teacher for being able to eradicate their Texas drawl, something she'd never been able to accomplish with her own students.

So. She had managed to come up with a few answers. She was in a hospital with French-speaking women nearby. Now if she could only remember what had happened to her to place her in a hospital, she would feel more in control of her situation.

She forced herself to think back, to discover her last memories. The effort needed to pursue her newest line of deductive reasoning made the pounding in her head increase its throbbing beat until it seemed to fill the room, causing the walls and ceiling to waver in time to the beat.

Unable to produce the strength to fight off the waves of pain, she allowed her concerns to slip away, allowed her mind to blank out into a shimmering silver screen of nothingness....

The next time she opened her eyes she felt a new sense of serenity. Although she didn't understand why, she felt safe and protected lying there in the spacious room. She had no more answers now than the last time she'd regained consciousness. Nevertheless, she knew that no one would harm her. How could she know that she was safe? Somehow her subconscious seemed to be reassuring her.

She lay quietly and stared out the window, enjoying the view of the tree outside her window. Springtime. The new green shoots were so delicate and determined. Springtime. Always a time of hope and renewal. She would get better. She would remember. Spring offered the magic of rebirth.... She faded away into a restful, healing sleep.

Hours later a slight noise drew her into wakefulness once again. She was no longer alone when she opened her eyes this time. A nursing sister stood beside the bed, checking the drip and making adjustments. The young woman glanced down at her. When she realized she was being watched, the nurse gave a start, her eyes wide.

"Oh! Madame DuBois," she said in French. "You're awake! Merciful God, we must let your husband know!" The nurse rushed out of the room, leaving her alone once more.

A sense of surprise stirred within her. She lay there, silently repeating what she had just heard.

Madame DuBois?

Her husband?

She tested the words and phrases, repeating them carefully in her mind.

It was no use. Neither the name nor the person meant anything to her.

They must have her confused with someone else. She no longer had a husband.

Why did that thought seem so painful?

She would have to tell the nurse when she returned that there was an obvious mix-up...some kind of mistake had been made. She didn't even know a Madame DuBois. She would be polite, of course. She always tried to be polite and patient with a person's mistake. After all, human beings were not created to be perfect, she often reminded her students. They were created to learn how to experience love and joy and the abundance of life.

So she would explain that she couldn't possibly be Madame DuBois because her name was—

She paused, feeling a little silly. Well, of course she knew who she was, she was just a little confused at the moment. Obviously the pain in her head had something to do with an injury she'd sustained. The constant throbbing was distracting. Her name would come to her. She knew it would. So she was patient and she waited, but nothing came to mind.

Nothing.

After several long inexplicably blank minutes passed, a queasy sense of panic began to form within her, as though trickling through her veins. What was going on? Just because her head was pounding didn't mean her brain couldn't function, did it?

Did it?

The panicky feeling inside her grew.

All right. She reminded herself that it was not surprising she might feel confused. Obviously she had been injured in some way or she wouldn't be in a hospital. All she needed to do was to stay calm. She would allow her mind to drift back, to remember....

She couldn't remember much of anything. Brief pictures without sound—like a silent film running too fast—flashed through her mind without a hint of explanation.

Was it possible she really had a husband, that she was actually Madame DuBois, even though she couldn't remember that name or her life? She squeezed her eyes closed for a moment, the pressure calling her attention to their swollen state. She forced herself to open her eyes slowly and with a certain amount of precision, as though in some way her sight might have an effect on the door to her memories. Perhaps the door had gotten jammed while she'd been unconscious and was now having trouble functioning upon command.

How long had she been unconscious, anyway?

The mystery was too much for her pain-filled mind. This time she actively sought oblivion, where there was no pain or confusion, slipping silently into a darkness no longer inhabited by sadistic, punishing demons.

The darkness now held only a soothing sense of peace and protection.

"Chérie?"

The sound of a deep male voice rumbling softly nearby irresistibly drew her from her place of painless safety, impelling her to seek out the source of the unusual term of endearment.

She opened her eyes.

Muted light from a small lamp nearby cast shadows over most of the tall, lean figure of the man standing beside the bed. The soft glow highlighted his long, tapered fingers resting on the railing. She couldn't seem to draw her gaze away from the sight of his large, capable-looking hands. His grip on the railing had caused his knuckles and the tips of his fingers to turn white. Drowsily puzzled by this obvious sign of tension, she allowed her gaze to wander upward, toward his shadowed head. The light glinted along the side of his face, bringing into prominence the plane of his high cheekbone and strong jawline, leaving his eyes veiled in shadow.

She licked her lips, painfully aware of how dry her throat was. "I—" She paused in her efforts to speak and swallowed painfully. Despite her efforts, she hadn't made a sound.

"Would you like some water?"

There! This time she heard the strain in his voice—his carefully modulated voice. She didn't understand why he had spoken to her in French.

She nodded and watched the graceful movement of his hands as he poured water from a crystal pitcher into a small glass with a bent straw. He brought the straw to her lips and waited while she gratefully wet them.

"How are you feeling, *chérie?*"

"My—um—my head...hurts." Her voice sounded strange to her ears, as though she hadn't heard it in a long while. She had answered him in the same language, but her tongue had felt awkward wrapping around the vowels, as though it were out of practice.

"It's not surprising, is it? You're lucky to be alive."

"What happened?"

He frowned, two vertical lines appearing above the bridge of his aquiline nose. "Don't you remember?"

She heard the surprise in his voice and was almost amused at the idea that anyone thought her capable of coherent explanations about anything. If she knew what had happened or why she was here she would most certainly share the knowledge with the handsome stranger standing so stiffly beside her bed.

As swiftly as her amusement surfaced, it disappeared, leaving her feeling confused and inadequate. She would very much like to have the answers to give to this stern, self-assured male. She felt a desire to impress him with a coherent summary of her present situation.

She frantically searched for something—anything—that might be flitting through her mind at the moment, but the images sporadically appearing were too fleeting to interpret.

"I'm sorry," she murmured after several uncomfortable moments. "I'm afraid I don't remember much of anything at the moment."

Silence stretched between them. She studied his grim expression, wondering who he was and why he was so concerned. She heard her own voice before she realized she had spoken her question aloud.

"What's your name?"

If anything, his expression grew more grim. "Raoul."

A strong sense of pleasure swept over her. "I've always liked the name Raoul," she replied with a tentative smile, then wondered about the medication she was being given. Her slurred words sounded as though she'd been drinking, and for some reason she had a tendency to blurt out whatever thought happened to cross her mind at any given moment.

"You don't know who I am?" he asked after another long silence.

Guess she was going to have to stay after school. She hadn't done her homework. He expected her to know him, she could tell. She tried to placate him with her most charming, conciliatory smile. "Please don't be offended. I mean, it isn't anything personal, you understand." She couldn't believe how difficult it was to enunciate each word. Pausing to gain some control over her tongue, she eventually confessed with a grin, "I don't even know who *I* am."

He didn't seem to appreciate her lame attempt at humor. When he didn't respond, her unruly tongue continued with

"Would I lie to you?" blithely ignoring the fact that she was obviously irritating her visitor.

He stiffened, a move that surprised her, since his ramrod-straight posture had seemed too rigid to be improved upon. "On many occasions," he muttered with poorly concealed bitterness.

She blinked at the obvious explanation for his inexplicable demeanor. This man didn't like her. From what he'd just said, he might have good reason. However, she had a strong impulse to argue with him. She might not know who she was, but she knew very well that she didn't lie. She'd always had an aversion to the idea. Lies could get so complicated. Truth was much simpler.

Impulsively she reached out and touched his hand. He flinched, but didn't pull away. "I'm sorry if I've hurt you. I'm afraid I'm at a distinct disadvantage here. I don't recognize you at all. Are we related?"

She heard a slight hitch in his breathing, but otherwise he gave nothing of his thoughts away. He seemed to be searching her face for some kind of answer before he murmured, "I'm your husband."

No! She could feel the immediate denial rising in her throat and she fought not to betray her reaction. How could she possibly deny their relationship if she couldn't remember exactly who she was? He seemed to be in no doubt as to her identity.

"I see," she responded after a moment, feeling very vulnerable. "So I really *am* Madame DuBois."

"Ah. Then you at least remembered part of your name," he replied with a touch of irony.

"I'm afraid not. The nursing sister called me that. I thought she must be mistaken." Unable to contain her curiosity any longer, she asked, "What is my first name?"

"Sherye."

"Oh! I thought you were using the French endearment."

"It's spelled S-h-e-r-y-e."

She allowed the name to circle in her head, saying it to herself several times. Why didn't it sound familiar? If she'd been called by that name all her life, wouldn't she feel some sense of positive identification when she heard it?

"How old am I?"

"Twenty-six."

She pondered that piece of information. Once again pictures flitted through her mind. "Have we been married long?"

"Six years."

Another surprise. She frowned. "Why, I was just a child when we married!"

The look he gave her was filled with cynicism. "I doubt that you were ever a child, Sherye. Not in the sense you mean. You began modeling when you were eleven years old. By the time we met, you were light-years away from the innocence of childhood."

There was so much new information in that statement that she had trouble taking it all in. Once again bitterness seemed to surround the man who claimed to be her husband. What kind of marriage did they have? She hesitated to ask. When she thought about the rest of his statement, she slowly rolled her head on the pillow in a negative gesture that renewed the pounding in her head.

"I'm not certain why you're so angry with me," she finally said, "but I do know that I couldn't possibly be a model. That you should suggest such a career for me strikes me as ludicrous."

Without a word he turned and walked away. She watched him go and wondered if she'd offended him by arguing with him. However, instead of leaving, Raoul opened a side door she hadn't noticed before and disappeared into another room. He appeared almost immediately with a hand mirror.

He returned to her side and flipped on the lamp beside her bed, then handed her the mirror.

Instead of looking at the mirror, she stared up at the man revealed in the light. Yes, he was very imposing... aristocratic...and no doubt arrogant, as well. His eyes were a dark gray, almost charcoal, surrounded by a heavy fringe of black lashes that in no way detracted from his masculinity.

She certainly had excellent taste in men. Too bad she seemed to have alienated him so badly.

"Aren't you going to look at yourself?" he asked, a strange note in his voice.

Reluctantly she raised the mirror and forced herself to peer at her reflection. If he was trying to convince her that she had the looks of a model, he'd certainly missed the mark. She'd always heard that love was blind, but he seemed more angry than in love. Maybe he just suffered from poor vision.

"Well?" he asked.

"Well, what?" she replied, lowering the mirror and looking back at him impatiently.

"What do you see?"

With almost a groan she forced herself to look into the mirror again. "A pasty-looking face with dark circles around the eyes. The most vivid and eye-catching feature I can see at the moment is the technicolor bruise that isn't completely covered by the head bandage." She made herself meet his gaze once again. "Why? What do *you* see?"

"A face that's been on every major fashion magazine in the Western world. With your wide-set green eyes, high cheekbones, pouting lips and—"

"Pouting," she repeated with a sense of renewed interest. She looked again. After a moment she murmured, "I wouldn't call them pouting, exactly. Maybe they're a little full." She squinted into the mirror, then widened her eyes without blinking. "At least you got the eye color right." She touched her bandaged head. "What did they do to my hair?"

"The doctor assured me he had to shave only a small portion that can easily be covered until it grows out."

She peered at the pale woman in the mirror again before she shrugged. "Well, all I can say is I must have looked considerably better at eleven than I do at twenty-six. What happened? Did I lose my looks and decide to retire at twenty and get married?"

"You didn't intend to retire right away. Unfortunately for your professional plans, your pregnancy—"

"My pregnancy!" His words set off a series of internal alarms, all clanging within her head with earsplitting dissonance. She pushed herself up on one elbow, her head spinning. She forced the next words, carefully enunciating each one. "Are you saying that we have a child?"

He nodded, watching her closely. "Yes. We have a five-year-old daughter, Yvette, as well as a fourteen-month-old son…Jules."

Too weak to stay propped up on her elbow, Sherye sank back onto the bed, but the move merely increased the spinning and whirling going on inside her head. She stared up at the ceiling, trying to find something tangible to hang on to in this strange new world she'd found.

"This is all just too bizarre," she muttered, finally. After another long silence she sighed, nodding her head slightly. "I know what this is. I'm having some kind of a dream. They've got me on pain medication and I'm hallucinating. I'll wake up in the morning and I'll laugh at this whole thing.…" She closed her eyes, tugging the sheet up over her shoulders. She lay there for several minutes, trying to regain her equilibrium.

"Well," she murmured to herself some time later as though she were alone, "this is quite a dream you're having. A husband, two children and a modeling career. If that doesn't win prizes for creativity, it should.''

She drifted off to sleep, glad to be escaping the confused feelings that had swamped her during the telling of this tall nighttime tale. As she drifted off to sleep she muttered, ''Boy, I've got great taste in dream men, that's for sure.''

Chapter Two

Sunlight flooded the room the next time Sherye opened her eyes. She was grateful to discover that the pain in her head was much improved, thank God. Not wanting to take a chance of reawakening the throbbing intruder, she carefully moved her head on the pillow—and saw her visitor from the night before asleep in one of the leather chairs.

She caught her breath, aware that her pulse rate had suddenly gone into overdrive. The man was real...she hadn't dreamed him, after all.

The light in the room revealed her visitor in detail, and finding him asleep gave her a much-needed moment to adjust to his presence, not only in her room but in her life, as well.

The man across from her was Raoul DuBois.

Her husband.

Or so he said.

As far as she was concerned, she had no connection with

Sherye or Raoul DuBois. The names meant absolutely nothing to her. Somehow she would have to deal with her new situation. Now that the pain in her head had lessened, she was feeling more capable of coping with this strange new world she had discovered when she'd regained consciousness.

She took the opportunity to study Raoul DuBois while he slept.

His long, athletically built frame looked cramped in the chair. His head rested at an uncomfortable angle on the back of the seat while his legs stretched out in front of him, one knee bent.

He wore a cream-colored silk shirt with chocolate brown trousers. A matching suit jacket lay across the arm of the other chair. His tie had been loosened and draped drunkenly across his chest.

This man was Raoul DuBois. Her husband, she reminded herself once again.

She shivered, remembering his attitude toward her. She wished she knew more about their relationship. Why had he acted so cold, so aloof, so bitter? Feeling as he so obviously did, why had he stayed with her through the night?

She stirred, restless, wondering if she dared try to sit up. How she hated feeling so powerless! She wanted to take charge of her life instead of passively lying there waiting for the next event to take place.

She had an unquenchable desire to find out more about herself…to find out all the missing pieces of her life and her past. Raoul had mentioned their children, a thought that created so much longing within her that she felt certain if she were to see them again she would remember at least their part in her life. She had always wanted children. She knew that without a doubt, even if she didn't understand exactly how she could have such strong and fixed opinions of who she was.

Take her present situation, for example. She felt just as strongly about who she was not. She knew quite well that she was not, nor had she ever been, a model. If they could be wrong about her profession, they were no doubt wrong about who she was, as well.

Obviously there must be some mistake in identification. She would discuss the mix-up with someone in charge of her case as soon as possible. There was no reason for her to panic. She would stay calm until she could—

As though on cue, the door opened with a soft whishing sound. A slight, trim man wearing a hand-tailored suit entered, closely followed by two nursing sisters. From the corner of her eye she saw Raoul stir and straighten.

"Ahh. Good morning, Monsieur and Madame DuBois. It is good to see you awake, my dear," the man said, striding to the bed and taking her hand. "Your husband has been extremely worried about you, as have we all." He nodded to the other man before returning his sharp-eyed gaze to her. "No doubt you have many questions, which we'll try to answer for you." He stroked her fingers while unobtrusively checking her pulse. "I'm Dr. Pierre Montand. You've been unconscious for several days and under my care since your husband had you transferred to our hospital."

She glanced at Raoul, who had risen from his chair and was running his hand through his thick, dark hair, a move that did more to tousle than to tame. From the doctor's comments she decided that if Raoul had arranged for her to stay in such luxurious surroundings he must care enough about her to want her well tended.

"How are you feeling this morning?" Dr. Montand asked, continuing to monitor her pulse.

"The pain in my head is much better, but I'm very confused at the moment. My memory seems to be in something of a muddle." She smiled at him in an attempt to lessen the appearance of criticism. "I really think there's been some kind of a mistake. Although I can't remember exactly who I am at the moment, I'm positive I'm not Sherye DuBois." She kept her gaze away from the man across the room, not wanting to see his reaction to her statement.

Dr. Montand's gaze sharpened. He gave Raoul a quick glance before returning his attention to her. "You must remember that you've received a fairly severe injury to your head, my dear. It isn't unusual that you may be somewhat confused." Once again his gaze sought out Raoul's, as though checking to see if the man wished to comment. When Raoul remained silent Dr. Montand continued. "I don't think you need to concern yourself with the possibility that your identity has been confused with someone else's. I understand that the police were able to identify you at the scene of the accident from the registration of your car, as well as the papers you carried in your purse. Even if there had been some doubt in the minds of the authorities, your husband recognized you as soon as he saw you."

Sherye looked from the doctor to Raoul, trying to read something in their expressions. If she wasn't who they said she was, what would be their purpose in lying? What she had to decide was whether or not she was going to trust these people to tell her the truth.

"I don't remember the accident at all," she explained with a hint of frustration.

"Which isn't uncommon in cases such as yours. I know all of this is difficult for you. I would like to recommend that you give yourself some time. A trauma of this nature can cause a multitude of problems. A temporary memory loss isn't unusual. Fortunately the mind has marvelous healing abilities. I'll be working with you during your stay here. We have proven exercises as well as counseling techniques that we can implement to assist you in stimulating your memory.'' He released her hand and gently laid it across her waist. ''Just be thankful that you survived with no more injuries than you received.'' He brushed his hand against her cheek. ''You're doing quite well, all things considered.''

She eyed him for a moment, wondering if this was the time to bring up the next item that was bothering her. Why not? If she was losing her mind as well as her memory, she might as well be aware of it now.

''Why is everybody speaking French?''

There was another exchange of glances between the two men, while the nursing sisters stared at her with varying degrees of astonishment and dismay.

After the brief, nonverbal exchange with Raoul, the doctor was the one who answered.

''Yes, I can see how confusing everything must seem to you. Your husband explained that you are an American, but since you've lived here in France for several years, you have a good command of the language.''

She stared at the doctor in disbelief. ''We're in France?'' she whispered, unable to disguise her shock.

''But of course,'' Raoul replied. ''Where do you think we are?''

''Texas!'' she blurted out, then paused, rubbing her head where the ache never seemed to go away, unable to understand why she'd thought about Texas. As soon as she said the word, pictures flashed across the screen of her mind—tall buildings, multilaned highways, azaleas in bloom, the state flag…

''That's a very good sign of your returning memory,'' Raoul pointed out. ''You're originally from Dallas. I understand you lived there for the first ten years of your life.''

The doctor frowned. ''Can you remember anything from that time of your life?''

She closed her eyes in an effort to recall something useful. After a moment she sighed and said, "Just brief pictures, I'm afraid. Nothing helpful."

Once again she looked to Raoul. "Can you tell me about the accident? Were you there?"

Her question seemed to catch him off guard. He hesitated, his body tensing, before he finally answered. "No. You were alone. According to the police investigation, you must have lost control of your car on a sharp curve. The car went over a steep embankment. Luckily you were thrown clear...since the car burst into flames upon impact. A passing motorist saw the flames and stopped. He saw you lying just over the edge of the embankment."

Sherye shivered at the thought of how close she had come to dying. "You're right. I'm lucky to be alive." At least she better understood why her head ached so badly. She must have hit it against something when she was thrown out of the car.

"Here," the doctor said. "Let's get these bandages off and see how your head looks. I'm sure you'll be relieved to know that we only had to shave a small portion of your hair...just the area around the wound. Luckily, because of the length of your hair, your scar will be covered." He smiled at her. "It would have been a shame to destroy that beautiful red hair of yours."

"But my hair isn't—" she began, then stopped, feeling foolish and uncertain. Nothing seemed to make any sense to her at the moment.

Only Texas seemed real to her. Nothing else. Not a husband, nor children, nor France.

The nurses efficiently unpeeled the bandages. The doctor examined the area around the wound, eliciting more than one wince from her. She bit her bottom lip to stop from groaning at one point.

"I believe we can leave the bandages off now," he said after a moment. "I'm quite pleased to see that you are healing nicely." He stepped back so that he could see her face once again. "I know you must feel overwhelmed. All you need to do at the moment is to rest and regain your strength. We'll give nature a chance to work her healing magic. You're really doing very well."

Feeling like a child who had been praised for eating all her vegetables, Sherye allowed herself to drift off to sleep once more, accepting the reassurance that everything would soon be all right.

Four days later she didn't feel quite so reassured.

Although the pain in her head had continued to lessen, none of her puzzling memories could be explained. Nor could she accept the fact that she had absolutely no memories—not even a glimmer—of anything having to do with France, her marriage or her family.

Her body continued to heal, however, and she was now strong enough to move around without help, which gave her some sense of progress. She could at least shower without assistance, as well as take care of her personal needs. Assuming that much control over her life and body was comforting, but her continued lack of memory unnerved her more than she would admit to others.

For the past three days Raoul had come to visit her each day. She felt ill at ease with him, given their circumstances. Her lack of any memory with regard to their relationship gave him an edge that made her uncomfortable. She didn't like having to ask him to tell her about their life together. It wasn't that she thought he would lie to her, exactly, but she definitely felt that she was getting only one side of their story. There was something about his attitude where she was concerned that made her wonder why he was so antagonistic. She found what he wasn't telling her—about her attitude toward him and their children—mystifying. Surely her memories could shed some light on their relationship and perhaps explain his aloof behavior.

She'd been glad yesterday when he'd told her that he needed to leave for a day or so, in order to check in at home as well as his business. According to Raoul, home was a château that had been in his family for over a hundred years. He had explained that they lived there with his widowed mother and a sister who had never married.

His explanation immediately conjured up some kind of foreign movie in her mind, possibly starring Charles Boyer…certainly nothing she'd ever lived.

The doctor had suggested that once she was able to return to the familiar surroundings of home her memory would no doubt become more clear. Perhaps he was right, but at the moment Sherye had no desire to leave the now more familiar safety of her comfortable room and the surrounding hospital grounds.

She wasn't ready to meet more people she should remember but couldn't. Every time she thought about her two children, she panicked. What must they think of a mother who didn't remember them? She kept hoping that she would wake up one morning and every memory would be back in place, plugging the holes in her mind that made her feel so hollow and disoriented. Most especially, she wanted to be able to greet Raoul when he returned with the news that she recalled everything about their relationship.

Now she needed to shower and prepare for a session with the therapist who was working with her. She walked into the bathroom, mentally bracing herself for a routine glimpse into the mirror. She still hadn't grown accustomed to her flaming red hair that cascaded around her shoulders and neck, giving her a strange, unfamiliar look.

She knew that her natural color was a very pale blond, almost white. She'd never worn it down, preferring to keep it pulled away from her face out of her way. She had memories of sitting at her dresser each night, putting it into a loose braid to sleep. The shorter length around her face and the color were all wrong.

When she had mentioned to Raoul that she wasn't a natural redhead, he'd told her that a photographer had convinced her to change the color early in her career to enhance the contrast between her light complexion and hair.

She still had difficulty accepting the idea that she had been a famous model. Sometimes she felt as if she was truly losing her mind. Either that, or she'd been given someone else's memories in some kind of cosmic brain implant.

After showering, she dried her hair, despairing of doing anything with it other than allowing it to fall about her face, framing her pale skin with fiery color. Her eyes seemed to gleam with added color, as well. She closed her eyes, picturing the person she knew herself to be—a slender woman who easily blended in with a crowd. She wore little makeup. In short, she did nothing to call attention to herself.

The seductive-looking woman staring back at her in the mirror was still slender, but the frothy underwear Raoul had brought her seemed to accent her slender waistline and the gentle curve of her hips. The bra was engineered in such a way as to thrust her breasts up and together into a provocative cleavage. The high-cut briefs made her legs seem longer and more shapely.

Raoul had explained that these were her clothes that she had purchased herself. He'd brought them from home. She studied herself in the mirror, trying to see herself shopping for such items, but couldn't. Turning away, she returned to the bedroom and slipped into one of the dresses he'd brought. The color matched the sea green hue of her eyes, its silky texture gliding down her body in a sensuous caress.

After a few quick strokes of a brush through her hair she

headed for the therapist's office, hoping that today would bring some much-needed breakthroughs.

"Ah, yes. You are very prompt, Sherye," Dr. Leclerc, the therapist working with her, said when she paused in the doorway of his office. "How are you feeling today?" He waved her to a chair across from him.

"There seems to be an inverse ratio going for me. The better I feel physically, the more frustrated I become with my lack of correct memories."

He casually clasped his hands on the desk in front of him in a relaxed manner and watched her with a slight smile. "Correct memories?" he prodded.

"You know—memories about living in France, being married, having children. Those memories."

"Instead you are having—what sort of memories, exactly?"

She sighed and leaned back in her chair. "I keep having these flashes of pictures as I drift off to sleep, or sometimes when I first wake up. I keep seeing myself standing in front of a classroom of girls, teaching, although I can't quite recall the subject. Sometimes I'm sitting on a small balcony watching a hummingbird feeding, or gazing at a skyline of tall buildings. I feel as though I live in a large city somewhere in Texas. I want to say Dallas, but I don't know if that's right. One time I was digging in a small garden, planting spring flowers, trimming around my rosebushes and azaleas."

"Is there ever anyone there with you?"

"Only when I'm in class. The rest of the time I'm alone...." She allowed her voice to trail off uncertainly. After a few minutes of silence she added, "Except the name Janine keeps surfacing."

"What does that name mean to you?"

"I see a pixie face with sparkling brown eyes and bouncy black curls as though she's seldom still. She's a

friend...a very good friend. She was there for me during
that terrible time when..." Once again her voice trailed off.
When she met Dr. Leclerc's eyes she was frowning. "I
can't remember, but something horrible happened that I
couldn't face, couldn't handle at all. Janine was there for
me. I wouldn't have made it through that terrible time without her."

"Do you remember the details of that event?"

After several minutes of probing into her thoughts she
shook her head.

"According to your history that your husband was able
to supply for us, you spent your early days in Dallas, so it
isn't unlikely that you are having flashbacks to your childhood."

She frowned. "Perhaps. But I feel as though I'm an adult
in these scenes. So is Janine." She shook her head in disgust. "This is so frustrating! I feel that if I could force
myself to concentrate more, everything would come back
to me." She shifted in her chair. "Besides, none of these
fleeting glimpses have anything to do with France."

Dr. Leclerc opened the file in front of him and thumbed
through some papers. He laid one of the papers aside and
examined it for a moment before asking his next question.

"Has your husband discussed with you the argument the
two of you had the night before your accident?"

She'd been staring blindly past him at a picture behind
the doctor's desk, inwardly probing for possible memories,
when he asked his unexpected question. Her gaze refocused
on him in dismay.

"No," she replied slowly, "he hasn't. He seems reluctant to talk to me about anything relating to our life together. Whenever he visits we generally discuss the activities of my day." She leaned forward in her chair. "Are
you saying that he told *you* about an argument we had?"

She could hear the criticism in her voice, but was unable to disguise it.

"In order to help you, Sherye, it was necessary for me to consult with your husband regarding your relationship within the marriage. He was understandably reluctant to discuss such personal matters, but eventually saw the necessity for it. It is possible that the argument may have contributed to the accident, as well as to your continued memory loss."

She leaned forward in her chair. "What are you saying? That perhaps I don't want to remember anything because of an argument I had with my husband?"

The doctor peered at her over his glasses. "The severe blow to your head," he explained in a patient tone of voice, "could certainly be responsible for your initial memory loss. However, it is the continued absence of all memories regarding any part of your life in France that leads me to believe that you—on some deeply subconscious level— may be blocking any memory that you are not ready to face at the present time."

She stared at him, fighting her frustration at this line of reasoning. "What, exactly, is so painful about being married to a handsome Frenchman, having two children and living in a French château? That sounds more like a fairy tale to me...somebody's fantasy of a dream come true...than a life that anyone would have difficulty accepting."

"Your husband—with a great deal of reluctance, I must say—gave me some of the facts regarding your recent history." He picked up another page and scanned it before he said, "It seems that you had a great deal of difficulty with your second pregnancy and were slow in regaining your health after your son's birth. Although postpartum depression is not uncommon, yours seemed unusually severe, and you—for all practical purposes—rejected the baby and would have little to do with him or his sister after his birth. Instead, you began to stay away from your home for long periods of time each day.''

Sherye stared at the kind-faced doctor in horror, wanting to refute the information he offered so matter-of-factly. She wasn't like that at all! How could she have abandoned a newborn baby and an innocent child? There must be some mistake, but she couldn't begin to understand where.

''Where would I go?'' she asked, hoping that she'd sought professional help somewhere.

''According to your husband, you began to socialize with people you had known during your career as a model.''

''Somehow I get the feeling that my husband didn't approve of my friends,'' she replied with a sigh.

''He said they indulged in frequent partying and he didn't find that he had much in common with any of them.''

''I'm beginning to get the picture,'' she said out loud. To herself she added, no wonder he was so distant with her. From all indications she hadn't been any great shakes as a wife and a complete zero as a mother. ''Did he say why we quarreled?''

''He wanted you to stay home that night.''

''But I ignored him, and went anyway.''

''Apparently.''

''So I drove my car off a cliff to prove my point, that I could do whatever I wanted. That seems a little drastic, don't you think?''

The doctor removed his glasses and pinched the bridge of his nose. ''What I think is that you left home angry. You did not return home that night. You did not contact your family the next day. When your accident was reported you were a considerable distance from home.''

''I'm sure I saw a story similar to that not long ago on television.''

''Sherye—''

"I know, I know, but this whole thing is so preposterous. If it wasn't for the fact that I have actually seen and talked with Raoul DuBois I would think you'd made the whole thing up. Everything is so dramatic. Don't you see? The former model, the aristocratic count or whatever, the scenes, the turmoil, the escape, the crash and then— Nothing. She can't remember any of it."

"Which brings us back to the crux of it all. What do you remember?"

"I've told you what I can. It's all disjointed and hazy. If I had to describe who I think I am, I'd have to say that I'm a very ordinary sort of person. I like to read, I like to work in my garden, visit with my friends, but I certainly don't do any heavy-duty partying...." She paused, then leaned forward, her hands resting on his desk. "Ever since I first woke up in this hospital, I have felt as though everyone is talking about someone else, not me. I don't feel any identification with the woman who ignored her children, partied with her friends and argued with her husband."

Unable to sit any longer, Sherye left her chair and began to pace. "Don't you understand? I can't begin to relate to a woman who behaves in the way you've described. I may have been stripped of my memory—that's certainly obvious—but I still have a strong sense of my own values. I would rejoice at the opportunity to have children and a home, to have a husband who loved me, an extended family who cared about me. Why would I deliberately behave in a way that would guarantee the loss of all that I hold most dear?"

Dr. Leclerc shifted in his chair and cleared his throat. "I believe there is a rational explanation for the facts in this case and your feelings about who you are and the behavior of which you are capable."

Sherye immediately sat in the chair she'd recently vacated. "Thank God. What is it?"

"There is no doubt that you almost died in your accident. In addition, you remained in a coma for more than a week." He paused and peered at her over his glasses, which were perched once more on the bridge of his nose.

"Yes. I understand and agree with that much, anyway."

"There is substantial evidence in the medical field, vastly reported, of what commonly has been described as near-death experiences. In many of the reported cases, the person who was near death later stated that he or she was given the opportunity to review his or her life from a less worldly perspective, in order to decide whether he or she wishes to make any changes. Whether this particular aspect of the phenomenon is true or not is immaterial. The fact remains that many people who have survived a brush with death subsequently have made radical changes in their life-styles...have strongly departed from previously set goals and priorities. In short, in almost every way possible they have become another person."

She eyed him with more than a hint of skepticism. "Is that what you think I've done?"

"What I find pertinent in your case is the certainty you've continued to stress about what you can remember and your strong convictions about morality and acceptable behavior."

"I would like to propose a hypothesis," Dr. Leclerc continued. "What if, as a result of your full-blown career at a time when a child is trying to discover her own identity, you drifted away from your early teachings and fundamental upbringing. You may have set up a deep-seated conflict within yourself that your mind could never quite reconcile. Because of the duality in your nature there has been a continual struggle as to which side would dominate your behavioral patterns."

He held her gaze without effort. "I am suggesting the possibility that the more unlike your early training your behavior became, the more intense this conflict within you became, until you eventually could no longer function.''

''Then you *do* believe the accident was intentional,'' she stated in a monotone.

''Perhaps not consciously, but since no one but you knows what you were feeling at the time, we can't rule out the possibility.''

''How do you suggest I work on regaining my memory?''

''Once you're feeling physically well enough to deal with the emotional situations that are going to occur once you leave here, I believe that confronting your life, placing yourself in more familiar surroundings, beginning a daily dialogue with your husband and family will all help you to recover.''

''You do think I'll remember eventually, don't you?''

He sat there studying her for several minutes before he said, ''I don't know what you were like before the accident, of course, but I feel that I've gotten to know you quite well since we've been working together. You've been under considerable pain and emotional tension, and I believe that you have handled it as well as anyone could. You strike me as a brave, courageous woman who's had to face some very difficult choices while dealing with traumatic events in your life. In my opinion, any retreat from life, regardless of how difficult that life might seem to you at the time, would only be temporary. In answer to your question…yes. I believe that you will regain your memory.''

Chapter Three

A week later Sherye sat near a majestic weeping willow and absorbed the panoramic scene around her. Rolling hills dotted with trees and lined with hedges and stone fences soothed her racing mind while the sound of the splashing water from the nearby fountain gave off a restful chatter.

The garden surrounding her was truly beautiful. The scented flowers added their touch to the day. She took a deep breath, absorbing the pleasing aroma, and waited for her mind to calm.

Raoul had left word with a member of the hospital staff that he would be returning today. She was to be released to his care tomorrow.

Each day of this week she and Dr. Leclerc had worked together in an effort to unlock the door of her memories. The work had been intense and draining, but it gave a sense of purpose. She'd grown accustomed to her daily routine here at the hospital. When she'd heard that she would soon be going home she'd been almost afraid of the next step in her recovery.

The truth was that she felt more comfortable with the doctors and staff of the hospital than she did with her own husband. She felt that at least she had gotten to know Doctors Leclerc and Montand on a limited basis. Raoul remained an enigma.

Just this morning Dr. Leclerc had assured her that she was more than ready to meet this next challenge. He felt certain that once she returned to her home and routine again, she would find some of the missing pieces of her memory.

What had stuck in her mind during their daily sessions was the real possibility that on some level she truly didn't want to remember.

Raoul was the key to many of the answers she needed in order to build some kind of future for herself. Now that she was going home she would be in his company on a daily basis. Since he'd assured the doctors he would cooperate fully in helping her regain her health, she should be glad to be taking this next important step.

Instead she was filled with trepidation to be giving up the sense of security she had slowly gained during her stay at the hospital. She had to prepare herself to face another group of strangers. She was being placed in a position that forced her to trust a man she didn't know, one with whom she had argued and, by all accounts, had walked out on in an anger she didn't understand. In the best of circumstances, the situation would be tense.

She found Raoul DuBois somewhat intimidating, which wasn't too surprising considering the role he played not only in her present recovery but in her life.

She could feel his dislike of her whenever he came to see her. To her his visits appeared to be made out of a sense of duty or obligation…possibly as a penance of sorts.

Perhaps she deserved his disdain and contempt.

Perhaps she didn't.

It was that last thought that gave her the necessary strength and motivation to keep pushing against the closed door in her mind.

She needed to learn everything she could about herself.

She needed to know how she felt about her husband.

Most of all, she had to know the true reasons that there was marital discord.

Raoul had told the doctor about her behavior since her son was born, which could be verified or disproven by others who had observed her actions at the time. If he was telling the truth—and he was intelligent enough to know she would be able to find out easily enough—she wanted to know what had happened between them to make her turn away from him and their family.

She had a hunch that this particular information, even if he told her, would be more difficult to verify.

She didn't like being in such a vulnerable position. Unfortunately there was nothing she could do about it except diligently dig into her head for answers.

Sherye rubbed her head, feeling her thoughts circling around and around inside her brain. She had come outside to enjoy the view, not to search for answers. Once again she swept her gaze across the panorama below her, consciously blocking her mind of any thought other than enjoyment of all that her senses were picking up.

Sometime later she knew she was no longer alone, although she had heard nothing to alert her to that fact. Sherye glanced around and saw Raoul standing a few feet away from her, so close to the willow that a few of the graceful limbs of the giant tree brushed his shoulder.

Feeling as awkward as a schoolgirl with her first beau, Sherye got up from the stone bench where she had been sitting and faced him. "Hello, Raoul."

He hesitated a moment before walking toward her. "You're looking much better since the last time I saw you. How are you feeling?" He paused beside her, his opaque gaze giving nothing of his feelings away.

"Fine, thank you," she murmured politely.

He glanced around the garden, then motioned for her to sit down again. When she did, he sat beside her, careful not to touch her.

"I apologize for not returning sooner. Some unexpected business detained me."

"How is everything at home?" she asked politely.

He raised his brow slightly. "You have remembered something about—"

"No." In a careful voice she went on. "I'm sorry, I didn't mean to imply that I..." She paused, searching for words.

Raoul looked away. "The doctor said it would take time."

"I was sitting here, trying to picture the children. It feels so strange to know I have children when I don't remember what they look like."

"They are doing quite well." He hesitated a moment before adding, "Would you like to see a photograph of them?"

Eagerly she turned to him. "Oh, yes, please!"

He reached into his pocket and pulled out a billfold. "I should have thought about bringing more from home," he said ruefully. "The doctor mentioned that seeing the children might trigger something, so I was concentrating on getting you home so that you could see them."

"I understand," she murmured, wishing that his aloof politeness didn't have such a strong effect on her.

He pulled two photographs out of his wallet and handed them to her. She studied the first one carefully. The professionally posed photo had been taken in a studio and revealed a young girl seated beside a toddler, her arm protectively around his shoulders. Both children had dark hair like their father. She couldn't tell from the photograph the color of their eyes.

The little girl looked very solemn, her eyes large in her face. She wore a ruffled dress that seemed too elaborate for her slight build. The boy seemed to be clapping his chubby hands together. She could faintly see a gleam of teeth in his smiling mouth.

She searched for traces of feeling within her, some hint of maternal love for these two children. Instead she felt as though she was seeing them for the first time.

"Well?" Raoul asked after a moment when she didn't say anything.

Slowly she shook her head. "I'm sorry. I don't recognize them."

He took the photo and carefully replaced it in his wallet without comment. She fought the impulse to ask to keep the images in front of her in order to memorize their likenesses. She knew any request of that nature would be futile, given the care with which he handled the treasured keepsake.

"Didn't you tell me their names are Yvette and Jules?"

"Yes. You said you'd always liked the name Yvette. Jules was named after my father."

She glanced at the second picture, her eyes widening in surprise. This one was a candid snapshot of her. She was leaning against the front fender of a bright red sports car with her legs crossed at the ankle. Her head was tilted back, showing the long line of her throat, and her hair was being tossed on the breeze. Her smile revealed sparkling teeth, while designer sunshades masked the upper part of her face. She wore a white jumpsuit that clung seductively to her body.

Sherye stared at the picture without any sense of identification with the woman.

"Is this a recent picture?"

He looked down at the photograph for a brief moment before glancing away without expression. "I took that several months ago. The car was a birthday gift."

"Was this the car I was driving when..."

"Yes."

She studied the picture of the woman who leaned so self-confidently against the car. This was a snapshot of the woman she faced in the mirror each morning. There was no doubt or chance for a mistake.

Had she really thought there was?

Sometime during the past week she reluctantly had come to accept Dr. Leclerc's suggestion that she unconsciously had blocked out years of her life rather than face the twists and turns it had taken. Regardless of what her subconscious had chosen to hide, she was determined to find out the truth about herself.

She turned to Raoul and reached for his hand. She could feel him stiffen beside her but she didn't let go. "I know this is very difficult for you. I wish I could make all of it easier somehow. I have so many questions and you're the only person who can answer them for me. As much as I know that going home is the next step, I find it a little unnerving to be faced with seeing strangers who are actually members of my family, people who know more about me than I do at the moment."

"I've discussed the matter with *Maman* and Danielle. Despite problems in the past, they have agreed to do whatever they can to assist you in adjusting."

Sherye came to her feet in agitation. She took a few steps away from him before she turned to face him. "What problems in the past?" she asked, her voice shaking. "I hate it when you imply all sorts of things, either with words or your distant manner. What is wrong between us? According to Dr. Leclerc, you told him that the two of us had argued the night before my accident. What caused the argument? Why did I leave? What was said between us?''

Raoul came to his feet, as well. ''The doctor also said that you should not get upset, that it will only retard your recovery. We'll have time to discuss everything that has happened between us once you are fully recovered. Believe me, I am as eager to deal with our relationship as you appear to be, but there's no reason to go into all of that today. I came looking for you to let you know that I'll pick you up in the morning about nine o'clock. We'll be able to talk on the drive home.''

''Is it far?''

''About four hours.''

''You mentioned earlier that you had business to attend to. What do you do?''

''The family owns a winery and vineyards that have been part of our holdings for generations.''

A winery…vineyards. She waited, hoping for some mental image to appear, but nothing happened. With a sigh she turned away from Raoul and looked over the pastoral scene that rolled into the horizon.

''Sherye?''

Reluctant to face him, she slowly turned and looked at him.

''I know that this is very difficult for you. I suppose what I want you to understand is that this situation is equally difficult for me. I'm doing the very best I can to deal with my own feelings at the moment. Just because you don't happen to remember what has transpired between us doesn't mean that none of it happened.'' His gaze grew bleak. ''Sometimes I find myself envious of your memory loss. You see, as badly as I want to I can't forget some of the things that you have said and done. Perhaps I could forgive what you have done to me, but I'm less able to forgive the pain you've caused the children…and *Maman*…and Danielle. I can't forget. I wish to God I could.''

He turned and rapidly walked away from her as though escaping her presence.

The pain Sherye felt as she watched him leave was not caused by her head injury. No, the pain was located in the region of her heart. She ached with the knowledge that she had hurt this man so badly. Only his polite good breeding had restrained his obvious contempt for and disgust of her.

How had her life become such a mess?

Whether the answer was painful or palatable she would be forced to pursue the answers. She offered a brief plea to God to give her the strength she needed to face the mistakes she must have made in her life to have brought her to her present dilemma.

Chapter Four

Raoul couldn't sleep. He'd been tossing and turning in the unfamiliar hotel bed for what seemed like hours, unable to shut out the scenes, the harsh words, the anguished feelings that continued to plague him.

Irritated with himself, he got up and went into the small bathroom off the bedroom and got a drink of water. He could try to kid himself and blame the bed, but he was too honest to accept the excuse. He knew exactly what was wrong with him.

He was dreading the next day when Sherye would be released from the hospital to go home.

He returned to bed and stretched out once again, his mind reliving the past.

From the time he'd received the call from the police reporting her accident, Raoul had been operating in a state of emotional suspension. He'd driven through the night to the hospital where she had been taken. He'd waited beside her bed for her to awaken. When the doctors had realized that she had slipped into a coma, they had warned him there was little more they could do for her.

Despite the rawness of his feelings where Sherye was concerned, he hadn't wanted her to die. Even though there was no chance that their marriage could survive, she was the mother of his children and, as such, deserved the best possible care.

He'd spent two days locating a private nursing hospital where she could receive the very best around-the-clock nursing available. For his own peace of mind he had to do everything in his power to save her.

Each decision had been based on the moment. He had not wanted to give any thought to the future.

Now he had no choice. Sherye was demanding some answers, answers that would immediately reflect the shambles of their relationship.

The irony of her having lost her memory at this time wasn't lost on him. On the contrary, had she been conscious and coherent when she'd been found, he doubted very much that she would have had him contacted. Hadn't she made it clear that she wanted no part of him—except for his money and position, of course? Given a choice, Sherye would probably have called one of the many friends she partied with, and continued with whatever plans she'd had that had precipitated their latest in a long line of quarrels.

Three months ago he'd offered her a divorce and she'd laughed at him. She'd made it clear that she liked her life exactly the way it was and that if he attempted to divorce her, she would drag his name through every scandal sheet in Europe.

Once again Raoul replayed their last scene in his mind.

He'd returned home earlier than usual one afternoon and had found her packing a bag in her room.

Her room.

Yes. Her insistence on moving out of the room they had shared since the beginning of their marriage had been the beginning of the end of their relationship, only he hadn't seen it at the time.

She had been in the last stages of her second pregnancy and very uncomfortable. She had complained that she couldn't rest, that he kept waking her up, so she had moved into the adjoining bedroom.

Once Jules was born, however, she had refused to return to his bed. Eventually they had resumed marital intimacies, but she rarely responded to him and he came to her bed less and less as time passed.

She had become involved with friends she'd known from her modeling days, people who partied more than they worked. At first she had brought them to the château on a regular basis, but gradually she'd taken to spending her time away from home. Whenever he'd attempted to discuss her behavior with her she had brushed him aside, ignoring him.

During that last afternoon he'd refused to be brushed aside. He remembered searching for her....

She was in her bedroom, packing a suitcase.

He leaned against the doorway between their rooms, his hands in his pockets.

"Going somewhere?"

She spun around and saw him. "Oh! You startled me. You're home early. Why?" she asked, tucking a wisp of satin and lace into the bag.

"You didn't answer my question."

She straightened and looked at him. "Nor you mine," she replied sweetly.

"All right," he said. "I'm home early so that I could have a word with you."

She rolled her eyes while she continued to fold resort

wear and place it in the bag. "By all means, say what's on your mind."

"I just received several statements in the mail today totaling charges you've been making. I consider them rather excessive."

"Do you, now? Don't you have the money to pay them?" she asked without looking up, a small smile on her face.

"That isn't the point, Sherye. We've discussed this before."

"I know. Don't you find it a tad boring, darling?" She gave a theatrical sigh. "God knows I do."

"Now it's your turn. Where are you going?"

"Don't worry. I'll just be gone overnight."

He straightened and walked over to the bed where she was busy. "Isn't that a considerable amount of clothing for overnight?"

She slammed the lid and locked it. "Don't worry about it." She turned and faced him, crossing her arms.

"I'd prefer that you stay home tonight, Sherye. I intend for us to talk about how much money you've been spending in the past few months."

"I really don't give a damn what you intend, Raoul. It's too late for me to change my plans." She patted one of his cheeks. "But don't worry, sweetie. I'll be back before you have a chance to miss me. I promise." She giggled. "Then we can have all the talks you want. Won't that be fun?"

"What if I insist on your staying?"

Her mercurial mood shifted into anger. "Why in the hell should I sit around here all day waiting for you to show up and bless me with your presence? It's boring, can't you understand that? I'm sick to death of entertaining your stuffy friends who barely tolerate me...sick of your aristocratic mother glaring down her nose at me and disapproving of every damn thing I do. I'm sick of your mea-

lymouthed sister cowering behind you and your mother,
refusing to stand up for herself and get her own life. I'm
too young to be buried alive in this blasted mausoleum. I
want to enjoy every minute while I can and I intend to do
just that. You aren't going to stop me.''

She grabbed her bag and purse and stormed out of the
room, slamming the door behind her.

He could have gone after her, but what was the point?
Their marriage had disintegrated into a series of stormy
scenes. Whatever love they had once felt for each other
was gone.

By the time he awoke the next morning he knew what
he had to do. He would call her bluff. He would see just
how serious she was with regard to her threat to harm his
reputation.

He went to see a lawyer about getting a divorce.

He'd had plenty of time to think while he'd sat beside
her bed after the accident. The accident really hadn't
changed anything between them. He'd known that once she
regained consciousness all the shared animosity between
them would be there waiting.

A divorce was the only sensible solution.

He'd known his choice would cost him financially, but
he could put no price tag on his peace of mind.

That's all he wanted from all of this now…peace.

However, fate had decreed otherwise—and Sherye had
awakened without any memory of him or their marriage.

During one of his interviews with the doctor he'd been
questioned at great length about her state of mind when
he'd last seen her, about the quarrel they'd had, and
whether or not he thought she had deliberately attempted
suicide.

No matter from what perspective he considered the matter, his answer was no. In the first place, she hadn't been

all that upset when she'd left, merely determined. She'd been like one of his horses—she'd had the bit between her teeth and nothing was going to curb her from doing what she wanted to do.

In the second place, she had no reason to want to die. She had everything she could possibly want, which he could easily verify by the thick stack of charges she'd run up lately. Where other women might have wanted a husband and two healthy children, Sherye concentrated on spending lavish amounts of money on herself...which brought him to his third point. Sherye would not do anything to mar her beauty. Even if she had chosen to do away with herself, she would have found a way to have remained beautiful even in death.

No. The accident had been just that, an accident, caused by the fact that as usual she was driving too fast and lost control of the car. In addition, as usual she hadn't been wearing her seat belt. Ironically enough, that habitual lapse of hers was what apparently had saved her life.

When Raoul had visited the doctor this afternoon, Dr. Leclerc had warned him that he would find some major changes in Sherye's behavior from the woman Raoul had described to him originally.

Raoul had hoped they would be able to prove that she was faking the amnesia. Unfortunately the tests were conclusively negative. She had no recollection of anything that had happened to her since she'd lived in France. For that matter, she had no memories of modeling, living in New York or traveling. The only memories they'd been able to evoke were around her childhood in Dallas, and those were sketchy at best.

The doctor had also mentioned some possible theories for Sherye's new and rather bewildering attitude toward life. She had almost died. Now she was being given a second chance.

Raoul wasn't at all certain that he wanted a second chance with Sherye. No matter what the doctor said, she was the same person who had caused so much grief in his home and his life. He'd been honest with her today. He didn't know if he could forget what she had done. He wasn't even certain he was willing to try.

However, the doctor insisted that she be returned to her home in hopes that the familiar surroundings would more quickly trigger something in her memory. Raoul couldn't deny her the chance to completely recover from her injuries. He could only hope that allowing her to come home wouldn't create additional turmoil for everyone concerned.

With that last drowsy thought, Raoul fell into a deep, exhausted sleep.

Sherye awoke the next morning with a sense of foreboding. She glanced around her, recognizing the familiar room with a relieved sense of safety before she recalled that today was the day she would be leaving the hospital.

She'd grown accustomed to being there. For all practical purposes, her life had begun here in this room, when she'd opened her eyes for the first time after her accident.

Her room had become a refuge for her to return to whenever the intense therapy regarding her lack of memory seemed to be too much for her to face.

In a few hours she would have to leave everything that was familiar and comforting to her. Her sadness wasn't eased by the knowledge that she would be leaving here with a man who was a stranger to her—a stiff, unbending man whose cold aloofness made her feel instinctively guilty without the slightest notion why.

She'd had trouble sleeping the night before, waking time and time again from some vague nightmare feeling of being pursued by ravenous animals.

Despite her anxiety, she needed to prepare herself for her

trip to a place Raoul called home, to meet people she couldn't recall, which included her children.

She felt hopelessly inadequate. She also felt as though she had knowingly and willfully let everyone down. She wished she had more confidence in herself. Surely her years of modeling should give her something from which to draw. Perhaps she hadn't been a very successful wife, but she'd been told that she was a very successful model.

She quickly showered and dressed, wearing another one of the dresses Raoul had brought for her. She must have gained some weight while she had been recuperating. The dress was a trifle snug. Studying herself in the mirror, she objectively noted the changes since she'd regained consciousness—her cheeks didn't appear so gaunt, her eyes had a healthy shine and her skin glowed with a light tan. The ivory silk shift she wore seemed to bring out the bright red of her hair and the green of her eyes.

When she returned to the bedroom she found Raoul standing by the window, looking out.

"Oh! I didn't hear you arrive. You should have let me know you were here."

Slowly he turned away from the window, his hands in his pants pockets. His gaze assessed her from head to toe without giving away a hint of what he was thinking. "I was early," he replied in a low voice. His face could have been carved from wood.

Her heart sank. For an instant Sherye felt the urge to plead with him to give her the opportunity to make amends for whatever she had done to cause him to treat her so coolly. Either that, or to allow her to go somewhere alone to continue her healing process, to a place where she would feel accepted and welcomed.

Of course, she didn't say any of what she was thinking. What good would it do? Instead she walked over to the bed and packed the last few articles that had been lying beside her bag. "I'm ready to go whenever you are." Her voice sounded as cool and calm as his, she was pleased to discover.

"You look tired," he surprised her by saying. "Did you sleep all right last night?" He reached past her and picked up the bag.

"Not really. I'm nervous about leaving here."

He raised an eyebrow. "Why?"

She didn't want him to know about her misgivings, but perhaps he would understand. "I've grown accustomed to being here. The hospital and the routine here are all that I can remember at the moment."

They were standing beside the bed, within touching distance of each other. He scanned her face as though searching for something. A slight line appeared between his brows. "The doctors warned me that I might see some pronounced changes in you since your accident. I'm beginning to see what they meant."

"I'm not certain I understand what you mean."

"In all the years I've known you, I've never seen you nervous or unsure of yourself. Even if you had been, you would never, ever have admitted it to anyone."

His voice hadn't warmed exactly, but his tone was more neutral than she had ever heard him. He sounded puzzled, as though she had presented him with a view of her he'd never seen and that didn't fit with any of his perceptions.

Impulsively she took his hand and said, "Raoul, it would help me so much if we—what I mean to say is…everything is so strange to me right now. I feel as though I woke up in somebody else's body, that I'm trying to live somebody else's life. What's worse, the more I learn of this person I'm being told I am, the less I like her." She looked down at their clasped hands, then up into his narrowed gaze. She almost lost her courage, but realized that she had to try to make him see how difficult all of this was for her. "I know that you're upset with me, but it's very difficult for me to deal with your attitude when I don't know what I have done to cause it. If I could go back and undo whatever actions of mine created the pain you mentioned yesterday that you and your family have suffered, believe me, I would. You said that you wished you could forget. Well, so do I. Unfortunately we're faced with the unfortunate circumstances where I can't remember what you can't forget, and we're going to have to accept that fact regardless of our personal feelings. I know I'm asking a great deal of you, but if we're going to get through today and the rest of the days while I'm working to recover my memory, we're both going to have to leave the past behind, at least temporarily.''

She waited but he didn't say anything, although he seemed to be considering what she had said. With a slight sense of hope, she decided to say it all.

''What I want to ask of you is…would it be possible for us to start over…to pretend we just met? As far as I know I saw you for the first time the night I opened my eyes and found you standing beside my bed. Can we just continue from there?''

She stopped talking when her voice began to shake. She hated feeling so emotional and so out of control. She hated feeling like a supplicant for royal favor. However, she also knew that she couldn't function with so much tension between them. She had to do whatever she could, say whatever was necessary, to effect a truce until her memory returned.

He continued to stare at their joined hands as though he found the sight unusual. Perhaps he did. After a tense, lengthy silence he carefully withdrew his hand from her clasp, put down her bag and moved away toward the window where she could no longer see his face. With his back to her, he said, ''I will do everything I can to accept as bona fide your offer of a truce between us. I'll admit that you have seemed very different since you regained consciousness. However, there's too much between us for me to pretend none of it ever happened. What I will do is attempt not to allow the past to color the present.''

Sherye felt as though a giant hand had just squeezed her chest so tightly that she could scarcely breathe. He had turned away from her but he'd been unable to mask the pain in his voice. She stared at his stiffly held back and for the first time felt as though she'd gotten a glimpse of the man behind the mask. He'd been hurt very badly, she suspected, just as she suspected she knew who had inflicted so much pain on him.

Despite his pain he'd seen that she was well cared for in those first harrowing days after her accident.

Despite his pain he was here today to take her home with him in an effort to help her heal.

Here was a man with deeply held convictions, a man who appeared to love deeply despite unknown—to her—but obvious setbacks. Whatever his feelings for her now, he was doing his best to deal with them without inflicting more of a burden upon her.

Sherye searched for something to say, but her new insight and understanding of the man could not help her to ease the tension between them.

After another prolonged, weighty silence she heard Raoul sigh before he turned to face her once more. His expression was carefully composed, his voice even when he spoke again.

''I will do my best to treat you with the respect you deserve as my wife and the mother of my children while you are in my home. I will assist in your recovery by answering whatever questions you may have in hopes that you will more quickly regain your memory. That is all that I can promise you.''

He stood alone, facing her, much as she suspected he

might face a firing squad—with fearless courage and undeniable dignity.

''Thank you, Raoul. I have a hunch it's more than I deserve.''

They stood there in the spacious room, he by the window, she by the bed, silently acknowledging their truce. Sherye could feel the tension ease somewhat between them. As though released from hidden restraints, Raoul strode to the bed and again picked up her bag. ''Come. We need to be on our way. We have a long drive ahead of us.''

The sunlight that greeted them when they stepped outside gave Sherye a buoyant feeling of hope that the day would bring answers that would ease the ever-present tightness in her chest.

Raoul escorted her to a silver luxury sedan and politely opened the door for her. She sank into the soft leather seat with a sigh, automatically buckling her seat belt, while he came around the car and slid behind the steering wheel.

They pulled out of the long driveway onto a country road. Although it was only midmorning she recognized that she was already feeling weak, which frustrated her. Perhaps it was the continued tension that so exhausted her.

Remembering that he had promised to answer her questions on the drive home, Sherye asked, ''What have you told the children about the accident? Did you tell them I don't remember them?''

''We told them you'd been in an accident. We didn't tell them about your memory loss. There was no need to alarm them more than was necessary.''

''We?''

''*Maman* and Danielle.''

His mother and sister who lived with them.

She recalled that the doctor had told her she had had

little to do with her children. "Do your mother and sister look after Yvette and Jules?"

"They spend as much of their time as possible with the children, of course, but we have a full-time nanny who looks after them—Louise."

"What sort of woman is she?"

"Very competent. She came highly recommended."

Once behind the wheel Raoul had placed shade glasses over his eyes, effectively masking his expression. She turned in her seat so that she could see him in profile.

"What I meant was…" She paused, searching for the most diplomatic way to phrase what she wanted to know. "What sort of person is she? Is she warm and laughing? Does she give them hugs and plenty of affection? Does she play games with them…maybe teach them little songs?"

Raoul gave her a quick glance, frowning. "Louise takes her job quite seriously. The children are well trained—obedient with good manners."

She sighed and straightened in her seat. What could she expect? If she had allowed another woman to care for her children, she couldn't complain about the way they were taught. As far as that goes, they could still be warm, exuberant children who had enough family around them to mask the absence of their mother's attention.

She prayed that was so and vowed to make up for her long absence by spending as much time with them as possible from now on.

"Before we arrive home," she began in a firm voice, "I would appreciate your giving me some kind of idea of our relationship. According to Dr. Leclerc, we quarreled the last night I was home. I also got the impression that you didn't approve of my friends."

This time she kept her gaze straight ahead, suddenly grateful that they were seated side by side so that she didn't have to look at him.

She could hear the tightness in his voice when he said, "I'm sorry that you had to learn of our relationship through a third party. I regretted having to discuss the matter with the doctor, but I understood his need to have some information about your past in order to work with you."

"Yes, he mentioned your reluctance."

She waited, silently reminding him that she was waiting for him to answer her question.

After several miles of silence Raoul cleared his throat. "I'm finding this much more awkward than I had imagined it to be. It's very difficult to discuss what you have said and done in the past when you have no way of knowing whether or not I'm telling you the truth."

Impulsively she touched his shoulder. "When I first regained consciousness I wondered about that, myself, but I feel that I've come to know you a little better now. I find that I trust you to tell me the truth, no matter how disagreeable you find the telling. I've already guessed that my behavior hasn't been anything to brag about. The thing is, I've imagined all sorts of things. It would be a relief to know the truth."

"Yes, but whose truth, you see. I want to be fair with you. However, you've never been one to explain the motives behind your actions so I have no idea why you've done the things you've done. You've refused to discuss your feelings with me. It's as though the woman I fell in love with and married became someone else during your second pregnancy. For the past two years I've lived with a stranger whose inexplicable, erratic behavior has created many problems in our household."

"So our argument wasn't unusual?"

"No. Over the past several months you've been spending a great deal of money without bothering to account for it. You've gone on shopping sprees that were excessive, even for you. You've been moody and unpredictable. Laughing one moment, snapping at someone the next.'' He massaged the back of his neck before he said, ''However, this was the first time you decided to go somewhere overnight.''

''You mean you knew I was leaving?''

''Yes. I found you packing, but you assured me you'd be back the next evening, despite the fact you packed a rather large bag, which made no sense to me. When I questioned you, you got defensive and sarcastic, refusing to answer my questions. I asked you not to go but you ignored me. I decided to face you when you returned and deal with our situation. Instead of your return, I received a call from the police reporting your accident.''

''Did I tell you where I was going?''

''No.''

''Or why?''

''No.''

She fell silent for several minutes before she asked, ''In the weeks that I've been at the hospital I haven't heard from any of my friends. Isn't that unusual?''

''I haven't given the matter much thought. I suppose it is, although we managed to keep a low profile in the papers. Perhaps they weren't aware of what happened.''

''But if I spent most of my time with them, wouldn't they have called for me at home?''

''Perhaps they have. I haven't asked.''

Sherye made no effort to fill in the silence that took over between them. At least she had a better understanding of their relationship, some specifics to go with the generalities the doctor had outlined for her. Unfortunately there seemed to be no one who could tell her why she had behaved the way she did.

After nearly an hour had passed, Sherye said, ''I have no explanations to give about my behavior. All I can do is repeat what I said earlier. I'm sorry for causing so much turmoil in your life. I keep thinking about something the doctor said to me—about second chances.''

He glanced at her. ''What do you mean?''

''Perhaps my accident was God's way of getting my attention and making me aware of my mistakes. Maybe I've been given another chance to look at my life and make some much needed changes.'' She gazed out at the passing landscape before adding, ''Perhaps we have been given the chance to begin again, as strangers, to get to know each other.''

When he spoke, his voice sounded gruff. ''That would be a little difficult, wouldn't you say, considering we've had two children together.''

She could feel the heat in her cheeks as she grasped the implication of his statement. ''I know...at least, a rational part of me acknowledges that you and I have a history together, but at the moment it's difficult to accept the fact that I have shared a life and a bed with you, when it feels as though we met only recently.''

''You needn't concern yourself about sharing my bed. You've had your own room since shortly before Jules was born.''

''Oh.''

''Given the present circumstances, I certainly wouldn't expect you to be a wife to me in the intimate sense. Perhaps I should have reassured you on this point much earlier. I suppose I keep forgetting that you truly don't remember anything about us.'' He glanced at his watch. ''Perhaps you should try to get some rest. We'll be stopping for lunch in little more than an hour. The doctor warned me that you would tire easily and that I should make certain you aren't overtaxed.''

In other words, she thought to herself, he was through answering her questions. Not that she blamed him. Nothing that she had learned had surprised her, but she was depressed to learn the condition of her marriage was as bad as she'd been told to expect.

The reason she was saddened by the confirmation was that she had discovered today that she liked Raoul DuBois. Given his perspective of their situation, she knew that he had handled himself well despite his personal feelings. She was sorry he had such a poor opinion of her, even while she understood why he did.

She adjusted her seat into a reclining position and closed her eyes with a sense of relief. Sleep had become her haven when she no longer wanted to face the life she had made for herself. For a little while she could escape.

Raoul awakened her sometime later. She opened her eyes and blinked, looking around in surprise. From the change in the landscape she realized she must have been asleep for some time.

They were on the outskirts of a village that looked as though it hadn't changed in a hundred years. Enthralled by the sight, she couldn't seem to look fast enough to see everything she wanted to see. Small shops, narrow streets, flowers in bloom…all of them caught her eye.

"Oh, this is beautiful. Where are we?"

Raoul told her the name of the town while he turned into a side street and parked. With his usual grave politeness he helped her from the car and guided her down the sidewalk to a small outdoor café.

A waiter immediately joined them, rattling off a list of the day's specials and discussing the wine list with Raoul.

Once the waiter left, Sherye leaned forward in her chair and asked, "Could you explain something to me?"

He sat across the table from her, still wearing the dark shades so that she couldn't see the expression in his eyes.

"I'll try," he replied.

"Tell me how we met. Help me to understand what drew

us together in the first place. There's so much I don't know.''

As though discussing two other people, he spoke in a matter-of-fact tone of voice. ''You were with a crew doing a modeling shoot on the Riviera. I was there on business. We met on the beach and began talking. You had just arrived, while I was scheduled to leave the next morning.''

The waiter appeared with their orders. While they ate, Raoul continued his story. ''I ended up staying another week, despite the need to return to my business concerns. I went with you each day and watched you work.'' His expression softened and his voice lowered. ''You were magnificent. You knew how to project whatever image necessary to make a man see you as the fulfillment of all of his fantasies.'' As though focusing on the present once more, he shrugged and in a hard voice said, ''You still do.''

Taken aback by his sudden bitterness, she could only ask, ''What do you mean?''

''You play the bewildered amnesiac so well. You've portrayed the woman I fell in love with most convincingly since your accident. I thought she was gone. I had accepted the fact that she had never existed anywhere other than my own mind.'' He picked up his wineglass and silently saluted her before finishing the wine. ''You have quite a gift, my dear. That's the way you ensnare us, you know.''

''I've done nothing, Raoul,'' she protested, sorry to see the grim mask appear once again.

''I know,'' he agreed immediately, surprising her. ''It's all second nature to you.''

When he didn't say anything more, she asked, ''How long did we know each other before we married?''

His cynicism hit her like a winging dart. ''Long enough for you to convince me that your career meant nothing to you in comparison to your love for me. I returned home when you flew back to New York at the end of your assignment. I needed to clear my brain, to try to look at the situation logically...sanely. But I couldn't resist calling you. We talked many times over the next few weeks. I wanted you, but was realistic enough to understand that we came from different backgrounds and cultures.''

Raoul leaned back in his chair and crossed his arms. ''You explained to me how you'd spent your entire life yearning for a home. That you had been raised by a single mother who'd had difficulty supporting the two of you. You finally convinced me that living with me and my family at the château would be a dream come true for you.'' His smile held no humor. ''I allowed myself to become convinced.'' He shrugged. ''And so...we were married.''

''And I set out to make your life miserable forever after, from the sound of things,'' she added.

He looked at her in surprise, taken aback by her unexpected response. ''Not at first,'' he finally said. ''You were very taken with the château. You said it looked like something out of a Hollywood movie. You said you felt like a princess living in a castle.''

Since that was the same reaction she'd had when she'd learned of her life in France, she remained silent. What she wished she could understand was what had caused her to change her mind about her life with Raoul.

The only way she was going to find out was to return to the château in hopes of having her memory triggered by familiar surroundings.

Chapter Five

Sherye didn't know how long they had driven before Raoul slowed the car and turned between two very old stone pillars just off the main road. She straightened in her seat and looked around, hoping against hope that something...*any*thing...would look familiar to her.

After following a winding lane to the crest of a hill, the car topped the hill, revealing a panorama that caused her to catch her breath.

Nestled among a growth of well-preserved trees, the château sat like an old but well-loved dowager, content to watch the passing of time from its comfortable perch halfway along a hillside across the valley from where they were.

"Oh, Raoul, it's beautiful...absolutely, perfectly beautiful," she breathed in awe.

"Yes."

His simple answer gave nothing of his feelings away.

However, his expression spoke volumes of the love he felt for his home.

How could she not remember such a place? she wondered. How could she have spent the past six years of her life here and ever want to leave it, for any reason? Without realizing her intention, she spoke her thoughts out loud with calm certainty. "I have never been here before in my life."

"You mean you don't remember," he corrected her.

"No. I mean that I could not possibly forget something so memorable and striking."

He made no comment, allowing the car to pick up speed once more. They drove for almost twenty minutes before they arrived in front of the château. Leaving the car, Raoul walked to Sherye's door and opened it, then guided her up the steps. He opened the door and allowed her to precede him inside.

The foyer soared upward two stories high to an arched dome, dwarfing the occupants below. Her gaze slowly fell from the ornately decorated ceiling to the stairway that wound downward from the upper floor. She saw a pair of wide green eyes peering down at them from around one of the balusters located in the upper hallway.

Sherye unobtrusively edged toward the stairway without taking her eyes away from the child crouched upstairs. She smiled and in a soft voice said, "Is that you, Yvette?"

The child edged away from the railing, her eyes, if anything, growing larger. Frustrated, Sherye looked over her shoulder at Raoul, who was speaking to a woman in a starched uniform. When Sherye glanced back upstairs, the child was gone.

A pang of loss hit her unexpectedly. Had she been mistaken? Or was her own child unwilling to come greet her mother?

"It is good to have you back with us, *madame,*" Sherye heard behind her, and turned. The woman standing beside

Raoul had spoken. "You are in time to join the others for tea."

Ready or not, here I come, she thought to herself as Raoul took her arm and escorted her into one of the rooms off the foyer. She had a brief sense of connection with the young child she'd glimpsed on the balcony. She felt as alone as the child had looked—alone and uncertain of her welcome.

The room she and Raoul entered was a formal salon from a much earlier and more gracious era. Each piece of furniture was a work of art, each accessory chosen by a discerning eye. She felt awed by her surroundings.

Why, the place should be roped off to visitors! And yet...somehow the room managed to invoke a sense of welcome and comfort to the weary, a soothing source of permanence and peace emanating from it.

"Ah, there you are," Raoul said and for the first time Sherye realized that they were not alone in the room. Two women had been seated in a grouping of chairs and love seats. Both of them stood when Raoul spoke.

There was no denying their relationship to Raoul or to each other. They had the same strong bone structure, similarly shaped noses and eyes. The older woman was dressed in expensive black silk, and her hair—a mixture of silver and black—was swept back from her face into a tidy knot at the back of her head.

Here was a woman who faced whatever life threw at her without flinching. She held her head proudly while she gazed at Sherye without blinking.

The younger woman was similarly dressed in black, but where the color was striking and dramatic on the older woman, on the younger one the color made her skin look sallow. She wore her hair in braids wound around her head in a coronet. She could be anywhere from Sherye's age to thirty years older. Without makeup or any attempt at fashion, she appeared older than her slender build and smooth complexion might indicate. She, too, looked at Sherye without speaking.

"Leandra will have our tea here shortly," Raoul said to the waiting women, while indicating that Sherye could sit on one of the love seats. Her knees had suddenly started to shake and she was glad for the opportunity to sit down before her nervousness was made obvious to everyone.

Raoul took one of the chairs nearby, facing the two women across a low, wide table.

"How was your trip?" the older woman said as though Raoul was alone.

"Uneventful."

Sherye clasped her hands in her lap, not sure what to do or say. She glanced up and saw Danielle looking at her with curiosity, but when their eyes met, Danielle immediately looked away.

A heavy silence seemed to fill the room.

"How are the children?" Raoul asked when no one seemed inclined to speak.

Danielle showed the first signs of animation Sherye had seen in her since they had walked into the room. "They're quite well. I spent most of the morning with them. We went for a walk, and I told them that—" her gaze darted toward Sherye, then away "—their mother was coming home today."

Silence filled the room once again.

Sherye realized that she felt more alone, now that she was at home, than she had all the time she was in the hospital. She could feel the animosity toward her from the two women and didn't have the faintest notion how to deal with it. She felt cut off from the world around her, an unwanted spectator attempting to discover where she fit in to the scheme of things.

The arrival of tea managed to ease the tension that had

seemed to build in the room. There was something almost cheerful about sharing food and drink with others. Raoul continued to talk to the women as though nothing was out of the ordinary about their situation, and they began to relax and respond to him. Feeling more like an invisible observer, Sherye noticed how well Raoul ignored the atmosphere. He appeared comfortably relaxed, voicing his relief to be home.

No one spoke directly to Sherye or included her in the conversation. If this was the way she was generally treated by the family, she could better understand why she'd reverted to the company of old friends.

She was actually relieved rather than more nervous when the children appeared with their nanny.

"Ah, yes, Louise," Raoul said, rising and heading toward where the trio stood just inside the doorway. "Thank you for bringing the children down." Sherye watched him walk over to the young, slim woman with reddish blond hair and attractively large blue eyes, and take the child she held into his arms. A little girl stood just behind the woman, shyly peering around her. Sherye recognized the green eyes and hesitant expression from her glimpse of the child in the hallway earlier. She felt a tug at the tightness in her chest.

"Hello, Yvette," she offered softly. Holding out her hand, she added, "Won't you come here to see me?"

With a dignity far beyond her years, Yvette walked across the wide expanse of rug toward her. Only her expressive eyes gave her away.

Raoul followed Yvette with Jules in his arms.

"Mama!" Jules announced gleefully. The exuberant word triggered unexpected tears and Sherye blinked rapidly in an attempt not to betray her reaction. When Yvette reached her side, Sherye pulled her stiff little body into the circle of her arms and hugged her daughter, feeling the rigidness of her spine beneath her fingers. Yvette suffered the hug but didn't lift her arms in response.

When she allowed her daughter to step back from her, Sherye looked up and saw Jules jabbering to his father with a great deal of waving. "May I hold him?" she asked, holding out her arms. Raoul moved closer to her and started to hand Jules to her, but instead of going to her, Jules clung to Raoul and whimpered.

Raoul's gaze met hers. "Perhaps we shouldn't force him," he said in a low voice. "He will need to get used to you."

"But he knew me! He seemed so glad to see me that I thought—"

"Oh, yes. He recognizes you. He just isn't used to being close enough to touch you."

With those simple words ringing in her ears, Sherye could feel all her hard-won courage to face the consequences of her previous behavior crumble. She couldn't control the tears that filled her eyes.

She turned her head away in an effort to hide her embarrassing reaction to her child's instinctive response to her. She swallowed in an attempt to speak around the lump in her throat. "I see."

As though taking pity on her, Raoul sat beside her so that they were shoulder to shoulder. Jules continued to cling to his father's neck.

Blinking away the tears, Sherye realized that Yvette was watching her intently. She gave her a wobbly smile. "Is your brother shy with everybody?"

Yvette shook her head.

"Are you shy?"

Yvette tilted her head in a way that immediately brought Raoul to mind. "Sometimes."

"Is this one of those times?"

Instead of answering the question, Yvette said, "You're different."

The statement seemed to bounce around the room like an echo. All the adults froze.

"I am? In what way?"

Yvette continued to look at her for a long moment. "I don't know, but you are."

Raoul reached out and tenderly brushed a strand of Yvette's hair off her forehead. "Your mama has been ill for a while, remember? She's better now, though, so she could come home."

Yvette turned her clear gaze back to Sherye. "Did you almost die?"

Sherye glanced at Raoul, unsure of what to say. He answered for her. "The important thing is that she's well enough to come back home." He looked down at Jules, who had released his death grip on his father's neck and was staring at Sherye from eyes as dark as his father's. "Are you going to say hello to your mother, Jules?"

Jules immediately hid his face in Raoul's shirt.

Danielle spoke up. "Would you like me to take them out into the garden?"

"I'll take them," Raoul said, standing. He looked down at Sherye. "Perhaps you could go upstairs and rest for a while. Danielle can show you the way."

"Doesn't she know where she sleeps?" Yvette asked, not missing a trick.

Refusing to start off with evasions, Sherye made an instant decision, instinctively wanting to be truthful with her daughter. "You see, Yvette," she said, taking the child's hand between both of hers for a moment, "I got a bad bump on my head, see?" She pushed back her hair and showed her the area that had been shaved. "Ever since then my memory plays tricks on me. I can't always remember everything that I used to."

"Do you remember me?"

Oh, help! she prayed, still not wanting to lie to the little girl. Sherye cupped her heart-shaped face gently between her hands and asked, "How could anyone possibly forget such a special person like you?"

Yvette's solemn stare seemed to look deeply into her soul. Then she grinned and threw her arms around Sherye's neck. "I'm glad you're home, Mama," she said, immediately backing away as though suddenly shy.

"Me, too," she managed to say.

She watched the tall man walk away from her, leading the little girl by one hand and carrying the boy with ease. They looked so comfortable with each other. Once again she had a flash of being alone and separate from her family.

"Very touching," her mother-in-law said once Raoul was gone. "Perhaps you should have gone into the theater. If I didn't know better, I would have believed you've really missed your children."

"Maman," Danielle murmured, her cheeks glowing.

"I know, I know, I told Raoul that I would accept her presence here," she replied as though Sherye wasn't there. "I'm afraid I'm not as gullible as these men you've managed to wrap around your finger."

Sherye blinked. "I beg your pardon?"

"And so you should, but seldom do. I'm talking about this act you're carrying on, pretending to have forgotten everything. It's most effective, to be sure."

"Maman," Danielle began, "please don't. There's no point in—"

"I know. She's here now." She turned back to Sherye. "I never faulted your intelligence, Sherye, and your ability to survive. It's beyond my comprehension how you were able to find out so quickly about Raoul's plans to divorce you. Now, of course, he must wait until you can—"

"Divorce me?" Sherye repeated in a whisper. She felt as though all the air had been knocked out of her.

"Don't try to pretend you don't know at this late date. You were certainly quick enough on your feet to fake an accident and pretend to helplessness before he could have the papers prepared, signed and filed."

Sherye managed to stand, although her knees were shaking so hard she wasn't at all certain her legs would hold her. "I knew nothing about a divorce."

"So you say."

"I'm sorry that you don't believe me. I'm not faking anything. As far as I'm concerned, this is my first time here. You and Danielle are strangers to me." She knew she had to get away from these people. She walked toward the door, praying that her knees would continue to support her.

"Sooner or later you'll give yourself away," her mother-in-law said behind her, "and you'll be out of here, out of our lives."

Sherye continued through the doorway, out into the foyer and as far as the newel post of the stairs before her knees gave way. She grabbed the post and held on, taking deep breaths. Thinking she was alone, she was startled when Danielle spoke from immediately behind her.

"I apologize for *Maman*'s outspokenness," she said, pausing beside Sherye. "She's been under a considerable strain. We all have."

Sherye straightened and started up the stairway on sheer determination and willpower. "She has every right to say whatever she wishes," Sherye replied. "This is her home, after all."

She could feel Danielle's gaze on her but she needed all her concentration to place each foot on the next riser.

"Yvette is right. You're different."

Sherye gave a tiny shrug. "I wouldn't know," she said indifferently. At the moment all she wanted to do was to lie down before she collapsed. When she finally reached the top she paused to catch her breath, gripping the rail.

"Your room is down this hallway," Danielle said.

Taking a deep breath, Sherye followed her.

Danielle opened one of the doors and stepped aside. "It's just that we love Raoul so much. It's been so painful to watch him deal with everything and not be able to do anything to help."

Sherye paused in the doorway and looked at her sister-in-law. Standing this close and in better light, she could see that the woman wasn't much older than she was. She couldn't be more than thirty. With her dark eyes and creamy complexion she could be very attractive. Sherye wondered why she dressed so severely and wore her hair in such an unflattering style.

"Thank you for showing me to my room," she said quietly.

"Dinner is at eight. We generally meet in the salon at seven-thirty."

"Thank you." Sherye closed the door and leaned against it, exhausted.

The room before her had been decorated in gold and white, with touches of royal blue. Once again she was reminded of an earlier era, where massive furniture did not shrink the size of the room. A large four-poster bed with a canopy that matched the drapes and spread stood at one end of the room, facing a fireplace. Floor-to-ceiling windows filled with leaded panes let in the light. She made her way across the wide expanse of carpet to the windows and looked down at a formal garden that stretched out toward a thick stand of trees.

She saw Raoul seated on a stone bench beside a fountain. Yvette leaned beside him, her elbow on the bench, her chin resting in her palm, listening attentively to him while Jules stood in the shelter of Raoul's knees.

She didn't bother to fight the tears that slipped down her cheeks. She had been counting on this day for so long. Dr. Leclerc had been so certain that her memory would be jogged once she returned home.

Nothing looked familiar.

She hadn't expected her mother-in-law's anger to be quite so aggressive. She hadn't expected to be accused of lying. Even more unnerving was the news that Raoul planned to divorce her.

She turned away from the window, unable to handle looking at a family that she would lose so soon after she'd found them. All her life she had yearned for a family of her own. She and Janine had often talked about—

Janine?

Her heart gave a sudden thump in her chest. There was that name again. The doctor had suggested that she was a childhood friend. Perhaps she was, but there was more to it, wasn't there? They were still friends.

Sherye closed her eyes in an effort to see Janine more clearly, to picture her surroundings, but all she got for her efforts was a pounding in her head.

Why did some memories seem to pop up without rhyme or reason, while others refused to surface, no matter how strongly she wanted them?

She hated the position she was in. If only she could remember why Raoul wanted a divorce. Of course the news shouldn't have surprised her. They had separate rooms and went their separate ways. She was obviously unhappy living here and after meeting her in-laws she had a much better understanding of why.

Yes, a divorce was probably the best solution. The problem was she didn't know where she would go or what she would do, particularly if her mind continued to play tricks on her. No doubt Raoul had decided to wait until they'd arrived home to tell her about the divorce in the hope that, once home, she'd suddenly remember everything and could discuss the matter intelligently.

He hadn't asked her if she remembered anything when they'd been having tea downstairs. As perceptive as he was, he hadn't needed to verbalize a question whose answer was obvious to him.

She didn't know how she was going to be able to face all of them again over dinner, but she had very little choice. In the meantime, she would rest.

After removing all but her underwear, Sherye slipped into bed, deliberately seeking oblivion from a cold and bewildering world.

Chapter Six

Sherye woke to shadowed light. For a moment she felt disoriented, unable to place where she was or why she was there. The wide, comfortable bed was nothing like the hospital bed she'd grown used to during the past few weeks. She lay still, allowing her gaze to wander around the large, high-ceilinged room with its opulent furnishings.

Was this how Sleeping Beauty must have felt, waking up after a hundred years? Nothing looked familiar to her, and for an agonizing moment she thought her memory had deserted her.

Then she remembered the events of her homecoming. She was at Raoul's château. She'd come upstairs to rest…now she remembered.

She propped herself up on her elbows to get a better glimpse of the clock. The hands pointed to a few minutes past seven. If she didn't hurry, she'd be late meeting everyone downstairs before dinner.

The rest had done her good. She felt restored, with no sign of the headache that plagued her whenever she grew tired or was under pressure to force a particular memory. At least she had time to shower and change before returning downstairs to meet her family once again.

She sat up in bed before she realized that she didn't know whether or not her room came with a bath. She hadn't taken time to explore when she'd come up earlier. There were two doors in the wall opposite. Perhaps one of them led into a private bath.

She slipped out of bed and silently crossed the floor to one of the doors. When she opened it she discovered not a bathroom as she had hoped but another bedroom. Despite the drawn drapes she could make out a figure asleep in the bed. How strange. Who else would be sleeping at this time of day?

The figure on the bed stirred and she froze, several realizations hitting her at once.

She'd been mistaken about the time of day. It was no longer evening, but morning…and the figure in bed was Raoul, sound asleep.

His movement had disarranged his covers and her startled gaze took in the fact that he slept nude. Only a small corner of the sheet covered most of his groin area, revealing a part of his bare hip and the long muscled length of his hair-covered leg.

Drawn to him as though by some magnetic force, Sherye moved on silent feet to the side of the bed. He looked much younger in his sleep without the lines that bracketed his mouth and marked his forehead. His dark hair fell across his forehead in a boyish way and her fingers tingled with the strong desire to brush it away.

She resisted the impulse. Instead she took the opportunity to study the body of the man she knew intimately, if only she could remember.

His body was tanned as though he spent considerable time in the sun without his shirt. Only the small lighter stripe across his hip gave her a clue to his natural color, which was still darker than her own. His skin tanned beautifully, all golden and sleek. She wished that—

His arm unexpectedly snaked toward her and he caught her by her shoulder, pulling her down onto the bed beside him. Caught off guard, she tumbled onto the bed in a graceless heap, embarrassed to have been caught looking at him. She had started to apologize when she noticed that his heavy-lidded eyes were scarcely open. He was still more asleep than awake.

"Mmm," he muttered in a wordless sound of satisfaction just before he wrapped his arms around her and tugged her against his bare body. Without a pause he rolled until she was beneath him on the bed, his thigh snugly tucked between hers.

"I've missed you," he murmured into the side of her neck, his lips brushing against her skin.

Sherye's heart pounded against her chest as she faced the situation that her curiosity had created. Raoul cupped her breast in his hand, lazily drawing his thumb across the lace-covered tip. His body pressed against hers, leaving her in no doubt of his early-morning arousal.

Her body seemed to come alive, vigorously reacting to the sudden onslaught of sensation. Somehow in all the movement her arms were securely wrapped around him and her fingers—as though unconnected to any thought—lightly examined the smooth expanse of back muscle, causing a ripple of sensation to run over him.

She tried to think clearly but her brain had gone dead and her sensory organs had taken over. She felt as though tiny electrical charges were going off all over her body, sending urgent signals.

Muttering something beneath his breath he shifted until

his lips found hers, then he seemed to take complete possession of her in a searing, mind-numbing kiss that promised her some passionate consequences if she didn't do something to stop him.

The problem was that she had no desire to stop him. Not now. How could she have thought him cold or aloof when the bedclothes must be singed and smoking by now by her heated response to him?

He nudged her mouth open and slipped his tongue inside, lazily exploring before he began a pulsing rhythm not only with his kiss but with his thigh that pressed firmly against the apex of her thighs, until she automatically pushed against him in a rhythm of her own. She felt like a victim of spontaneous combustion. All she wanted was to draw him closer and closer to the flaming center of her need.

Suddenly he stiffened and jerked his head up, staring down at her in shock. His eyes had darkened with passion, but now they were open fully and he was seeing her as though for the first time.

Like a man suddenly confronted with a deadly snake, he jerked away from her and rolled, coming up on the far side of the bed, his back to her.

"What the *hell* do you think you're doing!" he growled between clenched teeth.

"I—uh—" The change was too abrupt for her to get her mind to function properly.

"You must think you still have some control over me to try this one, Sherye! It won't matter how many times you seduce me, nothing's changed between us. Nothing."

Horrified that he thought she'd come into his room to deliberately— She moaned, his words sufficient to douse all the flames that had been started moments before. "No. I didn't mean— You see, I—"

Grabbing the sheet and twisting it around him, he turned and faced her once more, his gaze running up and down her body with a look of contemptuous lust. "Well, I see the trip must have been a success. You've regained your memory and hope to do everything in your power to erase mine." His gaze lingered on her breasts and she immediately crossed her arms in an attempt to shelter her body from his cold stare.

She shook her head, her hair tumbling around her shoulders and down around her face. "I'm sorry. It was inexcusable of me, I know, but I—I woke up and I didn't know where to find the bathroom, so I opened the door and I saw—" She dropped her head, wishing she could disappear without a trace. Never had she felt so humiliated.

He didn't speak. Nor did he move. She couldn't look at him, nor did she have the necessary nerve to get up and walk out of the room wearing no more than her lacy underwear, which revealed more than it concealed.

When he finally spoke, his voice sounded tired. "There's no reason for you to apologize. I was dreaming and I thought you were part of that dream, that's all."

She glanced up and saw that he was once again wearing his impassive expression, revealing nothing. She kept her gaze on his eyes, not wanting to visually explore the body that had been giving her so much pleasure only a short while before.

"But you're right. I had no excuse coming in like that, invading your privacy."

He stood, looking dignified and regal despite the fact that only a sheet protected him. He nodded toward a door and said, "We share a bath—through there."

There was nothing she could do except gather her courage and her dignity and walk across the room to the door he had indicated. Just as she opened the door he said, "Have you discovered anything—or anyone—that looks familiar to you?"

She could feel her face flame at the memory of how close

they had been to making love despite the fact that she didn't remember him at all. Unable to speak, she managed to shake her head before closing the door behind her.

This room must have been added at a much later date, or perhaps it was a dressing room that had been converted, because the bathroom fixtures were quite up-to-date and very luxurious. In addition to a whirlpool tub that could seat two quite comfortably, there was a large, glass-walled shower and a long marble counter with double sinks.

She might have moved out of Raoul's bed but she continued to share the intimacy of a bathroom with him.

Their encounter had shaken her, revealing a sensuous nature she hadn't realized she had. She rubbed her fingertips across her lips, feeling the slight puffiness caused by his passion. She traced her mouth with the tip of her tongue, tasting him, and shivered at the remembered sensation of him lying on top of her, his leg thrust between hers as though claiming what he knew was his.

She shook her head in an effort to shake off her memories and her embarrassment at her abandoned response before she turned on the water in the shower, adjusted the temperature and pressure, then stepped inside. Her skin was unusually sensitive while she soaped her body in a fruitless effort to forget how he had felt pressed so intimately against her. Was this how she'd reacted when she'd first met him, all weak and trembly, wondering what his lovemaking would be like?

He hadn't said, but she guessed that they had made love soon after they had met. Had their lovemaking convinced her to forget about her career in order to be with this man? If so, what could have happened to make everything go so wrong between them?

After she finished her shower, Sherye dried herself with a thick, overlarge towel before she returned to her room. By the simple process of elimination, the only door she hadn't tried must be her closet. When she opened the door she discovered a walk-in dressing room with two long rows of clothing for all occasions. The back wall was filled with shelves upon shelves of shoes of all colors and styles.

She was shocked by the amount of obviously expensive clothing and accessories. No one could possibly need so much. From the looks of things she wouldn't need to buy anything more until after the turn of the century.

Sherye searched through the clothing, looking for something simple to wear. By the time she'd looked through both sides of the long closet she faced the fact that there was no such thing.

Each piece of clothing she touched was specifically designed to call attention to the wearer. The shift she had worn yesterday was the most unobtrusive item in her wardrobe. She frowned. She certainly couldn't continue to wear the shift every day.

With a sense of the inevitable, she grabbed one of the outfits and put it on, more interested in getting something to eat rather than how she looked. Now that she was awake, her stomach was letting her know that she had missed dinner the night before.

She sat in front of the vanity to do something with her hair. She'd finally grown accustomed to the color over the past few weeks and no longer received that sharp jolt of unease whenever she happened to look into a mirror. She brushed her hair until it lay smooth, then in a practiced twist of her wrist coiled it into a neat knot at the nape of her neck. Unfortunately her hair didn't want to stay neatly coiled. Wisps of hair sprang around her face, determined to rebel.

After a light coating of lipstick she felt ready to face a new day.

Nothing like sleeping around the clock to make you feel like a new person, she thought, following the hallway to the stairway. *Or a passionate kiss from your handsome husband first thing in the morning to get all your juices flowing!*

When she reached the bottom of the stairs she looked around, wondering where she would find the kitchen in a place like this. She had a sudden picture of twenty-five or thirty men all dressed in white with tall, floppy hats racing around preparing food in a giant kitchen. Hadn't she seen that in a movie once?

Her biggest problem was believing that any of this was real—the château, Raoul, the children, the inflexible matriarch. Somewhere deep inside her lurked the inescapable belief that at any moment she was going to suddenly wake up to find herself back home in Dallas, having fallen asleep on the couch from watching a late-night movie and overslept…running the risk of being late for school. There would be—

Late for school?

Once again she saw the same picture of a classroom filled with teenage girls. She clung to the picture, trying to understand. She focused on a blackboard that was actually green, and saw handwriting—hers—conjugating French verbs.

She taught French?

She smiled to herself. That made sense in a surrealistic kind of way. If she taught the language, then she would be able to speak it fluently, and understand it, as well. No wonder she had been impressed with the Parisian French spoken by the nursing sisters.

Feeling as though she was finally making some kind of progress in her search for her own identity, even if it made absolutely no sense in her present environment, Sherye went in search of some coffee.

The first door she opened looked as if it was used as a

study. She made a sound of frustration and was closing the door when a voice spoke behind her.

"Good morning, *madame.* You are up quite early this morning."

With relief Sherye faced the housekeeper and smiled. "I'm afraid I slept through dinner last night. So I was hoping to find some coffee this morning."

"But of course. Breakfast is already set up in the dining room."

"Unfortunately I'm having a little trouble *finding* the dining room, which sounds strange, I'm sure."

"Not at all, *madame.* Monsieur DuBois has already explained to us about your head injury."

Sherye wondered what, exactly, he'd said. From her tone, the housekeeper sounded as though she thought the head injury had caused her to misplace a large portion of her brain, as well. Come to think of it, she wasn't far off. Her memory bank certainly had gotten jiggled around, if not completely erased.

She followed the older woman through a doorway that led into another hallway. Maybe she should make a map of the place so she could find her way around.

The dining room was in keeping with the rest of the house in that the furniture looked as though it belonged in a museum and the room was tastefully and richly furnished.

She also discovered that she wasn't the first one in the household to be searching for coffee. Danielle stood with her back to the room, facing the sideboard. She was filling her cup with a hot, aromatic liquid whose scent lured Sherye onward.

Danielle wore a tan shirtwaist dress, another unfortunate color choice that did nothing for her skin tones. Sherye waited until Danielle had set the coffee carafe down before speaking.

"Good morning."

Danielle whirled in surprise and faced Sherye with widened eyes.

Sherye glanced over her shoulder, convinced an ax murderer must be hovering immediately behind her to get such a shocked reaction. "Is something wrong?"

Danielle flushed a brilliant scarlet. "Uh—no. That is— I've never seen you up this early before," she stammered.

Sherye smiled at the other woman and nodded toward the tempting array of food on the sideboard. "I managed to sleep through dinner last night and woke up hungry as a bear this morning." She walked over to the buffet that displayed croissants and brioches, fruit juice and coffee. "Ahh! This looks wonderful." She filled a plate, poured a cup of coffee, inhaling the aroma with undiluted pleasure, and sat down across from the other woman.

"Raoul said that you were sleeping so soundly he didn't want to disturb you," Danielle said defensively, as though hearing an implied criticism in Sherye's comment.

"He was probably right. I don't remember rousing at all during the night."

Danielle kept her eyes on her plate and ate without saying anything more.

Sherye did the same. Since she wasn't much of an early-morning person anyway, she found the silence soothing. Danielle, on the other hand, appeared uncomfortable, giving Sherye brief glances before looking away to avoid making direct eye contact. Since she couldn't think of anything to say that would make the woman more comfortable, Sherye mentally planned her day as though she were alone.

She was on her third cup of coffee when Danielle finally met her gaze, her expression puzzled. Sherye smiled at her in hopes of putting her more at ease. The smile must have encouraged Danielle because she finally spoke, her voice soft and hesitant.

"I've never seen you with your hair pulled back like that. It makes you look very different."

Sherye touched the coiled mass of hair at her nape before she remembered how she was wearing it. Now that Danielle had called her attention to the style, Sherye realized that she had tried to wear it this way in the hospital but hadn't been able to keep it pinned back. In the following weeks it had grown enough to stay in place except for the short pieces around her face.

She had put it up unconsciously this morning out of some forgotten habit while her conscious mind had been focused on reliving the embarrassingly intimate scene with Raoul.

"I found this to be a comfortable style," she admitted. "Although you're right. Hairstyles can make a big difference in how a person looks."

It was only when the other woman's face flushed once again that Sherye realized Danielle thought she was making pointed remarks about her own choice of hairstyle. She almost groaned out loud. She hadn't meant anything by the comment, but how could she explain without making matters worse?

Sherye chose to let the moment go and continued to enjoy her coffee. She was admittedly surprised when Danielle spoke up after another lengthy silence between them.

"Raoul told us over dinner last night that you've been spending hours every day in therapy trying to regain your memory." Her voice was so soft that Sherye had to strain to hear her.

"That's right," she agreed in as pleasant a voice as possible in an attempt to encourage her shy sister-in-law's efforts at conversation, even though she didn't particularly care to be the subject of the conversation.

"You can't remember anything?"

With a sudden sense of recklessness, she grinned. "Actually, I do have memories, but they really can't be rationally explained unless I could prove that I'm not Sherye DuBois.''

Danielle almost choked. She set her coffee cup down, coughing, unable to take her eyes off Sherye, who continued to grin at her, encouraging her to share the humor in her comment. After a moment Danielle returned the grin, with a soft chuckle. ''You're joking, right?'' Her eyes filled with amusement.

Sherye was struck by the change in Danielle. She looked years younger, almost youthful. Sherye was delighted to see such an abrupt change caused by her attempt to defuse the seriousness of what had happened to her.

Danielle suddenly sobered, her expression stricken. ''I'm sorry. I didn't mean to laugh at you.''

''It's okay. I guess it was a silly thing to say, under the circumstances.'' With a lightness she didn't feel, Sherye gave an airy wave of her hand and said, ''Be my guest and laugh all you want.''

Danielle shook her head, obviously embarrassed once again. ''I can't imagine you thinking you're not Sherye, that's all. There are obvious changes in the way you wear your hair and your lack of makeup, but you can't hide your features, the shape of your chin, that sort of thing. If you weren't an only child, perhaps you might be able to pass yourself off as your sister. Otherwise...'' Her voice trailed off into another puzzled look. ''If you don't think you're Sherye, who do you think you are?''

Sherye paused for a moment, trying to decide what to say. She was pleased that she had somehow broken through Danielle's reserve. She decided to tease a little, despite the accuracy of what she said. In a pseudosolemn tone of voice she intoned, ''A teacher from Dallas, Texas.'' Her tone invited Danielle to enjoy the humor.

Sherye was delighted when Danielle erupted into a new round of giggles. She covered her mouth as though to obstruct the flow, which only seemed to make the laughter worse.

Sherye knew her statement sounded absurd under the circumstances and she began to laugh, as well. When she paused to draw breath she added, "I even know what I teach—French!" which immediately sent both of them into another round of choked laughter.

Raoul walked in as they were tapering off, his expression somewhere between shock and utter bafflement. Sherye had hoped to avoid him this morning, but in her enjoyment of getting the opportunity to visit with Danielle she'd lost track of time.

He walked over to the sideboard, shaking his head. "I can't believe what I'm hearing. As I was coming down the hallway I was convinced we must have company. The two of you sound like a couple of schoolgirls, giggling over secrets."

His remark was close enough to the truth that their gazes met in acknowledgment of the nature of their discussion... which set them off again.

Sherye was also enjoying seeing Raoul in a more relaxed atmosphere. He seemed pleased to see his sister enjoying herself, just as he seemed puzzled when he looked back at Sherye.

Whatever her relationship with Danielle in the past, she must have behaved differently toward her today.

Well, if so, that was too bad. She was growing rather weary of trying to live up to some unspecified form of behavior. For the first time since she'd awakened in the hospital she discovered that a lack of memory could be a sort of liberation from the past. She was free to behave in any way she wanted. What difference did it make, anyway? Even though he hadn't bothered to tell her, Raoul was already planning to divorce her. He'd made it clear that he didn't see any future in their relationship, so why should she attempt to work so hard not to incur his displeasure?

"If you will excuse me," she said to Danielle with a quick glance at Raoul, "I'm going to go visit the children." Before either of them could respond she left the room, feeling as though she'd set off a bomb and wanting to escape before it exploded.

Chapter Seven

Once again Sherye had to explore the château before she found the rooms where her children spent most of their time. The area was easy enough to find once she returned upstairs and listened for the sound of young voices.

She tapped and waited until Louise opened the door before she entered her children's domain. She wasn't certain who was the most surprised to see her—Louise or Yvette.

Her daughter sat at a small table eating, while Jules was in a high chair, obviously being fed by his nanny. Louise looked perfectly composed, far from the way Sherye felt. She felt like an outsider, hoping to be included in a highly selective club.

Louise was the first one to speak. "Good morning, *madame*. May I help you?"

So polite. Obviously she made a very good example for the children, but did she have to appear so cold? Perhaps she only behaved that way around her employers. Sherye sincerely hoped that the woman showed some warmth and friendliness to her two charges.

"I came to visit," was all Sherye could think of to say. She stood just inside the room and looked around.

A small frown appeared between Louise's brows. "I'm afraid the children are still at breakfast. Perhaps if you'd like to come back later—?"

Sherye displayed her most confident smile to the woman. "Oh, I don't mind helping with breakfast," she replied, walking past the woman and sitting across the small table from Yvette.

Yvette's eyes had grown wider during the conversation between her mother and her nanny. As soon as Sherye sat down, Yvette quickly stared down at her bowl of hot cereal.

"How are you this morning?"

Yvette glanced up through her thick lashes. "Fine."

"Did you sleep well?"

This time Yvette's gaze went to Louise before she nodded.

Meanwhile Jules had begun babbling again while beating his spoon on the tray of his high chair. Sherye grinned at him. "You're looking quite rested, little one. Would you like me to feed you?"

He bounced, giggled and waved the spoon. Sherye held out her hand and he gave the utensil to her. Before long she was making a game out of his food and Yvette was giggling at her silliness.

Louise had gone into the other room, leaving Sherye alone with the children, for which she was grateful. By the time Yvette and Jules had finished their meal they seemed to be more relaxed in Sherye's presence.

"Now what do you usually do?"

"We get dressed and when the weather's nice we go outside," Yvette responded.

"That sounds fun. Where are your clothes?"

Yvette hopped off her chair and headed toward the door where Louise had gone. Sherye cleaned Jules's face and hands and lifted him from his chair. "My! You're a big fella, did you know that? You're going to grow up to be a tall, strong man just like your papa, aren't you?"

Jules had gotten over his shyness with her and willingly came into her arms. He patted her cheek, touched her ear and talked to her in his very special and to her totally incomprehensible dialect.

Sherye smiled and nodded as though she understood and agreed with every word. It didn't matter. He was talking to her and beginning to accept her presence. She would spend as much time as possible with him until she could understand everything he said.

She hugged him to her, inhaling the baby smell of talcum powder, freshly laundered clothes and warm skin. Her heart seemed to swell in her chest with joy. She'd always loved children. When she was growing up she'd laughingly planned to have half a dozen or more. Unfortunately things hadn't worked out that way. She'd given up hope that she would ever—

Sherye paused, wondering where those thoughts had come from. When nothing more came, she shrugged and shook her head. She didn't have time to think about her memories and lack of them at the moment. She had an exciting day planned—to learn her children's routine and to become an integral part of their lives.

They went outside until time for Jules's nap, then Sherye offered to read to Yvette until lunchtime. Yvette gave her one of her favorite books and listened with shining eyes while Sherye read to her.

Sherye spent the morning with the children and, together with Louise, supervised their lunch. When it was time for Yvette to rest and for Jules's afternoon nap, she gave each of them a hug and a kiss, promising to come back later.

Their hours together had made a significant difference in the children's behavior toward her. She had played games with them and made up stories—enlisting Yvette's help in the creative process. She'd found gentle ways to tease them and was delighted to witness Yvette's awkward attempts to tease her in return. Yvette's giggles at Sherye's reaction touched a wellspring of contentment somewhere deep inside.

She found the children endearing and came away with a sense of well-being that had been absent in her life. For the first time in a long while Sherye felt good about herself, as though she had finally accomplished something worthwhile.

She entered the dining room smiling to herself at some of Jules's antics. What a little clown he was. Sherye was already in the room when she became aware that Danielle and her mother were already there. All right, here was another test, one she was determined to pass. *Think pleasant thoughts, set an example,* she reminded herself as she nodded to both of them and sat down, placing her napkin in her lap.

She turned to Raoul's mother. "I know how strange this request must sound to you, but under the circumstances I'm afraid it's unavoidable. What would you like me to call you?"

The woman blinked, stared at her for a moment, then nodded regally. "My name is Felicity. Of course, Raoul and Danielle—"

"Would never use your given name," Sherye finished smoothly, determined that she would not call this frosty—and unquestionably rude—woman *Maman.* "May I have your permission to call you Felicity?"

Taken aback by Sherye's forthright request, the older woman hesitated for a moment, then nodded.

"Thank you." Sherye turned next to Danielle. "I have a favor to ask of you."

An apprehensive expression crossed Danielle's face. Sherye could see her steel herself. "Of me?" she repeated timidly.

Oh, boy, I'm coming on too strong. It was because she was nervous and trying to compensate by sounding self-assured. *Take this one step at a time,* she coached herself. *You can't turn things around overnight. This is going to take time and you've got plenty of that.*

Sherye smiled at Danielle. "Yes. I'd like to go to town but I don't have any transportation at the moment. Besides, under the present circumstances I'd probably become hopelessly lost. I was wondering—that is, if you have some time in the next few days, if you would mind taking me to town."

Once again Sherye was painfully aware of being the outsider, and she watched Danielle and Felicity exchange glances. Felicity suddenly showed a great deal of interest in her salad fork, while Danielle slowly met Sherye's patient gaze.

"You want *me* to take you to town?" Danielle repeated carefully, seemingly convinced that she had misunderstood Sherye's request.

Sherye gave an inward sigh and nodded. "I just need a few things. There really isn't a rush, of course."

Danielle looked around the room and down at her plate before she finally answered. "I don't have anything planned—that is, if you'd like—this afternoon would be fine."

Sherye let go of the breath she'd been unconsciously holding. "Oh, good. I'll jot down a list so I don't forget anything." She looked at each of the women, experimenting with a neutral topic of conversation. "The château is breathtaking in its beauty and design. You must be very proud of it.''

Both of the women stiffened and looked away from her.

Oh, no. What now? Sherye waited but when neither one of them looked up or made an effort to respond, she grew impatient. ''What? What did I say? What's wrong?''

''You've often referred to it as a prison or mausoleum.''

Here we go again. She tried a light approach. ''The blow to my head has obviously improved my appreciation of classic architecture.''

One of the staff brought in their lunches and the three women ate their meal in silence. Sherye felt unbearably uncomfortable but forced herself to deal with her almost ungovernable need to bolt from the room.

By the time she had finished her meal, Sherye had developed a whale of a headache. No wonder. Tension had crept into the room, filling even the corners until she wanted to scream. No one made an effort to break the silence and she was at a loss to find a topic that didn't contain hidden land mines.

It was really too bad. She'd felt so good this morning, certain of her progress toward establishing healthier relationships with her children.

Perhaps she expected too much, she reminded herself. Just because she had no memory of these people did not mean that they could forget some of the things she must have said and done.

She fought the urge to blurt out apologies for her past behavior. She wanted to reassure them, to explain that she had changed, but she knew that would be pointless. What she would have to do was show them that the changes in her were real. Hopefully they would some day accept that, for whatever inexplicable reasons, she had experienced a major shift in her personality.

As soon as they finished the interminable meal Danielle

placed her napkin beside her chair and nodded toward Sherye. "Why don't we meet in the foyer in half an hour? I'll have my car brought around."

Although she had made no comment regarding the arrangements, Felicity made her attitude clear. She was suspicious of Sherye and of her motives.

Sherye could hardly blame her.

Nevertheless, there was so much that she didn't understand about the household and the routine. So many things that she wanted to ask about, but discovered an unexpected shyness.

She'd wanted to ask if Raoul ever joined them for lunch. She felt awkward that she knew so little about her husband's routine. Since no place had been set for him today, she decided to wait and ask him the next time she saw him.

She'd gained the impression that the two of them did not spend much time together. Actually, she was relieved...or at least, she should have been. From every indication, she and Raoul did not have a very close relationship.

Since he was practically a stranger to her, she couldn't be bothered by that knowledge. She'd been surprised at her own reaction to the news that he planned to divorce her. A relationship she didn't remember was ending before she'd had a chance to salvage it. She'd felt dismayed.

The bewildering question to her was why now did she feel so strongly that she wanted her marriage to work when her past behavior had shown a distinct disregard for her husband and his family?

Puzzling questions with no answers. She felt as if there was a swarm of bees buzzing around inside her head, making her dizzy and driving her to distraction.

Getting away for a while would help, she was certain. Anything would be better than the present oppressive atmosphere.

She went upstairs and, after painstakingly searching,

found a dress that she felt was more or less her style and changed into it. After checking the time, she quickly ran a comb through her hair and hurried downstairs so that she wouldn't cause Danielle to wait for her.

As soon as Danielle saw her come down the stairs she turned away and went out the front door, leaving it ajar for Sherye to follow. Not a great beginning, but at least Danielle had agreed to go. Wasn't that a start?

She found Danielle waiting in a late-model sports car, its sleek lines and bright metallic color unexpected for someone as quiet as Danielle. The woman had hidden depths. Sherye was encouraged to think she might—with enough patience—eventually reach those depths.

"Hi," she said in a casual voice. She opened the passenger door and crawled inside. "I hope you didn't have to wait long," she added, fastening her seat belt.

Danielle shook her head and made some noncommittal sound as they started down the long driveway.

"I like your car."

"Thank you."

"Did you choose it yourself?"

Danielle glanced out of the corner of her eye before asking, "You don't think it fits my personality, do you?"

Nothing like a hint of hostility to add richness to the occasion. Sherye caught herself counting silently to ten, gave her head a tiny shake and replied, "I don't really have an opinion of your personality, Danielle. The most I'm guilty of at the moment is attempting to make conversation, that's all."

They rode in silence for a long stretch, a silence that Sherye refused to break. Instead she admired the countryside as though this was the first time she'd seen it. At long last Danielle said, "I'm sorry." She seemed to be at a loss for words. In a sudden burst she said, "I realize I'm oversensitive. It's just that—" Abruptly she stopped speaking.

Sherye waited. When Danielle didn't say anything more, Sherye decided to push her luck with Danielle by prompting in a quiet voice, "It's just that—what?"

Danielle shook her head without looking at Sherye. Danielle's tenseness showed in every line of her body. When Sherye made no more attempt to draw her out, Danielle once again blurted out what she was thinking.

"I guess I'm having trouble adjusting to the difference in you."

Ah. Now we're getting somewhere. "In what way?" she asked casually.

"In the past you've always ignored me."

Whatever she'd been expecting, that wasn't it. "Ignored you!" she repeated slowly. "Why?"

Danielle shrugged, keeping her eyes on the road. "Oh, I understand. After all, we don't have anything in common. You're a famous model, while I—" Once again she came to a complete verbal halt as though anything she might add was self-evident.

Sherye felt sickened at being given another glimpse of herself. "How dreadful," she said in a low voice, feeling ashamed. "I've been going around bragging about being a famous model and ignoring my husband's sister? How embarrassingly rude!"

After a brief silence Danielle offered, "See? This is what I mean. It's your reactions that seem so different."

Sherye made a face at her faint reflection in the glass window. "Maybe the blow to my head knocked some sense into me," she replied with irritation at herself. "All I can say is, it's about time!"

Danielle chuckled, sounding more relaxed. "I must admit that you're much easier to talk to now."

Sherye leaned her head on the headrest and sighed. "I'm not at all certain I want to regain my memory if I'm going to discover that I've been playing the role of Queen Bitch of France.''

Danielle burst out laughing and after a moment Sherye joined her, finally seeing the humor in the exchange. If nothing else, they had managed to lighten the mood of their afternoon outing, which was a relief.

Once again Sherye felt that she had managed to pass a tough—because it was so nebulous—test.

When Raoul arrived home later that afternoon he found Felicity alone in the salon, working on her embroidery.

''Ah, there you are,'' he said, walking over and brushing his lips against her cheek. ''What are you doing sitting in here all alone?'' He glanced around. ''Where's Danielle?''

Felicity sniffed. ''Sherye complained over lunch that she had no transportation and demanded that Danielle drive her into town for her usual round of shopping.''

Raoul's jaw tightened. ''I'll take her to town tomorrow to get a car. Danielle shouldn't have to play chauffeur.''

''Exactly what I told her, but you know Danielle. She's always trying so hard to please everyone and ends up letting them run all over her. When I pointed out to her that she was just allowing herself to be used and she certainly wasn't responsible for the fact that Sherye had so carelessly destroyed her car, Danielle insisted there was no reason she couldn't help. She's so protective of you. She probably thought if she could entertain Sherye that you'd have an easier time of dealing with her once you got home.''

Raoul rang for tea before he sat in his usual wingback chair. ''I thought the two of them were getting along quite well at breakfast. I'll admit that I was surprised when I came downstairs this morning to hear them laughing together.''

''Well, they certainly weren't laughing over lunch,'' Felicity replied with a sniff of disapproval.

When the tea tray was brought in, Raoul poured each of them a cup, then sat back with his.

"Did Sherye say how she'd spent the morning?"

Felicity looked up from her own cup, her eyes snapping. "She didn't have to. I know what she was doing. She insisted on spending the entire time with the children."

Raoul lifted his brows. "All morning?"

"Yes. She totally ignored their routine. I could hear how excited the children were becoming while they played outside. She showed no sense of decorum. Instead she seemed to encourage them in their childish behavior."

He hid his smile behind his cup. "I don't suppose there's any real harm in that."

"Of course there is. She's just using them, and it's the children who are going to suffer for it in the long run because they'll think she's being sincere in wanting to become part of their lives. Of course, I see through her. I always have. She's trying to convince you not to continue with your plans for a divorce by pretending she's forgotten the past. She's hoping you'll forget it, as well."

Raoul thought about her remarks, weighing them, before he responded in a mild tone. "I might agree that there's possibly some truth in what you say if I'd given any indication to Sherye that I was contemplating divorcing her. However, I've never discussed the subject of divorce with her since the accident."

"Why not? Why shouldn't she know that you've made up your mind—finally—to get out of this ridiculous arrangement?" After a moment she added without looking at him, "Besides, I mentioned the divorce to her yesterday and she didn't seem all that surprised."

Raoul froze, his cup halfway to his mouth, his amusement gone. "You mentioned the divorce to her?" he asked in a carefully neutral voice.

"Yes, I did," she replied, filled with self-righteousness.

"She needs to know that you are no longer a fool who will continue putting up with her outrageous behavior."

Raoul fought not to show his irritation with his mother. He understood how many times Sherye's actions had hurt and embarrassed his mother, but she'd had no business discussing their personal business with Sherye, particularly under the present circumstances.

He set the cup down on the small table beside his chair. *"Maman,"* he began patiently, "there was no reason for you to discuss the matter with her. Until she regains her memory she—"

Felicity gave him a disapproving look. "Just what makes you think she has any intention of suddenly regaining her memory, when it's to her definite advantage to continue playing this helpless, pitiful role she's chosen?"

"You know, *Maman,*" he said, determined to stay calm, "she could have faked the amnesia without resorting to her abrupt attitude change."

"Of course, but it wouldn't have been nearly so convincing or effective. Sherye has always known exactly how to behave to get what she wants. She knew that her leaving when you asked her to stay would provoke you into taking steps to end the relationship. It's no wonder that she faked the wreck, faked the blow to the head, faked the amnesia..."

He shook his head and she paused in her recital of Sherye's latest transgressions. "The blow to her head was very real, let me tell you. I saw the wound and it was a nasty one. It easily could have killed her. She was very fortunate to have regained consciousness at all." He took his time refilling their cups before he continued. "I also believe her amnesia is equally real. I was there, *Maman.* I saw how she behaved. For one thing, she didn't believe she was Sherye DuBois. When we discussed who she was, she kept denying it."

Felicity stared at him in surprise. "Why in the world would she deny such a thing?"

"The doctor believes that while she was in a coma she somehow restructured certain events from a deeply subconscious desire—a yearning, actually—to escape her present life-style. He believes that those dreams became more real to her than the life she presently leads."

Felicity sniffed, shoving her needle into the material with short jabs. "Sounds ridiculous to me."

"Perhaps, but her new behavior supports the idea that she may truly wish to make substantial changes in her life. Spending her morning with the children, suggesting that she and Danielle spend time together this afternoon—all of this appears to me to point out some obvious shifts in her priorities."

"Obviously she's managed to impress you," she grumbled.

Once again his sense of humor surfaced. Raoul smiled. "Oh, I don't know, *Maman*. I don't think I'm all that easy to impress."

"We'll see."

He'd been home almost an hour when Raoul heard the front door open. Feminine laughter made it clear to him that Sherye and Danielle had returned, obviously in good spirits. There was a rustling of packages before he heard Danielle instruct one of the staff to take their purchases upstairs.

The two women appeared in the doorway. Raoul stood to greet them and Felicity gasped. "Danielle! What in the world have you done to your hair!" Her sewing slipped out of her lap unheeded and fell to the floor.

Raoul's gaze went to Sherye, who had a decidedly guilty look on her face. Then he glanced at Danielle and felt a small shock of surprise. He'd never seen his sister look quite so vibrant. Danielle's cheeks bloomed with color as she approached them. She raised her hand and lightly brushed her fingers across her cheek in a nervous gesture.

Her coronet of braids was gone. Her hair had been drastically shortened until it feathered in wisps around her forehead and ears, like a pixie. Shortened, her hair had an unexpected tendency to curl, softening her features and giving her a gamine look. Her eyes, always her best feature in Raoul's mind, seemed more noticeable, perhaps because they were shining with anticipation. She glowed. There was no other word for it.

"Do you like it?" she asked shyly.

Raoul glanced around at his mother. It was obvious she hadn't recovered from the shock of her daughter's drastic transformation. Danielle needed reassurance, and he could see that his mother was too taken aback to say anything.

He moved toward his sister, smiling, and took her hand. He raised it to his lips. "You look smashing. What a clever idea to make a change."

"Well, I got the idea this morning from something Sherye said."

"I knew it!" Felicity exclaimed. "I knew you wouldn't have done anything like this without someone forcing you to—"

"Oh, no! Sherye didn't force me in any way. Actually, I brought the subject up. I was the one who mentioned that I was thinking about experimenting with a new hairstyle. She just went along to the shop with me to give me a little extra courage. It was Pierre who suggested that I had the features to wear this style." She turned around and Raoul could see how the cut flattered the shape of her head. He could hear the hint of anxiety in her voice when she asked, "Do you really like it?"

Raoul glanced at Sherye, noticing that she was taking no part in the conversation. Instead she stood quietly by, watching the scene without comment. He returned his attention to Danielle. Still holding her hand, he gave it a gentle squeeze and said, "Yes, I do. Very much."

He stepped back and gave his sister an all-encompassing look. "Do I detect that you are wearing something new, as well?"

Color filled Danielle's cheeks. "Sherye happened to see this in a window we were passing and suggested that it looked like something I might enjoy wearing." She spread her hands along the skirt of her coral dress. "Since we weren't in any hurry, we went inside so I could try it on." She gave a nervous chuckle. "I must admit that I've never worn anything like it. The skirt is shorter than I'm used to wearing." She tugged at the pleats that fanned out around her. "It's probably too short."

Raoul smiled. "On the contrary. The men will appreciate the generous view of your shapely legs, Dani. I agree with Sherye. That particular color looks very becoming on you. You made a wise decision." He motioned to the grouping of sofas and chairs. "Why don't the two of you join us? We'll have more tea brought in."

Raoul waited until the women were seated before he said to Sherye, "You should have mentioned to me this morning that you wished to go into town. There was no reason to insist that Danielle take you."

"Oh, but she didn't, Raoul!" Danielle said. "Insist, I mean. I had nothing else planned to do this afternoon and Sherye wanted to see about—" She paused, looking uncomfortable. "Well, I suppose she can tell you...." She trailed off, her color heightened.

"Tell me what?" he asked abruptly, looking at Sherye without bothering to disguise his suspicions of her behavior.

This was not the time she would have chosen to have this discussion. Nor did she like the idea of having a marital discussion in front of Raoul's mother and sister. However, she saw no way to get around the matter. It was obvious that Raoul found nothing unusual about their lack of privacy.

Smothering a sigh of frustration, Sherye said, "While I was looking through my closet today I discovered that I have nothing casual to wear here at home. I want to be able to do some gardening. I find it very soothing and relaxing. I mentioned the idea to Yvette and she was excited about the idea and wanted to help me. I also discovered that she didn't have anything appropriate to wear, either. I decided to see what I could find for us to wear and surprise Yvette."

"Gardening?" Felicity asked faintly.

Sherye smiled. "Yes. I enjoy working with flowers and keeping a garden healthy." She paused, suddenly feeling confused. "Surely that isn't unusual, is it?" She looked around at the people watching her. "I remember gardening. I remember how much pleasure I get from it. Surely I—" She stopped, feeling as though she'd said or done the wrong thing again.

Felicity looked over at Raoul without comment. He ignored the look. "Tell me, Sherye," he asked, "how was your visit with the children today?"

Feeling as though this was a trick question, she studied him for a long moment before she quietly responded, "I enjoyed it very much."

He glanced at his watch. "It's almost time for Louise to bring them down to see us."

More tea arrived. Raoul sat back and quietly observed the interaction among the three women in his household. From his mother's expression he could see that she was still a little dazed by the changes in Danielle.

Now that the general attention had moved away from her, Danielle looked much more relaxed. She was animatedly telling Felicity about something she'd bought, and had lost her self-consciousness. Raoul took his time about studying the changes in her. He was really quite amazed. The combination of a new hairstyle, a brighter color and younger dress style seemed to take several years off her, leaving her looking vibrant and very attractive.

Whether the two younger women were willing to acknowledge it or not, he knew that Sherye's influence today had helped to create the changes in Danielle. She was the one who had first spotted the dress Danielle wore. She was the one who had convinced her to try it on, or, as Dani might say, encouraged her to try it.

He leaned back in his chair, pondering the ramifications of what he was witnessing. For years his sister had shown little to no interest in her looks or in her style of dress. If anything, she had seemed to go out of her way to be as unobtrusive as possible.

In the past Sherye had ignored her, dismissing the idea of a friendship with his sister, claiming that they had absolutely nothing in common. He hadn't tried to persuade her to change her mind because he tended to agree with her. His only request was that she show his family respect. To a great extent she had ignored them completely.

So what had brought on this new attitude of friendliness? Was his mother right, and she was trying to make sure of her standing in the family?

Now that he was thinking about it, he realized that Sherye was wearing something that looked out of character for her—a simple shirtwaist dress and low-heeled shoes. With most of her hair pulled back, leaving only escaped curls framing her face, she looked very young. Almost innocent.

While he sat watching her, Sherye glanced past him. He saw her expression change from one of social politeness into one of warm pleasure. He blinked, surprised at the change in her. He couldn't remember ever having seen her so animated since she'd regained consciousness. Raoul glanced around to see what had caused the transformation.

Louise had entered the room with the children.

Today Jules's sturdy legs carried him immediately to Sherye, his arms stretched out, while he babbled something incomprehensible. Laughing with obvious delight, Sherye scooped him up onto her lap, oblivious to the wrinkling effect on her clothes. She gave him a hug and murmured something too low for Raoul to hear from where he sat. Whatever it was made Jules giggle.

Yvette came directly to Raoul, hugged and acknowledged him with a kiss on the cheek, then immediately broke into an animated description of her morning with her mother.

A sudden sense of unreality swept over him and for a brief moment he had a flash of empathy for Sherye's dilemma when she seemed to have awakened in another world.

Had he been in the habit of fantasizing, the scene before him couldn't have been closer to what he could have wished for his family—Danielle looking young and pleased with herself, Sherye playing with their son, Yvette bubbling with plans she'd made to spend time with her mother.

Only *Maman* deliberately held herself aloof from all the changes. Perhaps she was feeling the same sense of confusion he was experiencing. How had Sherye managed to create such a difference in their family during one twenty-four-hour period in their lives?

What had caused such a radical change in her?

More to the point, how long would the change last?

Chapter Eight

Four weeks later Raoul stood at the window of his office at the winery, gazing out at the long rows of the meticulously kept vineyard, thinking about the changes that had taken place in his home since Sherye had returned.

The sound of children's laughter rang through the château.

Danielle had met a young man who seemed to spend an increasing amount of time visiting the château.

Maman had actually complimented Sherye about something over dinner the night before.

He'd never seen Sherye so happy.

Sherye's happiness was the most bewildering of all to him. Although she hadn't seemed to regain anything of her lost memories, she appeared content to spend each day enjoying her life.

Only with him did she maintain a polite distance.

After that first morning she had never ventured into his

bedroom. If anything, he got the feeling that she did her best to stay out of his way.

He remembered the day he took her to buy another automobile. She had strongly resisted the idea until he had pointed out to her that other members of the family might not find it convenient to provide her transportation whenever she felt the urge to leave the château.

She had given in, but had refused to consider any of the expensive sports models she'd been drawn to in the past. Instead she had found a sedan that she felt would be more practical when she wanted to take the children with her.

Although he still saw many changes in her, Sherye's stubbornness hadn't lessened in the slightest.

He had bought the car she wanted, fully expecting her to change her mind within a week. Instead she appeared delighted with it, installing an infant's seat for Jules as well as a safety lift seat for Yvette.

Sherye continued to spend most of each day with the children, until Louise had approached him wondering if he still wanted her to oversee them. Since he hadn't been certain how long this new phase would last with Sherye, he had assured Louise that her services were still needed and appreciated. He had suggested that she learn to enjoy having more free time.

Raoul had discovered something about himself today. He didn't know how it had happened, or when, because the change had been so gradual. He probably wouldn't have become aware of it even now if the attorney he'd consulted hadn't called him earlier in the day with regard to the status of the divorce.

He heard himself tell the attorney that he would have to get back with him and quickly hung up.

The truth was, he no longer wanted a divorce. The revelation had stunned him.

What he wanted was his wife.

Her flamboyant, shallow behavior in the past had effectively and relentlessly killed any of the feelings he'd had for her. Or so he had thought. However, he'd seen no sign of that behavior since her accident. Perhaps the close brush with death had frightened her enough to cause her to grow up a little and to appreciate what she had.

Whatever the reasons for her change, Raoul had discovered a disquieting fact—once again he was becoming more and more attracted to the woman he'd married, and he didn't know what to do about it.

How did a man begin to court the woman he'd been married to for six years? How did he go about convincing her that he wanted her back in his bed? How did he admit that she had managed to convince him that the changes he'd seen in her were real and long lasting?

He had to do something soon. The tension that he felt whenever they were together couldn't be entirely his imagination. She was just as aware of him as he was of her. Of course, there had always been a strong chemistry between them. The chemistry hadn't been enough for him, though, once she began to ignore the children and spend most of her time with her own set of friends. Now he would have to rethink the relationship. He would have to build on what had drawn them together in the first place.

Turning, he walked over to his desk and picked up the phone, irritated by the prickly realization that he felt like an inexperienced boy calling for a first date.

Sherye sat back on her heels and brushed her gloved hand across her forehead where perspiration had gathered beneath her straw gardening hat. Yvette was on her knees beside her, energetically pulling weeds, while Jules was busy nearby making hills and valleys out of the rich loam for his brightly painted wooden cars.

She smiled at the sight. Her children looked like little

urchins rather than the elaborately scrubbed and dressed miniature adults she'd been shown all those weeks ago when she'd first arrived home from the hospital.

She loved the change in them. Even Louise had commented on how happy they appeared, which had surprised Sherye. To get Louise to admit that anything Sherye had done was positive was a major accomplishment on Sherye's part. Nowadays the nanny didn't appear to be as threatened by Sherye's sudden participation in the children's lives as she had been those first weeks.

Now Louise enjoyed two extra half days off, knowing that Sherye took pleasure in entertaining the children until she returned in time to supervise their evening meal. Louise admitted to her that bedtime was quite pleasant now that Sherye had set up the routine of reading to them until they fell asleep each night.

When Sherye had first suggested the ritual, Louise had felt certain the children would be too on edge to sleep after another visit from their mother. Sherye had been pleased that Louise admitted she'd been mistaken in her assumption.

Sherye made certain that the children got plenty of fresh air and exercise each day, plenty of fresh milk and vegetables, and an abundance of hugs and kisses from their mother.

The summer sun had turned them both a silky tan even with the lavish sunblock Sherye put on all of them. Eventually she'd gotten herself included at bathtime, one of her favorite times of day, right up there with reading to them the hour before they went to bed.

Once she had set up a routine with the children, her life had taken on almost a dreamlike sequence. Each morning she woke up to find herself once again in her beautiful bedroom, knowing she didn't have to rush off somewhere to work, that there were servants who saw to the running of her massive home, who fed her family and looked after her children. She felt as if she was living the life of a princess in an enchanted castle, knowing that her dream was much too wonderful to last. Instead she woke up each day, looked around to make certain her dream hadn't suddenly vanished overnight, then gave a daily prayer of thanks to God.

She spent each day as though it might be the very last one she would have with each family member. She'd discovered a wealth of patience with Felicity, whom Sherye had finally understood from observing her behavior and remarks. The older woman was afraid of growing older, afraid of not being needed, afraid of dying.

Sherye decided to plan outings with Danielle where Felicity could be included. They took her shopping with them and out to lunch. Together the two younger women encouraged Felicity to find other women her age who were alone and lonely to get together and develop new hobbies.

Sherye enjoyed thinking about all the changes in her sister-in-law. All Danielle had needed was some encouragement and a stronger belief in herself. She had blossomed with new ideas and attitudes that touched Sherye deeply, because Danielle continued to give Sherye the credit for the changes.

Only her relationship with Raoul remained the same—distant and polite. There were times when she lay alone in her bed at night thinking about the wall between them. There was so much more than the physical wall dividing them.

Raoul's reaction to finding her in his bedroom her first morning home had made his feelings clear on the subject of their marriage. The only way he expected her to be in his bed was if he was dreaming...probably having a nightmare.

Over the past few weeks she'd had ample opportunity to

study the man who'd given her so much and asked so little for himself.

He worked long hours and yet always seemed to have time for his children, his mother and his sister. Being around his wife, however, seemed to create a wariness within him. She didn't know how to get past his aloofness.

Sherye wasn't certain she even wanted to, except for the times when he seemed so lonely. He gave so much to all of them and expected so little in return.

Once when Yvette had exuberantly thrown herself into his arms and given him an unrestrained hug Sherye had seen a flicker of expression in his face that stunned her. He'd been surprised by his daughter's affection. He'd also been touched by the unexpected gesture.

Because he was such a private man, Sherye had resisted the impulse to discuss Raoul with Danielle. Instead she contented herself by unobtrusively observing his behavior.

She watched and learned.

The more she saw the more her heart ached for him.

The more she learned the more she loved him.

As her love grew, she discovered that the most loving thing she could do for him was to give him the distance he so obviously wanted from her. Consequently she poured the love and gratitude she felt for him into loving those who were closest to him—their children, his mother and his sister.

A slight noise brought her back to the present, and Sherye glanced around to see her sister-in-law walking across the wide expanse of lawn toward them.

"So there you are," Danielle said, laughing at the sight before her eyes. "All three of you look as though you've been rolling in the dirt and having a grand time of it."

Sherye smiled. The dress Danielle wore reflected the newer, shorter style and showed off her slender build to a flattering degree. Her hair had continued to curl itself into a tousled look that was very becoming.

"Were you looking for us?" Sherye asked, coming to her feet and brushing off her denim-covered knees.

"Actually, it's Raoul who has called for you a couple of times. The last time I promised I would see if I could find you so that you could call him back."

Sherye felt a cold fear grab her. "What's wrong? Has something happened?"

Danielle looked at her, puzzled. "I don't think so. He didn't sound upset, if that's what you mean. Just determined to speak with you this afternoon if at all possible. I told him I was sure you were around here somewhere, since you never left the château without telling someone where you would be." She looked down at Yvette. "You're turning into quite an exquisite gardener, I must say. Did you plant all those pretty flowers yourself?"

Yvette bobbed her head and immediately launched into a description of her various choices. Sherye bent and scooped up Jules, who was liberally covered in dirt. "I'm not sure I can smuggle him upstairs and clean him up before anyone sees him or not. I don't dare call Raoul until I've found the little boy beneath all this dirt."

Danielle laughed. "Don't worry about him. I'll stay here with him and—"

"Not on your life. He'll have you all smudged and dirty, as well. If there wasn't an emergency, I'll get the children cleaned up before I call Raoul."

Both children were bathed and in bed resting before Sherye called Raoul from the extension in the nursery.

As soon as he answered, she said, "Hi, this is Sherye. Danielle said you wanted me to call you."

"Where have you been? I've called a couple of times this afternoon. Danielle said she'd have you call."

Sherye made a face at his irritated tone. Maybe she

should have called him first. "Louise has the afternoon off, the children and I have been working in the garden and, as a result, I had to bring them in and hose them down before I could respond to your message. Is something wrong?"

"Not at all. I wanted to suggest that we go out this evening. We haven't had any time together for several weeks and I thought it would do us both good to get away. I wanted to check with you before I made reservations for dinner."

"Oh!" Sherye was stunned. He'd never made any effort to spend time with her before. "Well, I—uh—"

"When is Louise to return?"

"She'll be back by six."

"Good enough. We'll plan to leave home around eight, if that's all right with you."

Sherye could feel her heart racing in her chest. Why was she being so silly? Hadn't she just been thinking about the man and how little time they spent together? Here he was offering to remedy the situation and she was reacting like a blushing schoolgirl.

"I'd like that, Raoul," she managed to say, her voice sounding hoarse to her ears.

"I should be home before much longer. I wanted to give you time to make whatever arrangements were necessary."

Sherye hung up and checked on the children. They were both sound asleep despite the fact that Yvette continued to insist she was too old for naps and didn't need them any longer. Even so, she was growing up so quickly. Both of them were.

She stood there for a few moments, enjoying the quiet moment before she went in search of Danielle.

As soon as she found her she felt unaccountably shy. Feeling foolish, she said, "I spoke to Raoul. He's making reservations for the two of us to go out tonight, and—"

"What a marvelous idea. I'm impressed that he thought

about it. He's practically been living at the winery these days.''

''I—uh—I'm pleased. I don't get to see much of him. What I wanted to ask was if you would mind listening for the children for me? I need to get cleaned up myself and I'm afraid I won't hear them if they should need anything.''

''Of course. I have some magazines I've been wanting to catch up on. I can read them just as easily in their rooms.'' Danielle gathered up her magazines and said, ''You haven't been out at all in the evenings since you got home from the hospital, have you?''

''No, I haven't.''

''Haven't you missed it?''

Sherye grinned. ''Not really. It's bad enough whenever we're out during the day and people I don't remember speak to me. Here at home everybody has gotten used to the fact that I feel as though I've only been here for a few weeks rather than six years. When I'm away from here, I'm suddenly confronted with people and situations I don't know how to handle.''

''Well, you won't have a problem tonight, not with Raoul with you. He's been working too hard. This will be good for both of you.''

Instead of a quick shower, which was her usual habit after working in the garden, Sherye showered to remove the soil, then filled the large tub so she could ease some sore muscles.

Raoul hadn't said what he had in mind for tonight, but she wanted to be rested and prepared. She wished she could stop all the butterflies in her stomach. No doubt she and Raoul had spent many evenings together, particularly before she became pregnant with Jules. It was perfectly natural for a husband and wife to spend an evening together, she reminded herself.

Who was she kidding? There was nothing natural about

her relationship with Raoul. They rarely spoke to each other, or saw each other, for that matter. Sometimes she had trouble realizing that they shared this room. By the time she was awake each morning he had showered, dressed and was downstairs. When she arrived downstairs for breakfast, he was already gone to his office.

She closed her eyes, feeling the soothing swirl of water caress her skin. *Stop trying to second-guess Raoul,* she told herself, *and enjoy the opportunity to spend more time with him.*

She didn't realize she'd dozed off until the sound of the bathroom door opening roused her. Raoul stood in the doorway from his bedroom looking as taken aback by her occupancy of the tub as she was at his sudden appearance.

"Pardon me, I didn't realize—"

"Oh! I'm sorry, I—"

They both spoke at once, then paused. Sherye sank deeper in the tub, thankful the swirling of the water from the water-jets had produced so many protective bubbles.

"I must have fallen asleep," she managed to say. "I'm sorry. I'll be out in a moment."

Raoul cleared his throat. "Take your time. I'm in no hurry. I just—" He seemed to run out of words and shook his head. "I should have knocked," he finally said before closing the door.

As soon as the door shut, Sherye climbed out of the tub and grabbed a towel, feeling like a complete fool. After carefully avoiding him for all this time, she'd allowed herself to fall asleep when she knew he would be returning home.

After rinsing out the tub and drying herself, she hurried into her bedroom. Glancing at the clock, she was appalled to see that it was already after six. How could she have lost track of time like that? Would he think she had been in there deliberately? It sounded like something the old Sherye might have pulled. She cringed, hoping he wouldn't be disgusted with her.

She slipped into underwear and walked into the closet, trying to decide what to wear. Tonight she could dress as glamorously as she wished. For some reason she couldn't quite explain to herself, she wanted to look her best. She wanted to remind Raoul that she was his wife.

After discarding several dresses with plunging necklines she let out a sigh of satisfaction and pulled out a sapphire blue gown of layered chiffon and delicate lace that had a high neckline and long, narrow sleeves, while the back was cut down to her waist.

She smiled to herself. A dress with its own surprise. From the tags still on it, she knew it was also a dress that she had never worn. The fitted bodice sparkled with tiny brilliants of the same color, giving a shimmering appearance that would change with every breath she took.

She sat in front of her vanity and carefully applied makeup with a light hand, then pulled her hair up high on her head, allowing it to cascade in back.

By the time she'd completed all her preparations, she felt ready to face the world with her chin held high. A light tap on the connecting door caused her to turn away from the mirror.

"Come in."

Raoul opened the door and she struggled not to show her strong reaction to his appearance. This was the first time she'd seen him dressed in formal wear. The suit had obviously been custom-made, showing off his well-formed body to perfection.

He seemed to be just as taken aback by her appearance. "I don't believe I've seen that gown before," he said slowly.

Since he was looking past her, she realized that he could

see the back of the dress in the mirror. "If you don't like it, I can change."

"The dress is lovely. I just hadn't seen it, that's all," he said.

"I must have overlooked it in the closet. It had gotten caught with another dress and fell from the hanger while I was going through the rack."

"You look—I'm certain you must know—quite beautiful, Sherye."

She smiled. "Thank you."

"I'm not certain how, but you look different from your modeling photographs." He came closer, his eyes narrowed as he scrutinized her face. "It must be the makeup or something."

"I've forgotten all the tricks of the trade, obviously." She looked everywhere but at him, feeling awkward.

"Actually, I like you this way much better. You seem more innocent somehow, with a sense of freshness that is very appealing."

"This is the first time I've gotten really dressed up since I've had any recollection of my life." She picked up her beaded bag and nervously dropped a lipstick and comb inside. "I'll admit I feel a little strange, given our circumstances." She forced herself to glance back over her shoulder at him and found him watching her intently, which did nothing to ease her nervousness. She turned to face him, holding her small bag tightly as though she didn't know what to do with her hands. She offered him a rather shy smile and said, "I've been feeling like I'm getting ready for a first date ever since I spoke with you earlier today."

He seemed to relax a little. "I know what you mean. I was feeling the same way when I made my invitation."

For the first time since he'd walked into the room she realized that he wasn't as relaxed as he appeared. "Was there a particular reason why you wanted to go out to-night?''

''Yes, but I'd prefer to wait until later to discuss it.''

She couldn't read anything in his expression or his tone of voice to hint at what was on his mind. Gathering her courage around her like a cloak, she said, ''All right. I'm ready to go whenever you are.''

He offered her his arm and they left the room together, Sherye's heart beating a double-time rhythm to their pace. She wasn't certain she was ready to hear what he had to say, but she also knew that she had to face without flinching whatever topic he wished to pursue.

Chapter Nine

When they reached the bottom of the stairway Danielle was waiting for them with a smile. "What a handsome couple you make," she teased. As soon as Sherye saw her sister-in-law she was reminded of the fact that she had left Danielle to look after Yvette and Jules. How could she have forgotten them!

"I forgot to look in on the children," Sherye said, echoing her thoughts, horror-struck by the omission. "Did Louise make it back all right? Do the children—"

"The children are fine, Louise is here and everyone wishes you a fine evening. Yvette did hope you'd stop in so that she could see you before you leave."

"Of course. I can't imagine how I could possibly have forgotten them." She shook her head with frustration and looked at Raoul. "If you'll excuse me, I won't be but a minute."

"Since I haven't seen the children today, I'll go up with

you. Quite frankly, that had been my intent when I came to get you, but, like you, I forgot all about my original intentions when I saw you.'' He grinned at Danielle. ''She looks far from motherly at the moment, doesn't she?''

Sherye knew she was blushing but couldn't help it. She turned away and returned upstairs, hurrying down the hallway to the nursery, Raoul's steps echoing a few steps behind her.

Louise was reading to Yvette when Sherye opened the door. When the young girl looked up and saw her mother, Yvette froze, her expressive eyes going blank.

Sherye hesitated at the door, caught off guard by Yvette's reaction. Her daughter hadn't worn that expression in weeks, not since Sherye had first arrived home. Had Yvette thought she'd forgotten about her, since she was the one who regularly read a bedtime story?

She crossed over to where Yvette sat watching her, still with no expression, and knelt beside the love seat. ''I'm so sorry I wasn't here to read to you, sweetheart.''

Yvette gave a tiny shrug. ''It doesn't matter.''

''Of course it does.''

Yvette looked at the dress Sherye wore. ''You're going out with your friends again, aren't you?'' she asked in a low voice.

''Actually,'' Raoul drawled from the doorway, ''your mother and I are having dinner out tonight. I hope that meets with your approval.''

The change in Yvette was indescribable. From being a frozen, inexpressive and stilted child, she became animated, her eyes glowing and her smile flashing.

''You're going out *together?*'' she repeated, obviously delighted. ''You've never done that before!'' She scooted off the sofa and gave Sherye a quick hug before darting over to Raoul.

Sherye was caught off guard and speechless. Slowly she

rose and turned in time to see Raoul catch his daughter up
in his arms, laughing. She felt a sharp pain in her chest—
as though her heart was being squeezed—at the sight of
Raoul's flashing white smile in his darkly tanned face.

"I want you to be a good girl for Louise, and go to bed
as soon as your story is finished, all right?"

Yvette gave a vigorous nod and asked, "Are you and
Mama going dancing?"

Raoul glanced at Sherye, lifting one of his eyebrows
slightly before returning his attention to Yvette. "Perhaps."

Yvette kissed him on the cheek. "I'm glad, Papa. I like
to see the two of you together."

"You do, eh? So. You are pleased with us, is that what
you're saying?"

"Oh, yes, Papa. Very pleased." She scrambled down
and dashed back to where Sherye stood. "You haven't gotten all dressed up in a long time, not since your accident."

Once again Sherye felt a pain in her chest once she realized why Yvette had reverted to her shell when she first
saw her. Yvette was afraid Sherye was going to start staying out at night once again.

"That's true," she replied in a husky voice. "I wanted
to wait until your papa could take me, and he's been very
busy."

Yvette took Sherye's hand and squeezed it. "You look
so pretty, *maman.*"

"Thank you, darling."

"Come," Raoul said briskly. "We must be on our way."

Sherye gave her daughter a hug and a kiss, smiled at
Louise and joined Raoul at the door. Yvette giggled when
Raoul took Sherye's hand and led her into the hallway.

Sherye could feel herself blushing like a silly schoolgirl
and all because her husband continued to grasp her hand
as he escorted her down the stairway and out to his car.

They were passing the gates when Raoul spoke. "Is there someplace in particular you would like to go?"

She couldn't seem to keep her gaze off his hands and the way his long fingers looked so capable wrapped around the steering wheel. She glanced up at his face. "Not really."

"Can't remember any of your favorite haunts?"

She stiffened. "Is that why you invited me out tonight, in hopes we can find something that might jog my memory?"

"Hardly. Quite frankly, I realized today that I'm not all that eager to have your memory return if your lack of memory means that you'll continue to behave as you have these past few weeks."

"What do you mean?"

"Oh, come on. You must know how you have the whole household buzzing, wondering what has occurred to make you behave so differently. It's almost as if you're a different person!"

"I feel like a different person," she replied in a low voice. "I continue to have trouble relating to the woman who's been described to me."

"Perhaps the blow to your head is proving beneficial in many ways."

"I take it you prefer me the way I am now?"

The smile he gave her was seductive. "Much."

"Does this mean that you no longer want a divorce?"

His smile disappeared and a small frown formed over the bridge of his nose. "I just know that I'm tired of being married without having a wife. If we're going to continue our marriage, I would like to see some changes."

"Such as?"

"I want more than a wife in name only."

She swallowed. "I see."

"However, I can understand that as far as you're concerned, you've only known me a few weeks, and in that time I've been considerably less than loverlike.''

She could find nothing with which to argue in that statement so she wisely remained silent.

''I realized that the only fair thing for me to do in this situation is to spend more time with you and allow you to get to know me once again.''

''I take it that you no longer expect my memory to return.''

He didn't respond immediately, obviously mulling over her comment. ''I have no idea. Neither, from all indications, do the doctors. Consequently we've been living in a state of limbo that is rapidly becoming untenable.'' He glanced at her before returning his gaze to the roadway. ''Everything could come back to you tomorrow. On the other hand, you may never remember anything before waking up in the hospital.''

She knew he was right. What surprised her was the realization that her memory loss wasn't as upsetting to her now as it was when she first discovered she couldn't recall anything.

''Perhaps I've been afraid to remember,'' she murmured.

She could feel him stiffen beside her. ''What's that supposed to mean?'' he asked.

''I'm not so sure that I want to know why I did some of the things I've been told about. My past behavior has been less than admirable.'' She smiled to herself, feeling wistful. ''All I know for certain is that I have enjoyed these past few weeks tremendously. The children are an absolute delight, I've gotten to know Danielle and feel that we are on our way to being friends. Which reminds me...''

When she didn't say anything more, he prompted her with, ''Yes?''

''I've been told by several people that I spent most of my time away from home with my friends and yet I have heard from no one but you and your family since I awakened in the hospital.''

''I wondered when you would notice.''

''Do you know why I haven't heard from anyone?''

''As a matter of fact, I've been puzzled by the same omission. I would have expected to have them calling you on a regular basis. The only thing I could think was that perhaps you had a fight with someone in the group and they are all punishing you with their silence.''

''I suppose that's possible. You did say that I was alone at the time of my accident?''

''Yes.''

''A passing motorist found me? A stranger?''

''That's what the police told me. You were already at the hospital by the time I reached you.''

She rubbed her forehead. ''Perhaps it would be worth remembering just to have some answers to so many puzzling questions.''

''There's another question you haven't asked that I've been waiting to hear.''

She looked at him in surprise. ''What is that?''

''Did I have anything to do with your accident?''

His matter-of-fact statement spoken in a quiet voice shook her more than she wanted to admit to herself. ''But you said—I mean, how could you have— You were at the château, didn't you say?''

''Don't you believe me capable of planning such an accident? Looking at it from one viewpoint, I certainly had enough motive to want an end to what had become an intolerable relationship. *Maman* mentioned that she told you I'd spoken to an attorney. I'll admit when you didn't regain consciousness and the doctors were uncertain of the outcome, I could see where a rather solid case could be built against me, given our circumstances.''

She stared at the road, aware of the careless ease with

which he followed its twists and turns. Was this really happening? Was she riding along with her husband while he matter-of-factly explained why he might want her dead?

She shook her head. "This is ridiculous."

"What is?"

"This conversation. You would not have discussed the possibility of a divorce with an attorney if you'd intended to do away with me. Besides, you told me that I left with very little notice and that you didn't know where I was going. So how could you have possibly arranged an accident?"

"Ah. So you *had* thought of the idea."

The blasted man actually sounded pleased that he was right!

They spoke no more until they reached the restaurant in a nearby city. They were greeted at the door by name with smiles from everyone who seated and served them.

"You must come here often," she commented after they had ordered.

"I bring business associates here on occasion. From the statements I used to receive, I would say that you and your friends spent a considerable amount of time here, as well."

Now that she sat across from him she could better judge his expression. The problem was that he had carefully masked his thoughts and feelings...much the way Yvette had earlier in the evening.

Was he afraid of being hurt? Surely not. Raoul DuBois was much too self-assured to feel anything other than at ease with their present situation.

"So these are familiar surroundings," she said, looking around the room with interest. "I wonder if there's anyone here I'm supposed to know?"

"If so, they're very carefully ignoring us, since you arrived with your husband."

There. Hadn't she caught a hint of feeling in that last

remark? A hint of—what? What had she heard for an instant? Sarcasm—oh, yes, there was always a hint of sarcasm in everything he said. Or perhaps it was mockery, although she could never be certain whether his mockery was directed at her or himself.

"The wine is exquisite," she said, hoping to find a more comfortable subject.

"Thank you," he said, lifting his glass in a slight gesture. "I'm rather proud of it, myself."

Her eyes widened. She glanced at her glass. "You mean this is from your vineyards?"

His smile flashed brightly in the dim lighting. "But of course. I would want to order our wine whenever possible, unless I'm checking the quality of our competitors."

She took another sip. How strange to be a part of something so traditional and not to remember anything.

"I keep getting the strangest prompting," she said after a moment. "I'll think of something that I want to mention to Janine before I realize that I can't place her and no one seems to know who she is."

"What is it you wish to tell this friend?"

"Oh, about all of this." She gestured toward the room. "I feel as though this is the first time I've been here, the first time we've been out together, and I want to share it all. I want to tell her about the children, and my gardening and about..." Her words began to slow. "My marriage."

"This Janine would be surprised?"

She nodded slowly. "Yes. Because none of it really exists for me. All of it is just a beautiful dream."

He held out his hand. "Would you like to dance?"

The music had been playing quietly in the background and she hadn't noticed other couples moving toward the dance floor. "But our food—"

"Will wait on us, I'm sure. In any event, we won't be gone long. For some reason I have a strong urge to hold you in my arms." He smiled down at her. "The urge proves to be irresistible."

Once again she could almost believe that she was in a Charles Boyer movie, listening to Raoul's fluent English with just a touch of his native tongue to add a subtle difference.

As soon as he placed his arms around her she caught her breath.

"Relax. I'm not going to bite you," he said, pulling her close to him. He kissed her ear. "I might want to nibble here and there, of course—"

She looked up at him in surprise to find his eyes filled with amusement.

He was flirting with her and she felt totally unaccomplished and vulnerable. He was so sure of himself, so comfortable in the exclusive restaurant and on the dance floor. Shouldn't she be at ease, as well? Wasn't this her lifestyle—her playground, so to speak?

Why didn't any of it feel natural? Why did she feel so self-conscious? Surely a model would be used to having people stare at her, and she had certainly garnered more than her fair share of looks and whispers tonight.

"Ah, I believe our order has arrived," Raoul whispered, and taking her hand he led her from the dance floor back to where they had been seated. Sherye was glad to returned to their secluded table.

"Why are all those people watching us?"

"You. They're watching you."

"Why?"

"You really don't know, do you? Have you forgotten how beautiful you are? How that dress dramatically displays your assets?"

"I should have worn something else! Something not quite so revealing, something that—" She ran down as she recalled that all the evening wear in her closet was designed to catch the eye.

Raoul reached across the table and took her hand. "Please relax and enjoy yourself. I thought getting out would be a treat for you. You've stayed home for so long."

"It *is* a treat, and I'm enjoying it, but I feel so out of place, nervous that I'm going to do something to make a fool of myself."

He laughed. "You could never do that."

"Wanna bet? I remember the time when I— When—" She stammered to a sudden halt, her mind blank.

"When?"

She shook her head. "I don't know. I had a flash of something but when I tried to explain, it was gone." She touched her fingers to the bridge of her nose. "For a minute there I saw something—remembered something—about school. Perhaps when I was going to school—or—" She waited, but nothing else came. She shook her head. "I can't remember. Whatever it was escaped me."

"Does this happen to you often?"

"Often enough. It's frustrating because the harder I try to remember, the more fleeting the memory."

"Let's enjoy our meal, shall we? I want you to relax tonight. We'll do this more often. I think I have everything under control at the winery. I'll take more time off and we can spend a few hours together each day. I feel as though I'm just getting to know you, too, which is a rather strange sensation. You rarely do or say the expected thing anymore. I find myself sitting back, waiting with a sense of antici-pation for what's going to happen next where you are con-cerned."

She tilted her head slightly, studying him. "You're dif-ferent, too."

"From what?"

"From the man that came to visit me in the hospital. He was cold…and arrogant…and sarcastic."

"You don't see me that way now?"

"Not as much. Perhaps you are wary, perhaps suspicious at times, but there are times when I catch glimpses of someone who intrigues me very much."

"Then I would say that we've made a good beginning for one evening, wouldn't you?"

"It's been a lovely evening. Thank you."

"You are most welcome. Now, then, if you're through with your meal, I would very much like to dance with you some more."

His gaze was filled with admiration. There were no shadows of wariness in their depths.

Sherye floated to the dance floor on Raoul's arm, convinced she never wanted this night to end.

Chapter Ten

The moon rode high in the sky on their way home. Sherye was content to lean back against the headrest and gaze out at the landscape brushed with silver light. She was enjoying the companionable silence between them. Raoul had seemed more relaxed—happier—tonight than she had ever seen him before. Without his stern visage he'd looked years younger. And what a dancer! Light on his feet, graceful, easy to follow.

She felt like an adolescent with a crush on a movie hero.

But Raoul was real…and he was her husband.

One thing had been evident tonight. He wanted her. He'd made no effort to hide his reaction to her body pressed so closely to his.

She'd been just as aroused. Perhaps both of them needed the long drive home in order to gain some control, although he'd made it clear earlier in the evening that he wanted more from her than their present relationship.

She couldn't think of anything she'd rather have than a workable marriage.

Wasn't it too soon? a small voice kept asking somewhere inside her.

Too soon for what? They had been married for years. Whatever had caused her discontent was mercifully blocked from her mind and her memory.

Perhaps she was being a coward, but she had come to the place in her life and situation where she preferred to keep her discontent at bay.

For the first time since she had awakened in the hospital she was ready to release her need to remember the past. Instead she prayed for her future, one that would include Raoul, Yvette and Jules.

"Shall I let you out at the front door?" Raoul asked as they approached the château.

She wasn't ready for the evening to end. More particularly, she wasn't ready to bid Raoul good-night at the moment, so she shook her head and said, "I'll ride with you to the garage."

He didn't comment, and since he was in deep shadow she couldn't see his expression.

Raoul parked the car with precision and walked around to open her door. He held out his hand and she took it. He made no effort to release her hand when they started across the driveway to one of the back entrances.

A night-light lit the hallway they followed to the front of the house. Raoul paused in the foyer and checked the small table at the foot of the stairway where messages were left for the household. There were no messages.

He turned to look at her, saying as they began to climb the stairs, "Thank you for a very pleasant evening, Sherye. I enjoyed it."

"So did I."

"I must admit that it felt unusual."

"How do you mean?"

They reached the top of the stairs and walked to her door, where he paused, taking both of her hands in his and study ing them as though looking for an answer to whatever was puzzling him.

After a moment he lifted his head and gazed at her. "I'm not certain. As a matter of fact, I was trying to figure out the same thing on our drive home. I believe it's something about your attitude."

She blinked. "You mean it's different?"

"In the past, anytime we were in public I always had the sense that you were very much aware of your image and appearance. Even while we would be in the midst of a conversation I invariably got the impression that you were conscious of the people around us, conscious of their stares, almost as though you were playing to an audience." He gave his head a tiny shake as though he hadn't quite found the words he wanted. "You've always been so conscious of yourself, so aware of your own movements and gestures, so that whenever I was with you I felt as though I was witnessing a well-rehearsed performance."

"Are you saying that tonight I didn't appear to be performing?"

"Exactly! Tonight your focus seemed to be on me, on what I said, on the conversation we were having." He gave a self-deprecating chuckle. "I must admit to feeling quite flattered. It's difficult to remain detached when someone so obviously enjoys my company."

"I *did* enjoy your company."

He grinned. "I suppose that's what made the evening so different. In the past I felt as though I was a necessary accessory to your entrance and evening—I was your escort. I had accepted the role without giving it a moment's thought...until tonight. Tonight I felt as if I was the focus of your evening, a vital, invaluable part." He slid his hands on either side of her jawline and cupped her face. "You made me feel very special tonight," he whispered. "I had never before understood what a touching gift a person's focused attention could be." He brushed his lips across hers, and the words "thank you" wafted between them before he kissed her again, this time with a possessive depth that pulled her into a very heated embrace.

His gentle cupping of her face made her feel treasured and protected while he teased and tantalized her with his lips and tongue.

Sherye leaned against her closed door, needing support for her weakened knees. With seeming reluctance Raoul eased away from her until he was no longer touching her. Her weighted eyelids opened and her gaze met his. His rueful expression caught her off guard.

"I didn't mean to get quite so carried away," he said. "I want to give both of us time to adjust to some of these changes."

She heard his words with mixed feelings. As much as she wanted to make love to him—and she was very aroused by his sensuous kiss—she also felt a sense of relief that she wasn't going to be forced into an intimacy that seemed too new.

For weeks Raoul had avoided her as much as possible, making his attitude toward her clear. Now he'd made a rather abrupt shift. She was having difficulty adjusting to the sudden changes.

Of course she wanted a healthier relationship with him. At one time she must have loved him very much to have given up her career and married him. However, their situation had changed over the years. From all indications both of them had been unhappy with their marriage and each other.

Until she could better understand why she had avoided him, why she had insisted on spending so much of her time with her friends, she wasn't quite ready to disregard totally all that she had learned in the recent weeks.

Raoul leaned around her and opened her bedroom door. "Sleep well, my dear. We have the weekend ahead of us. I am placing my time at your disposal to do whatever we can together."

"I promised the children a picnic tomorrow beside the pond. They're looking forward to it."

He nodded. "As will I." He paused, as though reluctant to leave her. He touched her lips lightly with his thumb, smiled, then turned on his heel and disappeared into the room next to hers.

Sherye entered her bedroom and closed the hallway door, her glance immediately going to the connecting door between their rooms.

The door was closed. She knew that it would remain closed, at least for now.

While she undressed she reviewed their conversations of the evening. She was surprised that he, too, had noticed the lack of visitors for her. How could she have been so socially active before her accident, not to hear from any of her friends afterward?

Another puzzling item to add to the list of mysteries surrounding her accident and loss of memory.

She waited until she was certain that Raoul had finished in their shared bathroom before she went in to remove her makeup and get ready for bed. Even without makeup her cheeks were flushed and her eyes glistening. Physically she was fully recovered; emotionally she was improving rapidly.

Her evening with Raoul had given her a great deal to think about.

Once again in her own room, she slipped into bed, convinced she was too keyed up to sleep, but the relaxing comfort of her bed proved otherwise.

* * *

"Papa! Watch me, watch me!" Yvette called, playing keep away from a gamboling puppy as he attempted to grab the end of the rope she trailed just ahead of him.

Raoul had been watching her all the while Sherye gently rocked Jules in her arms. Their picnic had been vigorously enjoyed, and the combination of a full tummy and the warm summer air had contributed to Jules's sleepiness.

Raoul had brought the adults a pair of folding chairs and after their picnic on the blanket he and Sherye had gotten more comfortable by sitting in the chairs.

"I'm so glad she's enjoying the puppy. She'll learn a great deal about responsibility now that she has something to look after," Sherye said softly so she wouldn't disturb Jules.

Raoul had been amazed earlier today when Sherye had appeared with the puppy in her arms. She had asked him if he would bring the children outside while she went to pick up a surprise she'd gotten for Yvette.

"That's true. She's repeatedly asked for a dog these past few months," he admitted.

"I think every child should have a special pet to love."

He made a sound of agreement while his thoughts raced. Could a lack of memory make such a profound difference in a person? On closer observation Raoul found more and more discrepancies between the Sherye he knew before the accident and afterward. It was almost as though she was an entirely different person.

How could that be? Of course she was his wife. Unless Sherye had a twin sister who could have stepped into Sherye's life at a very opportune moment, this *had* to be the woman he'd married.

The differences, mostly in attitude, continued to surprise him.

Take the puppy, for example. The woman he thought he

knew had ignored Yvette's pleas for an animal, insisting she didn't want a dirty, messy, noisy pet around the place.

Now today she surprised Yvette with a Brittany spaniel, having gone to considerable lengths to find one.

The way she treated their son was another radical change. After ignoring him most of his life, she now seemed to know what he needed before Jules did. She fed him, changed him, coaxed him to rest, all with the minimum amount of fuss, as though she'd spent all of his life by his side.

The changes in her appeared permanent, and to her they were quite unremarkable since she could remember no other behavior. At times like today, Raoul wished his memory could be wiped clean as well, so that he could enjoy his time with his family without questioning what was happening.

The children had already grown used to picnics and playtime with their mother. He could tell from their conversations that today was a routine occurrence.

The day was a revelation to him.

His eyes met hers and she smiled at him. "Would you like me to hold him for a while?" he heard himself asking. "He looks heavy."

"He's fine," she whispered. "I enjoy holding him, even when my arm goes to sleep. He's growing up so quickly. I can already see so many changes in him, just since I arrived home from the hospital."

Even the dullest person would be able to see how much she loved her son. If for no other reason, Raoul admired her for the changes she had made in the children's lives.

"What would you like to do this evening?" he asked.

"Oh, I haven't given it any thought."

"Would you like to go out somewhere?"

"Not particularly. I mean, of course I'll go if you'd like, but I'd just as soon stay in tonight."

He grinned. "All right. How about a game of chess?"

She frowned. "Do I know how to play?"

"A little, but you've never cared for it. I was going to see if that attitude had changed, as well."

"Ah, a trick question, I see."

"All right. You think of something we can do together."

He watched her cheeks darken to a rosy glow and fought to disguise his reaction to what she was obviously thinking. Perhaps he *was* being too reserved where their love life was concerned. For whatever reasons, Sherye was unable to articulate her willingness to resume their marital relationship, but she couldn't hide her interest in and awareness of him.

Every time she looked at him, his body reacted to her gaze as though she had physically touched him. Sherye had always been a passionate woman, using her beauty to get what she wanted. Her manipulative technique was another piece of her personality that seemed to have been lost among other misplaced memories.

Raoul found the nonmanipulative role she'd adopted since her accident more arousing than he could have anticipated. Her direct gaze withheld nothing, it seemed. Clearly she found him attractive. Equally clearly she had difficulty keeping her eyes off him.

What man could resist such a message?

What man would want to resist?

Now it was time for him to let go of his resentments toward her past behavior and accept the changes in her. He couldn't deny his hope that the changes would be permanent. Even if her memory returned, perhaps she would be willing to discuss the difference in her behavior.

Raoul vowed to be more understanding in the future. He wanted to rebuild the relationship he'd been ready to jettison. From all indications, Sherye was willing to help.

* * *

Sherye ran the brush through her hair while gazing at her reflection. She'd slipped on her nightgown after her shower and had intended to read in bed until she became sleepy. Unfortunately she was too restless to climb into bed.

She studied the woman in the mirror of her vanity dresser, wishing she knew her better. She could objectively note her assets and understand why people noticed her. The flaming red of her hair demanded notice. The color seemed to accentuate her fair complexion and call attention to the vivid hue of her eyes.

What puzzled her most was Raoul's seeming indifference to her particular charms. Remembering his physical reaction to their kiss last night, she amended her thought slightly. He was a healthy male and his body had certainly reacted to her, but it was his mind that made decisions for him.

Mentally he had rejected her.

She had no idea how to change his mind. She only knew that she wanted to…very much. Now that he had decided to spend more time with her, she was painfully aware of how attracted she was to him. Her heart beat faster, her need for air seemed to come more quickly and even the surface of her skin seemed to tingle with awareness of him.

Her problem was that she had no idea how to let him know, which was one of the reasons she was so restless tonight. She felt as if she was supposed to know how to go about seducing the man, but she didn't! What kind of femme fatale had she become since her accident?

A very inept one, to be sure.

She sighed, placing the brush on the small table, and stood. She turned toward the bed, and it was only then that she became aware of Raoul leaning against the jamb of the door between their rooms. From his relaxed position, with his hands in the pockets of his robe, he looked as though he'd been standing there for some time.

She could feel her embarrassment overtake her, even though she knew there was no way he could possibly know what she had been thinking. She fought to contain the wave of heat that seemed to engulf her. "I'm sorry," she said, her voice sounding rusty in her ears, "I didn't realize you were there."

He slowly straightened, his gaze seeming to go through her thin gown to the rosy skin beneath. "I'm the one who should apologize. I should have tapped on the door first."

She gave a nervous chuckle. "Nonsense. There's no need for such formality between us. Did you want something?"

The grin he gave her caught her totally unprepared. His expression was filled with mischief as well as a carnal awareness of the tension between them.

He moved toward her, his eyes focused on her face as though watching her expression for a clue to what she was thinking. Unfortunately her brain seemed to have rolled over in a dead faint as he approached her, leaving her feeling more vulnerable than she could ever before recall.

"Raoul?" His name seemed to singe her lips, the words coming out in a choked whisper.

"Hmm?" He paused in his approach, less than a hand reach away from her.

She attempted to swallow around the lump that had suddenly lodged in her throat. When she didn't say anything more, he tipped her chin up with his forefinger and placed a gentle kiss on her lips.

She shivered at his touch. She felt out of her depth with this sophisticated man who was her husband. She wanted to cling to him and to plant kisses all over his taut, well-hewn body. She wanted...

Everything with this man.

She flowed against him like melting wax against a contoured surface, molding her curves against him. Her unconditional response gave him all the encouragement he needed. With economical movements he swept her up in his arms and strode toward the bed nearby.

Sherye felt frantic with need. She'd waited so long, too long, for his touch and possession. She clung to him when he began to lower her onto the bed. He followed her down without interrupting the kiss. She made a low noise of pleasure deep in her throat as she felt the weight of his solid body on top of her.

Feverishly she brushed away the folds of his robe, eager to find him. Her touch made him lose any semblance of control he'd attempted to exert over his reactions to her. Raoul lifted the hem of her gown and ran his fingers along her inner thigh.

She couldn't lie still. She felt as though she was on fire. When he shifted she opened herself to him. He needed no further invitation.

With a tiny cry of triumph Sherye wrapped her arms and legs tightly around his muscular body as though reassuring herself he wouldn't leave her.

There was no chance of that, at least not for any time soon. Raoul fought for some semblance of control, not wanting to hurt her, not wanting their coming together to end too soon, but there was no way to slow the momentum of their coming together.

He felt as though he was burning up in the flame of her response to him. With a short groan of relief he gave himself over to an incendiary rhythm that guaranteed an almost immediate explosion. He fought to hang on but it was way too late for any attempt at control. Just as his body took over he felt the marvelously erotic contractions deep inside her that signaled she was with him—as she had been with him—every step of the way.

Raoul was still trying to come to grips with his unaccustomed loss of control when he became aware that he was still lying on top of her and that they were stretched across the bed sideways.

He hadn't been able to get them into bed properly before he claimed her. Not that there had been anything particularly proper in his behavior.

He wasn't at all certain that he was going to be able to move again, but he attempted to relieve her of some of his weight by shifting his arms to rest on his elbows.

Her arms tightened around him, holding him in place.

He tried to laugh, but was too weak. Fighting for breath, he managed to wheeze, "I'm too heavy for you."

"No."

She brushed her mouth against his ear, causing him to shiver. She nibbled on his earlobe and he felt the ripple of goose bumps race along his spine and over the backs of his arms and legs.

Still holding her as tightly as she held him, Raoul eventually managed to roll onto his side, amused to discover that despite his sated condition he was already more than half aroused again and still buried deep inside her.

He wasn't used to such a strong response, either in her or in himself. At the moment he was too involved with what he was feeling to attempt to analyze the differences he'd peripherally noted during the recent firestorm—a firestorm whose embers were already being fanned by the kisses she continued to lavish on whatever part of his body she could reach.

This time he tried to set a slower pace. Unfortunately, once control was lost it was tough regaining it, and Sherye wasn't helping in the slightest.

He cupped one of her breasts and nuzzled it, flicking his tongue across the pebbled peak, pleased to see the shimmer of awareness rise in her, as well.

She arched into him, causing his flesh to instantly harden within her. After that, neither could resist the rhythmic move of hips that increased the pleasure of being joined.

He kissed her, his tongue keeping the same inexorable rhythmic pace, steadily increasing the surging, life-giving movement that tossed them back into another explosion of mind-destroying pleasure.

This time they lay collapsed, side by side, their lungs gasping for air, their bodies slick with a film of perspiration. Raoul knew that they needed to move. They would grow chilled once their bodies cooled down, but at the moment all he could do was to lie there with Sherye in his arms and allow himself to drift into a pleasant space of satiated unconsciousness.

He had no idea how much time had passed when he opened his eyes again. The small bedside lamp was still lit and Sherye was curled beside him, her arms and legs still entwined with his.

Raoul couldn't remember a time in his life when he had felt so truly whole and complete. What had happened between them tonight was nothing short of a miracle. Never had he felt such a tenderness toward his beautiful and willful wife.

She'd shared her unabashed needs without shame, all the while making him feel as though he was the only man who could satisfy those particular needs. He lifted a long strand of her hair and watched it curl around his finger.

"Are you cold?" she asked.

He'd thought she was still asleep until her long lashes had lifted from her satiny cheeks. Her eyes were fuzzy with sleep.

"A little," he admitted with a half smile.

"We could get under the covers, if you'd like."

"We could." He didn't move.

She grinned. "Are you too comfortable to move?"

"Something like that."

She slid the leg she'd tucked between his thighs a few inches up...then a few inches down...his leg.

He tightened his arms around her. "I have an idea," he whispered.

"What's that?"

"We could go shower, then sleep in my bed for the rest of the night."

"Mmm."

"Is that a yes or a no?"

"Oh, I think it could definitely be considered a yes."

He sat up, pulling her up with him. Once on his feet he lifted her in his arms and carried her into the bathroom. There he allowed her to stand while he adjusted the spray of the water, then guided her into the shower with him.

With careful strokes Raoul lathered her entire body, blocking most of the water with his back, then stepped aside to allow her to rinse. Dutifully she took the washcloth and mimicked his ministrations until she had him so stiff he had to grit his teeth to keep from lifting her onto him right then and there.

He forced himself to turn his back and hurriedly rinse. Then he stepped out of the shower, grabbed a towel and in record time dried both of them off. This time he was determined to make it to bed and beneath the covers.

He made it, but just barely.

This time he placed himself on the bed and urged her to move over him. With a mischievous grin she knelt over him and soon had him gripping the sheets and clenching his jaw to stop himself from groaning at her exquisite touch.

When she finally eased herself down over him, engulfing him with her velvet-lined sheath, he was too far gone to do anything but grab her hips and encourage her to ride him fast and hard until she collapsed on his chest after they had once again reached their peaks together.

Raoul went to sleep with her bonelessly sprawled across him.

He was so soundly asleep that he couldn't seem to figure out how to quiet the jangling noise that impinged on his consciousness. The steady *brriinng* nearby wouldn't go away. He didn't know how long the noise had been going on before he was awake enough to recognize the sound of the phone.

Sometime during the night Sherye had curled up on her side, and he was tucked spoon-fashion beside her. With a groan he rolled away from her and reached for the phone.

"Yes?"

"Sorry to bother you," the housekeeper said hurriedly, "but you have a phone call from Perth, Australia. They insisted on speaking to you right away."

Perth, Australia? He had no business contacts there. Raoul shoved his hair out of his face, rubbed his jaw and said, "All right. Put it through, please." He glanced over at Sherye and saw that she was still sound asleep. No wonder, he thought with a grin of purely male satisfaction. He was already thinking of some fairly inventive ways he could wake her up a little later when another voice came on the line and he said, "This is Raoul DuBois."

Chapter Eleven

Sherye wasn't certain what caused her to awaken. She heard a low murmur nearby, then a sharp questioning sound that somehow broke through her wonderful dream and caused her to surface into awareness of her surroundings.

She blinked, surprised to see that she was not in her own bed before the events of the previous night rushed into her mind. She stretched, then winced as certain achy spots on her body forcibly reminded her of recent activities.

Smiling, she rolled over and reached for Raoul.

He was sitting on the side of the bed, obviously listening to someone on the phone. Unable to resist the temptation of that smooth, bare expanse of muscle, she placed her hand on his back.

He jerked away as though she had burned him and looked around at her with a grim, shocked stare. The combination of his expression and instinctive withdrawal sobered her.

What happened to the warm, loving, passionate man from the night before?

She stared at him in confusion. The tender lover of last night had disappeared as though he'd never existed. In his place was the cold, hard, aloof man that had been waiting beside her when she first opened her eyes at the hospital.

She could have wept if it would have done any good. What was wrong? What had she done? Was there some etiquette about sharing his bed that had been lost along with so many of her other memories?

Sherye forced herself to listen to his end of the conversation, for the first time wondering if the phone call had anything to do with his inexplicable change of attitude.

She couldn't tell much from his side of the conversation. He was asking short questions and receiving lengthy answers. Afraid to do anything that might further distract or annoy him, she lay quietly and waited for him to get off the phone.

When Raoul hung up and looked at her she knew that whatever information he'd received would affect her. She could feel a trembling beginning somewhere deep inside. She fought to control her reaction to the implacable mask Raoul now wore.

"What's wrong?" she finally asked when he didn't speak but continued to stare at her.

"I would say just about everything," he finally responded. He got out of bed and strode into the bathroom, closing the door quietly behind him.

By now the trembling had taken over her entire body. She knew that she needed to get up, to put on some clothes so that she wouldn't feel quite so vulnerable, but at the moment she was shaking too much for her knees to support her.

Within moments Raoul reentered the bedroom and, without looking at her, began to dress.

"I heard you say you'd be there as soon as you could. Is there an emergency at the winery?"

Once dressed, he walked over to the bed and stood at the end of it. He was studying her as though she was someone he'd never seen before. His stare unnerved her.

"Raoul?" she whispered, feeling as though her world was suddenly spinning out of control. How could she hope to adjust to such a wide range of moods as he'd exhibited in a few short hours? Was that why she'd ended up distancing herself from him in the past?

His first words wiped all speculation from her mind.

"The doctors and I should have listened more closely to you when you first regained consciousness."

She stared at him in confusion. "I beg your pardon?"

"During those first few days you kept talking about your home in Dallas, about your friend Janine, about seeing yourself in a classroom."

"Dr. Leclerc felt those images could be explained," she reminded him when he didn't say any more.

"Of course. Based on the fact that I identified you as my wife."

"Well, yes, that's true."

"But you didn't believe me. Or him. You were shocked to see that your hair was red. You were not comfortable with the clothes, you didn't recognize the children, the château, or Danielle and *Maman*."

"But I thought you said you no longer cared about my memory loss. You said—"

He made a chopping motion with his hand. "Forget what I said. Forget everything you've been told."

"But I—"

"I have just been informed that my wife—that Sherye DuBois—is presently in a coma in a Perth hospital. That she has been there for several weeks without identification. There would have been a more timely identification if there had been a missing persons bulletin out on her." He leaned closer. "But of course there would not have been a missing persons report filed, since I believed Sherye DuBois was living at home, showing an unusual amount of interest in my children, in my home and in my life."

He turned and began to pace.

"I should have known. You were too different from Sherye despite the physical resemblance between the two of you. If I'd been thinking at all last night I *would* have known. You are nothing like Sherye in bed...nothing! But I was so caught up in passion that I ignored all the evidence."

She felt stabbed by his offhand comment. She couldn't have said anything if her life had depended on it.

He stopped pacing and stood at the end of the bed once again. "The only thing that I do believe is that you haven't faked your memory loss. You were tested too vigorously to have faked such a thing." He ran his hand through his hair and frowned.

"I don't have time now to deal with who you are and how you came to be driving Sherye's car. I've got to fly to Perth and bring her back here."

She couldn't deal with what he was saying. She simply couldn't. One shock was falling on another. She wasn't Sherye? She wasn't married to Raoul? She wasn't the mother of Yvette and Jules?

"I—" She stopped, unable to go on.

He came around the bed and flipped the sheet away from her body. Instinctively she grabbed for it, but too late. He ran his hand over her smooth abdomen. "I bet you've never had a child. There are not stretch marks, something I didn't notice last night, but Sherye had several, here—" he ran his hand along her pelvic bone "—and here." He touched the curve of her hips.

Everywhere he touched her, her skin tingled, as though

remembering his touch during the long, heated hours of the night. She tucked the sheet around her, pulling it high on her chest.

"It's a little late for modesty, don't you think?" he drawled.

"Why are you being this way? Do you think I've done this on purpose? Do you believe that—" she choked on the words "—your wife and I planned this?"

He spun away from her and began to pace once again. "I don't know what to think...or believe. All I know is that I must leave right away and you—" He paused, and when he didn't go on, she prompted him.

"Yes? I what?"

"There's nothing else you can do but to stay here until we can find out who you are and how the hell you came to be here." He started pulling clothes out of his closet along with a bag. "I'll hire a private detective to see what he can find. I'll have him come here and interview you to see what you can dredge up from your memories that might give him some place to begin his search."

She rubbed her hands over her face. She was dreaming, that's all. This was some kind of nightmare. Any moment now she would wake up and she and Raoul would be able to laugh about her silly dream.

Tears slid down her cheeks. She couldn't seem to control them. They rolled faster and faster and she caught her breath in a sob.

He looked up from his suitcase, then slowly walked over to her. Sinking onto the side of the bed, he said, "Look, I'm sorry I'm not handling this very well. I should have realized the shock would be as great to you as it is to me, given our circumstances."

She wiped her cheeks with the heels of her hands. "I don't even know my name," she whispered.

As though he couldn't stop himself, Raoul took her hand

and massaged the knuckles with his thumb. "We'll find out."

"I don't belong here."

"But you'll stay here until we find out where you *do* belong."

The confusion as well as the unexpected kindness in his voice was her undoing. She could no longer hold back the pain.

The first thing she noticed when she opened her eyes was that she was back in her room. No. That wasn't right. She was in *Sherye's* room.

Dear God! This was even worse than the first time when she had awakened in the hospital. Now she had memories of a different sort, memories that shouldn't have been hers at all because she wasn't Sherye DuBois. Instead she was some nameless person who looked like the famous model.

Listlessly she turned her head on the pillow, aware for the first time of the lengthening shadows in the room. Raoul had given her something, hadn't he? She vaguely remembered a prescription for medication the doctor had sent home with her. Something to soothe her if she became too agitated. Raoul had offered her a tablet with a glass of water and she had been willing to escape into oblivion in order to avoid the pain of the moment.

Now she felt sluggish, her mind disjointed from her body and her surroundings. Raoul must be gone by now, gone to Australia to find his *real* wife.

She felt removed from the whole idea of Raoul and his wife who was in a coma. There was something to be said for being in a coma. At least Sherye could escape from a world she hadn't been able to face.

"Are you feeling better now?" Danielle asked, stepping closer to the bed.

"Oh. I didn't see you."

"Raoul asked me to stay with you. He didn't want you to wake up alone."

Not only had he placed her in her own bed, he had also slipped a nightgown on her. She closed her eyes, not wanting to remember the night they had spent together. Nor did she want to remember what he had said about their love-making. But she couldn't forget that he had known she was a fake. She hadn't been able to compare to Sherye when it came to making love with him.

Here was another humiliating aspect of her present situation. Not only did she not know who she was, she hadn't been able to successfully be someone else.

Her fairy-tale life had ended. Somehow she would have to pick up the pieces and go on from here.

Danielle took her hand and gently squeezed it. "Raoul explained that we were wrong about your being Sherye. I'm so sorry all of this has happened. I've grown to love you very much during these past few weeks."

She tried to smile, but she wasn't certain of her success.

Danielle continued. "Raoul contacted an investigator, who wants to speak with you as soon as you feel up to it."

"Yes. I need to do whatever I can to find out where I belong."

"In the meantime, we have to find a name to call you. Can you think of one you'd like?"

She shook her head and Danielle didn't push. After a moment Danielle asked, "Are you hungry? I could order a tray for you."

"I'm not particularly hungry but I know I need to eat." She tried to think. "Am I supposed to call the investigator to set up an appointment?"

"Why don't I call him and suggest he meet you here at the château in the morning?"

She nodded. "Thank you."

"We'll get through this together. You don't have to go

through any of it alone. I may not know your name, but you are my friend and will always be my friend. Try not to fret. I'll be back with something for you to eat.''

Once she was alone again, she slipped out of bed and went in to shower. She wanted to dress and feel more in control. She had to face the situation head-on and find the answers. Obviously Raoul had his hands full with this most recent news.

She stood in the middle of the room the two of them had shared since her memory began and thought of the man who had played a major role in her new life.

Raoul…who was no longer her husband…who had never been her husband.

Raoul…the man she loved.

Raoul leaned his head against the airline seat and closed his eyes. He'd managed to make good connections, but he had several hours of flying time before he would reach Perth on the western coast of Australia.

Perhaps during the ensuing hours he would be able to come to grips with this latest devastating news. The shock of the early-morning call had forced him to put all of his feelings on hold while he dealt with the practical details of the unusual situation in which he found himself.

For weeks he'd been living with a woman who wasn't his wife. The irony of the timing of the phone call hadn't escaped him. Twenty-four hours earlier and there would have been no intimacy between him and the woman he'd thought was Sherye. He could have apologized for his role in the misidentification, helped her find out her true identity and, perhaps, felt a touch of sadness that the woman he'd come to know—the kind, gentle, caring woman—was not, after all, a new incarnation for his previously shallow, self-centered wife.

Unfortunately he had been given that twenty-four hours,

which had compounded the inherent problems in the situation and added a distinctly painful side effect to everything that had happened.

He couldn't run away from the fact that he was in love with a woman with no memory of who she was. The only thing known for certain was that she was not his wife.

The authorities in Perth had made certain their proof of identity was incontrovertible before they had called him, not wanting to be held responsible for any possibility of a mistake.

Now he had to find some way to blot out the multitude of discoveries he'd made while making love to the woman he'd believed was Sherye—discoveries about how differently he viewed himself and his feelings and abilities to relate to others.

He had given himself in a way he'd never done before. He had shared all of who he was and accepted all of who she was...the woman who now held his heart in the palm of her hand.

He had seen her shock and emotional distress and had wanted nothing more than to stay beside her, holding and comforting her, reassuring her that somehow, some way he would make things work for them.

But he'd known better. He'd known from the time the authorities confirmed the identity of the woman in Perth that all the joy he'd discovered, the sense of unity he'd felt with another, his insight of how love transcends all boundaries would not matter now that he knew about the mistaken identity.

It could not matter. It must not matter because he had a duty to deal with life as it was, not the way he wanted life to be.

Hopefully the investigator he'd hired would soon be able to return the woman he'd left to her rightful life.

* * *

It was early evening, local time, when Raoul stepped off the plane in Perth. Passing through customs was a relatively simple matter and in a short while he was in a taxi on the way to the hospital.

He'd lost track of time. He didn't know if this was the same day he'd received the call about Sherye or the next one. He couldn't remember the last time he ate. He'd forced himself to nap on the plane, knowing he had to keep his wits about him. Despite his resolve, he could feel the bone tiredness pulling at him when he stepped out of the taxi in front of the local hospital.

Raoul paused at the front desk and asked for Dr. Parkinson, the name he'd been given by the police investigator who had placed the call to him. He was directed to the medical section—as opposed to the surgical or obstetrics section—of the hospital and told to ask for the doctor there, since he was logged in at the switchboard as still making his rounds.

When Raoul reached the proper area he paused at the nurses' station and identified himself to one of the nurses on duty.

The woman grew flustered when she discovered who he was. She quickly rushed into speech, assuring him she would find Dr. Parkinson right away and have him meet Raoul in Sherye's room. She escorted him down the silent hallway and paused in front of one of the doors, pointing out Sherye's room to him.

Raoul felt a sense of déjà vu when he pushed open the door and saw Sherye lying so still in the bed, hooked up to various tubes and machines. A creeping sense of unreality washed over him as he moved closer. Would this Sherye open her eyes and admit to having no memory of him?

There were differences, of course, in the layout and the

lack of luxury in the room. What he hadn't expected was to experience the oddest feeling that the woman lying there appeared to be more of a stranger to him than the woman he'd recently left.

Her hair looked dry, faded and lifeless; her skin looked gray and dehydrated. Sherye had always been in control of her weight because of her profession, but Raoul knew he had never seen her this thin—almost gaunt.

He also knew he was witnessing more than an extended bout of unconsciousness, such as he'd seen with the other woman in France. He felt a chill of unease as he studied Sherye's unnaturally still body.

One of her hands lay on her chest on the sheet covering her, while the other rested by her side. Her long, graceful fingers appeared almost transparent. Her nails looked brittle and unkempt.

Raoul couldn't be certain that he would have recognized her if he hadn't known who she was.

Whatever was wrong with her, it was damned serious.

He paced the room while he waited for the doctor to appear and thought about the information he'd been given during that traumatic phone call.

Now that he had seen her condition, more and more of the information he'd heard while in shock came back to him. For a little while he could distance himself from the emotional reaction. He'd had time to adjust to the intial shock.

While he paced, Raoul focused on what he could remember of the information he'd received on the phone.

Sherye had been brought to the hospital by two unidentified men. They told the doctor on call in the emergency room they thought she might have overdosed on drugs.

While one agreed to stay and answer questions for her admission, the other explained that he needed to move their car out of a no-parking zone and that he would return in a few minutes.

According to the report later given to the police who were investigating Sherye's case, the emergency room that day was filled with a miscellaneous assortment of injuries, including two heart attacks and a young boy injured in an automobile accident. These emergencies were brought in within the same hour as Sherye.

The nurse who was to get the information for Sherye's admitting form got called away before she'd had a chance to do more than jot down the words *Sherye* and *possible overdose* on a piece of paper.

After an absence of ten minutes or so—she'd later sworn it was no longer than that—the nurse returned to the desk and discovered that the first man had never returned and the second man was gone, as well.

Neither man had been seen again, nor were the police subsequently able to find them.

Raoul was told that in the weeks since she'd been there, the hospital staff had managed to stabilize Sherye's condition. However, up to the time of the phone call notifying him of her whereabouts, she had never regained consciousness.

After the inquiries into the whereabouts of the two men turned up nothing, the local police sent notices to enforcement agencies throughout Australia giving Sherye's first name and a general physical description as a possible missing person.

When the police saw that the first notice didn't produce any results, the crime lab came to the hospital, took photographs of Sherye and forwarded copies to every agency on the continent.

Because of the drug overdose, which had been confirmed at the hospital, the police decided not to take the usual missing person procedure of going public and flooding the newspapers and television with her picture, which the officer who called him had admitted hampered the progress of the investigation.

What they did do was consider the possibility that she was a tourist, visiting the country. Not knowing her nationality, they ran a check on every visa request for the past six months. In addition, they showed her photograph at every transportation terminal in the city.

No one recognized her.

According to the officer, one piece of luck in their favor was the city's relatively isolated position on the continent. A visitor to that part of the country would have limited access to it.

Although no one claimed to have seen her, the investigation turned up the seemingly irrelevant piece of information that a private, unidentified yacht had been spotted in the harbor at Fremantle, a seaport near Perth, on the same day Sherye had been brought to the hospital.

By the time the police decided the coincidence might be worth checking out, the yacht had been gone for some time without a trace.

The investigation had gotten stalled at that point.

Through sheer, unexpected luck, one of the female dispatchers in the Alice Springs police department kept looking at the picture they'd received—Sherye looked familiar to her. She went home and dug through several old magazines she'd saved. Ironically, she didn't recognize the famous model from any of her glamour shots. Instead she'd vaguely recalled seeing a candid snapshot of Sherye taken on a beach when she wasn't working. She'd worn very little makeup—and the photo was a close-up to verify the model's beauty in its most natural state.

For whatever reason, that photograph had stuck in the dispatcher's mind. As soon as she spotted it again, she knew she'd found the Sherye everyone was looking for.

The investigation had moved forward once again until it reached Raoul in France.

Looking at her now, Raoul was even more amazed that they had recognized her. Raoul reached out and touched her hand. "Sherye?"

There was no movement or sign of life other than the slight rise and fall of her chest when she breathed.

The door opened behind him and he turned to see a tall, middle-aged man walk in.

"Mr. DuBois?"

"Yes."

The older man held out his hand. "I'm Wil Parkinson. Sorry to keep you waiting for so long. I wanted to clear my schedule so that I'd have all the time we needed."

The two men shook hands. The doctor was the first to speak. "Although I'm sorry we have to meet under such sad circumstances, it's been a tremendous relief to all of us—police and hospital staff included—to finally locate Sherye's family. I want you to know that we're grateful that you responded so quickly. I can appreciate the fact that this is difficult for you."

Raoul nodded. "It's been a shock," he said, returning his gaze to Sherye.

"You must be concerned about her condition."

"Yes, I am."

Dr. Parkinson looked at the chart he held, flipping through his notes. "We have verified that her initial condition was brought on by a drug overdose. When we examined her, we found signs that she has been using drugs intravenously for some time."

Raoul spun away from the bed, feeling the jolt of shock-produced adrenaline hit his system. "You're positive of that? I mean, is there a chance you could be mistaken?"

Dr. Parkinson reached over and picked up Sherye's arm that rested by her side. Then he gently rolled the one on her chest until her inner arm was exposed. There were signs of old bruises on the inside of her arms from her wrist to her elbow, as well as needle tracks.

"I assume from your reaction that you weren't aware of her drug habit."

Raoul stared at her arms in horror, unable to reconcile what he was hearing and seeing with the woman he thought he knew. "She once mentioned that she'd become addicted to drugs when she was fourteen, but she saw what they were doing to her and after a couple of years managed to stop. I've never seen any signs of drugs since we've been married."

The doctor rested his hand over Sherye's. "I believe the evidence speaks for itself. She was in poor physical condition when she was brought in—underweight, dehydrated and anemic. While the police pursued the search for her identity we first worked to stabilize her vital signs and then began a form of therapy to stimulate her by various methods in the hope of bringing her out of her coma." He smoothed his hand over her hair in a comforting gesture. "As you can see, we haven't been successful, thus far."

"When was she brought here?"

The doctor checked his notes and quoted a date three weeks ago. "I know I'm being personal and I'm sorry to appear as though I'm prying into your personal life, but I've wondered how close you are to your wife. I believe the officer who called you explained that one of the obstacles they ran into in tracing your wife was the fact that there was no missing persons report filed on her."

Raoul contained his irritation despite the implied criticism of his behavior. "I can understand why this situation seems peculiar to you. I'll admit that I'm at a loss to explain some of the recent events, myself."

The subject had moved subtly from Sherye to Raoul. With that shift he realized that he could no longer hold on to his hard-earned objectively. His emotions surged suddenly despite his strong will to suppress them.

He disliked discussing his personal life with outsiders. Hadn't he already gone through this, for God's sake? First at the hospital in France and now here in Perth. He was being pressed and prodded to explain…to expose…to analyze an area in his life that had gone sour.

He knew he was oversensitive regarding the failure of his marriage. However, in recent weeks—up until the phone call he'd received several time zones ago—he'd believed that he'd been given a second chance, a chance to rebuild a shattered, hopeless relationship into something healthy and strong, a chance to resurrect a relationship and fill it with love and friendship, a new tenderness and understanding, a shared love of their children.

With one phone call, his life and his perception of his life, his values, his basic belief in himself—all of the pieces that formed the foundation of who he was—had been tossed into a chaotic swirl of events where the impossible had suddenly become not only possible, but had happened.

Raoul knew that he owed this doctor no explanations about his marriage. He also knew that sometime in the near future he would be facing a barrage of probing, in-depth questions from the local police if Sherye didn't regain consciousness soon in order to answer them herself.

He had no way of knowing how many laws—local and international—she had broken on her way to her capricious rendezvous with fate here in an Australian hospital, alone and unconscious. Just for starters, she hadn't cleared customs before entering the country. The evidence of habitual drug use was another red flag that would be investigated.

He had a hunch there was a much longer list involved.

Raoul realized that he had been standing beside her during his battle to override and suppress his emotions once again. He tested his control by looking into Sherye's expressionless face.

She knew all the answers to their questions. She was the one who could explain reasons, motivations, schedules, plots. She was the one who could explain why another woman was found with her car, her papers and wearing her clothes.

It was typical of Sherye to avoid confrontations that might lead to any unpleasantness. She'd always been skilled that way. She'd never been willing to assume responsibility for her behavior, either past or present.

Was her overdose an accident or had too many of her recent decisions produced a situation that got out of control? Had the consequences of her actions begun to catch up with her?

Knowing Sherye as well as he did, even if she were to regain consciousness he knew there was no guarantee that she would answer questions posed by the police.

On the other hand, she might find it amusing to play along, but then she'd never seen a need to tell the truth if a lie would better serve her.

No. He wasn't going to be able to ignore what he was feeling.

Raoul needed to talk to someone about all of this. Perhaps in the telling he would be able to make some sense out of what seemed to him at this moment to be an incomprehensible series of events, possibly orchestrated for nothing more than Sherye's own amusement. She'd carelessly played with all of their lives before blithely going her own way.

He turned away, unable to look at her without feeling his anger and frustration build. He was more than weary. He was exhausted. He didn't have the energy to deal with his roiling emotions on his own.

Dr. Parkinson had been quietly watching Raoul wrestle

with the conflict between reason and emotion within him, reading him fairly accurately as a result of his own wide and varied experience of dealing with people in crisis. He saw the moment that Raoul decided to trust him enough to share a part of himself.

Raoul looked around the room blankly, suddenly conscious of his need to sit down before he collapsed. As soon as he stiffly lowered himself into one of the well-padded chairs that furnished the room, Dr. Parkinson sat in its mate, leaned back and waited for Raoul to begin—at his own pace and in his own way—to discuss what must be a very painful and difficult subject for him.

"For the past year or more my wife and I have been having marital difficulties—since around the time our sixteen-month-old son was born. Approximately six weeks ago Sherye left our home, insisting she would be back the next day. The following night the police called and informed me that my wife had been in an automobile accident and had been taken to a hospital just outside Paris, where she was listed in critical condition."

Dr. Parkinson had started making unobtrusive notes soon after Raoul began. He looked up from them now with a puzzled expression. "I'm afraid I don't understand." His gaze strayed to where Sherye lay. "You mean she was already under a doctor's care weeks before she—" He paused, searching for words that might clarify what he thought he was hearing.

"No. What I am saying is that the woman found at the scene of the accident that night after Sherye left our home looks exactly like Sherye. She had the same hair and eye color, and the same physical statistics and features.

"There was never any doubt in my mind when I first saw her that she was anyone but Sherye. In addition, she was wearing Sherye's clothes, carrying her purse, driving her car. It was through the identification she had with her that the police were able to locate and contact me."

He could feel his body beginning to relax. He rubbed the back of his neck in an attempt to ease the tightness there. "No one thought it necessary to check her dental records, which I was told the police did as a final step in their positive identification of Sherye before they called me."

Dr. Parkinson had stopped writing and was staring—slack jawed—at Raoul. "This woman told you she was your wife?"

Raoul shook his head. "She couldn't tell anyone anything. Like Sherye, she was taken unconscious to the hospital. She'd received a severe blow to the head and remained unconscious for several days." He nodded to Sherye. "Ironically, the situations are quite similar except for the problem with her identity. That is, there was no problem of that nature until she regained consciousness and didn't recognize anyone.

"Unfortunately she couldn't identify herself, either. The doctors assumed her condition was the result of the blow to her head she received at the time of the accident. Her lack of memory was an unfortunate side effect to the accident, but the situation appeared staightforward enough."

Raoul's body was finally protesting the long hours and unbearable tension he'd been under. His head felt as if a tight band encircled it, and it continued to tighten as the minutes ticked by.

He leaned forward, placing his elbows on his knees and resting his head in his hands, which gave him some relief.

These were the painful memories, the ones that seemed to stab him in his gut. In a hoarse voice he said, "I thought I was bringing my wife home from the hospital last month. Until the phone call about Sherye, I'd been given no reason to doubt that the woman currently living with me was my wife.''

He knew he was lying, even as he heard the words. Some instinct deep within him had known that no one could make such a tremendous shift in her personality, beliefs and value system, but because he'd wanted so badly to accept and embrace all the positive changes in her, and because he knew there was no way she could be anyone but Sherye, he'd deliberately disregarded the wall that he and Sherye had placed between them so many months ago. He'd believed what he wanted to believe.

So what kind of person did that make him?

Dr. Parkinson had started making notes again, leaving Raoul the necessary space to deal with the pain as it surfaced. As the silence lengthened, the doctor finally accepted that he would have to help the man deal with the pain.

He glanced up from his notes and said in a casual voice, ''I would say that your story certainly explains the lack of a missing person report, but it certainly raises a great many other questions that demand answers.''

''Yes, it does.''

''You've been subjected to several bits of shock-provoking news in a very short time. Taken altogether, it's no wonder you've been severely shaken.''

''Yes.'' Raoul gestured toward the marks on Sherye's arm. ''How could I not have known that she was so heavily involved in drugs?''

''Oh, that part isn't so unusual. Addicts are extremely clever at covering evidence of their use, at least in the early stages. If, as you mentioned, there was some discord between you, I would imagine she had little difficulty in hiding her addiction from you.''

Raoul stood, needing to move, needing some privacy to deal with the turmoil inside him. He walked over to the window, sticking his hands into his pockets in an unconscious desire to hide, and stood there for several minutes in silence before Dr. Parkinson spoke once again.

"Do you know how your wife came to be in Perth?"

Raoul shook his head without looking around.

"Did the police tell you that there was a yacht seen in a nearby harbor close to the time she was brought in? No one on the ship contacted the port authority or immigration officials for permission to come ashore, so there was no official registration of their being offshore. Despite their efforts, the police could find no one who happened to observe or remember the name." He studied Raoul's shadowed figure, judging from his physical stance where he stood emotionally at the moment.

The man was almost reeling, he was so tired. Dr. Parkinson decided to press on. "Do you suppose it possible that she was on board the yacht? It's rather a long shot, but nothing else has turned up."

Raoul turned away from the window and leaned his shoulder against the wall, facing the doctor. "It's possible, I suppose," he mused, sounding a little more relaxed. And why not? The subject had veered away from him. His reactions were typical of most people, the doctor noted absently. He listened as Raoul continued without being prompted. "There has to be some explanation for her turning up here. I suppose that one's as good as any. I don't know many of her friends. Those I have met seemed to have enough money to afford to do pretty much as they pleased." He shrugged. "Whether one of them has a yacht is anybody's guess. I'm sorry. I wish I had more information for you."

Dr. Parkinson made several more notes before he looked up, shaking his head in amazement. "I don't believe I've ever heard of a situation like this before."

"Me, either." Raoul wearily rubbed his forehead in an effort to concentrate. "There is one thing that I thought of while I was on the plane coming over. It's something I'd forgotten about at the time of the automobile accident. I don't know that it's particularly helpful, but might suggest Sherye's plans if she thought she had managed to work out a plan where she could disappear without anyone suspecting.''

Raoul walked back to the chair and sat down. ''I came home early the day she left and found Sherye packing resort wear into a rather large bag. As I recall she was surprised to see me because I rarely get home that early. Perhaps she had hoped to be gone before I arrived. Now that I think about it, I'm sure she hadn't intended for me to see that bag.''

''Yes, that makes sense. Why pack a large bag if she's only going to be gone overnight?''

''My question to her, exactly.''

''What did she say?''

''Nothing. She ignored the question and left, which is customary behavior for her.''

''Did the bag show up at the scene of the accident?''

''No, but at the time I gave it no thought, since she was thrown—or, rather, I should say the other woman was thrown out of the car before it went over an embankment and exploded into flames. Had I thought about it, I would have assumed her luggage was in the car when it went over.''

''Is it possible the woman pretending to be your wife is feigning her loss of memory? Could she, in fact, be related to your wife in some way and agreed to take her place?''

''Anything is possible, doctor. I wouldn't begin to guess at the truth at the bottom of all of this. If the woman was part of the deception, something must have gone wrong in the plan because she was seriously injured. Since I was suspicious of what I considered to be a convenient memory lapse, I specifically asked the doctors to test her extensively in hopes of catching her out. It was their expert opinions that she was not faking her memory loss. Having seen the injury, I know that it wasn't faked.

"As for the possibility of their being related, all I can say at this point is—who knows? According to Sherye, she was raised by a single mother who had no living relatives. She never knew her dad. Sherye has never mentioned anyone in her family other than her mother, either when talking about her childhood or as she grew older."

"Would her mother be able to—"

"Her mother died when Sherye was in her early teens."

"Unfortunate at any time, but particularly devastating at such a vulnerable time in a person's life. I would hazard a guess that it was about that time that Sherye began to experiment with drugs."

Raoul looked at him in surprise. "Now that you mention it, I wouldn't be surprised if the two events were tied together. Getting back to the almost eerie resemblance between the two women, I took the time before I left home to hire a reputable and quite effective private investigator. I asked him to speak with the woman I thought was Sherye while I'm gone to see if some of her unusual and confusing memories would make more sense now that she knows she isn't Sherye DuBois."

"How did she take the news?"

Raoul attempted to block the brief flash of memory of the last time he saw her from his mind, but it was already there. He had held her in his arms and wiped away her tears. Since the doctor had cautioned him about the importance of not allowing her to get upset, Raoul had finally given her some of the medication the doctor had sent home with them.

He'd held her in his arms until she'd fallen asleep, then he'd searched out and found a new gown to put on her before carrying her back to her own room. There was no reason for anyone to know that she had spent the night in his room.

He knew that was one of the reasons she'd been so upset. Perhaps it was the only reason, given the circumstances. After all, the feelings she'd openly expressed toward him were perfectly natural toward a husband. Like him, she'd probably hoped to ease the tension between them. Fully believing they were married was grounds enough for her to have met him halfway in order to eliminate the strained atmosphere between them—despite the fact she had no memory of marrying him.

Whether she'd been a party to the deception or not, her lack of memory placed her in the role of victim. Unfortunately he had perpetuated her role by his foolhardy and premature behavior toward her.

He hadn't known, damn it! How could he have known? Wasn't he the planned victim in the scenario? The dupe? The unsuspecting, insensitive husband who wouldn't be able to tell the difference between his wife of six years and a total stranger?

The worst part of it for him was that it had worked...up to a point. Making love to the woman he'd brought home from the hospital had clearly shown him there'd been some kind of mistake, and he had made it. What gnawed at him was the question of whether—in his totally besotted condition—he would have had the integrity to admit to himself, to her and to the family that she couldn't possibly be the Sherye DuBois he'd married. Then he would have been expected to explain why he had waited so long and what had prompted his discovery.

It was a test he hadn't had to face. The early-morning phone call had rescued him. Now he didn't know what his choice would have been.

Sherye, and possibly this unnamed woman, had placed him in a position where he'd had to face parts of himself that had never been tested, parts that he'd never wanted to face.

He wasn't sure he'd ever be able to forgive either one of them because of it.

"The other woman," Dr. Parkinson repeated when Raoul didn't immediately answer him. Obviously he'd managed to touch on another painful part of the saga. "How did she take the news?"

"She was upset, which was a natural reaction. With no memory of her own, she accepted another woman's life. Now she has to start all over in an effort to find out who she really is. Since I have a strong desire to know as well, I fully intend to pursue the matter."

"Well, you certainly have a mystery on your hands. I don't envy you the task of unraveling it."

"My immediate concern is how to have my wife returned to France. Will she have to stay here until she regains consciousness?"

"If it was that simple, I would say yes, because she would then be able to answer some questions from officials. If she was brought into the country in her present state, she can't be held accountable for anything other than not having a passport and visa."

"You say 'if it was that simple,' meaning what?"

"Mr. DuBois, there is a better-than-average chance that your wife may remain in the coma for years without regaining consciousness. There's ample medical evidence to support the possibility that she could live out her natural life as she is now."

Raoul approached Sherye's side once more. She looked peaceful lying there.

Perhaps she had intended to die.

Perhaps she had accidentally overdosed herself.

Unless she was aware enough to answer, he might never know the truth.

Whatever the truth, Sherye had made good on her vow to prevent him from ending their marriage.

Once again Raoul faced the dark test of his belief in his own integrity. He knew that he could never divorce Sherye as long as she remained in her present condition because he wouldn't be able to face the knowledge that he could abandon her when she was helpless to care for herself. He took his marital vows quite seriously.

He'd promised to love and honor her. He'd been unequal to the task and he had failed.

He'd promised to love her in sickness and in health. Somehow, he would have to make up for his lack in other areas by caring for her now.

Chapter Twelve

"All right, Madame DuBois," Claude LeBeau, the private investigator, began once introductions had been made. "If you will, please tell me anything that you can remember prior to the accident, anything at all, so that I might gain some idea where to start my investigation."

"I'm not Madame DuBois," she replied in a quiet voice.

The two of them were seated in the salon. LeBeau had arrived promptly at nine for their interview, obviously eager to begin his assignment.

He looked pained by her response. Impatiently he waved his hand and said, "Yes, yes, of course. I quite understand the complexities of the matter. Nonetheless, we are faced with the problem of giving you some sort of address until we can ascertain exactly who you really are."

She looked down at her hands for a moment. "We call them Jane Does," she murmured, more to herself. LeBeau's hearing was acute. He leaned toward her intently.

"We?"

She looked up. "Oh. In Texas—in the States."

"Ah! There, you see. We have already discovered something important. You are an American, most probably from Texas, if that is the state that first popped into your mind."

She'd awakened with a headache this morning, fighting to resist the familiar sense of confusion and dismay that had accompanied her during these past few weeks. "Perhaps, but I was also told that Sherye was born and lived in Dallas when she was a child. Since I'd accepted the fact that I was Sherye I'm not certain how much of my thoughts are based on what I was told about me and how much are part of the life I led before the accident."

LeBeau made some notes, then tapped the head of the pen on the notepad several times. He spread several photographs of Sherye in a fan across the pad, looking at them, then at her, carefully comparing features.

"The one amazing coincidence in all of this," he mused, "is the astonishing resemblance between you and Madame DuBois. Is it possible that you are related?"

"I've been told that Sherye was an only child."

"Hmm." He made some notes. "I will have to follow up on what we know about her early life, as well. Perhaps we will discover a common thread." He looked at her for a moment in silence. "Do you remember if you knew her before the accident?"

"No."

"What do you remember? Anything? Anything at all?"

She tried to focus back to those first few days after she regained consciousness, before she had accepted her new life and become absorbed in the routine of the château.

"For a while I would get flashes of pictures—rapidly moving pictures—mostly with no sound. I couldn't make much sense of them without some context in which to place them."

"Did the doctors work with you to help you recall anything?"

"They worked with me, yes. However, they were trying to assist me in remembering someone else's life, although none of us recognized that at the time."

LeBeau rubbed his chin thoughtfully, pondered his notes, then asked, "May I make a suggestion?"

"Of course."

"A trained medical person might be able to work with you under hypnosis and further clarify some of these images for you, perhaps opening up memories that haven't surfaced in the course of natural events. Would you consider getting help in such a way?"

She was astonished to hear an obvious solution to a situation that had seemed almost hopeless to her for the past twenty-four hours. "Why, that's a wonderful idea! I wonder why no one suggested hypnosis before?"

"You must remember that there was no question as to your identity before, therefore there wasn't as big a need for you to explore your subconscious. Your identity had already been established, and no doubt the professionals felt it merely a matter of time before your forgotten memories would surface." He closed his notepad. "Now, you see, it is mandatory that we find out everything we can regarding your life prior to the accident. So. We delve deeper than we were willing to go before."

She nodded. "Yes. Of course you're right. I'll call the hospital where I recuperated. I'll explain to the doctors what has happened and see if they will work with me once again."

The investigator stood. "Fine. In the meantime, I will see what I can discover about Sherye DuBois's birth and her early childhood in Dallas, as well as look for any other information that might validate your own belief of having lived there." He held up a camera. "Before I go, I would like to take some photographs of you, if you will be so kind." He touched the professional modeling glossies. "These are a good likeness, but rather glamorous compared to the way you look this morning."

With a minimal amount of makeup, a shirtwaist dress and her hair pulled back from her face, she knew she presented an entirely different image from the pictures LeBeau held. "Of course," she replied with a nod, touching her hair. "I'll just— Oh! I just remembered something!"

"Yes?"

"When I first regained consciousness I was shocked to discover that my hair was red. I knew that my natural hair color was a very pale blond. Raoul said that Sherye was a natural blonde who kept her hair tinted."

"Ah. You were both natural blondes and you think you had kept your hair its natural color."

"Yes."

"Perhaps I can doctor a couple of these photographs of you today and see what difference that makes in your appearance." He reached into his pocket and gave her his card. "If you have any more thoughts on the matter, call me at this number. My associates will be able to reach me wherever I might be."

She walked with him to the door and paused on the front steps with him.

He looked around the grounds with appreciation. "It must be a grave disappointment for you to discover that you do not truly belong here."

"Somewhere deep inside of me I think I've always known that this wasn't really my home. I think I've been pretending for weeks to accept my place here. But you're right. I'm going to miss living here, miss everyone I thought was part of my world." She blinked back the tears, determined not to shed one more drop of moisture for what couldn't be helped. "Thank you for being so prompt. I'm sure Raoul will be grateful for your swift response to his request.''

He took her hand. ''Please keep in touch. Tell Monsieur DuBois that I will contact him as soon as I have something.''

She stood at the top of the steps and watched the investigator get into his car and drive away. She thought about their discussion, reviewing his suggestions and comments. Yes. She would call the hospital this morning. If they would accept her, she would leave the château, making a clean break between the life she had been living here and whatever might lie in her future.

She had discussed the matter with Danielle last night and they had both agreed that the children were too young to understand what had happened. She would spend this morning with them—one last morning that she would give to herself as a farewell present. Then she would explain to them that she would be making a trip.

Once Raoul returned with Sherye, the two of them could explain what had happened if they chose. She knew it wasn't her place to say anything.

With a sigh she turned back to the château to face another series of challenges that she wasn't at all certain she could handle with the dignity and courage she knew she needed. A betraying thought flitted across her mind—if only Raoul could be here to ease her through the next few days and weeks, as he had been there in the background when she'd first opened her eyes to a world that belonged to Sherye DuBois.

She'd been at the hospital a little over two weeks when the soft sigh of the door to her room pulled her attention away from the book she was reading. She looked up and saw Raoul standing in the doorway.

His unexpected appearance almost took her breath away.

Each day she had been at the hospital had been filled with consultations, hypnotic therapy, journaling and learning to live in the limbo state of her present existence.

She'd done her best to block out memories of the château and her life there—focusing instead on memories that were trickling back into her head.

Despite all her efforts, Raoul seemed to linger in the background of her mind at all times. Seeing him now, she thought her yearning to see him had conjured up his presence.

He crossed the room to where she sat and pulled up the chair beside her.

Seeing him up close she knew that their weeks apart had been as stressful for him as for her. His eyes were deeply shadowed, his expression grim.

She placed the book on the table beside her and instinctively reached out to touch him. Realizing what she had done, she paused with her hand hovering between them. "Hello, Raoul."

He grasped her hand like a drowning man and held it tightly, his gaze scanning her features. "How have you been?" he asked, his voice sounding rusty from disuse.

"I'm all right. How is Sherye?"

He gazed at her bleakly. "There's no change in her condition. I've spent every day of the past two weeks dealing with the Australian legal and hospital systems in an effort to have her released to my care. The red tape was indescribable. They could fill a thick book with transcripts of the multitude of interviews and interrogations I went through." He shook his head. "I never want to go through anything like that again."

"Where is she now?"

"I placed her in a hospital near the château. The doctors there have reviewed all her medical information. They refuse to make any predictions about the possibility of a full recovery.'' He shifted in the chair although he continued to hold her hand. She needed that small contact with him. His touch had always been able to soothe her.

"Do they know what caused the coma?"

He'd been absently studying her hand, and looked up at her question. "Oh, yes. She suffered a drug overdose. It seems someone was keeping her well supplied."

"Did you find out how she came to be in Perth?"

Once again he nodded. "We found out for certain a few days ago. It seems that she and a group of her friends were invited to spend the summer on a friend's yacht. They were under the impression that I knew where she was and didn't care. It's possible that she at least implied by her behavior that our marriage was over. I've spoken to Ted Andrews, one of the men who helped to get her to the hospital. He had to face police questioning once they found him because of the way Ted and the other man abandoned her at the hospital. By the time the police finished with Ted he was quite shaken. When I spoke with him and explained her present condition and my lack of knowledge regarding her whereabouts, he reluctantly agreed to tell me as much as he knew.

"He was understandably embarrassed to discuss the matter with me. I understood why when he explained that Sherye had boarded the yacht with a man she introduced as Mario, claiming that he was an old friend of hers and that she'd brought him along as her guest. It quickly became apparent to all those on board that she was flagrantly indulging in a flaming affair with him. None of them had ever seen him before and didn't know what to think of her behavior.

"When Mario found Sherye unconscious and reported it to the others, the ship's captain took them to the nearest port, which happened to be Fremantle. To avoid having to answer questions, Ted and Mario slipped ashore with

Sherye without going through official entry procedures. They flagged down a taxi and got her to the hospital.

"When Ted heard Mario tell the nurse he was going to move their car, Ted realized Mario's intentions and that he would be left to answer any questions about Sherye's condition. He admitted to me that he panicked and got out of there as soon as he could."

Raoul stated the facts and events coolly, giving no indication that he was emotionally involved with the woman he was discussing. She wondered how he could be so objective in the telling of what had happened.

Perhaps he still intended to divorce Sherye. She had certainly given him ample provocation. She reminded herself that it wasn't any of her business what he did. The DuBois family was no longer her concern. Not anymore.

"Have the police spoken to Mario?"

"No. They can't find him. He never returned to the yacht, not even to pack his belongings. I understand the owner of the yacht received a note requesting his things be shipped to a post office address in France. When local police checked, the box was no longer in use."

"Are you going to try to find him on your own?"

"It would be difficult, since they aren't certain he used his real name. I believe it would be a waste of time at this point. I have no reason to speak to him. According to Ted, he and Sherye spent most of their time on board away from the others. I think one of the reasons he bolted was because it's a good bet he was the one supplying her with drugs. If that's the case he's going to make sure his tracks are covered. He can't afford to be questioned."

"Do you have any idea how I became involved with all of this?"

He shook his head. "I'm afraid not. Only Sherye and possibly this Mario can explain how you came to be in her car. The authorities are now checking into the possibility that your accident may have been faked, that you might have been drugged and placed there. If so, whoever hit you on the head didn't know his own strength. That blow alone could have killed you.''

''Drugged?'' she repeated faintly.

''Yes. There were traces of a chemical in your bloodstream when you were first admitted that may have been an experimental drug currently being tested. LeBeau has been asking questions of the doctors, trying to find out more about it. He spoke with chemists and other scientists, who've concurred that the drug could have created lapses in your memory.''

She shivered. ''An experimental drug. How awful. I could have died there at the scene. Did whoever planned this scheme consider that? Did they care? What were they hoping to accomplish?''

''LeBeau and I have been trying to find a workable theory that covers all the facts we've gathered so far. One theory is that Sherye wanted to cover up the fact that she was going on that cruise. Her behavior these last several months has been increasingly difficult to deal with. We rarely saw each other. When we did, we ended up arguing. On one occasion I told her I wanted a divorce. She threatened to create a scandal if I pursued the idea. She didn't pretend that she wanted anything other than my money and social standing, but that was enough for her. However, she took me seriously and for a while her behavior improved to some degree. I believe that she wanted to go on that cruise and she knew I wouldn't tolerate the idea. That I would divorce her, despite her threats. Somehow, some way, she came up with an idea that would create a smoke screen to cover what she was really doing by providing someone who would be mistaken for her—at least on a temporary basis. Knowing Sherye, she probably expected to get away with it.''

Such a mess and there seemed to be no end to it. She felt so helpless, knowing there was nothing that she could do to make things any easier.

"The part that has been so confusing for me," she said, "is how Sherye got me to participate in the plan. I can't imagine ever agreeing to pretend to be someone else. Even if I had, what assurance did she have that I wouldn't change my mind and tell you the truth?"

"You'd have to know Sherye to understand the way her mind works. She makes up her own rules, changing them to fit her whims. If she got caught, she probably figured she could talk her way out of any problem it might have caused. She has a history of being able to get her own way. She probably enjoyed the challenge of trying it in order to see if she could get away with it."

"I'm beginning to understand your attitude toward me when I first recovered consciousness."

"LeBeau thinks you were given a drug that would induce at least a temporary amnesia to lessen the odds against my finding out that you weren't Sherye."

"You mean she counted on my not being able to remember anything?"

"Or at least you'd be confused and disoriented, which could be attributed to the injury you'd supposedly sustained as a result of the accident. All of it would buy her time."

She shuddered. "To go to such extremes just to have a few weeks away from her family. Such an elaborate ruse doesn't make sense."

"Not to me or you, perhaps. Remember, that's just one of the theories. There are others. We'll have to see what additional facts turn up in the investigation." Still holding her hand, he touched her cheek with his other hand. "Enough about Sherye. I came to see you to make certain you were all right and to tell you how sorry I am that I couldn't stay with you the day I received the phone call from Perth.''

"I didn't expect you to stay with me! Of course you had to go. She's your wife. The shock had to have been as great for you as it was for me." She looked down at their clasped hands, feeling his warmth and concern for her, fighting the almost overwhelming desire to throw herself into his arms and cling to his strength.

"We need to talk about what happened between us," he said in a low voice. When she didn't look up, he brushed his knuckles under her chin and raised her head until she was forced to meet his gaze.

"What is there to say?" she managed to say. "It happened. You thought you were reconciling with your wife. At least," she added with a tiny shrug of feigned indifference, "you discovered the difference once I was in your bed." She could feel the heat of her embarrassment sweep over her body.

His eyes darkened. "Yes. Given time to think about it, I would have known you couldn't possibly be Sherye."

She fought to hang on to her composure—determined not to let him know how much his words hurt—until she realized what he was saying to her.

"You were too open, too honest in your responses to be Sherye. You wrapped me in your flaming warmth and showed me what lovemaking could be—a free expression of pleasing and giving pleasure. You set me on fire and I lost all control but it didn't matter. I'd never experienced anything like it before. Sherye never had that effect on me, even at the beginning of our relationship."

He touched her cheek with his thumb and wiped away a tear. "I didn't mean to make you cry."

"When you told me that morning that you knew I wasn't Sherye when you made love to me, I thought I'd disappointed you. I—''

"On the contrary, you showed me what real lovemaking is all about. I woke up the next morning knowing I'd learned something valuable about myself and about you. I couldn't wait for you to wake— But then the phone rang and I discovered the new life I thought I'd discovered was an illusion. Nothing had been real. Except you."

She saw the pain he'd tried to mask and she ached with the need to hold him, to tell him how much that night with him had meant to her. She was touched beyond measure that he had shared his feelings about that night with her. He didn't owe her any explanations, but hearing them made such a difference to her bruised heart.

"Thank you for telling me this, Raoul. It helps, somehow, to know that what I felt that night wasn't one-sided."

They'd had one night together, a night that had opened her eyes to all that she felt for this man. She didn't regret it, not for a moment, but she knew that because of the circumstances, he didn't want to be reminded of what had happened. She cast around in her mind for another subject.

"How are the children?"

"Confused."

"Yes. Of course they would be."

"It's difficult to explain to them what happened and why, since we don't have many answers. It's particularly difficult when they ask questions, since we know so little about you."

"Not even my name or how I came to be in France."

"LeBeau is working on that."

"Yes. He calls almost daily to check with me and see what more I might have remembered."

"You must have friends somewhere who are frantic to know what happened to you."

"I can only recall the one name—Janine."

"Do you think there's a possibility that it's your name?"

"Danielle and I discussed that, but I really don't think

so. I see a face, a laughing face, whenever I think of the name.''

''I wish there was something more I could do for you.''

She forced herself to smile and say, ''You're paying for my stay here, which is very generous of you, considering that I was part of a plan to dupe you.''

''An unwilling part, I'm sure.''

''How can you be so sure? Perhaps Sherye paid me to pretend, then later made certain I wouldn't betray her.''

''That possibility has already been offered. I'm ashamed to admit that I briefly considered the idea, but I know better.''

''But how? You know nothing about me.''

''During the past two weeks I've had a great deal of time to think about all that has happened. It's true that I don't know your name, nor do I know how you became involved. What I realized was how much I've learned about you during the weeks we've been together. I watched you very closely, remember, convinced at first that you were putting on an act for reasons of your own. Gradually, however, I began to see how your mind works. Had I been completely honest with myself I would have admitted—at least to myself—that you couldn't possibly be Sherye. You are incapable of deceit.''

''Then you know me better than I know myself.'' She looked away from him. ''I've lain awake nights wondering not only who I am, but what kind of person I am. How could I be a part of something so shameful, involving the children, and Danielle and Felicity, not to mention the problems all of this has caused you? It's so scary, this not knowing.''

''Let me reassure you, then. Your name doesn't matter. What matters is how you live your life. I watched you day after day being gentle and kind to those around you who were being harsh and unkind to you. You accepted everyone in the family despite their strong judgments of you. You were not only recovering from a physical and emotional setback, you were attempting to find your way around an alien life-style, if we'd but known, and yet you never took your frustrations out on any of us.''

She didn't know what to say.

''I don't know who you are, but I know that during the weeks I spent with you I came to admire you very much. You've become a part of me, a very special part. Regardless of what happens, I want you to know that I will always be your friend. If you ever need anything…anything at all…I want you to contact me. You've taught me and you've taught my children to embrace life with open arms, to enjoy each and every day. Having you with us has been the only bright spot in our lives for a long while. There's nothing that I could do that would adequately repay you. I can only offer you my thanks and my friendship.''

''Oh, Raoul,'' she said, her voice breaking.

He reached for her and pulled her into his arms, holding her tightly. ''I didn't mean to upset you. I just wanted to assure you that whatever happens, I don't want you to feel that you have no one to turn to. We want to be your family.''

She pulled away from him, holding his hands in hers in an attempt to control her emotionally intense reaction. She couldn't handle being so close to him much longer without giving in to her need to cling to him. She did not have that right. She was not his wife. She was the impostor.

''Thank you for coming to see me, Raoul,'' she said in an attempt to bring his visit to a close. ''It was quite a distance for you to come and I appreciate it.''

''So you're sending me away,'' he said ruefully.

''Yes, because you have other responsibilities now. I don't want to be another one. I appreciate more than I can possibly tell you the fact you came to see me in the midst of getting Sherye settled and dealing with the aftermath of all that has happened. I, too, am grateful to have had the time with you and your family. All of you have added so much to my life. I will never forget you.''

He squeezed her hand and reluctantly stood. She followed his movement, not realizing until she stood beside him that she was much too close to him. Hastily she stepped back before she made a fool of herself.

She clasped her hands in front of her. ''Take care going home. Give the children my love. I miss them very much.''

He stuck his hands into his pockets. ''I'm in daily contact with LeBeau, so I will be able to keep up with the way his investigation progresses. In the meantime, please remember—if you need anything…anything at all…call me.''

He started toward the door, paused for a moment with his back to her, then turned and in a couple of steps was back in front of her. In an achingly familiar gesture he placed the palms of his hands along her jawline and tipped her face up to his. Disgusted with her lack of willpower, she closed her eyes and allowed herself to savor the touch of his lips on hers for one last time.

With a muffled sound she curved her arms around his waist and held him while his gentle kiss deepened and changed into a searing statement of their explosive emotions.

When he stepped away from her, she was visibly trembling. She caught her bottom lip between her teeth when he brushed a wisp of hair behind her ear.

''Take care of yourself,'' he murmured.

''I hope Sherye's condition improves soon. I know you'll help her to heal, just as you did me.''

She watched him walk out of the room and knew he was walking out of her life, as well. It was necessary. It was the only thing to do. At least they'd had this chance to meet once more, a chance to give their relationship a sense of closure.

She was the only one who knew that when he left, he took her heart with him.

Chapter Thirteen

Her name was Alisha Conrad. She lived at 412 Apache Way in Dallas, Texas. At the moment she was somewhere over the Atlantic, flying to New York with connections to Dallas.

Alisha sighed, wishing she could sleep, tired of thinking about all she had learned about herself in the past few weeks.

The continued regime at the hospital had helped her, but it was Claude LeBeau who had established her missing identity.

His search regarding Sherye DuBois's early childhood had netted as many questions as it had gained results. Convinced it was no mere coincidence that two women could look so startlingly alike, he had gone back to birth records, looking for twin births, adoptions, anything that would give him reasons to suppose that the women were related.

There were no twins born on April 10 of that year, but

he had found Sherye's birth certificate easily enough. She'd been born at home to Thelma Hopkins. In the space listed for father's name was the word *unknown*.

What caught his attention was the mother's listed occupation—midwife.

He had systematically followed the records of every baby girl born on or about that date in Dallas County, hiring researchers to follow every lead until they found similar statistics and descriptions.

Eventually they had found that Michael and Anna Matlock had had a daughter they'd named Alisha Marie Matlock. Alisha had been delivered at one of the local hospitals by a doctor whose name was signed at the bottom of the certificate as attending physician. Her vital statistics were similar to Sherye's, but her birth date was listed as April 11.

Because of the time constraints, LeBeau had made no more effort to follow up on a possible connection between Thelma Hopkins and Anna Matlock. Instead he had traced Alisha's records in an attempt to establish whether or not she was the woman they hoped to identify. He'd followed a paper trail through her childhood, her school years and marriage to Dennis Conrad.

Dennis.

As soon as she'd heard Dennis's name, memories had crashed down around her. Dennis had been the key to unlocking her past.

She'd met him during her senior year at SMU. They'd married two weeks after graduation. Four years later he'd been killed when a commercial airline tried to bring a crippled plane in to land at the Dallas-Fort Worth airport. Dennis had been one of twenty passengers killed.

When her memories returned, the pain of her loss felt new, as though she were reliving that time in her life.

It was Janine who had been there for her, Janine who

had stayed with her day and night those first few weeks. If Janine had not been with her, Alisha might have died the night she'd miscarried her twelve-week fetus and begun to hemorrhage.

The double loss had been more than she could bear, or so she had thought at the time. Why couldn't she have permanently forgotten that terrible time in her life? What was wrong with having selective amnesia?

At least she would soon be able to see Janine again.

She remembered most of her life now. She remembered when she and Janine had met, both of them freshly out of school, Alisha newly married. They had become instant friends, and the friendship had deepened over the years.

What she couldn't remember was how she had come to be in France, although there was a certain amount of logic in the idea that she might have chosen to spend her summer vacation in the country whose language she had majored in and presently taught.

The problem was, she couldn't remember. There was a gap in time, no more than a week or so, when she could remember nothing. She recalled the last few days of school, when she and Janine were looking forward to having time to themselves.

Janine had been invited to join a group that was going to tour Scotland for the summer months. Alisha had been invited to go, but she'd decided not to travel that year.

What had changed her mind?

So many questions, and so few answers.

Now it was the middle of August. She'd been found near Sherye's burning car the first week in June. The school was closed for the summer. Everyone employed by the school had scattered to enjoy their well-earned summer vacation.

If Janine had followed her itinerary, she should be arriving home within a few days of Alisha. Perhaps Janine could help her reconstruct some of those missing days.

On the other hand, maybe she couldn't.

Alisha knew that she had to find out.

In addition, Alisha intended to do some investigating of her own. She wanted to know more about Thelma Hopkins, the midwife who had given birth to Sherye.

She wanted to find out why the two of them were born in the same city only a day apart to different parents, although they looked like identical twins.

Alisha knew that she had to focus on something to blot out the loss of the family she had acquired in France.

Most of all, she had to forget Raoul DuBois, whose presence in her life had taught her how to love again.

When the taxi let her out in front of her condominium, Alisha felt a sense of anticlimax. She carried only a small bag, having left all but essential toiletries in France.

Everything looked the same and she wondered how she could possibly have forgotten the place she had lived for the past three years. She and Dennis had been renting an apartment when he'd been killed. After she'd lost the baby she had decided the only way she could face each day was to begin somewhere else.

With part of the settlement from the airline and Dennis's insurance, she had bought the condo, determined to make a home for herself, determined to get on with whatever life remained to her.

When she unlocked the door and opened it she found scattered across the floor an enormous stack of mail that had been dropped through the mail slot. She stopped, gathering up the envelopes and magazines, and carried them into the dining room, where she placed them on the table.

Her poor houseplants were dead and there was a film of dust over everything. She wished she could remember leaving here.

She checked the refrigerator and found it empty of anything that might have spoiled. She must have made preparations to be gone for a while.

After stepping out into her small enclosed patio area where the grass seemed to have grown a foot, Alisha felt a little overwhelmed with all that needed to be done. The heat and humidity drove her back inside. She was tired, that's all. Once she got a good night's sleep she'd be ready to tackle the dust and the grass. She'd be glad to have something to keep her busy until it was time for the school year to begin.

She decided to go upstairs and lie down for a while. There was nothing that needed to be done right away. Then she'd make a list of groceries and go out a little later to shop.

Halfway up the stairs the sudden ringing of the phone startled her, causing her to jump. She ran up the rest of the way. Her hand was shaking when she lifted the receiver.

"H'lo?"

"Ah. Then you have arrived safely."

Her knees buckled and she sank onto the side of the bed. What was it about a Frenchman speaking English that was so provocatively sexy? Her pulse rate doubled and she fought to take a calm breath.

"Hello, Raoul."

"When did you arrive home?"

"I've only been here a few minutes." She glanced at the bedside clock. "Maybe half an hour. How did you know when to call?"

"I didn't. The hospital told me you left yesterday and they weren't certain of your travel plans, so I have been calling off and on all day.

"How is Sherye?"

"There is no change."

"I'm sorry to hear that."

"And you? Does everything in Dallas look familiar to you?"

"Oh, yes."

"The doctors say that you've regained most of your memory."

"Yes, except that I can't remember anything about going to France. The last I remember I had intended to spend the summer at home. I don't know why I ended up over there."

"Have you spoken with your friend, what's her—oh, yes, Janine?"

"No. I remembered that she had plans to spend the summer out of the country. She should be back in a few days."

"Perhaps she can help with some of the blank spots that are left in your memory."

"Perhaps."

He sounded so close. She could almost feel his presence. She squeezed her eyes shut, fighting for composure. He didn't need to know how much she missed him.

"I, uh, want you to know that the doctors are preserving your confidentiality. Now that they know we are not connected in any way, they referred me to you if I had any questions. LeBeau gave me the information he'd turned up on you."

"I don't mind your knowing about my life, Raoul."

"I was sorry to hear about your husband. It was very sad how he died."

"Yes. Yes, it was."

"It makes me very angry that you had to go through so much this summer, in addition to what you've had to face in the past."

"It wasn't your fault. Besides, I didn't remember any of it then, and I don't regret my summer in France." Her throat closed and she swallowed. "I will cherish the time I had with you and the children. It was very, very special to me."

"You are certain that you are all right now?"

"Yes. Please don't concern yourself with me, Raoul. I'm a survivor. I'm used to being on my own."

"Of course. I forget about the independence of the liberated American woman."

He was teasing her! She hadn't heard that tone in his voice for such a long while. She laughed, but her laugh caught on a sob.

"Has there been any luck tracing Mario?"

"The police in France and Australia are investigating his role in the matter. As far as I know, he's still being sought for questioning, but I have heard nothing more about the investigation. Until Sherye improves enough to be questioned, there isn't much we can add for them."

"How are the children?"

"They miss you very much. They have accepted that your name is Alisha and that you only look like their mother. Because of your accident, you were told you were their mother. Yvette speaks of you often and asks about you. Jules is too young to understand why you aren't here, of course."

"Give them my love. I'll send them some colorful postcards to let them know I'm thinking of them." She bit down hard on her bottom lip. "This phone call must be costing you a fortune. I appreciate your concern, but I'll be fine now that I'm home. School will begin in a few weeks and I'll soon be back into my regular routine."

There was a silence on the line. She couldn't deal with his feelings as well as her own.

"Goodbye, Raoul," she said in a polite tone of voice. "Thank you for calling. I really must go."

She placed the phone back on the receiver and stared pensively at her last connection to Raoul.

Just as she had expected somewhere deep inside, the château and all those who lived there had been a wonderful dream, one that couldn't last. She was awake now and her real life had to go on just as before.

Three days later the doorbell rang. Alisha already knew who it was because Janine had called earlier to make sure she was home.

There had been several postcards from Janine in the stack of mail waiting for Alisha. She had put them in order by date to get an idea of the places Janine had visited.

Alisha opened the door and smiled at her friend, who seemed to be vibrating with energy and excitement. Janine was already talking as Alisha swung open the door.

"Gawd! But it's great to be home. Boy, did I get homesick. I can hardly wait to—" She had dashed by Alisha and spun around, her words jumbled together in one long rush until she looked at Alisha and came to an abrupt halt, her eyes widening. "What in the world have you done to yourself!"

Alisha frowned. "What? Do you mean my weight? I don't think I've—"

"No-no-no, not your weight. Your hair! What have you done to your hair! It's gorgeous, and the style looks marvelous on you. I've never seen you wear your hair down like that. You look downright glamorous, like some movie star or model or something."

Alisha grinned and shook her head. "C'mon, I'll pour us some iced tea and we'll go catch up on each other's summer."

Janine followed her into the kitchen, still staring. "But it's something else, isn't it? There's something else that's different. I just can't quite put my finger on it. You have a different look about you—softer, maybe. Almost a glow or— I've got it! You met a man while I was gone, didn't you? That's what it is! You're in love. I should have seen it right off. But there's a sadness there, too, that doesn't

quite fit with the glow.'' She tilted her head and lowered
one brow. ''I can see that it doesn't pay for me to turn my
back on you for a minute. You can't be trusted to behave
yourself when left alone.''

Alisha handed Janine a glass and they wandered into the
living room. ''You have a point there,'' Alisha said, sinking
into one of the stuffed chairs. ''I have a question.''

''Shoot.''

''Before you left, did I mention anything about going
away this summer?''

Janine's eyes narrowed. ''Don't you remember? You
wrote me a few days after I left. The letter arrived while
we were still in Edinburgh.''

Alisha leaned forward eagerly. ''What did the letter
say?''

Janine blinked. ''You're asking me? You wrote the
thing, don't you remember?''

''I'll explain in a minute. Can you remember what I
said?''

''Hmm. It was something about you'd gotten a letter
explaining a last-minute speaker cancellation for a teacher's
conference in Paris. It was all unexpected, last-minute stuff.
You were asked to fill in, your room and airfare were provided, and you'd decided to go.''

''Who was sponsoring it?''

''You didn't mention that part.''

''Where was it being held?''

''You mean, where in Paris? Gee, I don't know. I don't
think you said. Now then, would you mind telling me what
this is all about? When I didn't hear from you again I figured you were too busy to write, plus we were moving
around so much I thought you might have sent something
that never caught up with us.''

Alisha stared at her friend in silence for several moments.
Janine was her best friend and yet she was having trouble

trying to decide how to tell her what had happened. The whole story was too bizarre for words. Finally she leaned back in her chair and said, ''I have something to share with you that I don't intend to tell another soul. This will be our secret. It's nobody's business at school how I spent my summer vacation, but I have to tell someone.''

She began with waking up in a hospital, not knowing who she was.

She ended with Raoul's phone call on the day she arrived back home.

Janine had not moved or spoken during the entire unfolding of events. She sat there staring at Alisha with her mouth slightly open. When Alisha finished with her story she got up and went into the kitchen, retrieved the iced-tea pitcher and returned to the living room. Janine still hadn't moved.

Once her glass was refilled, Janine picked it up and drank as though she had been the one talking nonstop, as though her throat had gone completely dry.

''That is the most— That is the strangest— Can't you see Catherine Deneuve playing a part like that? Of course, she'd play a dual role. It's really a beautiful...and sad story...and—''

''And I want your help.''

''*My* help! What can I do?''

''I want you to help me find out if there's any connection between my birth and Sherye's.''

''Do you really think there is?''

''Of course I do! Don't you?''

''But Sherye sounds awful! I mean, she treats her husband like dirt, ignores her kids, she's rude to her sister-in-law, not to mention the fact that she happens to have what sounds like a nasty drug habit—''

''That doesn't mean that we might not be related.''

''You don't just mean related, and you know it. You're

talking identical twins here, which would be pretty tough to prove considering two different women gave birth to you.''

"That's what the birth certificates say, but Sherye's mother was a midwife.''

"So?''

"I remember Mother telling me that she had wanted to have me at home and that they had it all planned to have a midwife, but once she was in labor there were complications. My dad called an ambulance and had her rushed to the hospital.''

"So?''

"Don't you see? What if the complications included twins?''

"Oh, c'mon, Alisha. Isn't that a little farfetched? I mean, your mom and dad were there, for Pete's sake. Don't you think they would have known how many children she had?''

"Maybe. But they both talked about it later, about how scary it was. The pain was much worse than Mother had expected. My dad had panicked. Who knows what happened? But if I could find out the name of the midwife, and if it was Thelma Hopkins, I certainly think my theory would fly.''

"You think there was a baby born at home without your mother's knowledge and the midwife took it?''

"I know it sounds crazy, but there's got to be some kind of explanation why people who knew Sherye well could mistake us.''

"Did your parents leave anything in their personal papers that would shed any light on any of this?''

"No. After Dad died, Mom moved to Corpus Christi. I had to go down there after she died and pack everything. All the papers were standard stuff. My birth certificate has nothing unusual. If my mother did have twins, I don't think she ever knew about it.''

"How awful."

"Yes."

"Then Sherye could be your sister."

"I think so."

"Which means you're in love with your sister's husband."

"You certainly cut to the heart of the matter, don't you, Janine?"

"Well? That's what we're really talking about here. While you didn't have a memory you lived in Sherye's house with Sherye's husband and children. You, in essence, lived your sister's life."

"My alleged sister."

"Nitpick all you want, old girl, but you're in a real pickle."

"Don't be silly. Everything's been straightened out. Whatever happens, I'm no longer a part of it."

"Don't you care what happens to Sherye?"

"I've been thinking about that. I don't have any particular feeling about her, other than seeing such a wasted life. She's made some pretty poor choices over the years and her life is really messed up. Unfortunately her husband and children are suffering right along with her."

"Don't you want to see her, talk with her, try to get to know her?"

"No. I hope for her sake that she recovers and that she'll be able to get her life straightened out, but I have no desire to have anything to do with her."

"You sound angry."

"I *am* angry. It's my belief that Sherye somehow found out about me. I don't know how or when, but I think she used the fact that she had a twin to put in her place so that she could pull her disappearing act and get away with it.

If there was any way I could find out more about the so-called teachers' conference I was asked to attend—all expenses paid—I bet I could prove that Sherye was behind it."

"I hadn't thought of that."

"That's all I've had to think about since I found out that I wasn't Sherye DuBois. She used me, or at least she benefited by my being there. The doctors theorize that I was given some kind of drug that would cause amnesia, at least on a temporary basis. I can't fathom anyone being so wrapped up in their own needs and pleasures that they would manipulate and endanger another person's life."

"So you think she set you up?"

"Absolutely, even if I can't actually prove it."

Janine moved over to the sofa, sat next to Alisha and took her hand. "I'm sorry all of this had to happen to you. You've never done anything to deserve this kind of treatment."

Alisha gave her a weary smile. "Now you sound like Raoul. The worst of it is over for me. He still has to live with it every day, wondering if Sherye's ever going to regain consciousness or whether she'll remain in a coma indefinitely."

"You're very much in love with him, I can see that."

"I never said that."

"You don't have to. It shows every time you mention his name. From everything you've told me, he must feel the same way."

"It doesn't matter how either one of us feels. Nothing can ever come of it. I intend to put all of this behind me. Just to satisfy my own curiosity, I'm going to discover the truth about our respective births. Then I'm putting it all out of my mind. As far as anyone will ever know, I spent the summer here in Dallas. I know nothing about the former model, Sherye, her French husband or her fast life-style."

"Whatever you say. But some things aren't so easily forgotten."

As part of her teaching routine, Alisha regularly scheduled her annual physical the week before school started. She felt ready for her checkup this year. She'd been dragging around the house with no energy since she got home, blaming it on a combination of the heat, the humidity and the residual trauma from her head wound and amnesia. Either that or she had a permanent case of jet lag.

After dutifully turning her body over to the dubious delights of a medical examination, plus answering the doctor's questions and readily admitting to a lingering bout of lethargy, Alisha dressed and waited for the doctor to join her in his office. She hoped he'd offer some helpful suggestions on how she could boost her energy. Otherwise teaching a group of high-spirited girls was going to be a real challenge for her.

She'd been going to the same doctor for years and felt comfortable with him. When he walked into his office looking preoccupied she said, "I won't take up any more of your time, Troy. I know your waiting room's full and I—"

"Sit down, Alisha," he said, walking around his desk to his chair. He tossed her file down in front of him. "I'm never too busy for you, and you know it." He settled comfortably into his chair, tilted his head and looked at her over the top of his rimless glasses. "Besides, I think we need to have a little talk."

She'd made light of her head injury, admitting to occasional headaches that were becoming less frequent and less severe. There was no reason for him to look so worried. Determined to treat the whole thing as lightly as possible, she gave a little chuckle and said, "Uh-oh. I bet I'm anemic, aren't I? Actually, I'm not surprised. I seem to have lost my appetite lately and—"

"Alisha," he quietly interrupted her, "do you remember at the time you had your miscarriage that I told you there was no reason why you couldn't have a healthy, normal pregnancy?"

Pregnancy.

She froze when she heard the word. She'd ignored the possibility. No! She didn't want to think about it! She refused to consider that there was even a remote chance that she could be—

The doctor continued speaking as though what he was reporting was an everyday, run-of-the-mill occurrence. Of course, from his perspective, it was. "You've tested positive for pregnancy, Alisha. I would say you're close to six weeks along, making your due date around the last of March or first part of April."

Alisha stared at him in horror. No. He was mistaken. She couldn't be pregnant. She wasn't married. She was alone. She had a position of responsibility at a girls' school where she was expected to preserve, promote and maintain high moral standards.

Hadn't she had to deal with enough trauma in her life? Hadn't the events of the summer been difficult enough to overcome without long-term repercussions such as an unplanned, potentially explosive pregnancy to complicate matters?

The doctor watched her reactions with concern and compassion. After giving her a few moments to adjust to the obvious complications a pregnancy would create for her, he leaned forward in his chair and said, "As your doctor and as your friend, I guess the question I have to ask you now is—what do you intend to do about it?"

Chapter Fourteen

A strong gust of wind swept over the hillside, rattling the dry leaves that dotted the carefully groomed grounds of the cemetery.

Raoul stood beside the open grave while the priest's voice droned on, barely impinging on his thoughts. He held Jules with one arm while Yvette clutched his other hand with a fierce grip.

Danielle stood next to Yvette, while *Maman* stood beside Raoul. Few people had come to the graveside service. Raoul had kept the news of Sherye's death quiet, not wanting the media to sensationalize the family's troubles.

During the past four months he'd spent most of his time at Sherye's side. He had talked to her during the long hours as though she were aware of his presence. At times he asked questions. At other times he shared his pain and confusion with her.

He told her about Alisha, he asked how Sherye had found

her, how she had known of her existence. He promised her help and understanding if she would awaken.

Sherye never gave an indication that she heard him, but over the months he found a certain peace and release in expressing his turmoil over her behavior.

The early-morning call two days ago from the hospital saying that Sherye had slipped away sometime during the night had caught him unprepared to have his bedside vigil over. He'd felt a sense of rage from the knowledge that once again Sherye had escaped the consequences of her actions without ever having to face them. Now as he watched the final scene of her life being played out, Raoul could acknowledge how dearly Sherye had paid for her actions. She'd forfeited her life.

He doubted that he would ever know what drove her to such extreme behavior. It no longer mattered. He recognized his own sense of inadequacy that he hadn't been able to make a difference.

A rumbling in the dark gray clouds overhead drew his attention and he glanced up, hoping that the rain would hold off until the service ended.

He studied the people standing opposite the family. Most of them lived and worked for the château and winery. None of Sherye's friends were there. He had made no effort to contact them, since he hadn't heard or seen anything of them since she was brought back to France.

He had wondered if the man known as Mario would appear. Had he managed to stay in touch with the hospital to monitor Sherye's condition? Did he care? Did he feel any responsibility for what had happened to her?

The priest was concluding his remarks and the casket was slowly being lowered into the ground when Raoul returned his thoughts to the service. Yvette buried her face against his leg. Raoul placed his hand on her head and gently stroked her hair.

Jules had fallen asleep, his head tucked into Raoul's shoulder.

Later the family rode back to the château in silence, each lost in his and her own thoughts. The rain that had been threatening arrived, beating against the limousine Raoul had hired to provide the family transportation. In some way the weather seemed fitting, as though the rain was Mother Nature's tears shed for one of her lost children.

As much as Raoul had attempted to protect the children from the strain of Sherye's death, he knew that Yvette had been deeply affected. The bubbly little girl who had danced across the lawns with her puppy had said very little since the news of her mother's death. Whatever she was feeling, she kept it locked inside.

He knew that she had suffered from the loss of Alisha in her life. She had cried for her, as had Jules. He understood their loss but was helpless to combat it.

You are free now, the tiny voice in his head whispered, repeating a refrain that had been running over and over in his head. He hated the voice, hated the grinding guilt that immediately followed in the wake of the tempting siren's call.

He knew that the medical profession had done everything they could to help Sherye. They had explained that her abused body hadn't been able to fight the long-term effects of her drug use.

He hadn't wanted her to die, even though he knew that he no longer loved her. Perhaps he could have dealt with honest grief better had he still been in love with her. Now his grief was strongly interwoven with guilt.

They arrived at the château and Raoul spent the rest of the afternoon with the children. It was after dinner that night, after *Maman* had gone upstairs, that Danielle asked, "Did you let Alisha know about Sherye?"

They were seated in front of the fire. Raoul had poured each of them a snifter of brandy.

He stared into his glass for a long moment before he answered. "No."

"I think she would want to know, don't you?"

He shrugged. "Perhaps. Then again, perhaps she has already placed all of the unfortunate events of last summer behind her."

"Have you been in contact with her since she returned to her home?"

"Once, on the day she arrived. After that there was no reason to stay in touch. She said that most of her memory had returned, that her home and the city all seemed familiar. Hopefully, she's fully recovered from what happened to her."

"Are you aware she still sends the children notes and small souvenirs from Texas?"

"I would have to be deaf and blind to miss them. The only time Yvette is animated at all is when she's heard from Alisha."

"I was amazed at how quickly she formed a bond with them. Perhaps we should have realized that such an abrupt change in personality could not take place."

"According to the doctors, such changes are not all that unusual for some severely injured people who recover. I thought that Sherye had at long last recognized how much her family meant to her."

"Does Alisha have any children?"

"No."

"That's too bad. She's so good with them."

"All right, Danielle! That's enough. You're about as subtle as a sledgehammer! I doubt very much that Alisha Conrad would appreciate being offered the opportunity to become a permanent stand-in as wife and mother in this household."

Pleased that she had managed to break through his reserve and get him to express what he was feeling, Danielle hid her smile by taking a sip from her glass. After a long silence that seemed to stretch into the shadowy corners of the room, Danielle once again set out to shake Raoul out of his brooding mood.

"How do you know unless you ask her?"

"You're being ridiculous," he muttered.

"And you've buried your head in the sand like a silly ostrich, which tends to put a person into a very awkward stance. You're just asking for someone to come along behind you and kick you in the derriere."

"I take it you're self-appointed for the task."

"If necessary."

"The idea is preposterous. Alisha has her own career, her own circle of friends. She may be involved with someone else by now...possibly married."

"At least you've given the matter some thought."

He leaned his head back against the chair and closed his eyes, realizing how much he'd betrayed himself. For months he had sat beside Sherye and looked for her resemblance to Alisha, finding tiny touches of comfort when he noted them. What a damnably awkward situation. Alisha would never be able to understand that he had felt nothing but contempt for his wife and had only fallen in love when Alisha had taken on the role. He found it a little difficult to understand himself. All he knew was that it had happened.

"I think you owe it to yourself to see her once more now that you are free to make a new life for yourself."

"My God, Danielle, we just buried Sherye a few hours ago!"

"And I watched you for months bury yourself every day at the hospital while you sat by Sherye's side without her ever being aware of your presence."

"We don't know that for certain."

"Are you feeling guilty because you couldn't die along with her?"

"Enough, Danielle. Enough."

She got up and came over to him, kneeling beside his chair. "Stop sacrificing yourself, Raoul. Stop denying your own needs. Anyone who knows you and loves you as I do could see the difference that Alisha made in your life. It was not your fault that you believed her to be Sherye. Sherye herself must have been responsible. Surely you're not blaming Alisha, are you? Do you think she and Sherye planned it together?"

"No! She'd been drugged and struck a severe blow to her head. She could have died. Of course she had nothing to do with it."

"Then the two of you are innocent of everything but the natural and very human act of getting to know each other and falling in love."

"It was nothing so clear-cut as that. Alisha thought she was married to me, so she assumed she loved me. When she found out the truth, I'm sure she was embarrassed, as was I, and would just as soon not be reminded of the awkwardness of our situation."

"That doesn't take into account your feelings, though, does it? Don't you feel that you deserve a chance at happiness after all this time?"

"What is your point, Danielle? God knows you've hammered at this subject long enough. What do you want me to say?"

"I want you to admit your feelings for Alisha, at least to yourself, and then I want you to go see her. Tell her how you feel, find out how she feels. Create an opportunity where you can discuss the matter." She touched his cheek. "You've always been one to fight other people's battles. Now you need to fight for your own happiness."

He shook his head. "I can't believe we're having this conversation today, of all days."

"We are having this conversation today because it's the first time I've had an opportunity to see you for more than five minutes at a time since you returned to France from Australia last summer."

"You're correct in one regard. I spent most of my time during these past few months either at the hospital or with the children and I have a business to run. I don't have time to go dashing about the world chasing fantasies."

Danielle shook her head and stood. "I give up, Raoul. You are a hopeless case."

He looked up at her, his eyes shadowed. "Thank you for caring about me. I appreciate your concern."

"Good night, Raoul. I'm going to bed."

Bright sunshine and temperate air greeted Raoul when he stepped out of the terminal at the Dallas-Fort Worth airport four days after Christmas. He hailed a taxi and gave the driver an address he'd memorized months ago.

Raoul had spent the past two days in New York on business. When he left France he hadn't intended to fly to Dallas. There had been a problem with a major shipment of wine to New York that had been ordered for a New Year's celebration. He had flown to the United States to deal with the matter personally.

The face-to-face meeting with his client had gone a long way toward soothing injured feelings and any misunderstandings that had occurred. He had left the man the evening before, well satisfied with the outcome. The crisis had been successfully averted.

He'd returned to his hotel room with a sense of relief. He'd done what he'd set out to do. Now he could return home, having accomplished his mission. However, instead of immediately arranging for a flight home, his thoughts turned to Alisha.

Here he was in New York, on her side of the Atlantic, after all. A few hours' flight would put him in Dallas. There was nothing to prevent him from dropping by to see how she was doing, was there?

He considered calling her to make certain she was home. Schools were presently closed for the holidays. She could be out of town, visiting friends. He would be foolish to fly to Dallas unless he knew for sure that she would be home.

In the end, however, he didn't call. He knew he was being a coward. He wasn't at all sure she would have invited him to visit if he contacted her. She might not want to see him.

He didn't want to give her a chance to say no.

If she wasn't there, then he would return to the airport, get a room nearby and book a flight out for the next morning. In the meantime he would see the city of Dallas for the first time. He would get to see where Alisha lived.

To be able to visit the area where she lived, worked and spent her days would help him better visualize her life. Besides, he had nothing better to do in the next few days. The family didn't expect to see him until after the first of the year. He would treat the time spent here as a vacation. Even if Alisha wasn't at home, he might rent a car and explore the area on his own.

By the time the taxi turned down the quiet street where she lived, Raoul had convinced himself that it was perfectly natural to casually mention that he had been in the neighborhood and thought he'd stop by to say hello.

He got out of the cab and glanced around. Neatly manicured lawns, lush and green despite the December date, graced the area. He saw several shades of golden flowers in bloom.

"Would you mind waiting until I see if anyone is

there?'' he asked. Since he gave the driver a large tip along with his fare he wasn't too surprised when the man readily agreed.

Raoul carried his small bag up the walk, carefully set the bag down in an unobtrusive place and rang the doorbell. He waited, but there was no sound of movement inside. There was no sound at all—no music, no voices, no radio or television.

She wasn't home.

Well, what had he expected, after all? he reminded himself. He punched the bell one more time, glanced at his watch, then out to the waiting cab.

He felt as though his body had suddenly gained two hundred additional pounds. He wasn't going to be able to see her, after all. He was leaning over to pick up his bag when he heard a slight noise on the other side of the door.

He spun around in time to hear the bolt of the lock being moved. The door eased open. He fought to control his unruly emotions, which had been bouncing around for the past several hours like a roomful of yo-yos.

It was Alisha. Since the light was behind him, he knew she couldn't see his features clearly. He had a moment to stare at her before she recognized him.

She looked wonderful to him. Absolutely wonderful. She was wearing an emerald green robe that fell from her shoulders like a voluminous tent. She'd cut her hair into a shorter, more casual style and lightened the color to a soft red. He'd forgotten how green her eyes were.

He saw the polite question in her face and heard it in her ''Yes?'' split seconds before she recognized him. She froze, her eyes widening in shock. ''Raoul!''

''Yes. I know I should have called first. It was very impolite of me to show up with no warning, but I—'' He stared at her hungrily. ''I don't need to ask how you've been. You look won—um—quite well.''

She blinked, almost as though she fully expected him to disappear as a result of the action. He grew more anxious. "If you have company or if you are busy I'll just—" He waved his hand halfheartedly at the cab parked out front.

"Oh! I'm sorry, no, it's fine. I mean, you've just surprised me, that's all. I had no idea— What I mean is, you were the last person I expected to see standing on my doorstep."

"Would you mind if I let my taxi go? I'll get another one when I leave, if that's all—"

"Of course. Please. Come in."

He signaled the cabdriver, who saluted and pulled away from the curb.

Alisha stepped back, leaving the door open for him while she led the way into the first room off her hallway. Her lounging robe swirled around her as she turned and faced him. "As you can see, I wasn't expecting company. There's no school this week so I've been rather lazy."

Following her into the room, Raoul walked over to her and took her hands in his. "Please don't apologize. It was inexcusably rude of me not to call."

"Are you here on business?"

"Yes, as a matter of fact. Well, actually, I had to fly to New York on short notice and decided as long as I was there, I'd come on to Dallas on the off chance I might be able to see you."

She blinked again, this time with something like astonishment that he would consider a flight halfway across the country a chance to "drop in."

"Would you like some coffee? Have you eaten? I could—"

"I'm fine. Really. Please, have a seat. I won't stay long. I just wanted to visit for a while, if that's all right."

She sank into a nearby chair as though obeying his command, but she knew it was because her shaking knees would no longer hold her weight.

Dear God, what was she going to do! Raoul DuBois was here. *Here!* Right in her living room. She had never expected to see him again. There had been no reason to ever see him again, certainly not now. Not here.

He sat across from her and she had a chance to study him. He was much thinner than she'd ever seen him, and he looked older. His thick black hair had silvery flecks that were particularly pronounced over his ears.

"How is Sherye?"

His gaze was steady when he said, "She died almost two months ago."

"Oh, no! Oh, I'm so sorry. I didn't know."

"How could you? We kept her passing private. I saw no reason to make a media circus out of the circumstances surrounding her death."

Leaning toward him, she folded her arms and rested them on her knees. "Did she ever regain consciousness?"

"No."

She felt a tearing somewhere deep inside of her, as though something had been ripped away. She'd meant what she'd said to Janine. She'd never known Sherye and had no desire to meet her. Still...

Her eyes filled and she fought to control her tears.

"I didn't mean to upset you," he said quietly.

"It isn't that. I mean, of course I'm sorry she never recovered. Who knows how different she might have been if she'd been given another chance. It's just that—" She stopped and cleared her throat. "I've done some amateur sleuthing on my own, with Janine's help. I was able to prove to my own satisfaction that Sherye and I were sisters."

He leaned forward. "You have proof?"

"Looking at us is enough proof, wouldn't you say? I

don't believe in that kind of coincidence." She placed her elbows on her knees and propped her chin on her clasped hands, her knuckles white with tension. "I've been in contact with some of my parents' friends, as well as one of our neighbors at the time I was born. They remembered that my mother had insisted on having a home birth. Having a midwife and giving birth naturally was really being talked up back in those days."

His eyes narrowed. "I seem to recall that Sherye's mother was a midwife."

"Yes. Looking back it's clear that Mother wasn't aware she was carrying twins. Obviously Thelma Hopkins didn't tell her that she'd actually given birth to a child by the time the ambulance arrived and whisked her to the hospital, leaving the midwife to stay behind and clean up." Her gaze had gone inward as she recalled what she and Janine had discovered.

"A woman who knew Thelma told me that Thelma once told her that Sherye wasn't really hers. She'd said that Sherye's birth mother was a young unmarried girl who died during childbirth. Rather than turn the baby over to authorities Thelma decided to claim her as her own."

"You mean, no one ever questioned her about it?"

"The authorities had no reason to question a home birth and a single parent registering the birth."

"I wonder if Sherye ever learned the truth?"

"How else did she find me?"

"You mean she contacted you?"

"I don't know. All I know is that according to a letter I wrote to Janine I received an unexpected invitation to a teachers' conference in Paris, all expenses paid. I don't remember going, but it would explain my being in France at that particular time."

"Do you think Sherye had something to do with the invitation you received?"

"It seems likely to me. I don't like to speak ill of her. She's certainly paid for whatever she might have done, but whoever was behind it had carefully planned every detail, including dyeing and restyling my hair. No one but Sherye would have a reason to go to such lengths to duplicate her appearance."

"That's true."

"According to the people I spoke to who knew her, Thelma was always considered a little strange. Look what she did, after all. If she had any kind of conscience it must have eaten at her. From all accounts, she was obsessive about Sherye. I can't imagine what sort of childhood Sherye had under the circumstances."

"Sherye once told me that her mother was the one who was so eager for Sherye to model. That's how she got involved when she was so young."

"Thelma must have wanted to show her off to the world. If so, then she must have felt she successfully reached her goal, regardless of the long-term effects it had on Sherye."

"I can see that this episode didn't end for you once you returned home, did it?"

She shook her head. "I kept thinking about how it was for me growing up. I always wanted to have a brother or sister, but Mother never got pregnant again. If I'd had any idea that I had a sister, one who looked just like me, what a difference that would have made in my life."

"And in hers, as well."

"Yes."

Raoul couldn't keep his eyes off Alisha. There was a glow about her, despite her sad expression, that continued to draw his attention. When she caught him staring at her, he attempted to cover his lapse in good manners by hurrying into speech. "I wasn't at all certain you would want to see me again."

"Why?" She sounded honestly puzzled.

"Because I'm a reminder of what happened to you."

"That works both ways, you know. I'm even more of a reminder to you."

"Not anymore. Not really. You and Sherye have such different personalities that it is easy enough now to see how little you were alike. Physically, Sherye grew very frail during her last months, while you seem to be blooming with good health."

She flushed in embarrassment, which surprised him. He tried to figure out a cause for her uneasiness and kept the conversation simple. "I like your new hairstyle. The softer color is very attractive."

She touched her hair. "I've never worn my hair this short before. I decided to experiment, looking for an easy style to keep." Once again she inexplicably blushed.

There it was again. His presence must be making her uncomfortable, despite her polite acceptance of his unexpected appearance. Raoul glanced at his watch, then got up from the chair. "Well, I've kept you long enough, I'm sure. I just wanted to stop by to see you for a few minutes. The children have been delighted with your cards and letters. You've been very kind to remember them."

Alisha reluctantly came to her feet. "I've missed the children very much," she said softly.

He moved nearer. "And me? Have you missed me at all?"

She looked away, refusing to meet his gaze. "I've missed all of you, of course. I told you before that I enjoyed being a part of the life there at the château."

"Alisha, I know it's too soon to speak of this, and I—"

As soon as he began to speak she turned away from him and for the first time since he'd arrived Raoul saw her figure in full profile. The sight literally took his breath away.

She now had her back to him, walking behind the sofa

so that the piece of furniture was between them, effectively shielding her from his view.

"Please don't say anything, Raoul," she said quickly. "I appreciate your stopping by and I..." She paused and lifted her chin slightly before calmly continuing. "We can't pretend that Sherye didn't exist, nor can we pretend that I don't bear an uncanny resemblance to her."

Raoul interrupted her, growling, "Why not? Aren't you busy pretending that you're not pregnant with my child?"

Chapter Fifteen

She hadn't really thought she'd be able to hide her condition from him. Actually, she'd been unable to think at all from the time she opened the door and saw Raoul DuBois standing on her front steps.

She'd hoped the casual robe she wore would be enough camouflage to give her time to adjust to his presence, as well as time to come up with the explanation he was sure to demand when he discovered her condition.

She'd just run out of time.

The unexpected news about Sherye had distracted her from the ominous realization that she'd made a serious error in judgment when she'd decided not to notify Raoul when she first found out that she was going to have his baby. Janine had warned her at the time that she would be sorry if she decided not to tell him. She'd pointed out that he sounded like the type of man who would insist on his rights as well as on taking care of his responsibilities. She'd also pointed out that he didn't sound like the type of man Alisha would want to antagonize if it could be avoided.

There was nothing more annoying than to have a friend who was invariably right.

Now that Raoul was here in her living room looking his most intimidating, Alisha discovered that she would have much preferred to discuss the subject with him with an ocean between them rather than a sofa.

Unfortunately her discovery was too late.

Raoul stalked around the sofa, so that she lost even that dubious protection from his thunderous gaze.

She took a deep breath, held it, then slowly released the air in her lungs, intent on finding and hanging on to some semblance of calm. "You surprised me," she admitted with a hint of a shrug. "I didn't know what to say."

"I surprised *you!*" He took her by the arm and guided her around the sofa, silently indicating that she should sit down. He sat beside her, facing her so that their knees touched. She could feel the heat radiating from his body. "Why didn't you *tell* me!"

How could she have imagined such a scene? She had never expected to see him again. She tried to pull her chaotic thoughts together to form some semblance of order.

"I seriously considered contacting you when I first learned about it, but so much had happened. You already had so much to deal with that I thought—"

"You're saying you didn't want to tell me because you wanted to protect *me?*"

"Well, yes, that was part of it. You aren't responsible—"

"If I'm not responsible, then who is? Oh, and if you're going to try to convince me of another immaculate conception, you're wasting your breath. I know exactly who's responsible."

"I didn't mean— What I was trying—"

Unable to sit still, Raoul left the sofa and strode across the room, running his hand through his hair. He spun around and faced her. "What an unthinking fool I've been. I never gave the possibility of pregnancy a thought. Not once! I let you walk out of my life without once considering the fact that you could be carrying my child."

"Well, you—"

"When is it due?"

"Will…you…please…stop…interrupting…me?" she shouted, jumping to her feet.

He froze and stared at her as though she had metamorphosed into an alien monster creature.

He was close.

She couldn't remember when she'd been so angry. He wouldn't give her a chance to explain, to defend her actions, or to offer her apologies. Raoul DuBois might be the unanointed ruler of his own private kingdom in France, but he was in her home at the moment and he was badgering her.

Enough was enough.

She seated herself once again and folded her hands in her lap. "Now then," she said in a quiet—a very quiet—voice. "I can understand that you're upset, but if you will attempt to calm down for a moment, I'm confident that we can discuss the matter like two rational adults."

He strode over to the window and glared at the unsuspecting view, grasping his hands at his back. "Don't count on it," he muttered between clenched teeth.

She took another deep breath and began to speak. "I found out I was pregnant when I went for my annual pre-school-year medical checkup in August—"

He spun on his heel, redirecting the glare to her side of the room. "August! You've known *for months and didn't find it necessary to—*"

She held up her hand much like a policeman stopping

traffic. A muscle in his jaw jumped, but he said nothing more.

"I'd only been home a couple of weeks at that time. I knew that Sherye was in the hospital and that she was your first priority."

"Don't be ridiculous! I'm just as responsible for your condition as you are. Even though we thought we were married to each other at the time, I should have—"

Once again she held up her hand until he stopped talking. "I know what we thought at the time, but we were wrong. You were legally married to another woman. You are an honorable man. There was no reason to cause you any more problems than those with which you were already dealing. You see, there was nothing you could do at that point."

He looked at her in disgust. "So you were going to blithely carry on without any help."

She eyed him for a moment before making a sudden decision. "Very few people know this...and it isn't something I can talk about very easily...but I had a miscarriage not long after my husband was killed. Had I managed to carry that baby full term I was fully prepared to be both mother and father to it. I was devastated when I lost it. I knew that I wouldn't have any help, since both my parents and Dennis's parents were gone. But it didn't matter, then. I wanted very much to have my baby." She rested her hand on her softly rounded belly. "I still do," she said softly. "I don't deny that I was shocked to discover I was pregnant. I'd lost track of time and the possibility of a pregnancy had never entered my mind. But once I overcame the shock, I felt that God had given me another chance to have the family I've always wanted."

He studied her for a moment in silence, then sat in the chair across from her. She continued in a steady voice, praying he would understand why she'd made the choices she had.

"Because of the circumstances that occurred this summer, I knew there was very little you could do other than to help me financially. I don't need financial help. I'm perfectly able to care for myself. I teach because I enjoy teaching, not because I need to work." She gave him a rueful glance before saying, "I'll admit I told my classes that I had gotten married unexpectedly this summer—to a European who would not be moving to the States. I intimated that I would be spending my summers in France." She smiled, remembering that day. "I must say they found it all extremely romantic."

Raoul took his first deep breath since he'd discovered her secret. "Thank God for that. At least it will make things a little—"

She held up her hand and he stopped speaking as though she'd physically covered his mouth with her hand. In a very gentle voice she said, "I made up the story, Raoul. It is fiction…a fairy tale…something to protect the baby."

"Granted, but close enough to the truth."

"Close only counts in horseshoes and hand grenades, Raoul. As you know very well, we are not married. We were never married."

He gave her a heartwarming smile and said, "Which we can remedy immediately."

Sadly she shook her head. "I should have known that you'd feel honor bound to marry me if you could."

"True. I do feel honor bound. I can marry you…and I intend to marry you."

"No, you can't. Sherye's only been dead—"

"I can't concern myself about the conventions of the matter when there's a bigger issue here. You are carrying my child."

Of course she had known that he would feel possessive toward the child. She had gotten to know Raoul DuBois rather well last summer. In a conciliatory voice she replied,

"Yes. I know that. Perhaps next summer if everything works out I can fly over to visit with you and the family."

Once again he gave her a look that conveyed quite convincingly that he thought she had lost her mind. "You're joking, right? This is your idea of a joke. You will come to visit us during summer vacations and bring my child with you? How very thoughtful of you. So kind."

"Please don't be sarcastic."

"Then please stop being so ridiculous."

"I'm not. There are many children who only live with one parent, but that doesn't mean they can't learn to love both parents."

"You're being unreasonable."

"Not at all."

"I disagree with your logic."

"A marriage would not work between us."

"How can you say that!" he shouted, then paused when he saw the look in her eye. In a deliberate whisper he leaned toward her and said, "How can you possibly *say* that when we had a perfectly acceptable, enjoyable marriage last summer?" He gestured toward her protruding stomach. "How else do you explain, even justify, how you got into this condition? We obviously enjoyed each other's company. My mother and sister admire you, my children adore you. Getting married is the absolute best solution."

She was beginning to realize that she wasn't in control of this conversation. With a hint of desperation she said, "But don't you see? Marriage is totally unnecessary. I know you're a proud man, Raoul, and you always face up to your responsibilities. Well, I intend to face up to mine, as well." Unable to sit still she rose and stepped behind the sofa once again. Placing her hands lightly on the back for support, she said, "I really think we've covered everything that needs to be said." She fought to keep the tremor from her voice. "Thank you for stopping by. Please give the children a hug for me. Tell *Maman* and Danielle hello."

He stood and stared at her for a long, tension-filled silence. "You're right. You're not like Sherye. Even she would never have been so cruel as to deprive me of my child. I feel very sorry for you, Alisha. You are so determined to have your independence that you are refusing to see what you are doing to everyone else involved. You didn't become pregnant on your own. Our baby deserves a great deal more than you're willing to offer it. Our baby has a right to grow up with its brother and sister, to be a part of a loving family, but you in your wisdom—" he spit out the word "—feel justified in making godlike decisions for this innocent being."

She felt each word as a blow to her heart. Our baby. She had never thought of it that way. As soon as she'd learned of her pregnancy, it had become *her* baby, much as she'd felt about the baby she'd carried during those weeks after Dennis had died.

When she'd found out about this pregnancy Raoul had been dead to her, as well.

She loved him. Of course she did. But she hadn't considered the possibility of marrying him, even if he had ended up divorcing Sherye. The thought that Sherye wouldn't recover was one she'd refused to consider.

Now she had to face the unthinkable— Sherye was gone and Raoul was here, demanding in his usual arrogant manner to be allowed to do the "right thing." Was it fair to her baby, to their baby, for her to refuse him?

"Will you give me a little time to think about your offer?" she asked, her voice echoing in the tension-packed room.

His steadfast gaze touched her like a laser beam of light—probing, dissecting, judging. "If it will help you better understand my position in this matter, yes. If you intend to use the time to marshal more arguments against me, don't bother. I cannot force you to marry me. I can't think of anything that would be more inappropriate, given our peculiar circumstances. If you feel that being married to me will make you as unhappy as it obviously made Sherye, I'll leave now and promise to stay out of your life.''

His bleak words and matter-of-fact tone wrenched her heart. Of course he was angry with her. She had handled today's· unexpected meeting very badly. ''I think we both need a little cooling-off time,'' she said carefully. ''Our circumstances have changed dramatically. You've had two months to adjust to Sherye's death. I've only had a few hours.''

Raoul became aware of how pale she was. He was still getting over the shock of learning she was pregnant and learning that she had lost a baby earlier. How could he have lost his temper with her in her condition? What if she lost this baby? What if he didn't have her pregnancy as leverage to coax her into marrying him?

He shook his head, disgusted with his behavior. Once again he approached her, this time stroking her cheek with his thumb. ''I'm being an unmitigated ass, yelling at you…upsetting you.'' He brushed his lips across hers. ''I'm sorry. I'm never quite in control of my behavior when I'm around you. You trigger my deepest emotional reactions.''

His sudden and unexpected tenderness almost undid her. ''I should have realized how you would feel being confronted by the news without warning,'' she said, finding his nearness extremely distracting.

''I will give you all the time in the world to decide what you wish to do and I promise to accept your decision, whatever it may be.'' Once again he gave her a light kiss. ''For now, I will request the use of a phone to call a taxi and give you some space. Perhaps, if you don't mind, I will call you tomorrow to see what you have to say, hmm?''

Darn him. He knew very well how to charm her into agreeing to anything—to everything—he wanted.

"There's, uh, there's really no need for you to leave. What I mean is, I have plenty of room if you'd like to stay here."

"Are you sure that's what you want?"

"Well, it's rather silly to have you look for a place to stay, given our circumstances. Come. I'll show you the guest room and then I'll dress. You must be hungry by now. I can fix you something—"

"I would rather take you to dinner, if you don't mind. There's no reason for you to put yourself out, just because I dropped in unannounced."

"If that's what you want."

"Yes. Yes, it is."

She studied him for a moment, then nodded, walking toward the hall. He followed her and waited while she opened one of the doors for him. She gave him a brief, rather distracted smile, then turned and walked to the end of the hallway, where she opened the last door, closing it quietly behind her.

Raoul knew that the next few hours would be the most important ones he'd had to face. It was up to him to convince her to believe that they could make a relationship work, regardless of the irregularity of its beginning.

He retrieved his bag in the hallway and placed it in his room. The enormity of what he'd just learned hit him, causing his knees to buckle. Fortunately there was a chair nearby.

The most miraculous experience of his life had resulted in the beginning of another child. In the midst of tragedy and wasted lives, God had seen fit to offer him new hope and new dreams. He had to do everything in his power to win Alisha's trust and her love.

* * *

They had stayed out later than Alisha had expected, lingering over coffee and dessert while she shared some of her memories of growing up in Dallas, her schooling, a few things about her marriage and how she felt about teaching young daughters of prominent families.

Raoul had seemed engrossed in everything she had to say. How could she resist the captivating and flattering attention he'd given her all evening? He had driven them to and from a favorite restaurant of hers, following her directions without a sense of strain.

They pulled in to her garage and he helped her out of the car. "I'm sorry for keeping you up so late," he said when she fought to stifle a yawn.

She laughed. "I've enjoyed every minute of it. I'm just used to going to bed early because of my teaching schedule. I can sleep in tomorrow if I feel the need."

They stepped into her kitchen through the connecting door between the garage and her condo. "I enjoyed putting the frame of your background in context with the woman I know today. Thank you for sharing it with me."

She grinned. "I'll admit it's much more comfortable now that I have most of my memories, although talking about them reminds me of how ordinary my life has been." She glanced up at him, then quickly away. "Meeting you under such strange circumstances has been the most dramatic thing that has ever happened to me."

"If you'll excuse me," he said in a lazy tone, "there's something I've wanted to do all evening." Taking his time, he pulled her into his arms and kissed her. When she didn't resist, he held her closer, deepening the kiss.

This was what she'd been afraid of, Alisha told herself, in the back of her mind. This was also what she'd wanted very much. The rights and wrongs of their relationship were too much for her to deal with just then, and she gave herself to the moment.

When Raoul picked her up she didn't resist. Instead she clasped her arms around his neck and allowed him to carry her into her bedroom. There he carefully removed each item of clothing that she wore, placing kisses on each area of her body that was revealed, until he had her completely uncovered.

He pulled back the covers and placed her on the bed, then ran his fingers lightly over the contours of her body, coming to rest on her stomach. "You are so beautiful. I noticed the glow about you right away without understanding it. Perhaps it is wrong of me, but I am glad you are carrying my child. I am grateful that a part of me is now a part of you. I love you, Alisha, even before I understood who it was that I loved. I think I began to topple when you decided that if I was your husband that you had great taste in men."

She made no effort to cover her body, reveling in his enjoyment of her. When he reminded her of her embarrassing remark from her early days in the hospital, she couldn't control her blush. "I was hoping I hadn't really said that out loud," she admitted.

He grinned. "It was a startling comment totally out of character for my wife to make. Never wonder why I want to marry you, Alisha. I want you in my life because it is you that I love. The baby adds some urgency to the need, that's all."

"I've promised to work until the end of February."

"All right. I will return home and prepare the family, as well as take care of some business matters, then I'll come back here and stay with you until you are ready to go home with me."

"You'd do that for me?" she asked.

"There's no limit to what I'd do for you. You have become my heart. I do not want to be without you for any longer than absolutely necessary.''

She leaned up on one elbow and reached for his tie. ''One of us is wearing entirely too many clothes.''

He smiled. ''Does that mean you agree with my plans?''

Coming up on her knees, she pushed his jacket off his shoulders and began to unbutton his shirt. ''I've always had a weakness for anything French. How can I possibly resist you?''

Chapter Sixteen

Once again she was returning to the French château with her husband, Raoul DuBois. However, there were several differences from the first time she had turned through the stone gateway and followed the paved driveway to its end.

Summer had dotted the landscape with lushness the first time she'd entered those gates. Now winter had its grip on the surroundings.

She'd come the first time with no memories of the place and with the name Sherye DuBois. Now she had a great many memories of the place—wonderfully fulfilling memories—and she knew that her name was Alisha Conrad DuBois. She wore the wedding ring that confirmed it.

The first time she'd come here she'd been confused and a little afraid. Her confusion was gone, her fear was gone, but there was a residue of anxiety that still clung to her.

Raoul had reassured her that the family was looking forward to her arrival. He had convinced her to discuss with her boss the possibility of having her replacement take over the first of February. Then Raoul had come back to Dallas in time to appear at the school to meet her students and to allow them to practice their French with him. Every single one of them had fallen madly in love with him.

Who could blame them?

After overseeing the packing and shipping of those items she wanted to keep, Raoul had helped her to list her condo with a real estate agent and found a buyer for her car.

His help had been a godsend and she had found herself falling more in love with him each day, even though she'd protested his high-handed suggestion soon after she agreed to marry him that they be married immediately. Nothing she said could sway him from his determination to have her his wife at the first opportunity.

She still felt their marriage was too soon, despite her increasing girth, but she had given in because he'd been so adamant.

When they'd arrived in Paris he'd surprised her by announcing that they would be staying in the city for at least a week because he wanted a honeymoon with her. He'd also arranged for her to order a new wardrobe, pieces that she could wear in comfort for the remainder of her pregnancy as well as other things for immediately afterward.

He wanted her to fill her closet with items that she personally had chosen, and she had been whisked around the city for measurements, fittings and some sight-seeing. However, he'd made certain that she spent a considerable part of that time in bed.

Resting was only part of his carefully planned agenda while she was there.

By the time they reached the château Alisha felt pampered and well loved by the man who sat beside her in the car. She glanced at him, delighted to see how much better he looked now than he had little more than a month ago.

Besides looking more rested, he had gained back some of his weight, although he still appeared too thin to her. He smiled more now, which softened the rather harsh lines that had appeared on his face.

"Why are you looking at me?" he asked without taking his eyes off the road.

"I enjoy looking at you," she promptly replied. "Don't tell me it makes you nervous?"

"And if it did?"

She laughed. "I'll never believe that anything ever makes you nervous."

"You'd be surprised."

The truth was that she was the one who was a little nervous about the upcoming reunion with his family. "You did tell them that I was pregnant, didn't you?" she asked, more for reassurance than real concern.

He snapped his fingers. "I *knew* there was something I was supposed to do."

When he didn't look at her, she leaned forward to see his eyes. As soon as she did, she made a fist and hit him on the shoulder. "Oh, you!"

"I'm certain I'm wasting my breath, but I would like to point out that it really doesn't matter what anyone else thinks, you know."

Alisha nibbled on her bottom lip. "In theory, that's true. Practically speaking, it makes a big difference to me."

They pulled up and stopped at the front door. He immediately got out of the car and came around to help her out. She was rapidly becoming a size where she actually needed the help, particularly in a small car.

They were still in the foyer when Danielle came out of the salon. "I thought I heard you!" she said, dancing toward them. She hugged Alisha. "Oh, it's so good to have you back here." She drew back and looked at Alisha. "You're positively glowing with good health."

"I told you," Raoul pointed out, as though he was personally responsible for her condition, Alisha decided. Actually, he probably was, for the most part.

"You're looking rather glowing yourself," she said to Danielle.

Danielle laughed and held out her hand for Alisha to inspect the sparkling ring she wore. "For good reason. You've arrived just in time to help me plan a wedding!"

"That's marvelous! Oh, Danielle, I'm so happy for you." Alisha gave her another hug.

"It would never have happened without you," Danielle said, her eyes sparkling.

"Me! I haven't even been here."

"But you were here last summer and you befriended me, made me feel like I'm attractive, even if I'm not beautiful like you."

"Oh, Danielle. I can't believe you ever thought you weren't beautiful." Alisha looked up at Raoul. "Would you listen to her?"

Raoul hugged his sister, dutifully admired her ring and said, "I'm ready for something to eat and a chance to relax in front of a warm fire." He took each woman's arm and escorted them into the salon. "Ah, there you are, *Maman.*"

The older woman stood and faced them, her eyes on Alisha's protruding stomach. Slowly she raised her gaze until it locked with Alisha's.

Alisha didn't know what to say. She didn't know how to handle the blatant once-over. Then her jaw dropped when Felicity gave her a welcoming smile and held out her hands. "You must be very tired after your trip. Come, sit here by the fire and tell me how you've been doing. I want to hear all about Dallas and your students. Yvette has shared every card and letter with us."

Alisha walked over to the older woman and put her arms

around her. "Thank you, *Maman*. It's wonderful to be home again."

The same thought continued to run through her head several days later when she lay in Raoul's massive bed, waking up after a restful night of sleeping with his arms around her, holding her close.

All of her nightmares had been fought and dealt with. The children were so happy to see her. She couldn't get over the changes in them. Yvette was now going to school. Jules was no longer a baby. Instead he was a sturdy little boy with a very stubborn mind-set. He knew exactly what he wanted at all times and fought to get it, a trait he'd obviously inherited from his strong-willed father.

She stretched, missing Raoul. He'd left early, promising to be home early this evening. He'd insisted there was no reason for her to get up so early and she had obligingly gone back to sleep.

Everyone treated her with loving attention. No one referred to Sherye, or how Alisha had come to be at the château in her stead last summer.

Yesterday she had driven to the cemetery to visit Sherye's grave. She'd stood there a long time, and when she had left she'd determined to leave the past there in that peaceful spot.

The baby decided to shift at that moment and Alisha smiled, rubbing the spot and feeling a wealth of love and contentment sweep over her.

Driven by hunger more than a great desire for activity, Alisha forced herself to get up and face the day. When she reached the dining room, her setting was the only one left. Obviously everyone else in the household had been and gone.

She filled her plate with brioches and croissants and sat down, noticing for the first time there was a letter beside her place. Janine must have written almost as soon as Alisha had left Dallas.

She picked up the letter, smiling, before she really looked at it. Only then did she note that it had been posted in France and that the handwriting was unfamiliar. The letter was addressed to Madame Raoul DuBois. Puzzled, she opened the envelope, and several sheets of paper fell out.

As soon as she unfolded them she froze, staring at the top line with a sense of dread. Reluctantly she scanned the expensive paper containing the slashing scrawl.

Dear Sherye,
So you think you're too good to acknowledge an old friend, do you? Saw you earlier this week in Paris. You sailed past me like you'd never laid eyes on me. Sorry, babe, but it won't work.

I was glad to see you up and about these days. I don't mind admitting you had me a little worried with that fainting act you pulled last summer. From the looks of things you've decided to cozy up to the unsuspecting hubby. Nice try, but then you've always been a ballsy woman.

You owe me big time, babe. You missed the last two quarterly payments and it's getting hungry around these parts. I'll expect to see you at the usual place on Friday.

You wouldn't want me to tell the unsuspecting hubby just whose baby you're carrying, now would you?

Ciao,
M

Alisha had trouble reading the last few lines because the paper was moving. Only then did she realize she was shaking.

Somebody thought that she was Sherye. From the tone of this letter it must be the man known as Mario. She had seen him in Paris! She'd actually walked past him, unaware of his identity. Had Raoul been with her? She thought back over the week in Paris. He must have been. She'd never gone anywhere alone.

That's why he hadn't approached her.

He wanted money, and he didn't know that Sherye was dead.

She stared at the letter for a long time, trying to decide what to do about it. Her first thought was to ignore it completely. He couldn't hurt her. Raoul would quickly see that the man was arrested.

Wasn't any of this going to end? The nightmarish quality kept creeping back, despite all she could do to keep the past in proper perspective.

"Ah, there you are," Danielle said, coming into the dining room. "Mind if I join you? I'm ready for a cup of coffee and some advice."

Alisha tucked the letter into a pocket. "I don't know how helpful my advice will be, but I'm certainly willing."

Danielle filled a cup from a carafe and sat across from her. "Are you sorry that Raoul pushed you into a quick wedding?"

"Not sorry, exactly, but I felt it was somewhat rushed."

"No, I mean, didn't you want a big wedding with a long invitation list and bridesmaids?"

"That would have been totally inappropriate under the circumstances, but even without that, I preferred a small ceremony. My first wedding was headache enough with the friends and the few family members we had attending."

Danielle leaned over the table and said, "You know that very few people realize that you aren't Sherye. Because we kept her illness and death so quiet, people assumed she was away. Now that you're here, they think everything's back to normal.''

"I'm beginning to realize that. I'm not sure how to handle it.''

"Do you have to? I mean, it's really no one's business. I realize we're protecting Sherye's reputation as well as our own, but it seems so needless to put the children through any more heartache.''

Alisha forced herself to eat a few bites before she said, "What about Sherye's friends?''

"It's obvious they weren't friends in any real sense of the word. No one ever tried to contact her. Whoever she was traveling with obviously didn't want to be involved in what happened to her. That one fellow was the only person who gave us any information and he refused to name any of the others on board the yacht.''

"Danielle, did Sherye ever mention Mario to you?''

"Sherye never spoke to me about anything, why?''

"I just wondered.''

"Oh, I meant to see if you'd like to go shopping with me tomorrow. I want to have my hair trimmed and I thought we could have lunch, then browse. I need your idea on the type of gowns we could have for the bridesmaids. Plus, we want something special for Yvette and Jules to wear.''

Alisha smiled. "I'm not getting around very fast these days, but I'd enjoy going with you.''

"Good. Now, then. Here's some ideas I have about the wedding invitations.''

Alisha forced herself to listen to her sister-in-law and to forget about the letter that seemed to be singeing her pocket.

Alisha was thankful for the mild weather the next afternoon. She and Danielle had been in several stores before time for Danielle's hair appointment. They agreed to meet at the restaurant at an appropriate time and Alisha wandered through the shops, admiring the lace and looking at baby clothes.

Because she was tired of being on her feet, Alisha arrived at the restaurant early, thankfully finding a booth and ordering coffee. What a relief to sit down. She knew her ankles were swelling, even though she rarely caught a glimpse of her feet these days. Absently she rubbed her stomach and closed her eyes.

"Did you get my letter?"

Alisha opened her eyes and stared across the small table at the man who seemed to have materialized out of thin air.

"Where did you come from?"

"I saw you on the street and decided to follow you. When you came in here, I figured it was a good chance to say hello and make sure you got my letter."

Alisha looked at the man, trying to remember if she had ever seen him before. His skin was swarthy and he had glossy black hair and equally black eyes. He wore an obviously expensive suit and from his smile it was also obvious that he knew how good he looked. There was no denying that he was a very attractive man, if you cared for the type. To Alisha, there was no contest between this man and Raoul.

She didn't like the familiar way he was looking at her. She felt that he had stripped her with his eyes in one glance and obviously liked what he saw.

"Look, you've made a mistake—"

"No, Sherye, you're the one making the mistake if you think you can just brush me off like that. You and me go back a long way, babe, a long way. Don't you forget it. Haven't I always been there for you? Haven't I always risked everything for you? Hell, I even found that teacher dame that was your spittin' image, didn't I? Well, don't forget, doll face, that we both pulled that one off, and we could've gotten into some big trouble if the truth had ever come out." He laughed. "But it never did, huh? Damn, but you've got a devious mind. What a stunt to pull. I checked with my friends in Dallas last fall, you know the ones. Their daughter goes to that fancy school where the gal teaches. They said she was still there teaching school. So what did you tell her? Did you explain that it was a gag, that we didn't mean any harm?" He leaned back in his chair, crossed his arms and grinned at her. "From the looks of things ol' Raoul never suspected a thing. You're really something else."

"Ah, there you are. I'm sorry I was late, but there was this—" Danielle realized that Alisha wasn't alone and stopped talking. During the pause Alisha jumped to her feet and grabbed Danielle's arm.

"Don't worry. I think we'll still make our next appointment." She nodded at the man who was slowly pushing back his chair. "Don't bother getting up. I hope you enjoy your lunch." She practically dragged Danielle through the front door, out on the street and was almost running to the car.

"Alisha, what in the world is wrong with you? Have you lost your mind? If you don't slow down, you're going to trip and fall. What is the matter?"

"Please, just get in the car. I'll explain as soon as we're gone. Please!"

Danielle took one look at Alisha's face and said nothing more until they were in the car and moving. "All right, tell me."

"Would you mind driving me to the winery? I've got to see Raoul right away. I'd hoped we could just ignore it, but I can't handle this on my own. I've got to talk with him."

"Yes, of course. Who was that man back there? Did you know him?"

"No, no, I didn't. I'll answer all your questions once we get to Raoul's office, okay?"

Alisha could feel her heart pounding and she concentrated on slowing her breathing before she began to hyperventilate.

What a bizarre situation. Once again she was being mistaken for Sherye, by the very man who had helped to arrange the first switch. She didn't know what to do. All she knew was that she had to reach Raoul. He would know how to handle this.

Thank God she had Raoul.

Chapter Seventeen

Raoul was talking on the telephone when Alisha and Danielle arrived. He waved them into his office with a smile, finished his conversation, then came around the desk and put his arms around Alisha. As though he couldn't resist the opportunity, he kissed her rather thoroughly before looking over at his sister with a grin.

"This is quite an honor, having you drop by to visit. Have you eaten?"

Before Alisha could gather her wits after that blatantly sensual kiss, Danielle spoke up. "No, we haven't. If there's anything around here to nibble on, I'd appreciate it, because I for one am starved."

Raoul looked back at Alisha with a puzzled frown. "I thought the two of you planned to have lunch out today."

"We did, but—" She tried to think of a way to begin the story she had to tell him.

"We had unexpected company at our lunch meeting," Danielle said. "Alisha was upset, so…"

He looked down at her. He must have seen something in her expression because he immediately led her to a chair. "What happened?"

"Mario is here."

"Mario?"

"The man with Sherye."

Raoul stiffened. He nodded at Danielle to sit down, then leaned against his desk and folded his arms. "How do you know?"

Alisha felt so awkward. "I—actually, Sherye—received a letter from him yesterday."

Raoul lifted his brow. "Oh?" he asked in a neutral tone.

"The letter was addressed to Madame Raoul DuBois, so I opened it. The salutation was to Sherye and it was signed with an *M*. He said he saw me on the street in Paris and that I ignored him. He reminded me that I hadn't paid him the past two quarters and told me to meet him at our usual place. Otherwise he would tell you who fathered my baby."

Danielle gave a small gasp but said nothing. Raoul eyed her thoughtfully. "Why didn't you show me the letter?"

She had known he would ask that question. Impatiently she replied, "Because I chose to ignore it and saw no point in bringing it to your attention. There was no return address on the letter—no way to report his whereabouts. Since I had no idea where the usual meeting place was, I hoped that if I didn't show up he would leave me alone, assuming I was no longer interested in him."

"You mean that Sherye was no longer interested."

"Yes."

"So he isn't aware that Sherye died," he mused.

"Obviously not."

"What happened today?"

"He said he saw me on the street and followed me to the restaurant where I was to meet Danielle for lunch. He brought up all the things he'd done for me—for Sherye—

including finding the schoolteacher. He wanted to know if you'd ever discovered the switch.''

"Did you tell him who you were?"

"No. I couldn't think, I was so unnerved. As soon as Danielle arrived I made an excuse about having to go. We left immediately and drove straight here to tell you what had happened.''

"I appreciate your including me." His bland tone didn't fool either woman.

Danielle said, "Raoul—" but stopped abruptly when he turned his gaze on her. When she said no more, he returned his attention to Alisha.

"I'll notify the authorities that Mario's in the area. Perhaps you could give me a description of him.''

His voice remained smooth but Alisha could see he was exerting a great deal of control over his temper. All right, so she should have told him about the letter. She'd made a wrong choice. Now wasn't the time to apologize or explain any further. She'd done what she thought was best, after all.

Alisha gave Raoul a description of the man who'd sat down across from her. When she finished he repeated one of her words.

"Attractive?"

"Yes."

He glanced at Danielle as though to confirm Alisha's assessment and Danielle nodded.

"Is there anything else either of you can think of to help the authorities find him?"

After a long pause Alisha shook her head.

Raoul straightened. "Then I suggest the two of you go home and I'll discuss the matter with you when I get there. In the meantime, I'll give the information to the police."

He made no attempt to kiss Alisha goodbye.

The women wasted no time leaving his office.

"Whew! He was furious," Alisha said once they were in the car and Danielle was driving them home.

"He was worried about you and it showed."

"He's got such a temper!"

"Which he controlled admirably," Danielle pointed out dryly. "Under the circumstances."

"I know," Alisha admitted. "I should have told him about the letter."

"You didn't know that at the time. I happen to agree with you. What point was there in reminding him that his wife was seeing another man?"

"Exactly my reaction." She glanced at Danielle. "I've been trying to put the past behind us and build a new life with Raoul. I know it must be difficult for him to have me in his life as a daily reminder of his first marriage."

"I think you're more self-conscious about the situation than anyone," Danielle said, watching traffic. "Yes, you look like Sherye. There isn't much you can do about that. However, you need to remember that the family had several weeks to get to know you, Alisha. You helped us to overcome our reactions to Sherye. When we look at you now, we see Alisha. I know it's difficult for you to believe that, but it's true."

Alisha touched her sister-in-law's arm. "Thank you for saying that. At the moment I'm feeling anything but secure. Raoul married me because of my pregnancy and I—" She stopped speaking because Danielle laughed. "What's the matter?"

"I'm sorry, I didn't mean to be rude," Danielle replied, still chuckling. "I was just amused that you think Raoul married you because of the baby."

"He's an honorable man."

"And he loves you, Alisha. You. It's so obvious to the rest of us. You would have had to know what Raoul was like before to see the tremendous changes you've brought about in him. You've been very good for him.''

''I have?''

''Most definitely. I had no idea you were feeling so insecure. Obviously my brother needs to be a little more forthcoming about his feelings. I'm surprised he— What's this?''

A truck carrying crates of winter vegetables had broken down near the stone gates of the château. Three cars were pulled up in a line behind the truck and the drivers were shouting for the driver to get the thing out of the way.

Alisha chuckled. ''Sometimes these narrow roads can be a real hazard, can't they?''

Danielle stopped the car. ''We'll have to wait, since there's no other way to get to the château. By the time I finally get something to eat, I'll be near fainting.''

''I know what you mean. I—''

The door to the passenger's side flew open. Alisha's seat belt was jerked loose and she was hauled from the car before she knew what was happening. She heard Danielle's scream and fought to get her balance, only to find herself lifted into a pair of strong arms.

''What is—'' She couldn't get enough breath to finish the sentence.

Mario loped along the shoulder of the road until he reached a side road, more of a trail than a road. He opened the passenger door of a car parked there, shoved her inside, locked the door and ran to the other side.

''What are you doing?'' she stammered as he threw the car into reverse and backed out onto the roadway, then headed away from the château.

''I don't know what kind of game you're playing, Sherye, but I'm getting a little tired of it. It's a little late to be worrying about whether your sister-in-law sees us together or not, wouldn't you say? Forget about your need for financial security. You're carrying my baby now. That's more important to me than all the money in the world. We'll work all of this out together, somehow. You'll see.''

''But you've got it all wrong. I'm not Sherye. I'm—''

He glared at her before switching his gaze back to the road. ''Don't play games with me anymore. Okay? I can't take much more of this. After I left you at the hospital in Perth I was afraid to go back right away, for fear the police would hold me for questioning. When I finally managed to sneak in you were already gone. I've been trying to contact you for months. I didn't know where you were or how to contact you. Then when I finally do run into you, you ignore me, like I was dirt under your feet. Well, it's a little late for you to decide to forget about me. There's too much between us. You know that as well as I do.''

He was driving too fast and his agitated speech scared her. She didn't know what to do but she knew he had to calm down before he wrecked the car.

''Where are you going?''

''To a place I found. You've never been there but I know you'll enjoy it. I suppose we can expect Raoul to spend some time looking for you. Once he gives up, we'll be able to leave France, maybe go back to the States or wherever you want to go.'' He gave her a quick glance. ''When is the baby due?''

''In about three weeks,'' she replied absently. ''But, Mario, I can't go off with you like this.'' She had to think, had to stay calm. Getting upset would not help the situation and could harm the baby. Alisha didn't know how to tell him that she wasn't Sherye. If he discovered who she was, would he harm her in some way? *Think!* she told herself. What can you say to him in order to convince him to let you go? He was talking once again and she forced herself to listen to his rambling speech.

''I know you think you've got to stay with him for the

money and the prestige, but we mean too much to each other to keep on with this farce.''

Stay calm, Alisha, she kept repeating to herself. *Don't do anything that will cause distress to the baby. You're too large to try to run away. Danielle will get in touch with Raoul and he'll find you. If Mario's telling the truth, he won't do anything to harm you, at least not intentionally.*

''Please slow down, you're scaring me,'' she finally said, gripping the armrest.

Mario laughed. ''Who are you kidding? Nothing scares you. You've always been a speed demon. The faster the better.''

She fought to sound calm. ''I don't want to take any chances at the moment. I wouldn't want to do anything that might harm the baby.''

''Yeah, I guess you're right.'' He raised his foot off the accelerator and Alisha let go of her pent-up breath. ''Man, oh, man, I'm still having trouble believing it. Me, a daddy.'' He laughed exultantly. ''I was shocked out of my head when I saw you last week, let me tell you! All that time you insisted you wouldn't get pregnant because you were on the pill.'' He glanced over at her with a smug grin. ''Guess I showed you what a real man can accomplish, huh?'' He looked back at the road, still smiling. ''I always did have trouble keeping my hands off you. If we hadn't had that big blowup you never would have ended up married to that stiff Frenchman.''

''We've known each other for a long time,'' she said in a tentative voice.

''Yeah, we go back a long way. You got high for the first time with me. Remember that, babe? After that you were insatiable.'' He laughed again, sounding pleased with himself.

During their conversation Alisha watched for landmarks. If she could keep him talking, if, somehow, she could continue to allow him to think she was Sherye, he would have no reason to suspect that she wasn't happy to stay with him. She'd have a much better chance of making a phone call if she didn't give him any reason to become suspicious of her.

For the next hour she asked him questions that he seemed pleased to answer about what he'd been doing since last summer. She coaxed him into reminiscing about their past together, responding vaguely when he brought up places and happenings for her to remember.

She kept reminding herself that he wouldn't harm her as long as he thought she was Sherye. It was obvious that he loved Sherye very much. She knew he was going to be devastated when he learned the truth.

By the time they arrived at the small cottage tucked away in the hills, Alisha wasn't certain she could make it into the house unaided. The past few hours had taken their toll on her. The nagging ache in her back that had started in Raoul's office hadn't gone away. If anything, it had become more persistent. Her body wasn't used to carrying so much extra weight and she was in the habit of resting every few hours.

Now she had no trouble convincing Mario that she needed to lie down. He solicitously helped her into the bedroom, one of three rooms in the house, and encouraged her to rest.

Her heart sank when she saw no sign of a telephone anywhere on the premises. How was she going to contact Raoul? She was shaking as though she were having a chill. She was scared and the pain in her back wouldn't go away. She knew it was nerves and reminded herself to calm down. She had to think about the baby.

From every indication, she could see that she wasn't in any immediate danger from Mario, particularly as long as he thought she was Sherye. She'd played that role enough to have some understanding of what he expected Sherye to be. What she had to do was to keep Mario distracted until she could think of a way to get help.

Alisha knew she was too on edge to sleep, but at least she could stretch out and ease the strain on her back. She slipped off her shoes and lay down, pulling the folded quilt on the bed over her.

The soft mattress felt wonderful after the long hours she'd spent moving around today. She rolled to her side and pulled up her knees in an attempt to get comfortable. At this stage in her pregnancy, true comfort was only a memory. She placed her hand on the baby protectively and closed her eyes, willing herself to rest.

A kiss awakened Alisha sometime later and she smiled as she stirred, knowing Raoul would—

She opened her eyes and stared into Mario's smiling face. "Hey, sleepyhead, are you going to sleep the evening away?" He straightened. "I made us something to eat. We've got to keep up your strength, you know."

She was back in the nightmare once again. She was with Mario, and Raoul had no idea where she was. More important to her immediate well-being, she was physically uncomfortable.

Alisha pushed herself up until she sat on the side of the bed. "I, uh, need to—" She looked around the room, embarrassed by her situation. She was alone with a man she didn't know, the man who was responsible for her being in France in the first place. How could she hide her negative reaction to him?

"Yeah, sure," he said, nodding. "The bathroom's right in here. That's one of the things that sold me on this place. It's been modernized and updated but still manages to keep its rustic charm."

Thankfully Alisha found herself alone for a few very necessary minutes. She had to gather her courage. She'd been gone for several hours now. Surely Danielle would have immediately contacted Raoul to tell him what had happened. She knew him well enough to know that he would waste no time looking for her. All she had to do was to keep Mario from discovering her real identity. She would let him think she was ready to leave Raoul in order to be with him. She must do whatever she had to do to save herself and the baby.

When she could find no other excuse to linger, Alisha joined Mario in the kitchen. He'd set the table with colorful pottery and had a simple meal prepared.

"You know, babe, you're really looking good, nice and healthy compared to the last time I saw you. I guess maybe we kind of overdid our partying last summer." He shook his head, remembering. "I know you scared the hell out of me. I tried to convince myself you were just kidding around, but I couldn't take the chance. That's why I told the others. They insisted we get you to a hospital. I knew you'd be furious when you woke up and found me gone." He reached across and took her hand. "I'm sorry for running out on you like that, babe. Real sorry. I'll make you a promise. I'll never leave you again." He patted her hand and smiled, his eyes glowing. "I figure with us having a kid and all we need to back off from the heavy-duty stuff, kinda take it easy. Who knows? We might make damn good parents. Wouldn't that be a laugh?"

Alisha didn't know what to say. She didn't want to think about the results of their drug-using spree last summer.

Here she was, once again playing the role of Sherye DuBois. How could her life continue to be so bizarre? She felt as though she was in a nightmare. Instead of waking up, she kept finding herself in a new and different nightmare.

Alisha fought her panic. What if she couldn't make contact with reality again? What if she was doomed to play out various roles of another woman's life? What if—

"What's wrong? Are you feeling all right?"

She stared at the stranger sitting across from her and registered the worried expression on his face. "Not really," she murmured. "My back is bothering me. I can't seem to get comfortable and I—"

"Here. These chairs aren't the most comfortable things I've sat in. We'll go into the other room and sit in front of the fire. How does that sound?"

She nodded. He slipped his arm around her waist and helped her into the other room. "Your face is flushed," he said, lowering her to the small sofa. "Is it too warm in here?"

She leaned her head back and closed her eyes. "No. I'm just not feeling very well."

"I'm sorry, babe. I guess all of this has been hard on you, hasn't it? Me deserting you like that, leaving you to face your husband on your own. I've been a real heel, but I promise you things are going to be different for us. Wait and see. I'll be everything you need. I'll help you with the baby, I'll—"

"Mario, I—"

"Tell me what happened last summer after I left. I've got so many questions...like, how long you were unconscious, how you got back to France, what you said to the schoolteacher, did that stuff we gave her really work on her memory the way it was supposed to, did Raoul ever catch on to the switch? You know all the stuff we planned. Did it work out okay?"

She had to concentrate on what he was saying, not how she was feeling. She didn't dare think about the increasing frequency of her back pain, or the way her abdomen seemed to clench and draw, then release. It was too soon for the baby. She had to relax, that was all. She had to force herself to remember what he was saying. "The, uh, the schoolteacher went home," she panted, forcing herself to fill her lungs with air before releasing her breath in a sigh.

"Yeah, yeah, I knew that. Did she remember me meeting her at the airport as soon as she landed?"

That was easy enough to answer. "I don't think she remembered anything."

"Great, then the psychotropic drug worked the way it was supposed to. I kept telling you the guy who sold it to me insisted there was nothing to worry about."

He stroked her hair and Alisha fought not to react to his touch. If only—

"What a touching scene," came a voice from the doorway, a voice that had never sounded so wonderful to Alisha before. She almost cried out with relief when Raoul walked into the room and paused beside the sofa. "That happens to be my wife you're mauling, Pirini." He didn't look at Alisha. Instead he kept his attention on Mario.

Mario had risen at the first indication that someone was in the room. He stared at Raoul in shock. "How the hell did you find us?"

"I alerted the police that you were somewhere in the area as soon as my wife mentioned seeing you."

Mario spun around and glared at Alisha. "You told him? You actually told him that I was here?" he repeated incredulously.

Raoul went on. "Fortunately my sister had enough presence of mind when you showed up again to follow you on foot until you drove away. She memorized the license and described the make, model and color of your car to the police."

Only then did Raoul sit beside her and take her hand. "I've been worried about you." He searched her face, frowning. "Are you all right?"

She was so relieved to see him that it was all she could do not to throw her arms around him and burst into tears. She'd been so frightened that he wouldn't find her. At the moment all she could do was bite her bottom lip and nod her head.

"Of course she's all right. She's been with me, where she belongs," Mario said, striding back to the sofa. "I guess it's time for you to hear some unpleasant truths, DuBois. Sherye always insisted that you would divorce her if you found out about us. Well, that's exactly what I want." He gestured toward Alisha. "Surely you aren't so stupid as to think that's your baby. Sherye would never have had another one of your brats. She could barely tolerate living in the same place as you."

Raoul didn't move from Alisha's side. He looked up at Mario, standing belligerently in front of them, and quietly said, "She could have left at any time. I never forced her to stay."

"Maybe *you* didn't," Mario sneered, "but your money did, and your prestige did. Sherye always wanted a home and family, that was her dream...until she got it and realized what a boring life that was. She needs me to help make life more exciting for her. Now that we're finally together again, I don't intend to give her up, to you or anybody. We belong together. We're going to become parents together. We're going to build our lives together. I'm the man she truly loves."

Raoul's eyes met Alisha's and she saw compassion and understanding for the other man in his eyes. He was aware that whatever this man had done had always been for Sherye. Whether Sherye had deserved such devotion was irrelevant.

Alisha knew that the relationship she and Raoul had established had gone a long way toward his accepting the truth about Sherye and his marriage to her. Somewhere along the way he must have come to terms with and accepted Mario's presence in Sherye's life.

Raoul looked over at Mario and nodded his head to one of the chairs. "Sit down, Pirini. I've got some bad news for you."

Warily the man sat down across from them, glaring at Raoul when he slipped his arm around Alisha. "Yeah? What sort of bad news?"

"Whose idea was it to have someone take Sherye's place last summer?"

Mario looked at Alisha, frowning, before glancing back at Raoul. "You found out about that?" He clearly wondered why Alisha hadn't warned him.

"Just answer the question."

Mario looked at Alisha again, shrugged and admitted, "We both thought it up, didn't we, babe?"

"How did you find Alisha Conrad?"

"Who? Oh! You mean the schoolmarm." Once again he shrugged. "Hey, we got lucky. I guess that's what first gave us the idea, right, Sherye?" Alisha kept her eyes focused on her hands, refusing to meet his eyes. When she didn't answer him, Mario continued. "I was visiting some friends in Dallas last spring and their daughter was showing us a bunch of pictures she'd taken and I got a glimpse of the teacher. Except for her hair color, she was a dead ringer for Sherye. I asked if I could keep one of the pictures to show a friend, and I got the lady's name." He scratched his ear and said, "Of course, she isn't as beautiful as you, babe. No one could be, but she came close by the time we colored her hair and put her in some of your clothes."

"That's kidnapping, Pirini," Raoul said in a low voice.

Mario straightened in his chair. "So who's gonna complain? Don't forget that Sherye's in this up to her neck. You gonna tell the police on me? You think I won't explain how she was just as much a part of it as me? And for what!

Nobody was hurt. The teacher's back home, happily teaching her little classes, me and Sherye are getting that divorce you're so willing to give her, so everything's working out fine without the police having to know anything about what we did. After all, there was no harm done.''

Raoul stood, placing his hands in his pockets as though to prevent himself from reaching for the other man. ''I'm afraid it's not quite that easy, Pirini. You see, you and Sherye did too good a job. I identified Alisha as Sherye just as I was obviously meant to do. While you and Sherye took off on your cruise I spent those weeks with Alisha. I fell in love with her.''

Mario got a pained look on his face. ''So why are you bothering to tell me all this stuff? Who cares? No wonder you're so willing to let Sherye go. I can't believe you're standing here telling me all of this right in front of her. So what have you been waiting for, her to have my baby so you can kick her out and chase after the other gal?''

''There's no easy way to tell you, Pirini. Sherye never recovered from that drug overdose last summer. She died in November of last year.''

Mario stared at him, looked over at Alisha blankly, then returned his gaze to Raoul. ''What is this, some kind of sick joke?''

''There's no joke.''

Mario looked back at Alisha. ''C'mon, Sherye, explain to the man. He's suffering all kinds of delusions or something. Tell him the truth.''

For the first time since Raoul had entered the room Alisha spoke. ''He's telling you the truth, Mr. Pirini,'' she said quietly. ''I'm not Sherye. I'm Alisha and I taught school in Dallas. When I regained consciousness in the hospital I didn't remember who I was. Raoul convinced me and the doctors that I was his wife, so I went home with him and spent several weeks there.'' She touched her stomach. ''That's when I became pregnant.''

Mario jumped up from the chair. ''But that's impossible! You—Sherye—whoever—doesn't sleep with him. You haven't slept with him in years.''

She looked him in the eye and said, ''I did. He came to see me in Dallas several weeks after Sherye died. When he discovered that I was pregnant he insisted on marrying me. That's why you saw us together in Paris.''

Mario's skin turned a pasty gray. ''Sherye's really dead?'' he whispered. ''She died? No. That isn't possible. She couldn't have died. I would have known somehow. She wouldn't have done that. She wouldn't have left me....'' He sank back into the chair as though his legs would no longer hold him.

Alisha caught a movement out of the corner of her eye and turned. Two men stood in the doorway, one wearing a police uniform.

Raoul looked at Alisha and said, ''Are you ready to go home?''

She nodded and he helped her from the sofa and past the two men. When she glanced around at Mario, she saw that he was sitting hunched over, his hands covering his face. She wasn't certain whether or not he'd seen the other men, or if he was aware that she and Raoul were leaving.

Once they were in the car Raoul said, ''Are you sure you're all right? I've been out of my mind with worry.''

''He wouldn't have hurt me. He thought I was Sherye. That's why I decided not to try to explain. He was too convinced and I was afraid of what he might do if he knew the truth.''

''Danielle thought he was rough when he grabbed you out of the car. I was afraid he might accidentally injure you.''

''I can't deny that he frightened me, showing up that

way, but he was really very gentle with me.'' She sighed. ''I'm glad it's over…I mean, completely over. All the questions have been answered. I can't help but feel sorry for Sherye. She never understood how blessed she was, how much she had.''

''Each of us has a different idea of what it takes to be happy. Hers was different from yours.''

''That's really obvious. Even without my memories, my life seemed so perfect to me last summer. I was living the life I had always wanted…only to discover it wasn't my life, after all.''

He reached over and took her hand in his. ''It is now.''

''I do have one rather minor problem.''

''What's that, love?''

''I'm afraid this child has decided not to wait any longer to become a part of the family.''

Raoul jerked his head around and peered at her in the shadowy car. ''Alisha! Are you having labor pains? When did they start? How far apart? Do you need to get to the hospital now?''

She closed her eyes and counted for a brief moment before she sighed and said, ''I know that first babies usually take their time, but this one seems to be in something of a hurry. Since I'm not nearly brave enough to have it at home, I think we need to go to the hospital.''

''A simple yes would have done it,'' he muttered, stepping on the gas and shaking his head. ''I can't believe you never said anything. How long have you been—''

''I'm really all right, Raoul. Stop worrying. We've got plenty of time.''

He brushed his palm against her cheek for a brief moment before returning it to the wheel. ''That's true, love. We've got the rest of our lives.''

Epilogue

She fought her way to the surface, knowing there was something she needed to do. She hated to leave the soothing, restful place where she had found peace, but it was time—time to surface and face whatever it was that awaited her.

She opened her eyes. The room seemed to be filled with golden sunshine, pouring through a large window. She blinked from the brightness and waited for her eyes to adjust. Once she could see, she discovered that she was not alone in the room.

Raoul stood next to her bed, holding her hand between both of his. He looked tired, but extremely pleased with himself and with her. Sleepily she peered around the room, recognizing the faces of Danielle, *Maman* and Janine.

"Janine," she whispered. "What are you doing here?"

"Making the acquaintance of your family and gazing with a great deal of awe and admiration at that handsome young son of yours."

Alisha smiled. "He *is* beautiful, isn't he? Just like his papa." She squeezed Raoul's hand. "We did it, didn't we?"

"I was very proud of you," he said gruffly.

"Thank you for staying by my side."

"I wouldn't have missed it for anything."

She smiled at the others. "I'm sorry I'm so groggy. I finally asked for something to take the edge off toward the end."

Raoul grinned. "Yes. Now the delivery room staff and I have a very good idea what sort of drunk you make... very, very jolly."

Her eyes widened in horror. "Oh, no!"

He nodded, his eyes filled with amusement. "Oh, yes. You serenaded us for a while, in both French and English."

"How embarrassing! I'll never be able to face any of them again."

"Nonsense. They were amused but not particularly surprised. People react differently to medication. Fortunately, what they gave you was quite mild. I had an opportunity to talk with your doctor about your susceptibility to drugs. We're really very fortunate that you recovered as well as you did from the drugs you received last summer."

Danielle leaned over and said, "The authorities called this morning to say that Mario gave a full statement about what occurred and is cooperating with them, so they won't need to bother you or Raoul anymore with the matter."

Alisha caught Raoul's eye, and he returned her gaze while he kept a firm grip on her hand.

Maman spoke up. "Yvette and Jules are delighted to know that their new brother has arrived. They have all manner of things to show him when he gets home."

She smiled, thinking about the children. "I'm eager to get home to see them. I already miss them."

"Right now you need your rest," Raoul said. "You've had a rather exciting last few days."

Each of the women kissed her on the cheek and left, leaving her alone with Raoul. He pushed a wisp of hair behind one of her ears. "I was thinking as I stood here watching you sleep about the time when I was actually seeing you for the first time. You were lying in a hospital, much like this. You were very pale and wearing a head bandage. I thought I knew you. Then you opened your eyes and my life was never the same again. You turned my thinking upside down...you kept me confused and on edge. You woke me up to my own prejudices and set opinions. You made me reassess everything about my life and myself."

"I didn't mean to. I was just trying to find out who I was."

"Well, you helped me to find out who I was, as well. Thank you. I thank God every day that He sent you to me." He leaned down and gave her a tender kiss. When he would have stepped away she tightened her grip on his hand. She met his gaze as she said, "I thought of a name for the baby."

"Ah. We never talked about names, did we, thinking we had some more time. So? What have you thought of?"

"Michael René. I wanted him to have your name—the René. Your mother mentioned once that was your middle name. Michael was my father's name. I always hoped if I had a boy that he could carry part of my father's name, since he never had a son."

Once again Raoul kissed her. "Whatever you want, love, is fine with me."

She looked up at him. "Are you going to always be such a mellow, accommodating husband?"

"If I'm not, I'm sure you can whip me into shape in no time."

She yawned, then laughed at her sleepy state. "I think you're perfect just the way you are. You see? I have wonderful taste in husbands."

* * * * *

A Note from the Author

I hope that you enjoyed Alisha's story. Her story has circled in my head for several years. It was one that I knew I had to tell at some point in my writing career.

Have you ever wondered what would happen if you lost your memory? Would the person you are still be there, hidden away from your conscious mind? Just think about how unnerving it would be to have the people around you tell you all sorts of things about you that were painful to hear, things that made no sense to your idea of the kind of individual you feel you are.

It would take a very strong personality to withstand such an onslaught of confusing information. The most heroic thing a person could do, in my opinion, would be to hang on to a belief in yourself when no one else believed in you.

Raoul is a man of honor and integrity faced with some very tough choices. His quiet strength and stubborn tenacity intrigued me. I knew that he would have to be a very special man, because Alisha is a very special woman.

Coming in May 1999

BABY *Fever*

by
New York Times Bestselling Author

KASEY MICHAELS

When three sisters hear their biological
clocks ticking, they know it's
time for action.

But who will they get to father their babies?

**Find out how the road to motherhood
leads to love in this brand-new collection.**

Available at your favorite retail outlet.

If you enjoyed what you just read,
then we've got an offer you can't resist!

Take 2 bestselling
love stories FREE!

Plus get a FREE surprise gift!

Clip this page and mail it to Silhouette Reader Service™

IN U.S.A.	IN CANADA
3010 Walden Ave.	P.O. Box 609
P.O. Box 1867	Fort Erie, Ontario
Buffalo, N.Y. 14240-1867	L2A 5X3

YES! Please send me 2 free Silhouette Desire® novels and my free surprise gift. Then send me 6 brand-new novels every month, which I will receive months before they're available in stores. In the U.S.A., bill me at the bargain price of $3.12 plus 25¢ delivery per book and applicable sales tax, if any*. In Canada, bill me at the bargain price of $3.49 plus 25¢ delivery per book and applicable taxes**. That's the complete price and a savings of over 10% off the cover prices—what a great deal! I understand that accepting the 2 free books and gift places me under no obligation ever to buy any books. I can always return a shipment and cancel at any time. Even if I never buy another book from Silhouette, the 2 free books and gift are mine to keep forever. So why not take us up on our invitation. You'll be glad you did!

225 SEN CNFA
326 SEN CNFC

Name	(PLEASE PRINT)	
Address	Apt.#	
City	State/Prov.	Zip/Postal Code

* Terms and prices subject to change without notice. Sales tax applicable in N.Y.
** Canadian residents will be charged applicable provincial taxes and GST.
   All orders subject to approval. Offer limited to one per household.
   ® are registered trademarks of Harlequin Enterprises Limited.

DES99   ©1998 Harlequin Enterprises Limited

Coming in June 1999 from

Silhouette Books...

Those matchmaking folks at Gulliver's Travels are at
it again—and look who they're working their magic
on this time, in

HOLIDAY
Honeymoons

Two Tickets to Paradise

For the first time anywhere, enjoy these two new
complete stories in one sizzling volume!

HIS FIRST FATHER'S DAY   **Merline Lovelace**
A little girl's search for her father leads her to
Tony Peretti's front door...and leads *Tony* into the
arms of his long-lost love—the child's mother!

MARRIED ON THE FOURTH   **Carole Buck**
Can summer love turn into the real thing? When
it comes to Maddy Malone and Evan Blake's
Independence Day romance, the answer is a
definite "yes!"

Don't miss this brand-new release—
HOLIDAY HONEYMOONS: Two Tickets to Paradise—
coming June 1999, only from Silhouette Books.

Available at your favorite retail outlet.

THE MACGREGORS OF OLD...

#1 *New York Times* bestselling author

NORA ROBERTS

has won readers' hearts with her enormously popular
MacGregor family saga. Now read about the MacGregors'
proud and passionate Scottish forebears in this
romantic, tempestuous tale set against the bloody
background of the historic battle of Culloden.

Coming in July 1999

REBELLION

One look at the ravishing red-haired beauty and Brigham
Langston was captivated. But though Serena MacGregor
had the face of an angel, she was a wildcat who spurned
his advances with a rapier-sharp tongue. To hot-tempered
Serena, Brigham was just another Englishman to be
despised. But in the arms of the dashing and dangerous
English lord, the proud Scottish beauty felt her hatred
melting with the heat of their passion.

Available at your favorite retail outlet.

HARLEQUIN®

Available June 1999 from Silhouette Books...

World's Most
Eligible Bachelors

LONE STAR MILLIONAIRE
by Susan Mallery

The World's Most Eligible Bachelor:
Cal Langtry—oil baron, financial whiz,
ladies man...father?

When gorgeous wildcatter Cal Langtry discovered he
was a daddy, he turned to his trusty assistant for family
lessons. Sweet Sabrina's job duties soon skyrocketed—
from part-time helper to full-time lover! Can the
wealthy bachelor stop himself from asking for one last
favor: "Be my wife"?

Each month, Silhouette Books brings you an irresistible
bachelor in these all-new, original stories. Find out how
the sexiest, most-sought-after men are finally caught.

Available at your favorite retail outlet.

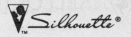
Silhouette®

Strong, seductive and eligible!

THE AUSTRALIANS

Stories of romance Australian-style, guaranteed to
fulfill that sense of adventure!

This June 1999, look for

Simply Irresistible
by Miranda Lee

Ross Everton was the sexiest single guy the Outback had to
offer! Vivien Roberts thought she was a streetwise Sydney
girl. Neither would forget their one night together—Vivien
was expecting Ross's baby. But irresistible sexual attraction
was one thing...being married quite another!

*The Wonder from Down Under: where spirited women win
the hearts of Australia's most independent men!*

Available June 1999
at your favorite retail outlet.

HARLEQUIN®
Makes any time special ™

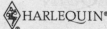